FRONT SIGHT

ALSO BY STEPHEN HUNTER

BOB LEE SWAGGER SERIES

Point of Impact

Black Light

Time to Hunt

The 47th Samurai

Night of Thunder

I, Sniper

Dead Zero

The Third Bullet

Sniper's Honor

G-Man

Game of Snipers

Targeted

EARL SWAGGER SERIES

Black Light

Hot Springs

Pale Horse Coming

Havana

The Bullet Garden

RAY CRUZ

Dead Zero

Soft Target

OTHER NOVELS

The Master Sniper

The Second Saladin

Tapestry of Spies

The Day Before Midnight

Dirty White Boys

I, Ripper

Basil's War

NONFICTION

Violent Screen: A Critic's 13 Years on the Front Lines of Movie Mayhem

Now Playing at the Valencia: Pulitzer Prize–Winning Essays on Movies

American Gunfight: The Plot to Kill Harry Truman—and the Shoot-out That Stopped It (with John Bainbridge, Jr.)

FRONT SIGHT

THREE SWAGGER NOVELLAS

STEPHEN HUNTER

EMILY BESTLER BOOKS

ATRIA

NEW YORK LONDON TORONTO SYDNEY NEW DELHI

EMILY
BESTLER
BOOKS

ATRIA

An Imprint of Simon & Schuster, Inc.
1230 Avenue of the Americas
New York, NY 10020

First Emily Bestler Books/Atria Books hardcover edition January 2024

EMILY BESTLER BOOKS/ATRIA BOOKS and colophon are trademarks of
Simon & Schuster, Inc.

Simon & Schuster: Celebrating 100 Years of Publishing in 2024

For information about special discounts for bulk purchases,
please contact Simon & Schuster Special Sales at 1-866-506-1949 or
business@simonandschuster.com.

The Simon & Schuster Speakers Bureau can bring authors to your live event.
For more information or to book an event, contact the Simon & Schuster
Speakers Bureau at 1-866-248-3049 or visit our website at
www.simonspeakers.com.

Interior design by Alexis Minieri

Manufactured in the United States of America

1   3   5   7   9   10   8   6   4   2

Library of Congress Cataloging-in-Publication Data has been applied for.

ISBN 978-1-6680-3036-3
ISBN 978-1-6680-3038-7 (ebook)

For Franny and Alice
And new arrival Hank,
Linebacker to the world!

It takes equipment.

—Raymond Chandler

CITY OF MEAT

AUTHOR'S NOTE

I N THE 1930S, IN THE NEW YORK OFFICE OF THE *NEW MASSES*, DEEP THINK-
ers in Trotsky glasses called it social realism, no matter the medium.
They saw it as one more siege engine in the destruction of capitalism,
and a party duty. However, Americans wanted stories, not lectures.
STIX NIX PROLIX PIX. Hollywood, then full of clever, quick-thinking
pulse-readers, got it right. They called the genre, in its cinematic form,
the message picture. Although that meant a hard look, through drama,
performance, and cinematography, at some part of the system gone
wrong, crushing the common man, it also promised more picture than
message. Moguls hated it—"If I want message, I'll get Western Union!"—
but enough writers and directors prevailed, and greatness sometimes
followed: *I Am a Fugitive from a Chain Gang* in '32, *Wild Boys of the
Road* in '33, on to *The Grapes of Wrath* in '40. The pictures were solid,
progressive but not preachy, straightforward and without stylization, and
deeply heartfelt. *City of Meat* is a shot at that brilliant tradition.

CHICAGO, 1934

CHAPTER 1

THE BICKERING GOT SO BAD, FINALLY, THAT THE DIRECTOR CALLED BOTH Sam Cowley and Mel Purvis to Washington to talk out the command difficulties in the productive but messed-up Chicago field office of the Justice Department's glamorous Division of Investigation. A good airing-out was called for, under the Director's prodding. Rumor insisted that the Director also wanted to have a come-to-Jesus meeting with Melvin, whom he did not want to lose—after all, Mel was widely if vaguely credited with getting Dillinger—but also whom he did not want to be giving unauthorized press conferences and leaks, and taking credit for work that had been done by the whole field office.

As far as Charles Swagger was concerned, none of this had anything to do with him and he bore no grudges for attention denied him, or celebrity he was owed as the man who actually killed Dillinger. He had just done the job. He bore down, continued his duties, particularly teaching new agents firearms skills, tracking their talent, skill, and dedication, so that the office could put the best shooters in the firefights and not end up with somebody who'd never fired a Thompson facing off with Thompson master Baby Face Nelson. As well he worked long hours checking out the odd tip that came in and running down sightings and so forth, as did the other, younger agents.

In Sam's absence, who took over but Hugh Clegg, and again that was of no concern to Charles. He'd do the work as it arrived, no matter who assigned it to him. His only orientation was to the task before him—ultimately finding Baby Face—and that was all he cared about. It drove out many discouraging thoughts and the disturbing memories that any man-killer might have.

One afternoon, however, one of Clegg's people came by his desk and told him the inspector wanted to see him.

Charles went quickly, wanting not to be the source of any friction or behavior for which Clegg, Mel's man, not Sam's, could find cause to criticize him. And as it turned out, Clegg was entirely reasonable. Perhaps he too wished to dial down the rancor a bit.

"Please sit down, Sheriff. A little something has come up."

"Yes, sir," said Charles.

Clegg couldn't help the Old South style he had; it was natural to him, as, of course, he was Old South. But that Old South–New South, Georgia-Arkansas gap was between them and always would be, as the one mistrusted the other's foppishness and aristocratic airs and longueurs, while the other detested the boot-poor pig state origins of the other and the fact that talent, not breeding, had brought the man before him. That's the way it was and would always be.

"I have reports from three sources that Baby Face Nelson is working as a cowboy at the Chicago stockyards."

"Yes, sir."

"This is not the first time such reports have come in. We've had batches of them twice before, once just after Little Bohemia and once two months before in February. In both those cases we sent large, heavily armed teams, combed the place out, kicked in a few doors and roughed some folks up, interviewed aggressively, and found nothing. The Union Stock Yard and Transit Company Police, who run the place, raised bloody hell with the mayor and we were much criticized for it in the newspapers."

"Yes, sir."

"Since Dillinger, we have been getting largely positive press. I think it behooves us to keep that situation going."

"Yes, sir."

"So I'm not going to raid, like the last time, and give the papers cause to laugh or mock."

"I have it."

"I'm not even going to send two agents, as I would normally, for exactly the same reason. Do you see where this is going?"

"I think so."

"Of all the men, you're the most prepared to work on your own, as you've proven. You don't seem to need anyone backing you up, and of course I'd prefer to keep the other men on their assignments."

Charles seriously doubted Nelson could be at the stockyards: too many witnesses, too many guns and people who knew how to shoot them, too much, if other stockyards were any guide, mud and shit. Someone as dapper as Nelson wouldn't be able to put his shiny Florsheims into such glop.

"So what I want you to do is go down there and nose around. See what you can pick up. If he's there, there'll be a buzz. With your western Arkansas accent you'll fit in and attract less attention than any of these law school kids with the dainty fingers and the Boston Brahmin tonalities."

"Do you want me to dress down?"

"Don't go full cowboy, I don't see the point. But I'd wear work or field boots, as you know what cattle produce in abundance. No need for a tie, as it'll set you apart and maybe give the cowhands pause. On the other hand, have no reluctance to pull badge if someone braces you, but I would think you'd avoid announcing yourself from a tabletop and demanding cooperation. If something comes up, I'm sure you can handle it, whether it's Baby Face himself or helping a sow give birth to cow quadruplets."

"Yes, sir."

"It may take several days, a week even, for them to trust you and for you to see into this thing. That's fine, though of course if something that requires your gun skills comes up, we'll get in touch. I've called, and the Fourth District Station, on Cottage Grove, near the Yards, will know you're in the Yards and their switchboard will take care of you. I've also called Chief Mulrooney of the railroad yard police to tell him you're coming and asked him to assist as necessary. That's by way of making up for the previous turmoil, so you'll have to get along with the railroad detectives."

"Yes, sir."

"Be forewarned, they're not the most cooperative. Most are ex-cops who lost their jobs over dubious enterprises and came to rest with Union Stock Yards and Transit Company. They basically answer to no one except big shots in New York, so they tend to be heavy-handed. Lots of rough stuff. Tough guys. They deal mostly with road hobos and thieves. Their answer to every problem is a billy to the head."

"Yes, sir."

"But at the end, we want a report for the files. If by God it turns out later he did go to earth down there, we have to show we took all the reports seriously."

"Yes, sir."

"And needless to say, if you strike gold, either kill the bastard or call up here for troops, so that the Division gets the credit. Leave the Chicagos and the railroad detectives out of it."

That was the Division: yes, solve the crime, but that was only the beginning; the next priority was winning the publicity contest.

CHAPTER 2

HOW DO THEY KNOW? HARD TO SAY. MAYBE IT'S THE MOLECULES OF blood in the air, and, inhaled, those molecules tickle some ancient cell cluster in the not-terribly-sophisticated bovine cerebellum. Maybe it's pure instinct, acquired over thousands of thousands of years of obediently awaiting their execution, passed, somehow, from generation to generation. Maybe they're reading the behavior of the men who herd them, seeing that it's oddly different this time, not meant to soothe their fears, as happens so frequently on the range; instead, meant to hurry them, to push them in a certain direction into a certain cattle trace and up a certain narrow ramp, and somehow the human sweat and fear at the presence of so much death is something they themselves have learned to sense.

There is no mooing. Only cows moo, and there are no cows on the ramp today at, for example, Nugent's Best Beef, Building 44, Exchange Avenue, Chicago, purveyors of fine canned meats including stew, chili hamburger, hash, gravy—as they say, everything but the methane. Cows are bred to produce calves and dairy. On this ramp, or any ramp, there are only moo-less steers and heifers, and if they dream, surely it is for the life of a cow, to snooze in clover and daisies, to sniff sweetness in the spring air, to never hear a voice raised in anger or urgency, and to squirt milk. These animals are cattle. These animals thrash, and twist, and occasionally gore; sometimes one will slip or break a leg, throwing the whole routine off. They are components. They are not insensate, however. They cry.

The cries—more bellow, full of rage and fear, fully knowledgeable of the approaching horror—rise and mingle, and all who hear it know that today is a day and this is a place where living animals will become pounds of beef. The agitation is not ideal anywhere, but it is a fact of death at Nugent's and other low-end packers far from the industrialized efficiency of big boys like Armour and Swift. Those big boys know it is much better, commercially, to process the animals in a state of calm. Too much uproar, as at Nugent's, riles the blood and darkens the meat, precludes the release of lactic acid, and that product, known as "darkcutter," is tougher and less flavorful and must be sold at deep discount.

On the killing ramp, the steers and the heifers are all between twenty-four and thirty-six months old, and they mingle indifferently. There is no gender or age separation here. To the degree that each has a consciousness, another animal is simply "a member." It has no meaning. It is not a friend or an enemy. It's a part of the herd, that is all. No cuddling, no foreplay, no sex. There was never any chance of sex because of course the steers have been castrated since birth and the heifers have not been bred, so both sexes die as virgins, which to a certain kind of imagination might seem tragic. But to the cattle's point of view, there is enough tragedy without the loss of a frolic in the meadow.

Up the ramp they are forced, pushing, shoving, responding to the calls, sticks, and belts of their drivers, who want it orderly but are incapable of managing order. The ramp narrows, and at its peak, where it enters the kill house itself, there is only room for one beast. He or she—it—squirms through. And finds itself suddenly halted, its neck somehow restrained by a mechanical yoke that rises from the floor. Since the animals differ radically in their size, sometimes the yoke fits perfectly, sometimes it doesn't, being too large, so the neck must be forced unto choking, or too small so that the animal can squirm.

This is the ultimate moment. Restrained, more or less, it is about to receive the killing stroke. The instrumentality is not meant to be cruel, though it can be; it is not meant to be kind, though it can be; it is meant only to be efficient, for such places process cattle in the thousands each day.

A good knocker is hard to find. He needs strength in abundance, particularly in forearms and wrists, but as well through the chest and back. But strength is not enough. He needs dexterity and highly developed hand-eye coordination, for it is no easy thing to raise four pounds of dead iron on a two-foot wood shaft well above his head and bring it down in the perfect spot, time after time, at full extension, at full force. His target is an imaginary meeting of imaginary lines between left eye and right horn and left horn and right eye. That X, above and not between the eyes, drives all force into the center of the animal's brain and, again in the ideal, is planned to completely destroy its mental capacities, such as they are. Well and truly struck, it goes down, hard, to the floor, and there, is quickly attended by handlers, one of whom, another specialist, wielding a razor-sharp knife, quickly bends and slits the throat, severing jugular and carotid, producing gallons of blood. Others close in. These men are also noted for their strength and efficiency, for their job, literally, is to wrestle the carcass into a posture where it can be turned into food or leather or chicken feed. They hoist it, until a hook can be driven between the Achilles tendon and the ankle bone of its right rear leg, and then the mechanics of processing take over. That is, now on the power of ball bearings, chains, rails, and grease, the hanging carcass is pushed dangling by hook from station to station; it is bled—gravity helps—it is beheaded, its guts and organs are cut out. The inedible products are captured beneath, swept up, and set to dry on sheet steel, then ground into meal that is of some commercial use and sold at pennies per ton to the Pulverized Manure Company right next door. As for the animal, it is at last sundered totally, "split" in the patois, each half getting its own hook and place on the line. It is no longer an animal, it is now a side of beef, and in plural such entities are called "beeves." Of the thing that was, nothing is left, only bisected halves, to be skinned, washed, dressed, chilled, ultimately butchered and sent to the aging house.

Of course sometimes the knocker's blow is off; the animal is not immediately stilled, and it's not rare for living beasts to be hung to bleed out squealing and moaning and thrashing, spraying blood and shit and piss everywhere, going into convulsions and contortions before finally finding themselves with no more blood to spray, no more shit to shit, no more piss to piss when it finally stops hurting. On the line of any slaughterhouse in the year 1934, such spectacle is barely noted. Nobody cares.

CHAPTER 3

LATER THAT AFTERNOON, AS TWILIGHT WAS FALLING, HE ARRIVED AT the vast Union Stock Yards, a mile south and west of the Loop, a straight shot down Halsted. He turned right on 41st, and that road led him directly to the absurd pretend-castle entrance gate that someone who thought he had wit had erected in the last century. Though much of the traffic through the gate was still on horseback or in unruly herds, the road accepted his automobile easily enough, and he drove on, on a street named Exchange. He quickly found himself exactly where he didn't want to be: No Man's Land. Fire being first cousin to war in its destructiveness, the great stockyard blaze of May 19 had scorched to ash and dirt at least eighty structures, including restaurants, hotels, a newspaper office, banks, an office building, and packinghouses, as efficiently as a hosing by German howitzer. It was emptiness everywhere, the occasional spar still standing, maybe a wall or two. But he drove onward, passing then into open land where the flames had not reached. It was its own astonishment—not so much endless, though it seemed so, but blank and featureless, unwilling, somehow, to admit its secrets without careful study. It was somehow the emptiness of intellectual weight, a metaphor for something as yet to be categorized.

Ahead, down Exchange, appeared a constellation of light where surely temporary HQ for the various necessary administrative functions had been relocated so that business could continue to hum post-conflagration.

About this time, the famous bovine bouquet of the place slapped him in the face. It smelled and felt thick, all those unguents that had passed through all those digestive systems and then been eliminated into the soil, all the tons of grass and hay and feed that kept the herds alive, all the filthy water from the Chicago River that kept them unparched. Then, the undertang of char, from the fire. And finally, mixing in but unescapable if you recognized it, the smell of blood too. The blood, it was said, at highest efficiency, ran inches thick on some floors. That blood stench would not go away.

He entered the city of blood and slaughter, but it seemed mostly like any other city from the outside appearance, a maze of industrial architecture thrown together ad hoc, without a thought for coherence or consistency, relics of what buildings had been, forecasts of what they could be. Not too much farther down Exchange he found a building that had certainly once been a packinghouse but now wore a crude sign outside that said "Union Stock Yard & Transit Co. Division of Police."

Charles parked, got out of his car, and walked on in, finding the milieu to be city police department, with the shabby furniture, messy desks, signs pointing out the lockup and the phone bank, the faces of many wanted desperadoes on the walls, their mug-shot gloom filling the air with a general odor of the miscreant, the drunk, and the recently robbed. Amazing how fast the cops had made their new headquarters into a replica of their old.

He showed his badge to one of the few men on duty at this late hour, made inquiries, was taken to the captain's office, and there met Captain Mulrooney, who ran the place, a beefy, practical fellow with a bourbon nose and brown teeth. He was cop through and through, with the dead eyes and the dead face, and the bulk that suggested abundant muscle and the will to use it. He wore an executive's suit and tie, as opposed to a uniform, as Union Stock Yard & Transit Co. cops had no need to present buttoned tunics to polite society. Only those assigned to a big station dressed as something other than a farmhand with a badge.

"Baby Face again?" the captain snorted, when Charles had explained his presence. "Well, at least this time you guys didn't bring the riot squad and tipped me off that you were coming."

"Maybe a lesson was learned, Captain Mulrooney."

"I hope so. Of course we don't have an index of all the boys who work the herds here, since they're hired by individual companies, who rent pens from us abutting their own processing plants. So I can't do no paperwork checking for you. And on top of that, we're all messed up because of the fire. We're still basically making it up as we go along."

"I got that."

"But as I mentioned, this has happened before."

"I've seen the reports."

"Good. I can tell you, after the fact, that all these Nelson sightings seem to come from the same area of the Yards. It's a big place, believe me. Here, look at this."

He showed Charles a map on the wall, a huge thing broken into segments and grids, three-quarters encircled by and penetrated by the busy crosshatched lines that meant railroad track, each and every space or unit designated by code, all of them in different colors. The areas currently in ruins—about a quarter, the whole northwest corner—from their date with flame were x-ed out in black crayon.

"Swift is red, Armour is blue, Hammond is orange, Morris is yellow, and it goes on and on. So you can see, it's plenty complicated, even with the fire damage, and you need to know what you're doing."

"Any help is appreciated."

"Last two times it was mainly in the southwest quadrant, where the tracks come in from Oklahoma and West Texas. I have to tell you, the fellows down there are a tough lot and they don't cotton to outsiders, so you won't be greeted with open arms."

"I'm used to that."

"If you get yourself into a jam, you'll have to get yourself out. Most of my boys are on the trains now, looking for hobos and thieves. It's rough work and they have to bust a lot of heads, but I can't just dial up a squad room and send out reinforcements. Sorry, but that's just the way it is."

"I was a sheriff for many years. I'm used to handling things on my own."

"By the way, if you do see boys digging through ruins, don't worry. They're mine. There's a rumor running around that way before the fire burned him out, one of the richer Jews buried gold under his kosher kill house. My boys heard about it and you know what gold does to an Irishman. So every spare moment they're poking around."

"To my mind, Baby Face is the treasure."

"Okay, I'll have Cracker take you down there by wagon, at least as close as you can get. Whatever you do, be careful of your footing and balance. A stockyard is a dangerous place and these animals can turn killer in the blink of an eye."

"I was raised on a farm. I know animals enough to stay away."

In a few minutes, he was sitting next to an elderly black man who offered him nothing and hardly noticed them. A slatternly old pony pulled their little cart along, driven by the casual slash of a whip Cracker snapped into its flanks. The pony, which could only be called You Poor Thing, pulled his wagon to the right under Cracker's ungentle mandate, and they left the administrative city behind, entering the pens. Unprotected by the bubble of his car, Charles experienced the smell full on. It seemed to double or triple, like a palpable cloud, a tear-bringer, like a phenomenon of the weather. It was everywhere and could not be avoided. Worse still, its fetid promise of nourishment brought flies in the billions, even some carrion birds silhouetted on bare branches, ready to pounce on the gobbet of beef, a foot, an eye, whatever spillage there was.

Penland again. Charles felt himself lost in the featureless landscape of a place that had to be the bovine capital of planet Earth. He saw now that it was an infinite checkerboard, with cows, in pens, as far as the eye could see, one and then another out to the horizon in all directions. But it was not one-dimensional. Giving it depth and yet more confusion, viaducts for cars, walkways for humans, and ramps for slaughter arose here and there indiscriminately, and most of the fences had narrow walkways nailed to their top board, so that a fellow could progress from one to the other—carefully—without actually entering the dangerous confined spaces. The skyscrapers of the city loomed formidably a mile and change away, dominating one quadrant, and to the east the industrial might of the big meat factories stood, Armour's belching smoke through stacks, but the others empty except for the low silhouettes of the poverty-row meat-packers. Few details proclaimed themselves, only a kind of restless shifting behind the pen fences, where the masses of cattle simply drifted aimlessly, emitting that low moan, louder now that he was among them, and waited until it was time to die. Now and then the cart passed under a viaduct where traffic still ran, since no one could actually drive through such a jumble of square mile as the Yards.

It seemed to go on for hours, but in what the clock said was a mere fifteen minutes, Cracker halted the poor pony with a swift, merciless pull on the reins and gestured. A set of wooden steps led up to a catwalk that spanned three or four pens.

"The cap, dis where he tell me drop you, suh," Cracker said.

"Take the catwalk?"

"Yas suh. Cowboys be gathered over at the shower house."

"How do I get back?"

"I guess you have the boss call the office, and someone poke me, and I come on out here and gits you."

"Okay. Don't know how long I'll be. If he don't call, don't worry about it. If I get back to that road, I can just follow it to the castle."

"Yas suh."

Charles gave the old guy a couple of bucks, then got off, climbed the steps, and faced a long skywalk. The carpentry seemed solid, though there was a little bounce and sway, and the railings could have been stouter, but it was no ordeal by ready danger. The cattle paid him no attention as he passed over their little chunk of paradise. They seemed mindless.

The walk took him over six pens, all but one full, and deposited him in a wide, dusty yard outside a makeshift wood building, very frontier-looking in the helter-skelter way the slats were hammered against its frame. Those peculiar cowboy brands—squiggles, letters forward and backward, pictographs, some symbolic, some indecipherable—had been fried randomly into the building's wood. It looked all crazy to Charles. A single pipe issued smoke, presumably from a fire that kept the water inside hot. A sign said "Showers 5 cents." It was a trip back to 1873, a city named Dodge or Laredo. Cowboys lounged everywhere, either just in from herding and waiting for their time in the showers and then off to the nearest bar, or already showered and waiting to gather up, outfit by outfit, clique by clique, for the same night on the town.

He walked over to the nearest group of loungers, who eyed him on the approach. They were all thin young men, brown-red from weeks in sun and dust, seemingly assembled out of gristle, leather, and bandanna cotton, all held tidy under a hat with a crown too tall and a brim too wide. It wasn't love they showered on him; he was the outsider and they knew it, and they wanted him to know it.

"Fellas," he said, pulling open his lapel to show where he'd pinned his badge on the inside surface of the flap, "federal agent, Justice Department. Looking for a fellow, got a photo of him, care to take a look?"

"You going to arrest him all by yourself, federal man?" someone wanted to know, a little leather in his voice.

"Hope to," said Charles smiling, "but if he don't want to come, I guess

I'll have to shoot him. I ain't yet decided whether to put the bullet through his left eye or his right."

He pulled back on his jacket and showed his .45 in its carved S. D. Myres shoulder rig, the holster tied down to the belt, the pistol cocked and locked, the strap disengaged. It was a serious, fast man-killing setup, and he knew these boys would get it. They'd seen man-killers before and understood that you don't dress like a gunslinger unless you are a gunslinger, and if you are a gunslinger they wouldn't want to mess with you. It was the Way of the West.

The picture was circulated, looked at earnestly, and returned without any luck for the man hunter.

"Thanks, y'all."

"I heard Johnny Dillinger got shot in the back."

"Funny, I heard he was pulling a Colt .380 when someone put three into him faster than you can say 'Jack Boo.' Johnny was fast. This federal man was faster. You wouldn't want to go to leather on that boy." He smiled again, and there wasn't an ounce of back-down anywhere in him, and all knew there was no way a fellow got sand in him like that without spending time on the trigger when others were shooting at him.

He moved on, group by group; he showed the picture of Nelson to the geezer who ran the shower house, and the geezer who chopped the wood and loaded it into the furnace that warmed the water. Nothing, and he was just about to call it a lost day, when a fellow did say, "I'd go a couple of pens over that way. There's a West Texas outfit called Rocking-R. They think they too good to mingle with the common, but you never can tell."

"Thanks, cowboy. I'll do just that."

Another catwalk took him three pens in a certain direction, though by now it was dark, and the cattle had settled considerably, so it was just like walking a gangplank to a phantom ship. He came to a larger area, lit by firelight, and saw cowboys here too. He didn't think anybody saw him in the dark. So as not to excite any reconnaissance by fire, he hollered out, "Law officer, coming in."

He found twenty hollow young faces on him, eyes wide and lit red by the fire.

"Federal agent, Justice Department. Got a headman?"

A rangy fellow, mostly leg and arm, all vested and booted up and one of those big hats, came over.

"My name's Charles Swagger," Charles said. "Justice Department Division of Investigation."

"Lutie Crone, Rocking-R foreman. Sir, my boys all good. We only take the best at Rocking-R, anybody tell you that."

"Just hoping you've seen somebody. Got some calls, said this fellow was out here. Take a look, if you don't mind."

Lutie looked, then said, "Oh, hell. That's what I thought it was. Hey, Mort, where's Shorty, they done going to arrest him again!"

The cowboy chorus laughed, for evidently this was a joke they'd heard before.

"Shorty's sleeping," came the answer.

"Well, wake him up, goddammit. Before this here fellow pulls out his tommy gun."

In a few minutes, Shorty approached, called Shorty, of course, because he was about six feet four inches tall. His hat added six more inches, his boots two more. He was all string and no bean.

"Here's your Baby Face Nelson, Mr. G-man. Take him away, I'm sick of this."

Charles beheld the man and tried to get the mystery of it all. He saw a handsome cowboy, all hat (the cattle were all around), with a sleepy face, cracked lips, and blue eyes that communicated not much in the way of clever. He was in faded jeans so tight they could have been on him since birth, and his boots were all covered in mud and straw.

"What's your name, son?" Charles asked.

"Harrison B. Harris, sir. Born in Lubbock twenty-one years back. Like horses, cows, girls, and payday. Do an honest day's work, never no trouble. Everybody calls me 'Shorty' 'cause I ain't no kind of short."

"Hmm," said Charles to the foreman, communicating his confusion.

"Shorty, take off your hat."

It was the hat. It elongated the head and cast a shadow on the features and contributed a whole new context that confounded expectations. Under the hat, Shorty was just another cowboy.

Unhatted, Shorty's head proved to be oddly small and squarish, proving that most all of the crown had been empty. He had a rough mess of unruly blond-brown hair, and without the hat, by God his features soon assembled themselves, in Charles's eye and particularly in the red flicker of the fire, into something very similar to Baby Face Nelson's. Shorty had the pug nose, the freckly Huck Finn guile, the square pug jaw, everything symmetrical and conventionally attractive.

"You look a lot like a certain fellow," said Charles.

"I know, sir," said Shorty.

Charles saw how it happened. Shorty arrived once every couple of months with the Rocking-R bunch and, over the course of a few days' hard labor in the pens, would take his hat off to wipe a brow clean or some sweat from his eyes, or to take a swat at a particularly obnoxious fly. Someone would catch a glimpse—Baby Face's face was well enough known among newspaper readers—and then look back to check, by which time Shorty had re-planted his ten-gallon, so the illusion was lost. But sooner or later someone would say, "Hey, I think I saw Baby Face Nelson out there," and the story would embellish itself as it moved from pen to pen and outfit to outfit, until someone finally called the cops or the Division. But by the time the Riot Squad arrived, Rocking-R would have headed back to Lubbock or wherever.

"You get in much trouble on account?"

"Spent nights in jail all along the rail line. Don't know nothing about this Nelson, except he robs and kills. Don't even own no gun, 'cept my granddad's '92. But every sheriff in the Southwest has thrown me in the crap hole."

"He's got papers backing up his name?"

"He does. They don't work Rocking-R without papers."

"May I see them, son?"

"Yes, sir," said the boy, and produced a leather wallet, which contained documents verifying him to be exactly who he said he was.

As he handed them back, Charles said, "Not for me to tell you what to do, but you look like you got enough bristle on your face to grow some hair. Until we get this damned Nelson, and even a few months after, you might think about a beard or something. It might just change you up enough to end all this nonsense."

"I been after him for months but the damn fool won't. He thinks the gals like him better with his pretty mug all buck naked."

"Shorty, ever hear of a fellow named Gable? He does okay with the gals behind his toothbrush. You got enough lip to grow one like he has. I'm just saying looking all smooth and handsome might get you killed by some trigger-brained cow-town deputy who wants to run for mayor."

"You hear him, Shorty? That's Uncle Sam himself talking," said the foreman.

"I'll give it some thought, sir."

"That's the boy," said Charles. "And now my business is concluded, so I will leave Rocking-R territory to Rocking-R folks. Didn't even need my tommy gun."

He and Lutie shook hands, Charles turned down an escort for the two-catwalk trek back to the main road. Charles figured a half-an-hour walk, then a half-an-hour drive, and he'd be home before midnight for a bath and a cooldown. Oh, figure in dinner; he'd have to pick some up.

He made his goodbyes, found the steps, and got himself back to the shower house; from there, he found the steps to the catwalk back to the main road of this quadrant and proceeded without incident.

That catwalk trek, wobbly as it was, dumped him on the wide straight pull between the pens that headed back to the admin buildings and the yard dick office. It was too late to do his shoes any good, so he just clomped ahead, picking up mud and straw with every step even if he watched carefully to avoid obvious puddles, cow pies, and mud slicks. On and on he went, under a calm sky, the cattle soothed in their nighttime pens and most on haunches for a night's rest, to dream cow dreams of green meadows and clear brooks and blue skies. No moon stood up to amuse them, and perhaps the veil of dust and stink blurred the air, for the stars were dim pricks of illumination, what few of them were visible.

It was a trek through nothing until at the halfway point it turned suddenly to something.

FEBRUARY 1934

CHAPTER 4

THERE ARE ALWAYS PROBLEMS IN MEATPACKING. UNION PROBLEMS, fire problems, animal quality problems, rail problems, track repair problems, maintenance problems, theft problems, federal inspection problems, payoff problems, and on and on. No day is without its problems, but the problems at Nugent's were particular.

"And what can be done, then?" asked Thaddeus Nugent, owner and president, of Oscar Bentley, manager and make-it-happen guy of the house. The setting was Thaddeus's rather dingy office high above the killing floor, but not above the stench of blood and shit. They were considering the most ominous darkness ahead: the future. Theirs was black because the numbers were red.

Thaddeus was not happy. He was not really suited for the hustle and bravo of big meat. Moreover, he hated the Yards in winter, when, as now, the months-long blanket of snow, which this year, as all years, had fallen in Chicago, revealed the true nature of his enterprise and destiny: contaminated by yellow and brown stains, everywhere, everywhere, it revealed the site as a vast animal toilet. Most here got used to it; Thaddeus never did.

"Hire better guys is the only thing I see," said Oscar.

It was true enough. Being low to profit margin and just basically scuffling by, Nugent's Best Beef could not afford to hire experienced herders at nearly the hourly rate Swift and Armour and Morris paid. Plus, no man gifted in handling the beasts would consider working for a low-ranker like Nugent's in the first place, and the fact that its ramshackle spew of pens and passageways and process lines and kill rooms and other necessities was right next to the Pulverized Manure Company on Exchange Avenue, far from the shine of the big boys, was not an attraction either. The place looked as if had been designed by Charles Dickens's dumber brother, when in fact—*designed* wasn't quite the right word—it had been assembled by Thaddeus's smarter grandfather Phillip.

"I cannot get them to run the kill chute operation any better," said Oscar. "They are incapable of it. They are, to a man, quite stupid, easily rattled, afraid of falling amongst the cattle and being smashed to death, fast and sloppy. Immigrants, not cowhands. What can a Czech or a Pole know of beef except 'Don't step in the shit, don't get skewered on the horns'? Thaddeus, it's the quality of the man that determines the quality of the meat. We have terrible men. Thus we'll have terrible beef. Thus our sales will—and have—dropped. Thus we'll never get big contracts for railway or restaurant, thus our cannery will be of second quality, the odd can splitting, the spoilage rate high, the art on the can pitiful. Thus no sales to the big chain groceries like National Tea, or Atlantic and Pacific, that now predominate, and we will make our living, as we do, on the outskirts of the industry, shufflers and lurkers and hustlers, racing after the odd local chain to stock our products. We'll sell, as we do, mostly to institutions that don't require quality as they don't produce quality. Negro hospitals and schools, the same on Indian reservations, prisons of course, faltering steamship lines and trunk line railroads. We will stay where we are and are lucky to have survived this long through the Depression. The only hope I can see is that there'll be a big war and it will be as good to us as the Great War was. So pray for war, sir. Say, doesn't this happy little fellow in Germany look promising?"

Oscar was entirely too practical and truthful a chap to make jokes, so his Hitler line was delivered quite earnestly. To him, the greasy little agitator with the flop hair and the smudge mustache was the only hope for getting out of Packingtown and up to Winnetka, where Thad already lived, though barely.

"No one ever accused you of steering off the truth, Oscar. I wish I were rich enough to fire you and be done with your damned pessimism, but I'm not and I will never be. Besides, I knew all this already. You merely grind it into the bone, so it hurts."

"I do."

"Is there no hope of surcease? Perhaps Swift will buy us out?"

"To acquire our lucrative Rhode Island penitentiary contracts? I doubt it."

"Let us then try to think creatively."

"The word 'creative' frightens me, Thaddeus. It leads always to ruin."

"I have been thinking."

"God help us," said Oscar.

"Now, see if you can poke my logic. Run at it hard, without respect. Crush it, then tear it to pieces. Try to make me cry. We'll see what remains."

"I would without instruction. That is my way."

"All right, then. The problems begin at the chute. Bad chute management sets the ball of catastrophe rolling; that seems to be the root of our problems. Is that not correct?"

"That is correct."

"Thus far too much of our meat can be categorized as of the darkcutter variety. It isn't good and will never be good."

"Correct again."

"But we can't afford better men."

"We cannot."

"We cannot afford better cattle."

"We'll never experience Rolling-R stock except at the better restaurants."

"What if—"

"Yes, sir?"

"What if we could come up with a fast way to soothe the beasts. I mean extra-process."

"I'm not—"

"Chemical!"

For once Oscar had nothing to say. It was beyond his horizon. He knew nothing of chemicals. He knew everything of the giant animals whose deaths in the tens of thousands were his to manage, but nothing of chemicals.

"I have been in contact with Marjory's brother. He is a veterinarian. He believes it is possible to apply a certain solution to the cow that, no matter his condition in extremis, will calm him. Thus the chute itself, the ignorant foreign men with their clubs and straps, the crowding, the blood in the air, the smell of the shit, his hunger and thirst—none of it will matter. He will go happily up the chute and accept the sledge without rancor. Hence, quickly, our percentage of darkcutter is all but destroyed. Hence our brand becomes tasty, then popular. We all end up in Winnetka, even our knockers."

"There must be a flaw."

"There is. Anesthesia is inherently tricky. Anesthesia is close on euthanasia. It is so tricky that among humans, it can only be applied by a specialist MD. Only a specialist DVM may handle it as applied to the bovine. Or the canine or the feline or the . . . well, you're getting the picture. It can kill."

CHAPTER 5

CHARLES SAW THE FIGURE EMERGE FROM A TRACE BETWEEN PENS AND arrange itself against a fence, in seeming repose. But he knew at once it was no cowboy, for cowboys were seldom of Africa, and seldom dressed so big-city, with a tan jacket over a blue workingman's shirt, and a fedora. He was tall, thin, well put together, with the ropey muscles that the blacks have in abundance. Not enough light here to see his features, but Charles read his body and saw tension, spring, readiness, and presumed that no-good was on the fellow's mind. It was a good place for no-good too, as no witnesses were in evidence, not even the dozing cows, and not a human soul awake or sober in a square mile. Charles figured the man was on the hunt for a drunken cowboy ambling back to his outfit, and meant to leap upon him, maybe clonk him with a cosh or hold a knife to his throat and make off with a wallet or a half-full bottle before the victim realized he'd been jumped.

As he approached, the fellow lifted himself off the fence and set himself on two feet, weight evenly distributed, an action-ready set that also spoke of trouble.

"Hold on there, brother," said Charles, coming to a halt. "What's this about? You lost?"

"No, suh," came the voice, and the man took a step closer. "You gots my money."

"Partner, I never saw you before."

"You gots it and I need it back. Here, now. I gets it or I be sending you to glory."

"I am a law officer," said Charles. "I am armed, and though I mean you no harm, I will shoot to defend myself."

This news was greeted sullenly. The man wilted at the complication, and some readiness seemed to drain from his limbs. Again, though some distance remained between them, and Charles could not read features, he had the impression of anguish, of disappointment, of realization that a fragile plan had just been demolished. But then readiness squirted back into his frame, maybe this time fueled by desperation, and he squared his shoulders and took another step.

"I need my money," he said. "Mister, you give me my money, or goddammit, I'll take it from you." His hand disappeared and came out with a knife, and its blade caught what little ambient light fell from the stars above. It was a long, wicked blade, meant for stabbing deep or cutting wide. It was designed to open bovine throats.

But before the knife came to *en garde*, Charles's fast right hand blurred into his coat where he carried his Great War Colt pistol in the fancy S. D. Myres's No. 12 shoulder holster. And from that stash to its own *en garde*, this time with Colt's automatic equalizer pointed straight to the chest of the man, the thumb having snicked off the safety in mid-blur.

"You put the weapon down and lock on the fence and I will cuff you, and you will live to see morning," Charles said.

"You think you can drop me before I get seven inches of blade into you?"

"Not many could, but it's to your misfortune that I am one."

"I needs my money," the man screamed, radiating a singularity that had to be a form of insanity.

He launched himself, fast as an animal leap, and while most on the receiving end of such an assault would have cinched up in panic and made ready to die, Charles shot him three times. The flashes, each a fraction-second's spurt of incandescence, caught an increasingly desperate expression that blinked from rage to fear to wide-eyed dumbfounded-ment, and like Johnny, this fellow could not stand against hardball three times, and he corkscrewed left and drove himself like an awl into the mud and shit at a fence line.

Charles pivoted, put a foot on the knife, which was still in the hand, pinned it, and knelt through the stench of burned powder, a relief from the other atmosphere.

"What a fool thing," he said. "Nobody runs at the pistol."

"Tell my wife I am so sorry what I done, what happened."

He reached out, groping, for human touch as he died, and Charles transferred the pistol to his left and kept it leveled to the head on the ancient principle of trust but verify, caught with the other hand and held the man's, felt its tightness and warmth but also felt the exact instant death reached through the arm to the hand, when it went limp. He laid it across the chest.

He rose, holstered, and looked about. Where the Johnny Dillinger kill had excited the known world, this one seemed to have had no impact at all. The universe was as empty as an abandoned attic. In a few seconds, however, cowboys in various stages of undress edged out of the darkness and approached.

"He shot a dark one, looks like."

"Mister, you okay?"

"He must be a cop."

"Sounded like a machine gun."

"Look at the knife that boy got. Man, you dropped him hard."

"Black boys are crazy in this town."

"All right," Charles yelled. "Y'all stay back. I am a law officer and this is officially a crime scene. We don't need you trampling it up. Someone call or run for a police officer. We need to get this handled properly."

In time, two yard bulls showed, coming from nowhere, certainly not from the direction of the station. Odd or not? Possibly just off the scurry for the Jewish gold. Anyhow, big men, sullen of face, dressed like the hobos they usually billy-clubbed, but with badges on the chest too ceremonial for the clothes. The badges had scrolls and columns and maple leaves. The two paid no attention to the dead man, because, after all, he didn't mean a thing to them.

"We heard shots. What's going on here, bub?" asked the one, another Irisher lit red by internal fires, so red that it showed in the darkness.

"He plugged a coon," said the other.

"Jump you, is that the story?"

"My name's Swagger, Justice Department Division of Investigation. I have a badge too." Charles flipped his lapel. "Isn't as fancy as yours. What are you, archdukes from Ruritania?"

"Ease off on the lip, bub," said one. "We don't want to have to send you to silly-land."

"Feds," said the other. "They think they sit at God's right hand."

"Let's just get this done," said Swagger.

"So spill. You were on the trigger, not us."

Charles—who hated to explain—explained. The boys took no notes, made no show of listening, and afterward asked no questions. Open-and-shut, closed, let's go home.

"Only one thing," said Paddy, or was it Paddy? "See, it don't matter what we say, but it matters what New York says. Our outfit is owned by that town, and they have funny rules. I'm thinking they might not like some federal fancy-pants coming directly on our property and plowing somebody under, colored or not. Not good for business. Scares customers. Got rich people here at our big steak restaurant, the Stock Yard Inn. Scare them off, business could drop."

"You are headed in the wrong direction, Father O'Toole," said Charles. "You and your pal Father O'Shaughnessy, you try to shake down a federal officer, all the leprechauns and all the archbishops in the world won't save you."

"See, he's got it backward," said one.

"Bub, it's like this. Some New York lawyer gets on this, and our giant company owned by the most powerful men in America, they come after your division. They scare everybody. Next thing you know, you got press, you got Congress, you're giving depositions the night long, you're testifying. First, I'm thinking your nancy-boy boss"—first time Charles had ever heard this one, but he let no surprise show on his soldier face—"won't like it being said his boys shot down a colored for no reason. He won't like the way it interferes with business. Then, somewhere, this pipsqueak machine gunner Nelson, he'll be laughing as he mows down more Indiana bankers and their wives and kids while the man who got Dillinger—yeah, we figured that out, bub—is tied up in court."

"Let me tell you mugs, you do not want to get in my shade. I'm one of those stubborn West Arkansas bird dogs who never lets anything go and never forgets. This will come around and bite you hard."

"Here's the solution. We have a charity. It's called the Widows and Orphans Fund of the USY and T Police Division. Now, maybe you make a contribution, all this could go away, and we end up drinking suds together and singing 'Oh, Tommy Boy' until the wee hours."

"Sounds like a good idea to me," said the other. "How much you got on you, gunfighter?"

But before Charles could answer, another player slid into the circle. He was a Negro, and a Chicago policeman, in tunic and severe visored cap low over hooded eyes. He was tall and broad and rather athletic-looking, and his pride of person was evident. He was no buckler, and it was the first time Charles had encountered a black man in uniform and badge and cap of authority, independent and freestanding, working among white people as if he were any citizen at all.

"What's all this?" he said. "I see a dead man, two bulls, and a standing-tall, no-backing-down agent of some sort. You, Mulligan, you want to explain?"

"Slim here dropped a colored with a knife. He says he's federal, so it's okay. We're just clearing it up."

It was an astonishment that Charles had never seen. The black man himself was standing tall, no back-down.

"Who are you, sir?" asked the black.

"Swagger, Justice Department. Out here on official business. This poor man came out of the dark with that knife. I had to put him down." He watched as the officer knelt at the body, turned it over, peeked at the wounds in the chest.

"Sir, you must be a good shot. You put three in the same inch in the center of his heart. The boy was dead and gone and in hell before his knees even bent on the way down."

"I have done some shooting before," said Charles.

"We heard the Division people were all well advanced in the pistol."

"Some are, some aren't. It happens, and too bad for this fellow that I know a thing or two."

"Say there, Cap," said one of the bulls, "this here is railroad property and no business of Chicago Blue. If I's you, I'd head on—"

"The name," said the officer, "is Sylvester Washington. You may know of me."

The Irishers eyeballed each other briefly.

Washington stepped forward, coming squarely into what light there was, and his big hand rested casually on his revolver, immediately visible because it had ivory grips. By the thickness of its frame, Charles saw that it was no dowdy Colt but instead Smith & Wesson's .38 on a .44 frame, extra strong to take a new higher-powered cartridge somebody had just put out. It was a revolver for stopping fights fast.

"So you'd be Two-Gun Pete," said one of the Irishmen.

"That's me," said the larger man, "but feel free to call me Officer Washington."

"All right," one said, "the great man-killer himself. You want this, you've got it. We'll read about it in the papers."

With that, they eased off into the night and in seconds were gone.

The black man turned back to Charles, and Charles saw the second .38-.44 frame on his left side, same ivory gleaming like a polished bone, though with grip facing out so that the man could go to it fast across his body with his right hand instead of fumbling through a reload.

"I've seen enough to read the scene," he said. "From the position of the shell casings, the shape of his footprints in the mud signifying speed, as in a rush, and yours steady, signifying stillness, and finally that pig sticker still tight in his dead hand, I can tell he was the aggressor and you the defender. So it accords with your account. I have no problem accepting it as self-defense."

"Appreciated, Officer," said Charles. "Now I suppose we wait till detectives and Coroner's Office people arrive. We'll be here all night, I'm guessing."

"That's the issue to be decided," said Officer Washington. "This can run two ways. Easy and hard."

"What's hard?"

"I call it in as justified homicide. That means, as you say, detectives, maybe somebody from City Attorney's, fellows from the morgue to photo, then chart the body and the scene. Even with the yard bulls out of the picture, it's still complicated. I write my report and I give a statement. All the police Irish try to figure out what politics might be involved, how it could be played to advantage, and some inspector named O'County Cork sees a way to leverage the Division, and maybe games are played and it does get complicated. All the Irish run the same game. Some of it is simple mischief; they just want to see what advantage they get out of it. Oh, and all this won't even begin till morning, because no senior detective is going to come down here and ruin his shoes in the mud and shit, like you have ruined yours. We have to wait till morning when some new junior comes in, and they'll send him so they can laugh at what it does to his shoes. Still, the upshot is that bosses are involved, yours and mine and Union Stock Yard and Transit Company's, and since I'm a Negro my bosses hate me and won't listen to me and will take this where it pleases them and where it gains them something. As to what your bosses make of it, sir, I wouldn't know."

"It could get complicated at that end too," said Charles, thinking of Hugh Clegg and his own hungers for leverage and conspiracy.

"The other alternative is, you go. I mean, you leave, however you came, as if you were never here. I call this in as a John Doe Negro, found facedown in the mud. One more dead Negro in the city of Chicago is hardly going to set the town afire again. When the meat wagon gets around to it, they pick him up and hang a toe tag on him. He gets the only private room of his life, a drawer in the morgue, and if nobody comes to identify him, he goes to the city Negro cemetery and is planted under no marker whatsoever. He is gone forever. It's not a tragedy, it's only a fact. They die all the time and nobody hardly notices. My job is to make sure it doesn't disturb the Irish machine, and as long as I do that, I will have food on the table. But, telling you a secret now, my real work is to find some justice now and then for the Negro. I am telling you that as you never called me 'boy' or 'Sylvester,' but 'sir' and 'Officer.' I return the respect by telling you the truth."

"You are quite the fellow, Officer Washington, I can see that. You pack two big guns and have no fear of dark places, alleys, or offices full of Irish. I will take your advice willingly and call this poor man a Doe." He felt as if sixteen tons of cow flop had just been removed from his shoulders. He imagined having a shot of bourbon while smoking a cigar on his fire escape before shutting it down for the evening.

"Agreed. Life's short enough without the Irish," said the Negro officer.

"But I do have a question I'd like to put to you."

"Please go ahead, sir."

"I have killed before, possibly too many times, but always it made some sense. It was war or he was a known criminal. It was easy to put away afterward. This fellow, whoever, he stood face on to the muzzle of the automatic and was warned of the consequences. Yet still, crazily I would say, he jumped me. I suppose he hoped I'd knit up and he'd have the advantage, even though I warned him against it. But on he came and down he went."

"Maybe he was hopped up. These folks down here, they'll put any-thing into their systems for the pleasure it gives them, and hang the consequences later. Perhaps he had juju in him or the white powder or some other chemical. But I would say, no responsibility affixes to you, and try to forget it. It's only the Fourth District, that's all, Agent Swagger. Nothing matters in the Fourth District."

CHAPTER 6

HE WENT STRAIGHT TO THE OFFICE, ARRIVING AT 5 A.M., AND TYPED UP his report. That got him to 7 a.m., and the report would be there for Clegg when he got in, with carbons for Sam and Mel's daily piles, to be read or just filed when they returned. He made no mention of the shooting and the agreement with Officer Washington, though, to be safe, he'd noted Washington's badge number and written it down in his notebook, along with Washington's phone number. Then he left the office, found a diner for eggs, juice, and bacon, but stayed off the coffee as he worried it would keep him awake. Fed, he took the El back to the near north side and his little studio and went upstairs and slept a few hours. At 2 p.m., he called in and Clegg seemed satisfied and told him not to bother to come in, and he'd see him tomorrow.

That was fine with Charles. He'd left his shoes on the fire escape, and now he examined them and concluded that they were beyond salvaging. So wearing field boots, he went out and checked into a few shoe stores, and remembering Sam's admonition that quality is cheaper in the long run, he bought a nice pair of brown oxfords in what was called Scotch grain, all pebbled like a football, with six outlets for the thick, strong laces and thick soles, made by a firm he was told was the best, called Cheaney, an English outfit. They were claimed to be waterproof.

That effort accomplished, he had a steak for dinner, then called his wife, to whom he hadn't spoken in a number of weeks.

The reports were not happy. Bobby Lee was cutting himself again, and she'd taped the drawers with the knives closed, hoping it would dissuade him. If he wasn't cutting himself, the boy hid in his room, drawing rocket airplanes and singing in a strange language. He was getting strong and seldom responded to her. She was afraid of him. What would happen if—

"I can't come home, dammit," said Charles. "We are in the middle of a campaign here and I have people relying on me. I can't let them down, just like in the war."

"Why did you take that job? You only took it to get away from Bobby Lee. But what does that leave me, stuck in a house with a boy who needs help and could do something terrible at any moment. He needs your love and guidance. Since you've been gone, he's gotten worse."

"I'm hoping to parlay this into something bigger and better for all of us," Charles said. "We can get Bobby Lee some top-drawer help and make him better. If he is beyond help, we can put him somewhere nice, not some state home where he's in a snake pit with violent lunatics and deviates."

"Charles, you always say you're doing things for us, but it's only you that reaps the benefits."

They had been down this road many a time, and it always ended in a bitter dead end after some screaming. He did not feel up to it tonight.

"You are getting the money regular, right? I could call the judge and I'm sure he'd add some dough to the kitty. After all, in a way, I am working for his interests too."

"Charles, be careful. Don't get yourself in city trouble you can't shoot your way out of. Those people have tricks you never heard of."

"I'm fine. Anything from the other boy?"

"Earl said that he was in a battle finally, and that he came through okay and was told he done well."

"I know he has it in him to make an excellent Marine," said Charles. "You should have told him that instead of browbeating him so often."

That one again.

"He had a stubborn streak. He had to learn to follow orders. I'm sure the lessons I taught him have done him well in Nicaragua or wherever else they send him."

There wasn't much more to say, and the conversation ended on a sour, unresolved note. Charles hung up, realizing that his life made no sense at all, and he decided the cigar on the fire escape wouldn't please him a bit. Instead, he decided on an early bedtime, as he was feeling a yearning for whiskey, and it was best to escape in the sheets. He hoped he wouldn't see a Negro with a knife in his hand coming hard at him in his dreams and dozed off.

He was lucky. No Negroes visited that night. Only the usual—Germans with bayonets.

It was the same everywhere in the city, except that here all the men were colored. Charles had never seen so many in one geographic location; it was like an alternate universe gone completely black, different but the same. The men were just as bitter, sweltering, and angry as any American men—it's just that they were shade. Sylvester Washington drove carefully, finally easing the cruiser into a parking space fronting on a row of brick tenements, low, gray buildings in the low, gray light, the grass all gone to thatch, the trees hung with parched leaves, the bushes bristly.

Washington got out. They were at a street corner, 75th and Roosevelt, far in the city's south side, a few miles beyond the Stock Yards. The street here was empty. The weather was hot, forecast hotter. The asphalt repairs to the gritty streets looked like melting licorice. You stepped in it, you might not get your new Cheaney shoe out.

Charles followed Washington as he led the way into one of the buildings. It was a scabby place, flat-roofed, raw brick, needing paint, a gray wooden stairway that creaked on the way up, the second floor yielding a hallway with a few doors on it, amid stark shadow lattices cut by a bare bulb on a cord. Washington went to the middle left, knocked twice.

Charles trailed him in. A grim woman awaited, in a baggy print dress. Her face was sunken and no light showed in her eyes, only resignation. Two children sprawled at the kitchen corner. They looked at Swagger with the deadest eyes he'd ever seen. The place was illuminated by sunlight as electricity was too expensive to waste on reality.

"Miz Roberts, this here the investigator I told you about. Looking into the death of your husband, George. I told you, now, you just answer his questions, maybe we get to the bottom of this."

The woman did not know that George Roberts had come at Charles with a knife in the Stock Yards and Charles had shot him dead. She only knew that that night George didn't come home, nor the next nor the next. On the fourth day, she went to the Chicago morgue and watched as a body was pulled from a file cabinet of corpses, unzipped from its rubber bag, and there was the man who had fathered her children and supported her and them extremely well by the standards of the time until . . .

Did she want to take possession of the body? She had no money to pay for a funeral, much less an undertaker, and so that was that, without apology. She filled out a form that permitted the city to do what it was going to do whether she signed it or not and left the building, knowing that George's next stop was an unmarked site in potter's Negro field.

"Someone killed him," she said. "I know who. Even if it was some other man wif a gun, it happened because of a certain man."

"Ma'am, to help you I need to hear about it. Maybe something can be done."

"Nuffin' can be done," she said. "World don't work that way."

"There can be exceptions," said Charles.

She looked at him, mournful and solemn. Her eyes were blank to possibility, her body torn by gravity. She had no place to go, no money, and though it was hotter now than wind from the devil's ass, a bitter Chicago winter was coming on.

"What you care?" she asked.

"It's what my department does," he said. "Now, please: What was going on with George? Who do you think killed him, or put him in a situation where he got killed?"

What made him charge the gun? Why did I have to put three hardballs into him and watch him die in the cattle shit of the Stock Yards?

She told it. George Roberts had been on the slaughter line for Armour. He was not without skill. He was a knocker. It was a good, steady job, at 9 cents an hour. The issue was the workday, which was usually fourteen hours, six days a week.

George was a member of Amalgamated Meat Cutters 173, however, and 173, in concert with many other union locals in the Yards, was on the agitation for an eight-hour workday. Finally, a year ago, 173 went out on strike for the eight-hour day, along with six other unions. It was a long, tough strike, with more than a little picket-line violence, more than a few heads broken on each side of the line (the company brought in scabs from the South, men just as desperate as the strikers). After six months of the workers making do on the tiny union relief fund, the strike was settled—for a penny raise on all hours over eight per day.

Everyone knew Union leadership—that is, the Italians—had been bought off by Armour or had sold out the workers, but no one could do anything about it. All those who'd campaigned against signing the new contract had been subject to intensive goon violence. The contract passed, but just barely, with charges of a rigged election. And everyone who voted against the agreement was mysteriously fired the next day, then blackballed and couldn't get jobs in the industry. George was desperate for money to move his family back to Mississippi, where he'd heard the steel mills were hiring, but he couldn't afford the tickets for the Illinois Central. It seemed that the three biggest institutions in his life—Armour,

Amalgamated Meat Cutters 173, and the Illinois Central—were dead set on destroying him.

"He was near crazy. He be in such a hurt. Man thought his babies goin' starve."

"You said 'because of a certain man.' May I ask who?"

She looked hard at Washington, and it was as if some strange Negro information passed between them no white person could ever understand.

"I didn' mean nothin' or nobody. Certain man. *The* man. You know, they all different, they all the same. Holdin' us down, killin' us if need be, always gittin' away with it."

"I see," said Charles. "So what's next for you?"

"You lookin' at it, sir," she said. "When winter come, we freeze here in this hole, pray fo' warm weather and a break or two."

"Do you have anything in Mississippi?"

"It ain't gonna happen."

"What about a job in the other mills, for the cotton?"

"How I git down there? Illinois Central ticket fo' us three cost near on fifty dollah. Then what? Where I put the boys when we gets there, while I look fo' a job, then a place to stay? Maybe I don't start fo' a week. Who feed us then?"

"Do you have people there, Miz Roberts?" asked Washington.

"My mama, and George's. But hard on them too, just barely keeping alive. I don't see nothing but the street fo' me, if I can git the state to take over the boys, but George Jr., he weak, you know, he ain't no tough one, and if he go into a home he gwine git hurt."

"All right," said Charles. He reached into his pocket, pulling out the last of the money he'd gotten from the mob people as the Dillinger bonus.

"I'm giving you two hundred dollars in cash money."

Her eyes went all wide, maybe crazy.

"Suh!"

"You listen here. That's money to get you back to Mississippi, to support you while you get settled and employed. You guard this money well. Don't give it to anybody, don't tell anybody. Don't show anybody. Don't let anybody hold it. It's killing money, down here. Lots of thieves and slickers in the world, and they feed on folks like you. Do you get it?"

"Yes, suh. Oh Jesus, you must be an angel and—"

"Now, stop with that kind of talk. I'm just a sinner, vain and proud and stubborn, like any bad man. But I do want to help, for my own reasons. You take the money, you get out of this town as fast as you can and start over where it's better or at least warmer. Don't waste money on a new hat, you don't need a new hat. But before you leave, you take these boys to an eatery and get them fed on meat and potatoes, do you hear?"

"Yes, suh."

He turned to Washington, who looked at him in utter surprise.

"Our business is done here. Let's go. Good day and good luck, Mrs. Roberts."

"Suh, Jehovah himself will take you into heaven."

"I doubt that," said Charles.

They went back out to the car wordlessly and settled into the drive back to Comiskey Park, where Charles had parked his Pontiac.

"Never heard of that," Washington finally said.

"It's between you and me, right? You're not going to spread the story."

"No, sir. I swear it."

"Something's going on down here, and it smells real bad. It needs to be looked at."

CHAPTER 7

HE FIRST HEARD IT AT THE LOCKUP NEAR COMISKEY PARK. WAS IT SAID straight-out, or in parts from which he inferred its meaning, or had he imagined it? Didn't want to appear too curious at all. Made no sign of noticing, which was hard among the cops, for they survived by noticing. Still, was it real or a phantasm?

He had come down here to pick up just such a clue, telling Clegg and then Sam that he wasn't sure about Baby Face and needed more time to poke around. As office star, until another one came along, he got that freedom without trouble. That was the nature of an office.

He mingled, he wandered, he made friends, he answered questions when asked, and nobody seemed to care. That was good. He meant to overhear what was being said unofficially, in the squad rooms or showers, by the cops. No need for reports to brass, no need for press attention, no need for badge showing. But cops know stuff, somehow. These boys knew—magically, it seemed—he was the one who had put Johnny down. In their world, that made him a hero, if for no other reason than it meant that was one less tommy gun for them to face if it came to pass.

"I went to the library and looked at that Negro newspaper, the *Chicago Defender*. It seemed the South Side had gotten much more violent this year. More murder among the South Side folks, more assaults on police, more times one of you had to drop one of them. Lots of anger on both sides. Or am I wrong?"

"What are you looking for, federal man?" asked the sergeant, as Irish as a map of Dublin. "We just do what has to be done and that's that. We're the blue wall. Keep the black people from edging uptown into white areas like the Loop or the North Side and everything is fine. If their deaths go up a little down here, it doesn't matter, and that will happen because your Negro is a moody lad under the smiling, and sometimes on no account, he gets angry. Takes it out on wife, best friend, stranger, nearest police officer. In the latter case, he earns three in the chest, and don't tell me you didn't put three in the chest of that boy in the Stock Yards, no matter what Sylvester Washington's report says."

"I know how it goes, O'Brian, and I'm not down here to upset apple carts. I'm no reformer—no reports are going to the Loop. I just want to know how things are in case we have to operate down here against Baby Face."

It took a few visits before they got to trust him, or at least be less guarded in their chatter. Yet one time he went back to his Loop office with a new phrase banging around his brain—had he heard it, or had he heard parts of it and inferred the rest? Hard to tell, hard to remember. But if he bore down with whiskey as a reward, he could maybe get something coherent, and he did: the phrase was "the Night Train," as in "Was he ridin' the Night Train?" "Had to be. They don't act like that straight up. It was a Night Train Express the whole way."

What was the Night Train? To the blue Irish, it seemed to be code for the train to oblivion. Life being too hard, the black man just gave up, climbed aboard, and the end of the line was a better place.

Then one day a Costello shot a Johnson dead after pulling him over for erratic driving, and after the afternoon's cop celebration at a bar so Irish it seemed built of potato was over, Charles intercepted Costello as the crowd broke up, finding him more than a little drunk.

"You know who I am?"

Costello laughed. He was young, enjoyed being a hero at least for a day, and had gone three over his limit and switched to whiskey.

"I do. Yes sir, you was pointed out to me. The man who shot—"

"Never mind that. Just tell me about the man you shot."

"Nothin' to it, Mr. Federal. He's bouncing from curb to curb in that boat he's driving. I pulls him over. He's stinking of the hooch, he is. He hands me his license but sure, I can tell even more he's six sheets into the wind. I'm hoping to take him to lockup where he can sleep it off. He'd be what you call a 'good Negro,' if you know what I mean. So nobody needs to get hurt on account."

"What happened?"

"He changed. In a flash. He gets out of the car and I say, 'Whoa, there, big fella, back inside, keep them hands on the wheel.' His face all strange now. Didn't look crazy at all. Looked like he was already a corpse. Eyes all dead. But he's a big fella, almost two hundred fifty, while I'm a runt Irisher at a hundred or so less. 'Whoa,' says I, 'back off now, big fella, you too sloshed to be moving about.' He don't say a thing, but he just leaps and gets me pinned against the hood, and throws them big paws around me neck—here, look—"

The Irishman shoved down his tunic collar and indeed Charles saw the bruising, purple/yellow, rotted like fallen fruit.

"I'm dead, but I think clear enough to draw me pistol, and though I don't remember neither doing it nor hearing it, it seems I drilled him four times up through the gut to the heart and that was it for him. He lets me go, takes two steps, and hits the pavement like a sack of cement. Going to see the Cubs tomorrow."

"Who're they playing?"

"The Giants."

"Sounds like a good game. So this fellow had a name?"

"John J. Johnson, Jr. Was an undertaker, of John J. Johnson and Son, on Cottage Grove. By their standards, a big man. No record, deacon at Baptist Ebenezer. Taxpayer, Shriner, big contributor to Mayor Cermak. Don't know what could have made him go loco like that, but I'm hearing it happens more and more."

"The liquor, you think? Holding it isn't something they do well."

"Could be, sir. But they've always had liquor and this thing seems new so maybe it's something else, or maybe it's some red college student from the university is stirring them up to hating the white."

"They just crack and attack?"

"Used to be your better black fellow both respected and feared we Irishers in blue. That seems to have changed, the boys say. This year. All of a sudden."

The last time he'd seen it was the night he put Johnny down at the movie palace. Then it had been mobbed, with crowds and photogs and other press frogs and radio cowboys about. Everybody wanted to see the great Johnny Dillinger laid out on a slab, his toes poking free, the exit wound from Charles's head shot a blister below the right eye. It was like the premiere of a big new picture: *The World Without Johnny Dillinger*.

Now, late on a hot August afternoon, the building was just nondescript brick in a cluster of buildings of the Chicago Gigantic Style. It was hardly noticeable among the big boys of the county hospital complex, which looked like its own downtown sprouting off a mile or so west of the skyscrapers. The Cook County Morgue's location was Harrison Street, about twenty blocks due west of the lake.

His badge got him in, that plus the name of the pathologist who'd done the autopsy work on Johnny under the eyes of most of the Midwestern Division brass, Mel and Sam at the head of the party, there to make sure the man who had so bedeviled them was in fact dead. In a while the doctor appeared, balding, wire-rimmed, no different from any of the many white-coated death professionals heading this way and that.

"Doc, remember me?"

"I sure do. Special Agent Swagger of the Division, right? You brought down Johnny last month."

"Well, two fellows were with me, and stopping Johnny turned out not to be that important. Still some bad ones, especially that Baby Face, on the loose."

"I have no doubts I'll see Baby Face on the slab soon enough. But what's doing that brings you here?"

"Actually, another case. I'm aware that a new client arrived here yesterday evening late from the South Side. He was colored. Name of John J.—"

"Yes, Mr. Johnson. A very fine man. I cannot for the life of me figure out what got into him."

"I'm assuming no autopsy."

"The four bullet holes are autopsy enough. The family, grief-stricken to be sure, wants the body back. Obviously they have an interest in sending him off in grand style. Good for business."

"Yes, sir, I do see their point and don't want to tie anything up and make their difficulties more pointed. However, because it relates to something else I'm working on, I'd be gratified if you could pull a blood sample for me. Just enough for the Division chemists to examine."

"Special Agent Swagger, you would need a court order for that."

"Yes, I'm aware. But as I say, it's not in regard to Mr. Johnson, but to a John Doe who died under similar circumstances. His body is some weeks underground now, and getting to him would involve major effort on the part of several reluctant bureaucracies. I want an unofficial baseline so I can determine if pulling the Doe out of the ground is worth the effort. I'm shortcutting, you see, as the Nelson situation is number one on our list, but I don't want this one to be lost and forgotten."

"So nothing official. I'm happy to assist, but I don't want to get bitten on the ass."

"It's a favor, not a Division request."

"Well, favors I can handle. Paperwork from Justice Department officials is another story. Let's see what we can do about it, then."

It only took a few minutes to relieve Mr. Johnson of an ounce of his fluid. At slumber in a horizontal human filing cabinet in the Big Room, he did not appear to mind. The doctor quickly inserted a syringe, withdrew the dark liquid, squirted it into a tiny bottle already marked "Johnson," and handed it to Charles. Mr. Johnson, both fat and dead, lay in sublime stillness, his eyes gently closed, his face relaxed, and his composure serene. As the sampling was accomplished, Charles noticed how manicured his fingers were, how polished his nails. Even his toes were at their finest, his pencil-thin mustache razored up to perfection, his hair marcelled neatly back, and except for the four holes, he looked as if he were napping between ceremonies at the John J. Johnson Home. Put a mourner's jacket on him, a white shirt and dark tie, he'd be ready for business.

"Doc, what would make a man of such clear distinction and respect not only within his own society but even ours suddenly try to strangle an officer of the law?"

"His blood may tell you, may not. But if not, you'd need a psychiatrist used to dealing in race matters. I know and work with many of them, most fine, just as few bad as among our own, and I still have no idea what really operates deep in their brain. Maybe well concealed hatred for us; maybe some disposition from the plains of Africa where they were bred; maybe just a life-long pattern of now and then making bad decisions, though that's more a feature of the lesser ones than a fine man like Mr. Johnson, who certainly seemed to have his ducks in a row."

"I know I'm pressing here, but someone's got to analyze it, unofficially of course. If I have to send it to Washington, it could end up on a refrigerator shelf for a month. Maybe the State Police, but their headquarters is—"

"I'll call Jack Hallowell. He's at the Northwestern University med school off Michigan Avenue, just beyond the Loop. They've started a forensics lab more as a teaching device than as a state organ. But they'll handle some of the overload. This would be perfect for them. Good practice for the interns and it helps a field officer by avoiding paperwork and wait."

Other duties still occurred. A call from Sam brought him back to the main office, where he was told St. Paul police were close to tracking down Homer Van Meter, of Dillinger gang fame. The Division wanted a man there and that man was Charles. This meant a Tri-Motor flight to the Minnesota city, and a hunting party the next day that consisted of three others with heavy artillery. He didn't expect to take a big part in the arrest and didn't, learning soon enough that it was more a murder squad than a civil transaction team. The three, with Charles standing by, .45 in hand, caught up with Van Meter at a St. Paul intersection. No shouts, only shots, and it was the shotguns that finished the gangster, even if the man on the Thompson then used him for target practice, while civilians scampered away. Three fingers shot off. But that was St. Paul, a gangster city through and through. Nobody wanted Homer talking to strangers.

By the time he got back to Chicago, the message had arrived that the analysis was done.

"Yes, sir," said Hallowell, the boy doctor. "We found slight traces of pentobarbital in the blood. That's a category of drug called a barbiturate, more or less new to the practice of medicine. It's basically a sedative, that quiets a man down. Too much of it can be fatal, which is why it must be very carefully controlled."

"Is this stuff unusual or rare?"

"It could be. It could also be prescription. For a man of the decedent's age, seizures may be a problem and his physician might have prescribed a tiny daily amount in order to keep him on an even keel. Did he have such a prescription?"

"I'll have to find out."

"I see. It's a criminal case."

"It may be. What if there's not a prescription? Any idea what it would be doing in there?"

"Unlikely he'd have taken it accidentally. The bottle would be vividly marked. Possibly he took it intravenously, but I didn't see the body for marks. Maybe in some tablet or syrup form. Even as a suppository."

"Somehow I don't see this prosperous fifty-five-year-old man doing that."

"Well, you never know. But otherwise I'd be at a loss to come up with an explanation. Its potential lethality makes it too dangerous to use as the kind of substance one would take at a party or to have an enjoyable relaxation period, as one might do with marijuana or cocaine. It's much too dangerous for the usage a heroin addict puts his drugs to. An overdose, even by a tiny margin, can be fatal."

"Could he have been poisoned?"

"The blood can't tell us how he got it, only that it was there."

"Of course. I'm not thinking straight. But as for sporting use of a drug, he wasn't the type for that sort of thing either, unless he had some kind of secret life."

"Many do. It's not so uncommon as you might think."

"I was for many years a sheriff in a small town. I do know of such things. But now I'm thinking maybe he was suddenly facing a crisis of some kind and he needed relaxation from the worries that beset him. He was of a status that might put him in contact with many doctors and he might have had friends among them willing to come to his immediate aid."

"That's a good possibility, I would say. They could get him a onetime amount to survive the crisis. The only thing is, there are much safer drugs that provide the relaxation effect, so I'm wondering who would set up such a risk."

"Are there side effects?"

"Many, none good. Obviously, a dreamy period, very enjoyable, perhaps enough so to become addictive. But also behavioral alteration. Not in everybody but enough to warrant concern: a sudden, dramatic increase in aggression. This could mean increased bickering with his wife, increased irritability on the job or with family members. In extreme cases—"

"Combined with alcohol?"

"Indeed, either accidentally or on purpose. But he could seem to change personality and do something beyond accountability."

CHAPTER 8

FRESH SNOW HAD FALLEN AND TURNED THE YARDS INTO A NORTH POLE, WITH cows instead of reindeer and Thaddeus as Santa Claus. The view out his window was wondrously white, with mounds of the still-glowing stuff heaped everywhere. It was a balmy fourteen degrees out, and the lakefront had frozen itself for two hundred yards offshore.

"It does have a flaw," said Thaddeus.

"And that flaw—" began Oscar.

"The flaw being essentially it causes things to die," said Thaddeus.

"Not good," said Oscar.

They sat again in his Dickensian office above the killing floor.

"On the other hand, that is what we do here. We kill things. We turn animals into canned stew. We are death professionals. So we must not shy away where others might."

"Thaddeus, this is worrisome."

"Here's my thought. Just listen to it. It might be our salvation."

"It might also be our trip to the gallows."

"Through our registered veterinarian—what's his name again?"

"Tibbits, I think. I haven't seen him for quite some time."

"He's around somewhere."

"Maybe you fired him in the last round of cutbacks."

"Hmm, note to self: check on Dr. Tibbits. Anyhow, we acquire, legally, the substance, reason to put diseased cattle down."

"By definition—our definition—there's no such thing as diseased cattle. If it moves, we kill it and put it in cans and sell it."

"Oscar, please let me finish. We run a brief program with our magic medicine. At the cost of three or four heifers, we find out the dosage. What kills them, what doesn't affect them, and what is the magic place in between that soothes them but keeps them on their feet. That is where we want to be. We simply add a step in the pen before we start to process. Something simple and—"

"Thaddeus, do you imagine giving each beast an injection? Good God, that would be a nightmare. That would be another choke point, another cause of stress and anxiety, the result being more beef classified darkcutter, not less."

"Well, yes, that is a problem to solve. With your practical mind, I expect you'll come up with something rather quickly."

"Grind it into their food? No, no way to regulate how much food they consume at the trough. Eyedrops? Preposterous. Run them through a room where the stuff is in gaseous state? Give it to them by the spoonful?"

"I was thinking . . . by the noseful."

"How do you turn it into gas?"

"You don't. You soak cotton muslin in a solution. As they enter the chute, a man swabs each nose with it. It's said to be very fast acting. They enter cuckoo-land. They mosey up the ramp, where a good knocker sends them on to the next world. No dark blood in the meat, plenty of lactic acid. We are saved. You move to Winnetka. Your children—what is it now, twelve or thirteen?"

"Four, actually."

"Your children go to a great upper-gentry high school and then on to Yale. You retire to a large estate in upper Michigan and spend your comfortable days hunting and fishing, and being visited by grateful little Oscar grandchildren."

"Or I climb the gallows stairs, explaining to the guards and the hangman, 'It seemed like a good idea at the time.' "

It took three heifers and a steer to get it right. The first heifer dropped like a rock tossed into a well. The second staggered before she went down, permanently. The third—this was 1cc of pentobarbital in fifty-fifty glycol and alcohol—wobbled, grew mellow, even tame, and seemed to be enjoying herself a great deal. Then she hit the deck sound asleep and couldn't be roused for six hours. On the chute this would be somewhat destructive. The point was to drug the cattle, not give them naps.

Finally, on 0.8cc pentobarbital in the glycol-alcohol solution, the research team at Nugent's Best Beef, all three of them, found what appeared to be the proper proportions.

"Are you sure this is legal?" said Dr. Tibitts, who had been found in the lounge of the Transit House Hotel, not completely sober.

"It is not illegal. It's an additive in levels too small to be harmful to human beings," said Oscar.

"No, but to test it, we need replication."

He looked at the steer whose muzzle he'd just engulfed in the solution, who seemed and indeed was calm enough to pet, whisper endearments to, even name if you wanted to keep it in the family barn. It gazed back with doleful but benevolent eyes, actually sighed, and radiated beams of goodwill and benevolence.

"That would take time, man," said Thaddeus. "We'll be out of business months before you'd be satisfied. But since you'd be out of a job by the time you'd be satisfied, I'd recommend signing on, Doctor. After all, you've been paid a goodly sum to pretend like you work here."

"Well, at least notify the Food and Drug Administration."

"I think we can handle the FDA," said Thaddeus. "I am close with Charlie Oliver, their senior agent."

"Meaning Thaddeus has kept the man in prime cuts of filet and fine wines over the years," added Oscar.

"Look, Doctor. Oscar, you listen here too. Let's do it on an experimental basis and keep track of the results. We'll ship the improved meat only to prisons. If that works out, then we'll go on a wider scale. We'll call it 'Roasty-Toasty Flavor'! We'll go with it until it gets us out of the money jam. Then, with that accumulated capital, we'll invest in a higher grade of beef and better men. It'll be a turnaround for Nugent's Best Beef! And in time, everybody here, including the cow, will forget our little trick."

It worked until it didn't. All through February and March, Nugent's salesmen pitched "Roasty-Toasty" to their Northeastern prison accounts. "Radical new flavor." "Prime beef flavor at tinned beef prices." "New processing ups the flavor without upping the price!" The boys in the iron-bar hotel ate it up, literally, demanding more.

Finally, after a glorious run, Thaddeus called his veterinarian out of the Transit House Hotel bar.

"We're going to apply it to the whole line."

"Thaddeus, are you certain?"

"Two months and not a problem—except banking the profit." Since Tibbits had a stock portfolio chunked with Nugent's Best Beef, he bit down any remorse. He'd seen the stock grow in value, in an era when few did.

"So what's the problem?" he asked.

"We need more. Lots more."

"You can't buy that stuff in large quantities without attracting attention. Even legally. That's how dangerous it is. You have to be very careful here." Tibbits licked his dry lips.

"So . . . can you look around to the various pharmaceutical houses? Maybe somewhere there's one on the margins of the business, where the recordkeeping has gone sour. They need the business; they're so far from the center of things nobody pays attention. Maybe they're about to go under. You'd know. You could smoke it out. Maybe we could apply a few cash gifts to key players and move things along a bit. That's always worked with Food and Drug."

"I am not a criminal, Thaddeus."

"Nor am I. I wouldn't consider if it weren't so important to my family, my workers' families, and, yes, your family. We're just cutting corners a bit, we're not stealing, embezzling, extorting, blackmailing—nothing nefarious or dangerous."

"I just get scared sometimes, Thaddeus."

Thaddeus mentioned a sum.

"Feel braver now?"

"Uh, yes, but still not quite—"

Thaddeus upped the offer.

"Now, that wasn't hard, was it?"

CHAPTER 9

"ALL RIGHT, OFFICER WASHINGTON. GOT SOME WORK FOR YOU."

"Yes sir," said the black officer.

They were sitting in Charles's parked car on Washington's 4th District beat.

"You heard, of course, of the case of poor Mr. Johnson."

"I did. I knew him. A fine man."

"I can't help but think of the similarities between this case and the man I shot. They were from different levels of society, of course, but in both cases, of a sudden they had a kind of rage attack and went hard at a police officer and were shot for their efforts. Both leave confused relatives behind. And you're telling me that such incidents have become a commonplace on the South Side?"

"I count ten total, but nine beginning in early June."

"So nine in two months?"

"That's correct."

"You saw the pattern, but nobody else."

"They may have seen it. It mattered to them none."

"It matters to me."

"Agent Swagger, you are a bafflement. I can come to no accounting for your ways in regards to the Negro.

"I spent way too much time in the trenches of the Great War. There I saw many—again, too many—men blown up. I learned firsthand that no matter the color of the skin, the insides of any man look the same as any other man. If that is the case, then the Negro deserves the same justice as the white. And the poor Negro, like the man I killed, deserves the same as the rich Negro Costello killed. That's all it is."

"Are you a man of hard faith?"

"Yes, but only in the .45-caliber pistol I carry."

"You wanted something of me?"

"Yes. I know that Mr. Johnson, as a well-known member of the community and a funeral parlor director as well, a highly revered position, will lie in state amid flowers and silk in his own establishment. But wouldn't you think there'd be a more private farewell among his friends in his neighborhood, the other black professionals, doctors, lawyers, and such? And wouldn't that be at his home, not in a public building? People like that expect to be cosseted and told of their importance."

"I am sure."

"Could you attend?"

"Two-Gun is welcome anywhere on the South Side."

"That is what I was counting on. Here's what I want you to do. Two kinds of investigation. The first is in his medicine cabinet, maybe his nightstand. I'm looking to see if he had on hand by prescription a soothing drug called pentobarbital. It would be prohibitively marked as poison, its daily intake limited."

"Yes."

"Can you do it? Slip away on some pretext to use the bathroom. Run your eyes over the vials and bottles, looking for this pentobarbital?"

"I can do that."

"And second, I need details on Mr. Johnson's situation. Had he recently had reverses or was some ugly family business brewing? Our first fellow had lost his job and had no prospect of getting one back. If such a thing was happening to Mr. Johnson, that would be another parallel. Under those circumstances an illicit substance that offered a soothing and comfort more abundant than whiskey might suddenly be attractive, and he might partake for the relief."

"I'll put ear to ground."

"And a third thing, I suppose. Tell *me* what to do. My business in the stockyard was done on the first day and I can't keep hanging around here much longer. They're beginning to ask at the office, even if Inspector Clegg told me to take my time. So I only have a few days left, unless Baby Face is spotted and my gun is needed immediately. So I want to use my time wisely."

"Here's an idea, Agent Swagger. It seems to me that the kind of violent craziness you're interested in might not only be directed at the police. So maybe you could go through the newspaper files in the library for cases of domestic violence, for sudden shootings at crap games, gambling halls, houses of ill repute. Maybe there's much more of our type than just the nine shot-by-officers."

"Excellent idea, Officer Washington."

CHAPTER 10

SAM, BACK FROM D.C., ASKED CHARLES TO DROP BY WHEN CONVENIENT, which was his style, even if everyone took to interpreting *when convenient* as *now*.

"Please, Charles, update me, if you will. I hear from Inspector Clegg but I discount him. I don't talk much with Mel anymore, so if he's pulling your strings I wouldn't know of it. Let me know and I'll get those strings cut."

"No, I'm fine, sir. Still taking boys to the range three times a week. If it doesn't help their shooting, it helps their morale."

"Nothing helped their morale more than the bullets you put into Johnny. I would call that an excellent morale booster."

"Thank you, sir."

Sam was an open-faced, squared-headed man under a thinning but far-from-vanished layer of brown-blond hair. He was Mormon, as all knew, meaning that he worked harder than the devil, prayed devoutly, and believed in the cause and would fulfill his obligations to the death. But he had more than a little sly in him as well, which is how he was gently pushing the highly publicized but somewhat flighty Mel out of the office. He didn't hate Mel. He didn't hate anybody. His religion wouldn't allow him. It was just that he knew effective people were to be treasured and advanced, while those less so were to be eased into positions where they could do no damage.

"Call me Sam, Charles. You're too valuable to be troubled with formalities."

"Thank you, Sam. I do have something to discuss with you. I wanted to wait until you called me in rather than rushing to you with something and getting the office into a hubbub over what."

"Nobody ever said you weren't clever, Charles. Is this the stockyard thing?"

"It is."

"I have heard, not from this office but from those in some others I know, that you've been spending some time in the Fourth District, encompassing the Yards and the South Side."

"That is so."

"Still looking for Baby Face down there?"

"He's not there. Seems there was a cowboy who looked a little like him with the hat on. I managed to talk the boy into growing a mustache, and he has a much bigger lip than Nelson, so it won't be mistaken for Nelson's little wisp of child's fuzz."

"Excellent. Then what has been keeping you there?"

Charles told Sam about shooting George Roberts.

"The Fourth District Negro Chicago police officer who covered the scene advised me against making a formal report because it would involve a lot of politics and paperwork. He was willing to see it as a John Doe. It seemed not to matter. So I made that judgment, maybe wrong."

"But maybe not. You get Chicago Irish involved, games become complicated and it's easy to lose time, effort, and ultimately control to them. They are our allies, but they are not. You clearly understand that."

"I want to see what caused that man to attack. It was stupid. Everyone is stupid now and then, some more than others. Maybe that's all it was. Still, I killed him and I can't just walk away from it. I have to know why.

Was he just that way, always a hair from explosion? Was it alcohol? That stuff they drink is kin to poison and it may have driven him to something ridiculous like this. He had just lost his job, unfairly as I hear it, and maybe that rage pushed him to it. Or maybe—well, something he took for relief instead made him insane."

"So you think another mechanism was involved than booze and the anger of the black man."

"I do."

Charles took him through the rest, especially Washington's late discoveries and his own, based on hours reading the Police Blotter column of the *Chicago Defender*.

"According to the Blotter, the deaths by violence within the Fourth District since June are up close to 40 percent over the same period last year. That's to say nothing of beatdowns, screaming fits, various sorts of discord that threaten but don't quite reach the level of lethal violence."

"But you think there's an agent involved? Something physical, a drug, a potion, I don't know, a voodoo curse of the sort that might inflame certain folks."

"The undertaker Johnson had a drug called pentobarbital in his blood. He had no prescription for it, so it couldn't be medical. He was also being sued by his younger brother for rights to the estate of his father, the original John J. Johnson, who founded the home. Lots of stress, anger, fear in that. He turns to something called the Night Train for fast relief. Only one day he takes too much or maybe not enough. The result: a fine man is dead. In the case of the man I killed, George Roberts, we have a fellow bitter over his loss of a job as a knocker in the meatpacking industry. And his realization he's been blackballed in that industry. He can't feed his family. He too turns to the Night Train, whatever it is, whoever is selling it, and the results are the same. Only it's Sheriff Swagger who's elected to be the triggerman. In most cases it would pass unnoticed. It's just that Swagger has done a lot of killing in his time and doesn't want to do more unless it's absolutely necessary. Johnny for sure, Baby Face I hope, but a poor workingman of the slums, no, sir, not if I can help it."

"And I suppose it could be construed as under our mandate on account of Roberts's attack on a federal agent."

"That's how I would look at it."

"Okay, how's this for a suggestion. You continue your shooting lessons for the boys and you keep yourself available for trips such as the one to St. Paul. But when those aren't scheduled, you mosey on down to the Fourth District. You and Officer Washington continue to investigate. You make reports to me alone. Whether or not we put the official stamp of the Division on the investigation is to be seen. In the meantime, I'll endeavor to keep the odious Clegg off your back."

"Thank you, Sam. A question you could answer but I can't: Should we alert the Food and Drug Administration people? I mean, to some extent we are intruding on their territory, since this appears to be about food and drugs first and foremost. Moreover, I know how quickly things can get complicated if some outfit feels it's being usurped in its own backyard."

"My answer would be no, at least not yet. The FDA is held to be among the worst of the 'old' bureaus. So involving them, at least at this stage, when you don't know who's what or why they're that, might turn out to be highly counterproductive. Let's discreetly build a case, then bring it to them, gift-wrapped, so they can't subvert it a priori."

"I understand." It was exactly the response he'd wanted.

CHAPTER 11

A WANING GIBBOUS MOON REVEALED ITSELF INTERMITTENTLY BEHIND racing clouds, a sliver of celestial illumination usually bone-white in color but here, owing to the contamination of the air, a bilious brown-orange. It was Chicago's Golgotha, by name the Cook County Cemetery for Unclaimed Negro Cadavers, a ripple of hills not far from the dump that absorbed its part (there were six others) of the city's daily accumulation of trash and produced a stench akin to the Western Front under German gas attack. It was far from the glamour of Chicago, being southwest of the Loop, almost out of the county, and far, far in the distance, thousands of miles it seemed, the skyscrapers at lake's edge announced their presence in beads of light clustered at the horizon.

In this place, records were poorly kept, if at all. Thus Officer Washington could only go by the daily logs that were marked crudely on paper, somewhat flimsy as a basis for progress. His reckoning was that Roberts had been killed on a certain day and by law his remains must rest at the city morgue a two full weeks awaiting a claim. Then, if unclaimed, they would have been transported here and buried in an area only designated roughly. The log recorded only one reception that was in accord with fourteen days from the death of Roberts; Washington and Swagger were here, alone in the place, with a lantern, shovels, and high, if melancholy, hopes.

"Agent Swagger, this is the kind of work usually left for black folks."

"Black, white, I don't care. If Two-Gun can pitch in, so can I."

"Even Two-Gun feels wormy to the bowel on this one."

"I'll do the horror part. If killing is happening, it must be stopped and the killers punished. Without that formation, all else goes away. I will do what must be done."

The lantern light revealed nothing, only unkept grass and weed, without marker or number or stake or anything testifying to the presence of what used to be a man.

"Since it's recent, Officer, wouldn't you expect that the soil would be tilled? It might not show up so well in this bad light. But to the touch, perhaps."

"I hear you. Do you want me to—"

"We'll both go to knee and feel about."

On hands and knees they roamed the plot, their fingers searching for newly turned or possibly newly patted earth. It seemed to take hours but in fact only took one, at the end of which, Washington exclaimed, "Agent Swagger. Here, try this."

Charles went, and yes, Washington had located a patch where the earth was loose to the scrape and seemed not to have been packed down with any enthusiasm. The lantern light revealed a six-by-three-foot disturbance.

"I can't imagine the gravedigger would put much effort into his labor," said Charles. "Perhaps this won't take too long at all."

"Then you get some blood out of him?"

"Correct, but not easily at this stage. It's called livor mortis, meaning that the blood has sunk to the lower parts of the body under the pull of gravity. So we have to get into the lower half and do some scraping."

"So no need of a needle?"

"He thought the needle insufficient. I have to do something more primitive. It pains me and I'd prefer not to, but my preferences aren't on the table."

They dug from each end and sure enough found the soil easy to move, and in time a box emerged, not so deep down. Whatever it contained would be gone shortly enough. Maybe it was even too late.

They did not bother to remove it, but Washington leaped upon it and, using his shovel as a pry-tool, managed to snap off the top quarter of the lid. The lantern spotlighted what appeared to be a head wrapped loosely in muslin cloth.

"I suppose he is beyond caring."

"Let us hope so. Otherwise, he would be bothered at what's about to happen."

Washington took a pocketknife and sliced open the masking, peeling it back.

Charles examined by light of lantern. Was it him? Seemed so, though he'd really only seen the face for a minute or two before firing. But he saw gauntness and fury, which seemed to sum up the man named George Roberts in late stage, and if he saw nothing confirmational, neither did he see anything non-confirmational. He peeled further, to reveal chest. Yes. Three blisters dead center, close enough to cover with a cup.

"Agent Swagger, you are one hell of a shooter."

"I've had too much practice, Officer Washington."

Now came the terrible part.

"Were you in the war, Officer Washington?"

"Too young."

"Well, as I said, I was. On a few occasions it got to close work. So it is that I have killed men with a shovel. If you have not, I would advise you to turn away. It's not a pleasant thing."

"Agent, I am in this all the way. I will help anyhows I can."

"Just hold the lantern, so that I can see what I am doing and it's no worse than it has to be."

Washington adjusted, arranging the lantern over the face of the dead man.

Charles took a deep breath, turned his spade so that its blade ran parallel to the corpse's closed eyes, its spear-point dead even with the fragile bridge between the eyes, took another breath, and then drove forward, feeling the blade bite and slip.

He looked. The head was desecrated to be sure, but the bridge had held, and no blood appeared anywhere on the now-skewed face.

"One more time," said Charles, and tried to remember the German sergeant he had killed in 1918, holding the entrenching tool sideways and delivering the shovel's corner like a hatchet strike. He supposed it was all right because the sergeant had tried to kill him with one of those wicked bayonets the Huns affixed to their rifles and Charles had just barely deflected it. He'd heard bones crack and saw blood spurt that time. Not this.

Another hard stroke, and again it bounced off, tearing dead skin and bringing destruction to the face, but no blood.

The third drive broke bone, caving in the brow above the bridge of the nose.

"You have done it," said Washington

Charles bent and saw in the shattered plate of bone a kind of density that had to be brain. Now the awful part. He withdrew a vial from his coat pocket, unscrewed the lid, and, holding it in one hand, with the other he reached into the cavity and ripped the brain forward. It was like handling rotted fruit, though it came to his pull easily enough. All that was and all that ever would be George Roberts was clutched in his left hand, yielding the texture of a banana, that balance between hardness and softness, fiber and mush, and with his right he was able to insert the vial and scrape through the swampy terrain at the back of the skull, where the blood had collected. He withdrew the vial, saw that it was half-full, and realized that was all he could take.

He screwed the vial shut.

"Agh," he said, "now let's clean up and get out of here."

"Mr. Swagger, you let me finish this here thing. I make it nice and tidy. You sit over there and relax."

Charles had nothing to say, and did what he was told.

He dropped the blood off at Northwestern and then went to the firing range at Chicago Police HQ, where he instructed new members of the field office on the theory and practice of the handgun. As always, the men had been issued weapons in accordance with their place in line, not in any accordance with their physical characteristics. That's what the book said, that's what the Division did. Charles spent twenty minutes dispensing with that nonsense and in the end had matched gun to hand, so that the bigger boys, with stouter paws and stronger forearms, would carry the government Colt .45 automatic and the thinner, slighter fellows the Colt .38 revolver. That way, neither classification would fear or detest their own guns and be reluctant to practice, so necessary to retain skill.

Then they shot—some well, some not so well. It was athletic. Some had the gift of hand-eye coordination and found it easy to keep their shots centered, and the others were less fortunate, spewing holes all over the silhouette.

"Remember," said Charles, "in a fight, you will default to your worst self. So look at the poorest shot you took, and that's the one you'd fire to save your life. For that reason, you want all your shots to go where you want to place them. This isn't cowboys and Indians. This is full-blown, hard-as-nails man's work, and the better your skills, the more is the chance you'll survive."

That done, he returned to the office to find a phone message that read: "Call Dr. Hallowell from Northwestern University."

It took a little phone runaround before the two were connected.

"Yes, Doctor?"

"Well, though the blood was heavily decomposed, I was able to detect the same pentobarbital. Actually, in larger percentages than the previous cadaver. This fellow would have died shortly, gunshots or no gunshots."

"I see. That's very helpful, Doctor. I suppose my next step ought to be to focus on the drug."

"Is your idea that someone is selling this stuff for some kind of sporting use?"

"Yes, sir. I'm hearing, or at least picking up, that they call it 'the Night Train.' It seems to provide a very hard wallop and takes a fellow immediately from what problems he faces in our world on a magical journey to a land of candy and happiness. Not sure yet how it's applied, who's distributing it, where it comes from. So far it's only sold to the dark people, as if those behind it know that if it starts killing white people there'd be a fuss, maybe a riot. But just selling it in the Fourth District means that nobody shines a light on it; the cops don't ask, the federals don't care, and the only way to track it is via the police blotter page in the Negro newspaper."

"I can't begin to tell you how dangerous that would be. And how irresponsible. It's far deadlier than heroin. The body can sustain surprisingly large amounts of heroin, but just a bit over the limit on pentobarbital and death is the result. It could be used as an execution method."

"That's what those of us who are looking are seeing. And here's some other mystery to it. Usually, drug usage leaves considerable litter. Any cop, big-city or small, knows the signs. Heroin: needles, bent spoons, rubber tubes for tying off the arm to swell out the vein. If it's cocaine, there's always spillage, and so you see grains of white powder everywhere. You see crumpled up paper from the wrapping. You see matchbooks or razor blades, anything with a hard, sharp straight edge, for arranging the stuff in straight lines so that it can be sniffed hard via some little cardboard funnel. You see the funnel too, discarded. Because after he's had his hit, he doesn't care much about security. He just wants to enjoy his state. With opium, though I suppose this is mostly in Chinatown, it's long porcelain pipes, or water pipes, by which the smoke is inhaled through a vessel of water of some sort, called a hookah. No pipes, no hookahs. Nothing at all to suggest Asian involvement, and believe me, the people here would notice Asian."

"But nothing like any of that here?"

"Nothing like anything here. No trace of usage sites. No debris, no litter, no left-behinds. No Asians. No whites. Maybe, then, it's a sip out of a bottle."

"Too risky. Two sips and the dealer has a corpse to dispose of."

"So they've come up with some new way of distribution and ingestion. It leaves no traces or it is easily policed up in the aftermath. I'm interested in a kind of rage or madness it produces. We got onto this from too many cases where people go crazy, they attack others, often armed policemen, and the result is death, as you say."

"That would be the pentobarbital side effect. And the more widely spread the consumption, the more incidents."

"So where would someone get substantial amounts of pentobarbital?"

"Most hospitals have a small supply, under lock and key. Perhaps someone is stealing it. But not in any meaningful quantity. Another possibility is a pharmaceutical supply house. They would have a larger supply, but again, the security would be quite tight. You could only order it under license, and you'd have to be either an MD or a DVM affiliated with an accredited institution. Still, a large supply would certainly attract significant attention."

"I see."

He almost lost something there. But he caught it.

"By the way, what's a DVM?"

"Doctor of veterinary medicine. For large animals, it's widely used as both a euthanasia mechanism and an anesthesia."

"I don't—"

"I'm not being clear. For animals. One would use it to put them down or to relieve them of pain. By 'them,' I mean, cattle."

It simply confirmed his suspicions.

But then the doctor said, "If you want to track these bastards down, I see only one path. Through a pharmaceutical supply firm."

CHAPTER 12

"AND WHAT HAPPENS," CLEGG WANTED TO KNOW, "IF WE GET A BABY Face sighting and need our top gun on the arrest team, but he's off hanging around with a colored officer named 'Two-Gun'?"

"Charles," said Purvis, "what Hugh is saying is that your talents are such that not only are they a necessary part of any action, but your presence gives the young and less experienced men much more confidence."

It was come-to-Jesus time in the Bankers Building, and Charles sat before the Pontius Pilate of the Justice Department Division of Investigation and his Roman overseer.

"I do understand that, sir. I am not meaning to be rebellious or insurrectionist or anything like that. I swear to you. If you'll check, you'll see that I call in my whereabout to Ed Hollis frequently. If something urgent comes up I can get there under Fourth District siren as fast from the South Side as from the Loop. Then, second, I would say, we usually know in advance of an encounter and an opportunity. That was so of Dillinger and Van Meter. I believe it will be so of Floyd and Nelson. We get a tip or develop a piece of evidence or break down a pattern, and we have time to set the operation up."

"Okay, Charles," said Purvis, smiling in his mild way, "I do understand you have a passion for this case in the Fourth District stemming from an attempt on your life. I do understand how an officer can make a crusade out of something personal. I don't want you becoming bitter at being pulled off it. I do understand that it's the dog days of August and not much happens in August, even among our gangsters. Can I only say, please, as a personal favor to me, can you bring the Fourth District thing to a close as quickly as possible?"

"You have my word, sir," he said, which is why he said to Sylvester Washington an hour later over the phone, "I am getting under more and more pressure to stay here in the Bankers Building and let what happens down there happen."

Washington skipped a beat, then said, "That means more black folks dying before their time and the engineer of the Night Train getting richer and richer."

"I cannot accept that. There's got to be a way. How would Two-Gun handle it?"

"Break down a user. Find out where it's coming from. Go in hard one night, guns blazing. Disappear with the dawn. Just like the raids you led in the Great War."

"It may come to that. So yes, your job is to try and find somebody on the stuff who'll talk. I will, as my job, go on a phone safari, calling the twenty-nine pharmaceutical houses in the Midwest who could have moved a large quantity of pentobarbital. If we can find out who bought it legally, we can get one step closer to who is using it illegally."

Of all the sour jobs a detective did, this was the sourest. If you call blindly off a list, maybe you get someone impressed by your affiliation and maybe you don't. Maybe they lie to you and maybe they don't. Maybe they only tell you half the story and maybe they don't. Maybe they're intrigued by your questions, maybe they're not. The hardest part is, lacking a face across the tabletop to read, a set of eyes that shift or don't, a tongue that's too quick to dry lips, a swallow before each answer—it was hard for the detective to get a sense of the other man or woman.

So after twenty-nine calls, he had only three where he detected apprehension at his probe. Of those three, two were in Downer's Grove and could be visited in a single day, one was in La Crosse, Wisconsin, and would demand at least a day and a night. Ninety-nine out of a thousand cops would have bagged the day-night ordeal because, after all, the evidence supporting it was entirely theoretical. But Charles was of a sort who, when he got a bug in his shirt, he wasn't satisfied till the bug was squashed and dead and on a slab in the morgue.

So on his official Saturday off, he headed at 5:30 a.m. to La Crosse, two hundred miles and about eight hours northwest by car, and found the most blank of all blank buildings he'd ever seen, a nondescript brick unit by the railroad tracks called Magellan Medical and Pharmaceutical Supply.

"As I told you on the phone," said Dr. Magellan, owner of the place, "it's a mess. It was another bright idea of mine that fizzled. Well, didn't fizzle, but didn't sparkle either. It was a wash. I'm one of those dreary people who never quite succeeds and never quite fails. I just sort of mosey along."

"It's my feeling," said the tall, strong detective to the short, dumpy physician–failed capitalist, "that most people just mosey along."

"Well, then, Special Agent, let's go down to Accounting and mosey through our somewhat disheveled records and see if I can satisfy you on the issue of pentobarbital."

"Doctor, I'd like to see the stuff, if possible. Helpful to know what I'm hunting."

"Of course," said Dr. Magellan. "I do hope if nothing else you'll be impressed by our security regarding dangerous drugs."

"I'm sure I will," said Charles, and sure enough, he was. The vault occupied one corner of the larger supply room and was of small-city-bank proportions, surrounded in a fortress of seemingly impenetrable-short-of-artillery brick. The doctor—"I'm the only one who knows the combination, and thus I open it only when an order must be filled, making certain there's no pilferage"—diddled with the mechanism for a bit, had some trouble remembering if it was two turns before 36, or three. Three, as it turned out, and the heavy door yielded a tidy, shelved room well stocked with temptation and death.

"I call it Pandora's box. All the troubles of the world are here. Your medical heroin, cocaine, and even marijuana. Yes, it's prescribed! In certain cases of high anxiety coupled with a tricky digestive system. Oh, and sleeping pills and potions, anything to get a fellow off to dreamland instead of marooned in the land of jumping sheep. All dangerous, indeed, if overused. But here is the pentobarbital, the most dangerous of all."

He gestured to a shelf where cardboard cartons held rows and rows of tiny vials.

"Go on, Special Agent. Pick one up."

Charles did, seeing the black skull and crossbones as the primary feature of the label, with the identifier of Upjohn Pharmaceuticals of Framingham, Massachusetts, and the subscript "25 CCS SODIUM PENTOBARBITAL, HIGHLY DANGEROUS. TO BE ADMINISTERED BY MDS AND DVMS ONLY."

The bottle was brown, and the cap had a rubber center, through which a syringe could be inserted and a tiny amount, suitable for injection, could be withdrawn.

"It only comes in liquid?"

"As a sleeping aid; it's marketed differently in tablets, much cut. They call it Nembutal and there are other active ingredients. The idea is to nudge you into unconsciousness, not hit you in the face with it. Do you want to see a package? Yellow Jackets, I believe, is the slang term. Some criminal usage, alas."

"I'll skip," said Charles. "I assume you keep track of the in and out of all this stuff."

"Well," said Dr. Magellan, "officially yes. And officially the Food and

Drug Administration checks us once a year to make certain everything is as it should be. But the FDA is, uh—"

"A problem, I've heard."

"Let us just say they are not to the higher standards of the Justice Department. Actually, I haven't seen one in four years. And when he did come, Charles Oliver by name, he was usually in some kind of rush."

"What are the ramifications of his disinterest?"

"Well, without threat of annual examination, I'd have to say our discipline may be subpar."

"That means the records aren't reliable?"

"I would have to say so, yes, I'm certain. It's on Mabel."

"And Mabel?"

"Well, as we move on to Accounting, I'm afraid you will have an encounter with Mabel. My wife's brother's wife."

"Accounting" looked as if it were more likely to be called "No Accounting." Piles and stacks of paper on empty desks, some of it dusty, some filing cabinets half-closed, ashtrays heaped with butts from a week ago, the bathroom issuing a stockyard-caliber stench.

"The hub of my empire," said poor Dr. Magellan.

"I am, however, appreciating your time and effort here on my behalf, and without lawyers and local law people breathing down my neck."

"Well, let it be said I tried to do one good thing today."

The files, it seemed, were kept by this Mabel, who had her own way of doing things.

"Even with pentobarbital?" asked Charles.

"Mabel isn't much interested in our supplies with regard to danger. To her, it's all product, and she makes no further distinction. Ridiculous, I agree, and yet if I made an attempt to replace her, I'd suffer family issues more disturbing than anything the federal government could bring against me."

"Well, then, let's see what Mabel has cooked up for us."

Mabel! Mabel, Mabel, Mabel! Mabel, you idiot! What the woman had cooked up was chaos compounded by lassitude compounded by disinterest. Files must be kept regularly or they are of no use, and Mabel's dereliction was rife, a day here, two not so much. Worse, she seemed to have no organizational principle.

"Maybe we could call her and get her down here?" asked Charles.

"Oh, good heavens, no. She would complain to her husband, who is my wife's brother, it would get to my wife, and there'd be hell to pay."

Pull badge, rant, get tough, or no? He decided no.

"I am looking for a series of drug-related events that seemed to commence in May, maybe early June of this year." He was dating it to the May 19 fire in the Yards, before which there had been no documented rise in 4th District violent episodes.

"Hmm," said Dr. Magellan. "Okay, some of it is alphabetical by purchaser, some of it chronological by purchase."

Lots of pulling and scanning finally located the month in question, but there were no big sales, determined via the invoices marked "PAID" in that month.

"All right," said Charles, "a pause here. Let me think harder on this one."

"If you think someone is misusing pentobarbital and it *started* after May," said the doctor, "it seems like whoever is doing this would have had access to it earlier. Because they would have had to do some experimentation on dosage, then distribution, then finally going on the street at a later date. Though I do believe that all of my clients offered the proper documentation for their acquisition of the material."

"All right," said Charles. "Then let me add a factor. I'm seeing now this may relate to the fire in the area in May. That's exactly the kind of confusion and mess that experienced criminals could use to disguise their operations. But for them to take advantage of the fire, the stuff had to already be there. So let's see if we can find March and April."

Success! They found March, they found April.

Failure! No pentobarbital sales in March, no pentobarbital sales in April.

And February was no place to be found even if January was, and it also yielded nothing.

It went on, eating up most of the afternoon, trying various organizational principles, all of which, if they yielded paperwork, yielded no results.

"I'm so afraid it's come to nothing," said the doctor. "It seems wrong, given all your effort."

"That's the way this business works. You dig and dig and dig and, more often than not, hit nothing but more dirt. You've tried hard and I appreciate your candor and—"

"Wait a minute," said the doctor. "In February, Mabel was gone for two weeks. Hospital, 'woman's business,' is all I know. Stella took over. I can call Stella, because she's not family. She's actually the storeroom floor manager, but she's first-class. Let's just see."

A few minutes later, in Dr. Magellan's office, the doctor put down the phone in beaming satisfaction.

"She knew how disorganized Mabel was and she didn't want any of her work disappearing into the morass. So she never filed it."

"So where—"

"It's in her desk!"

MARCH 1934

CHAPTER 13

THADDEUS HAD SPENT THE AFTERNOON AT THE STOCK YARD INN, BUYING a lunch of thick fresh sirloin grilled to order as preferred by the purchasing agent of the Schenectady County, NY, prison system. He'd moved an order of three hundred cases of Nugent's New "Roasty-Toasty Beef Stew, Just Like Ma Used to Make," because the convicts had loved the first fifty cases that Nugent's had offered at deep discount.

"You put U.S. prime in that stuff, Mr. Nugent, and still sell it to us at nineteen cents per gallon tin?"

"Nope. New top secret processing trick," Thaddeus said warmly. "Now all the big boys want it too. May eventually sell to the highest bidder, but I am so enjoying my celebrity and prosperity. It's been a long time!"

After port and cigars, the two parted, a New York State check for $3,200 in Thaddeus's pocket, to be deposited at Bookkeeping. He was so happy the corrupted traces of snow, in unmelted drifts and piles, and desecrated here and there in piss yellow and shit brown, attended as well by the whiffs of the post-elimination product, didn't even register. He happily turned the check over to Accounting. After this pleasant task, he went to his office, decided to smoke another cigar, and have another glass, not of port but of newly legalized rye whiskey. It burned clean and pure on the way down, and only the smell from the Pulverized Manure Company next door marred his pleasure.

Then a knock hit the door, urgent, maybe itself full of panic, and Thaddeus's world changed, possibly forever.

"Thaddeus? Open up, goddammit."

It was of course his house manager, confidant, and co-conspirator Oscar Bentley, for no one else he employed dared address him so informally.

"Yes, yes," said Thaddeus, "it's open."

Oscar spilled in, urgency powering his moves, stripping him of grace. He was, as always, in corduroy work trousers, heavy boots, green cotton shirt, green tie tight at the neck, and ever-present fedora.

"Now, now," said Thaddeus, still mellow from the big Schenectady County sale, still looking forward to what was left in his glass of Pikesville. "Calm down, Oscar, have a drink, what could be—"

"Seven," said Oscar, passing on the drink.

"Seven what? Cardinals? Home runs? Weeks till baseball season?"

"Dead."

"It's a tragedy but hardly a catastrophe. People? Heifers? Hopes and dreams?"

"Prisoners."

Thaddeus knew what this meant.

"Shawshank, Maine. The big joint up there. Food poisoning, they say. Seven convicts in the last week. Never happened before."

"And we—"

"Yes, we."

"How much?"

"Two hundred forty cases. A gallon a tin, eight tins to the case."

"When?"

"Three weeks ago."

"It might not be us."

"Doubtful."

"That doesn't mean we're responsible. Maine, what can they know of sanitation?"

"What's to know? Boil the food, wash down the kitchen with convict labor every night using antiseptics. Works for the whole civilized world. All of a sudden—"

"Who knows about this?"

"It was a small item inside the *Tribune* today. My wife saw it and called me."

Thaddeus hit the intercom.

"Virginia, I need a copy of today's *Tribune*. Fast, please."

"Yes, sir."

MARCH 15, 1934

CHICAGO TRIBUNE,

THE WORLD'S GREATEST NEWSPAPER

PAGE A-23

SEVEN DEAD IN MAINE PRISON, FOOD POISONING SUSPECTED
Shawshank, Me., (UNITED PRESS)—Seven convicts have died within a week in a large state prison here, authorities say.

"We suspect food poisoning to be the culprit," said Warden James J. Bliss. "There was no pattern other than consuming victuals in our food facility. The victims appear to be randomly affected without regard to national origin, race, length of sentence, and so forth."

The warden stated that state forensics experts are now closely examining food products and preparation procedures, as well as checking the kitchen staff for infectious diseases.

"There is no evidence that this occurrence has potential to spread beyond prison walls," said Col. Robert Mayhew, Commandant of the Maine State Police. "It seems isolated within Shawshank where we are taking aggressive steps to make sure that's where it remains."

All of the deceased have been transported to Bangor for autopsies.

No other prisons in Maine, nor in the greater New England region, have reported difficulties of this nature, the United Press has learned.

"We should hire lawyers right away," said Oscar. "We have to be ahead on this one, not behind. Or we'll end up in prison." An edge of breathlessness afflicted his voice.

"Now, let's think this through," said Thaddeus. "Maybe there's a madman poisoner in that facility. Somehow he got ahold of some killer drugs and got it into the food supply or the water, just to see the folks stop breathing. It's his idea of fun."

"We could never be that lucky," said Oscar.

"Okay, okay. Consider this. More logic to attack. Tell me how I'm wrong. Rip it to pieces if you can."

"Yes, yes," said Oscar.

"A large prison kitchen must have hundreds of food items on hand, and the stock is always coming and going. Tinned goods, staples, vegetables, meat itself, condiments, seasonings. It would take them months, maybe years, to test them all, one at a time. So time is on our side. What we have to worry about is some kind of outbreak in another institutional kitchen. Because that will narrow their inquiries considerably. They have merely to look for products common to both prisons. A third prison outbreak would narrow the possibilities even further. Then and only then would we, should we, feel as if we'd end up targeted."

"But, Thaddeus, don't you think it behooves us to come clean, admit our mistake, pay a fine, and hang our heads? Hang our heads, not be hung by our necks. Thaddeus, we probably killed those seven men."

"Prisoners," said Thaddeus. "Not schoolchildren, nuns, war heroes, amputees, I don't know, symphony musicians. Don't get overwrought. Whatever they are in jail for, they probably did far worse. It's justice in a way."

"I don't think the law will see it that way."

"So let's quietly withdraw Roasty-Toasty. This will blow over, you'll see. And the money we've already made may keep us afloat. I know: we'll keep the TR line going, but we'll cut the pentobarbital out of it. It'll be months before we start losing business again!"

"What if it was the pento that made it taste so good?"

CHAPTER 14

WINNETKA. TOWN OF LAWNS AND ELMS AND GIGANTIC, STATELY STONE houses among them. Not rich-rich—that was Kenilworth—but rich enough. Law partners, doctors, corporate vice presidents, that comfortable level of America where nobody dressed for dinner but nevertheless the dinner was excellent. Most of the local New Trier High School grads went Ivy League. Some of the big houses—not quite mansions—even had a lakefront over which to peer at the calm blue each summer day. Everything here was of highest cotton. About twenty miles north of Chicago, either by car up Sheridan Road or by the Northwestern Railway. Beyond Evanston, beyond Wilmette, beyond No Man's Land, beyond Kenilworth.

Charles pulled up to 344 Stoneleigh Road, two blocks west of the lake. This one, swaddled in the green froth of the trees and nestled in vines and flowers and boasting a lawn as green as the ones in Arthur's Camelot, dozed in the late summer sun. Somehow the quiet beauty of Winnetka prevented the town from ever getting dead hot, since there was no tar or asphalt to melt, no black boys in ragged undershirts to lounge about with slack faces, no sweaty chubuncular cops named Wykowski or Janoskovsky to keep the lid on. There was no lid.

He walked up the stone path and rang the doorbell. Better to catch him unexpected, without time to prepare defenses. Inside, some hustle and finally a not unattractive woman of higher order opened.

"Charles Swagger," Charles said, "Justice Department Division of Investigation. I'd like to speak with Mr. Nugent, please."

"He's dressing for golf. He has a tee time at Indian Hills at four."

"This won't take long, madam. And it is official business regarding a criminal investigation."

Floridly dressed in yellow plus fours and a cream shirt with a tie emblazoned in regimental stripes of the sort Charles—but not Mr. Nugent—had seen in the Great War, he was in argyle stockinged feet, carrying brown-and-white spiked shoes with him.

"Sir, I'm Thaddeus Nugent," he said, though with a little friendly mellow in the tone. "Tell me, please, how I can help. Do sit down. Drink? No, duty? Lemonade, water, Agent . . . ah . . . ?"

"Charles Swagger."

Nugent was affable, of regular symmetry and good dentition, wore a slicked-down haircut and in all respects seemed what he claimed to be, a member in good standing of the upper gentry, secure that he had contributed to his nation and it had provided in turn for him.

"Sir, you said Justice Department. In my business we have regular dealings with the Food and Drug Administration but never Justice. The agent in the Yards is named Charlie Oliver."

"This is a different part of the law than would come under jurisdiction of Food and Drug. This would be criminal law, hence our engagement. Our headquarters are in the Bankers Building in the Loop."

"Yes. Aren't you mainly pursuing these bandits? I think you were the folks who killed Dillinger last month."

"It was people in our office, yes, sir. But we do handle other cases. It's not all waiting for gunfights."

"I hope I'm not in any trouble. I'm just a businessman. I can assure you—"

"If you were in trouble, I'd have a warrant and a team. You would be advised to call your lawyer. No, we're just checking on some material that was shipped to you that has potential of much harm."

"Of course."

"Let me go to particulars here, sir, if I may. You are Thaddeus Nugent, CEO and owner of a firm called Nugent's Best Beef, purveyor of tinned meats to primarily institutional clientele."

"Yes. Hospitals, prisons, YMCAs, that sort of trade. No four-star restaurants, but Nugent's Best turns out a fine can of beef stew, which we sell in large tins for cafeteria usage. That's our main product. Of course the animals have other uses, such as lard, chicken feed, swine feed, soap, even belts and shoes. As we say, we sell everything but the squeal. Or moo, as the case may be. We're strictly a beef house."

"According to the records I've seen at a place in La Crosse, Wisconsin, called Magellan Pharmaceutical Supply, your firm in March of this year acquired a large—unusually large, I think—supply of a drug called pentobarbital, very closely regulated for its potentially fatal effects."

Charles thought he saw a kind of involuntary tremor pass through Nugent, of exactly the sort a professional would never permit. Even worse, a dry little swallow quivered in the man's throat.

"Yes, that's true. All legal, under signature of my board-certified house veterinarian Claude Tibbits, with copies submitted, as required by law, to the FDA. Did they—"

"No, the information is from another source. Anyhow, I'm told it is common for animal husbandry businesses to keep a small quantity of pentobarbital around to put down distressed animals without violence—"

"A steer with a broken leg can be very dangerous, too dangerous to apply the sledge. You can't shoot because the noise might cause the animals in the pen to panic. It would be Claude's job—and he was well paid for it—to soothe the animal and inject the drug into the carotid. The beast dies painlessly within a minute or so. I do not believe in hurting the animals. Nor did my father, nor his father, who founded Best."

"I can see that. But since the fatal dosage on a steer is two ccs of pentobarbital and you bought more than four hundred eight-cc bottles, I'm wondering what you had in mind."

"Yes, I can see how that might seem suspicious. Actually, it's a follow-on to what I just told you about not hurting the animals. We'd been having trouble getting them up the chute into the house for processing, and it occurred to me we might find anesthetic to calm them down. For their sakes as well as our own. A side of beef from a distressed animal is called darkcutter. Its meat is tough and chewy. We saw our sales dropping, we saw Armour going into the institution kitchen provision end of the business, and we thought we could diminish our darkcutter problem by giving each animal a whiff of the pento before sending him up the ramp. Is there a problem? Have there been complaints?"

"It seems that in certain precincts of the city, a drug based on pentobarbital has made considerable inroads. It kills some folks; it drives others so crazy they either get themselves killed or kill someone else."

"Good God, that stuff is too dangerous for human ingestion in any setting except carefully applied medical supervision."

"So you understand the government's interest?"

"I do. I wish I could help. But, Mr. Swagger, our plan went nowhere because in mid-May Nugent's Best Beef as well as eight million dollars' worth of buildings, businesses, hotels, restaurants, and even the amphitheater burned down. The drug went up with everything else. It's now a wasteland. I can only say, thank God for insurance."

CHAPTER 15

BILLY THE HAT WAS A BONES GUY. HE WAS OTHER THINGS TOO, RUNNING a stable out of a house on Maxwell Street, occasional strong-arm boy for rent, freelance armed robber, occasional grifter, but damn his shoes he did so like the skitter and click of the devil's cubes in his fist, the flash as they bounced across the asphalt, the suspense as their meaning was read, and the elation when they came up his way. When a floating game threw itself up in an alley along his way, he'd most always join in, winning some, losing some, but feeling so mother-fucking *alive* it made his toes jingle.

The game was street craps, as distilled from the classic form of casino craps, so simple a fool could play it. You rolled a number. It was then onto you to roll that number again before you rolled the house's 7, except there was no house and you were only betting against the other boys. It could go on for minutes, hours even, when neither your number nor 7 came up, signifying victory or loss. Each fruitless toss racked up the suspense a good degree, just like in a story. Meanwhile others bet for or against you and you bet for yourself against any who'd go your way.

He was hot. Who knew why? Maybe God had something to do with it, but Billy, thirty-four going on sixty-five, up from Mississippi and hacking a living off the street in the 4th District for close now on fifteen years, thought not. He had been born hardscrabble, sharecropper Baptist outside of Greenville, not that he remembered much of that life, but he still believed in the one true God up there—he just thought that Our Father must have had better things to do than control the flip and flop of the little cubes on South Chicago alley asphalt, amid an array of cement garbage boxes all packed solid and stinking hard of rot, four or five other miscreants who should have had better things to do, and the countless rats who diddled and munched decay in the shadows.

"Okay, baby," Billy incanted, "baby, baby, babybabybaby!" And with that he flung the well-rattled ivory-and-ebony pair in his hand to the scabby alley at the center, watched them tumble this way and that, and come to rest showing—nothing.

He was on 9, and it had been a while now, maybe five passes, and yet no 9 and no 7 had showed.

The dice came back to him. He held them close to his nose and eyes as if to communicate with them, squeezed them up tight, rubbed his fist against his cheek, then commenced the rolling spin that was his trademark. He was feeling good. He'd had a sniff an hour ago and taken his trip on the Night Train, and its artificial confidence lingered in his body, making him feel a part of the universe, a force in the universe if you will. He still had to attend to Charlotte, a high-yeller in his stable he'd heard was hanging out with a boy named Hop. That girl needed some attention. His pimp hand was the same as his gambling hand, kept strong.

"Crap out against the boy," said the man immediately across the circle from him, another pimp, this one named Jack Razor, who threw down a five against him.

"Here she come," said Billy, and the two bounced from his hand, spun on their axis this way and that, and came to rest signifying—damnation!—nothing. Not a 9, not a 7, but a 5.

"You don't get no money off me, sucker," said Billy.

The money stayed where it was. It was the poke, growing larger on each throw.

"I take all your bread, fool, you keep on rollin' that way," said Jack Razor. Considerable professional animosity lay between them over gals, territory, hats—Billy chose a big felt fedora, creamy and smooth, but Jack irked him by going for a straw in roughly the same shade, only closely giving up its identity as a tropical weave—as well as bright haberdashery, but most of all and most dangerously, R.E.S.P.E.K., and perhaps it had not been a wise idea for them to sit across from each other over the devil's bones. But it had happened and started before either had noticed, and now there was no backing down.

"You watch this, then, and prepare to pay down." More money went into the poke from all concerned.

Billy shook and shook and heard the bones rattling. They banged and smacked and dusted each other, picking up mojo, and Billy went to his whirl motion, that he was so known for, and unleashed the pair, and they lightning-flashed across the asphalt, and finally came to a slow halt, and—

"Yo mama!" hooted Jack Razor. "Lawdie, lawdie, you done Jack so good. Hey, little man, them bones ain't no friend of yours. I take yo wad, hear? That's the way it is, right, boys?"

Billy the Hat wasn't sure why what happened next happened next. It wasn't rage. It wasn't a gash of crazy. It wasn't the fever that killed his father in 1906. It wasn't watching his mother die in the cotton fields, wasted from the labor, beat so down they wasn't no up. It was just what it was. Something pushed him to the edge, and then over.

He had a pimp's special—that is, a silver bicycle gun in .32, with pearl grips. He pulled it out, cocking it. For no other reason except to right something so wrong in the universe he shot Jack Razor under the left eye. He did it quick, because Jack was known to be himself quick with the blade that gave him his name.

Jack's eyes welled wide in surprise, for this was no move ever seen before. But then the blood began to spill as if pumped from the hole under

Jack's eye, and Jack pitched hard to the alley, hitting one of the bones just right so it skittered away.

There was silence. Billy the Hat reached over and scooped the poke up, crumpled it, and wedged it tight into the pocket of his coat.

"Be mine now. He don't need it."

"Billy," someone said, "you'd best run off. You can't be just doing that, right here, in the daylight. Cops be on you, word gits around. Best head back south. They never chase a nigger south."

"He ain't lying, Billy. You know them Irish donkeys want to smack you down so hard you don't come back until Tuesday."

A chorus of "Uh-huh's" and "That be the truth's" and "Yassuh's" arose so as to urge him onward. He rose. He turned. His mind was all messed up. He tried to see through his problem to a solution, and somehow the words *train* and *south* and a mental picture of the big Illinois Central depot with the tower where he'd gotten off all those years ago rambled through his mind. He'd just get on and ride the same train back south to Greenville. He had the money.

But where was the depot? He hadn't seen it since that day. He walked into the street, saw people run in horror from him. That's because he still had the silver pistol in his hand. He tried to solve the following problem: if he put the gun away and the Irish showed, he might not have time to get it out. On the other hand, if he carried it openly, folks would run, sooner or later an Irish would arrive, and that would be that.

Damnation, he wanted a sniff. That would settle his ass down. That way he could think it straight. That way all things could work out. He tried to remember where the Man was. It wasn't that long ago. He tried to remember today's magic number, but it got mixed up with yesterday's and some others too, like Uncle Clevon's birthday. He spun, the blue sky whirling above him, the sun a blast of bright flame, a whisper of dizziness turning into a shout, went to one knee. He heard a siren.

Man, this was all fucked-up. He'd killed Jack for what couldn't have been more than a hundred's worth of crumpled green bills. And now what?

Then he remembered. 5-4? Was it 5-4? Yes. 5-4. It was 54th and Halsted. The Man was at a place called Nickle's, two blocks down. Still there? They didn't stay in one place too long. Too much attention. But he had no place else to head, so he elected for a shot at Nickle's.

He made it clean, gun in hand, people still running from him, sirens rising. Riot Squad? Yeah, sure, cops with tommy guns for serious work on the colored. It didn't matter. He was now focused on another whiff, another fine ride on the Night Train. That would make it all right.

He busted into Nickle's, a no-count place that sold cheap beer and shots of dubious origin, with sawdust on the floor and nothing else in the joint, no pictures, no nothing. It was just a hooch joint, straight and harsh, for a man who wanted to blur out his life and possibilities, both of which being nothing.

People scattered before him. He raised the pistol, fired one more precious bullet, meaning he had but four left for the whole Riot Squad.

"Where he be?" he screamed. "Where the ticket man? I needs me a ticket."

Somehow the bartender's shaking hands communicated the idea of the crapper, and Billy headed there, walking like Moses through the parted sea as folks opened a way for him and fled once he was past them. He reached the toilet door, but then it occurred to him the barman had a sawed-off underneath, and as he turned he rotated a little to the left and the blast of buckshot ripped up his left arm bad. The barman went into a hoochie-mama dance of trying to reload, but his hands trembled too hard and the shells dropped to the floor.

He looked at Billy, who shot him in the throat.

There! That be that.

Billy turned back to the door, slammed it hard, and it popped open. The Man sat terrified on the commode, his pants down to his ankles, the shakes jabbering through all parts of his body. He'd been wearing a cream suit and the pants were crumpled at his feet, but Billy could see he had on white-and-brown spectators, because the Man always dressed to the nines, as befit his importance.

"Take the money," he squeaked, holding out a large wad of greenbacks.

"Fuck that shit," said Billy. He suspected he was beyond money now. He shot the Man in the face, just like Jack Razor. The Man wasn't a man no more; he was a dead man.

Billy bent, saw the briefcase, and snatched it up.

He spun, as a shitter was no place to do the ritual.

He pulled a jar out of the briefcase. Inside was about half-a-jar's worth of cotton patches awash in about a quarter-of-a-jar's worth of solution. He shook it up real bubbly, then unscrewed the lid, reached in, and with more delicacy of touch than you might have figured on, plucked a patch, damp with fluid. He brought it to his nose, breathed deeply, feeling its powers rush through his nostrils to his lungs and finally his soul.

Yes, sir!

Glory be to the Negro man!

Heavenly Father, there you be!

Your servant Billy be on his way. He didn't mean no harm, but on these streets a man's got to do what's there for him to do.

Sniffed, the fluid vapors burst across his brain in a surge of sweet. Everything turned to gold and candy and his mother's scrapple and corn bread on a cold Sunday morning when they didn't have to go to the fields. The music began to rise, all gospel, all flourish, and the spirit pulsed through him. He saw his Heavenly Father and Jesus the son, and of course as he had known all along they were Negro men. They gestured welcome to him. His mother stood off to one side.

Hi, Moms! Damn, you looking good.

She smiled.

He'd never seen her smile before.

Lord, he felt fine. Never been so happy! World never been more won-derful!

And he had a jar, or half at least, of the stuff!

He tightened the lid, slid it into his pocket, adjusted his cream felt fedora, picked up his nickel-plated bicycle gun, and headed out.

There the Riot Squad awaited. Four Irish in blue, looking as big as giants, all with the rat-a-tat guns with the big round bullet-holders snapped in place. They crouched before or leaned against the Black Maria by which they were known to travel. Otherwise the street was empty.

He smiled and raised his pistol.

CHAPTER 16

THERE WERE FEW PLACES IN THE CITY WHERE A WHITE MAN AND A BLACK man could meet as equals, share a beer or a cup of coffee and chat, at least not without arousing suspicion. One, however, was the cafeteria at the University of Chicago in Hyde Park, amid a somewhat more cosmopolitan milieu than all elsewhere. There, white and black, though far from predominating, were a part of the mix, as were folks from all over the world. Moreover, it was a jibber-jabber place, where voices were never still and often rose in debate or even quarrel. The voices were so loud because the stakes were so small.

Charles and Sylvester sat at a far table, away from the general thrust and jab of argument from the more animated occupants. They sat over half-eaten scrambled eggs and cold coffee. Sylvester wore civilian clothes because it was still an hour before he went on duty and he kept his uniform at the station. Yet even lacking the bold pronouncement of self that the two ivory-gripped .38-44s conferred, he still radiated considerable force, vitality, Gable power, whatever you call it. Well, Charles knew what you called it: swagger.

Charles, meanwhile, had his one suit, the jacket necessary to conceal his automatic, his tie tight because he was a tight-tie man. But he had taken his fedora off, revealing a thatch of once-blond hair that four years of war had turned a dingy gray. He didn't like slippery stuff in it, so, unkempt, it stood up like flowerless rosebushes all over his head.

"What have we learned from this 'Hat' fellow?" he asked.

"Not much," said Sylvester. "They hit him so many times with them fat bullets, he was a mess. Looked like the Capone mob did the job on him."

"The Irish do love their machine guns."

"By the time I got there, our detectives and patrol officers were all over the place. It was far from the kind of crime scene you could get a whole lot out of."

"Give me what you have, Officer Washington. Maybe it'll fit in somewhere."

"What I saw was basically an Irish wedding party. The boyos were quite happy with their work. Lots of whooping, hollering, joy-jumping. They almost busted out into a jig."

"You and I both know such antics are far from uncommon among the Irish police."

"Yes, sir. I do think I have some good news here, on how the people selling this stuff distribute it and control the litter," said Sylvester. "I'm told he had a jar in his pocket, though a bullet had smashed it. It contained a mysterious batch of one-by-one cotton patches, soaked in some kind of fluid. The fluid, of course, was contaminated by all the blood. The Hat—the late William Francis Robinson—was hit by thirty-three out of the forty rounds that were fired at relatively close range."

"The St. Paul coppers didn't even put that many into Homer Van Meter. Anyway, follow on your thought."

"So as I see it, the pusher man has a jar full of cotton patches soaked in whatever medium they are using for the pento. You pays him your dollar and he picks one patch out of the jar, maybe with tweezers. That's your hit. You put it to your nose and do a big jitter-dance of breathing. The stuff goes straight to the brain, and you on the Night Train. Maybe you just chug through happy land, maybe you drop dead, maybe you go chimpanzee and attack someone you love or, if it's a police officer, someone you hate. You get a bellyful of lead if it's the cop."

"Yeah, that makes a lot of sense. And part of the transaction would require the user drops the patch in a bag or something right there on the spot, so there's nothing left to suggest a drug transaction took place. It's slick. And speaking of the pusher man—"

"It looks like Billy the Hat shot him in the face, just like he did Jack Razor. But Billy was so gone by that time, he'd gotten sloppy. He must have hit him in the jaw or cheekbone or at some strange angle. Reports of a big man in a cream suit holding a kerchief to his face running down an alley in the next block about that same time. Blood dripping everywhere, even on his brown-and-whites."

"Can you think of a next step?" Charles then asked. "I'm plumb out. I know there was a quantity of pentobarbital shipped to the Yards, but it went up in the fire. So that one, which looked so promising, yielded nothing. I am now officially at loggerheads, and fear that at any moment I may be called away to shoot someone the government knows to be a gangster."

"Well," said Washington, "here's something. A fellow like that, in a nice suit and shoes, it pains him something awful to see it get messed up. I'm thinking the suit's a lost cause, but the shoes, maybe he is hoping to clean up. In the Fourth District they do love their shoes. So it seems he might take them to a cobbler down here and have that man do some work, you know, get as much of the blood out as possible, then repolish over the stain that's left."

"That's good," said Charles. "You're thinking better than I am. So you go around to all the Fourth District cobblers, looking for someone who fixed up some brown-and-whites. From that we get a name, and maybe instead of busting him, we watch him. We see where he leads us. He's got to get his stuff from somewhere, somehow. Then we tail that fellow and on and on to the next."

"Yes," said Washington. "I will get on it soon, figuring he might not go to the cobbler's until it all dies down."

"Just a thought that occurs to me while we're on the subject of haberdashery. It's that these dealer-men, they're amateurs. One-timers. Someone goes to a respectable fellow, respectable enough to be well dressed on a steamy August afternoon, and says, My friend, care to make some easy cash? Who doesn't? You go to a place. You have a jar. Some mysterious way people know you are today's man. Your customers know not to crowd or push or line up. One at a time, they come up to you. Say in a place you never been and never will go back to. Your clients give you the money, you give them the patch, then make sure they toss it in the bag. End of day, you've got a heap of cash money, but because you're no criminal hard-ass, you won't be tempted to take off. You pay off, you get your swag, and that's that. You never see them again, they never see you again."

"It is slick," said Washington.

"It would mean the formation of no network of meeting or communications that the law could penetrate and follow to the core people. Naming it the Night Train means the cops all think it's just Negro code for having given up, so they're not hard on the trail of a phantom."

"Whoever worked it out knows a thing or two. He is a tricky one."

"And here's the biggest trick of all," said Charles. "The whole thing is based on the proposition that nobody cares what's going on down here. Colored people dying in various ways, falling dead on the street, getting blasted by an out-of-town Division agent in the Yards, being machine-gunned by the blue Irish on the street, the numbers running higher and higher, it matters to nobody. Death, death, death, just like in the war. On and on, more and more. And nobody cares. Newspapers don't care, police don't care, federals don't care, politicians don't care. The money just keeps rolling in, easy as can be."

"Ain't gonna change, not soon, anyway, Mr. Charles."

"But just this one time, Officer Washington, just this once, of no overall significance in the long run, wouldn't you like to see this bastard go up the hard way in righteous flame?"

"Praise to glory," said Officer Washington.

CHAPTER 17

IT WOULDN'T LEAVE HIM ALONE. IT SHOULD HAVE, BUT IT NAGGED AND scratched and punched its way into his dreams. All that pentobarbital. So close to where it would ultimately come to do its great harm on the streets of the 4th District. Yet all of it gone on May 14, in the $8 million fire that turned a large section of the Yards into a view resembling No Man's Land. So they had to get the stuff from somewhere else.

He sat in his undershirt on his little fire-escape balcony on the North Side, with a pack of cigarettes and a bottle of Pikesville late into the summer night. Since it was so hot, the cityscape was alive with open windows in which people sat to avoid the temperature that collected in their rooms. This meant yells, radio music, even trombone playing filled the night. But the alternative was the room itself, a threadbare rental of the sort a man who wished to kill himself might take.

Another cigarette, another sip of whiskey, and the mallet of the hooch hit him again, knocking him a bit dizzy. A little ice might have helped, but his allotment had melted and another delivery wasn't due for three days.

He tried to sort it out.

A possibility: desperately needing money, maybe this Dr. Magellan had put the whole thing together. He'd used the Best Beef shipment as a guise to ship twice as many vials of pentobarbital to the Stockyards.

Nugent got his, and whomsoever the other purchaser was got his, at exorbitant rates, and went to business in the 4th District. The plot was hidden behind Mabel's suspiciously convenient ineptitude.

Note to self: check with Food and Drug boys on this Dr. Magellan.

Another possibility: insurance scam. Somehow, for a little cut, Nugent got Dr. Magellan to go through the formal paperwork but ship nothing except old newspapers to Chicago. The fire goes up and that order of expensive drugs is claimed as a loss. It ups the payoff by the insurers considerably. But that would imply the fire was started by Nugent and, being an incompetent, he hadn't figured it right, and so it burned and burned until $8 million worth of pens and cows and pigs and offices, bidding rooms, sales headquarters, a hotel and two restaurants and one brave man were destroyed. It probably wouldn't matter to him. It was a farewell to a business that he had inherited and run poorly, almost driven into bankruptcy by shrewder meat folks. He did very well by the fire, inheriting freedom from the Yards, particularly the next-door presence of Pulverized Manure, as well as so many other demons, plus inheriting Winnetka forever.

Note to self: check with Chicago Fire Department on arson possibilities of the big May fire.

And still another theory: mystery man Oscar Bentley. Having checked, Charles knew that Oscar had left town and now lived in Florida, far from the smell of meat and manure. Oscar was said to be a sharp man, who'd kept Nugent's Best Beef running against the habitual uninterest and absurd schemes of its owner. He could have been shrewd enough to put the thing together, but . . . why would he have left? One thing such a plan would require is close eyes upon its operation, as its manager would know it to be a fragile setup. It could not operate with an absentee boss unable to make snap decisions to correct unanticipated misfortune. Again too, if Oscar was involved, he'd have known that fleeing would certainly attract attention his way. In fact, leaving town was almost a proclamation of innocence, seemingly an act committed in complete naivete. It wasn't either as if he'd disappeared; he'd taken the chunk of insurance that Thaddeus had given him for his years of loyal service and departed for the sunshine, but burned no bridges behind him, leaving address and phone number.

Note to self: no note to self.

Finally there was the Organization, well developed, well muscled in Chicago, perhaps rightly thought by some to be the city's true ruling class. Unless it was sanctioned, the scheme would certainly cut into their profits as steady users of their powders might be drawn away by the cheaper, easier-to-administer diluted anesthetic. The mob would never stand for that. Their turf was always inviolate and had sent many a man for a swim in the lake with his new friend, an automobile radiator, tethered to his ankle. Moreover their intelligence sources would have tumbled to its existence much earlier, and they would have either destroyed it or absorbed it. That river of illicit money was far too much for the Italians to leave alone. But why had they? Did they own a part of it? It then occurred to Charles that the way it was set up—amateur, one-day dealers, no necessity of a safe house for shooting up, no real locality to find and raid, all of those things that made it so hard for law enforcement to even notice—might have been equally planned to keep the mob guessing. But how long would that last? Somebody always talked, and when they did, things fell apart fast.

That suggested another ramification. This was planned as a onetime, quick-in, quick-out effort. Whoever was doing it had no belief in it as a career, but only as a short campaign. Take the money and run. Hmm. That would seem to suggest that perhaps the supply of pentobarbital was limited to the four hundred bottles supposedly swallowed by fire. When gone, they'd be gone, and the Night Train would cease to exist, leaving no tracks to be followed, nobody to answer to either law or the Italians. Risky? Very risky on both counts. But certain people could see a big blast of cash as worth the risk, because—well, because of what? Because they weren't going to be around? Such a person knew his time in this town was limited. He'd decided to beat the system, take the dough and be gone.

Another blast of hooch. What if—

But someone knocked on the door.

"Yeah?"

"You got a phone call, Mr. Swagger," came the voice from the other side.

Charles trudged down the hall to the public phone, the earphone hanging loose by cord. He picked it up.

"Swagger."

It was Officer Washington.

"Just found the man in brown-and-white shoes."

"Oh, that's good."

"It isn't. He's dead."

CHAPTER 18

I T WASN'T A BIG DEAL—NO FOUR-MAN MACHINE-GUN FROLIC FILLING THE fellow with an abundance of lead. Instead the ambulance and two cop Fords, the second unusual for a floater, but belonging to Officer Washington. Charles parked, found his colleague.

"A couple walking on the beach called it in."

The lake lapped against the shore, turning the sand it overcame to black sherbet. Off to the right, beyond the busy roadway, loomed the great museum as left over from the world's fair of 1904. It looked, in silhouette, as if a battleship had washed ashore. Like sentinels, the lifeguard stands marked the beach, white against the darkness of the night and the gleam, nevertheless, of the water.

The man in the brown-and-white shoes was on the gurney, not yet inserted into the ambulance, which would drop him at the morgue. A medic stood next to him, filling out the paperwork. Farther back, two black women, mother and daughter, stood arm in arm in support, battling grief.

"Wife and daughter?"

"Yes," said Washington.

"Hope to ask some questions, then."

"We'll hold him till you release him," said Washington.

He asked the medic, "How long was he in the water?"

"I'd say twenty-four hours or thereabouts."

"Yesterday evening. He pushed dope all day, got his dough, went home to steak and potatoes. Medic, how do you read this?"

"I've seen dozens of floaters. Sometimes it's a dumb kid slipped off the rocks or some wild teen showing off for his girlfriend, gets caught in a riptide. But a well-dressed fella dressed for a casual night at home, his shoes still on, almost always turns out to be suicide."

"Name is Ralph Hughes, dentist by profession," said Washington. "Reasonably successful. Some money in the bank."

Charles pulled back the sheet, saw the face, distended by immersion, but still featuring a slice across the right cheekbone.

"That's where the Hat's bullet went. He used up all his luck on that one."

The man was heavyish, not heavy; had he lived, he would have gotten heavier. His hair was marceled over his pate, its natural zigzag beginning to assert itself against the diminishing discipline of the chemical. He had a pencil mustache. The suit was gone, but he was nicely enough dressed, in a short-sleeve Hawaii-style shirt and a pair of linen pants, tan going on brown. Just to make sure, Charles flipped the rest of the sheet off, to look at the shoes. There they were, as promised, a solid, well-built pair of oxfords, so tightly tied they'd defied the suction of the lake, thick soled, not cheap. Looking closely, Charles saw the traces of spots that could have been polished over in the white.

"He sure did like those shoes," said Washington. "He dumped the suit, but he made sure to keep the shoes. Florsheims. Nice. I can understand his pride."

"See anything unusual?" Charles asked. "Any signs of violence or force, any indicators of illness, anything that could suggest the intercession of another party?"

"Looks clear as glass to me," said the medic. "Only that scratch on his cheek. He didn't bang against no rocks or anything."

"Could the rocks have caused the scratch?"

"No, sir. It was all dry and scabbed up. If he'd done it on the rocks the cut would still be bleeding."

"Okay, now I'll talk to the two women," said Charles.

Washington ran interference on the transaction.

"Mrs. Hughes, this man here is a federal officer. He'd like to ask you some questions if he may."

"No white man never cared a thing about what happened to us before," said the widow, her face tight under the weight of the emotion. "Why would this be any different?"

"Because I say it is. And you know who I am."

"You Two-Gun. But them fancy guns didn't do my Ralph no good."

"Maybe they will if you cooperate with the agent here."

Charles showed her his badge—she didn't bother to look at it—and said, "Ma'am, I hate to interrupt you at such a rough time, but we'd like to get to the bottom of this and make sure everything is on the up-and-up."

"I know what they say. They say he killed himself. That way, they done with him and that's that."

"Mama, you shouldn't talk to a federal man like that. Git you in trouble."

"I don't make trouble," said Charles. "I don't work that way. But you say you doubt it was a suicide? Why, if I may ask?"

"He was happy day before yesterday. He came home, said he'd won a bet. He had a thousand dollars. He was going to take us to a nice lake in Wisconsin, he said. Get away from the big city and just relax."

"I noted some kind of injury—more a scrape, I guess—to his upper right cheek. Did he have that on his face when you last saw him?"

"Yes, sir. He said he was so happy when he won the bet, he jumped for joy. He was getting too big for that kind of silliness, and his foot slipped when he landed. He fell, cutting his cheek on the corner of a table."

"Was he—"

"Sir, Ralph was not a drinking man! No, sir. He hadn't had a drink, nothing wobbly about him, no odor of the liquor. I know, because my daddy drank hisself to death. Ralph was a hardworking man, a good dentist, made us a good living, no one can say nothing bad about Ralph."

"Yes, ma'am, I understand."

"Don't you be saying nothing bad about him, sir."

"Ma'am, I wouldn't think of it. Can you please tell me what happened the last night? It might be important."

"Night before, he was nervous. Don't know 'bout what. Wouldn't say nothing. But he went out, usual time, and everything was just as it always be. He was early getting home, and all excited about winning the bet."

"Was his suit in any way bloody?"

"Wasn't wearing no suit. Had them pants and that crazy island shirt. Come to think of it, he *did* leave in his suit. The clothes he had, they were new. Never saw such a shirt in my life. That wasn't him. He was what you call a serious man and he dressed serious, wearing a suit to his office every morning. He was proud of being a dentist and showed it every day. But he was so excited I never noticed that then. He was so happy!"

"Did he want to take you out to dinner?" asked Washington.

"Wisconsin was what he was happiest of. He was so happy. We don't spend much because we have to pay the tuition for Regina at St. Josephine's. Ralph worked hard to put his daughter through a good school so she go on to college."

"I've been accepted at the big state university," said Regina. "That made him so happy. The trip to Wisconsin was to be our celebration, before I was to leave for Champaign."

"Tell me why he went out that night. He doesn't seem the type to go to bars or clubs."

"He got a phone call. I had the feeling it was from somebody he know. I answered, he—"

"White or colored?" asked Washington.

"White. Nobody I'd ever heard from before. But wasn't no gangster voice. It was kind of sloppy. He didn't say his words too clear."

"Okay," said Charles, "please continue."

"He just smiled. He said, 'Just got to check on something. Be back in half an hour.' And that was it until the police called tonight."

Charles nodded, writing it down in a cop's shorthand.

"Is that all?" she said. "I'd like to say goodbye to him and go to church."

"Of course, ma'am," said Charles. "Here, finally, is my card and a phone number. If you should remember anything more, please call me."

"I hear you," she said. "Thank you."

"No need for thanks, ma'am. I just try to do my job."

CHAPTER 19

I T WAS A HOLE ON WELLS STREET, JUST BEYOND NORTH, FORMALLY A speak, now legal. The booze hadn't improved any.

"So I found out a good deal about him," said Charlie Oliver, Food and Drug Administration senior agent and well-known fixer, rascal, and of the easily bought. "I do know lots of people, been working for the government close to forty years now."

But Thaddeus didn't care about Charlie's career, how Charlie had found out, when Charlie planned to retire, or any of it. He just cared about one thing: what was going to happen to himself.

"Who is he?"

"Some sheriff from down south," said Charlie. "He was a legendary gunfighter. The Division brought in a bunch of gunmen when it realized what it was up against, namely the motorized bank boys, with their machine guns and automatic rifles. They needed cool hands."

"So it was never intended that he handle general investigations. He was strictly there for the gun battles. Should I be worried? Does he know anything about investigating?"

"You should be worried. Sheriff of a small town learns all kinds of things. He sees most kinds of crimes, from husband-wife murders to bank embezzlement. They say he's smart, he notices, he remembers, he can put pieces together. He did an analysis of that robbery in South Bend that made him a big man even before the Johnny Dillinger thing."

"I don't know what you mean. What Dillinger thing?"

"He was the guy who got Dillinger, not Mel Purvis, who was across the street in a dress store."

"So what's he on my case for? Why isn't he at the range, practicing for Baby Face?"

"He's pretty much the office star now. That means he's free to do as he pleases. You know how it is in an office. The best man gets all sorts of freedom."

No, Thaddeus didn't know, because the only office he'd been in he was the boss of, by virtue of inheriting the firm. But he got the implication.

"I'm guessing he can't be bought off."

"Wouldn't even try. You'd end up in the can."

"Could your boss at FDA write his boss at the Division and make the argument that the Yards were under jurisdiction of the FDA, not the Division of Investigation? Get him kicked out of there by administrative politics, I'm saying."

"See, here's the problem. That colored fellow that attacked him the first night, the one he had to kill, that was an assault on a federal officer, making it a federal felony. So that would be the justification for his investigation."

"And if he found out about our, er, problems with the Roasty-Toasty line, he'd be able to follow up on that?"

"How would he find out about it?"

"Well, people talk, word gets out, maybe he sends a bulletin out on me, and someone somewhere puts two and two to—"

"Thaddeus, I'm telling you, he's interested in the drugs getting into the Fourth District, and you are clear on that one, owing to the fire. He's done with you."

"But suppose—"

"If it came up, and it won't, you could make a case that the Maine business was in FDA jurisdiction and he'd turn it over to us. We could bury it."

"But just to be sure, what should I do, Charlie?"

"I'd hire a lawyer."

"Sounds like I need an assassin."

CHAPTER 20

THE RAILROAD DETECTIVES—YARD BULLS, DICKS, WHATEVER, THAT IS, the official police arm of the Union Stockyard & Transit Co.—were not helpful, but he expected that after his run-in with the shakedown thugs the night of George Roberts's death. He didn't see those two bog-dwellers about the run-down station, only a dozen or so near-perfect replicas, and nobody acknowledged the flagrant wrongdoing. Instead, he was shunted to the same chief, Captain Mulrooney, as had briefed him before, the whiskey-faced Irisher with a nose the size and color of the setting sun, and those dark, restless eyes that all the good cops seemed to have. They would notice everything, and could, if necessary, melt through anything.

"Agent Swagger," the chief said, "I think I told you this a few weeks ago. We pretty much specialize in the 'transit' part of Stockyard and Transit Company. You would not believe how much pilfering goes on against a railyard. So my people spend ninety percent of the time patrolling the track areas"—he pointed to a large wall map of the mile-square, his finger sweeping the dense filigree of track that surrounded the place on three sides, complete to switching yards; dockage sites; single lines deep into the pens exclusive to the big boys, Swift, Armour, and Morris; engine and car repair shops; the whole thing being the envy of any middle-sized country—"and conking heads. Lots of heads to be conked in the mile-square. Sure, sometimes we tie in with the Chicago department, and most of the boys are ex–Chicago cops, but it's more like the Wild West of lawmen versus train robbers than anything else."

"So you are not notified of the contents of shipments and asked to pay special attention to potentially dangerous ones, such as heavily regulated drugs?"

"Can't say the system is that developed. Inbound, mostly it's cows. Lots and lots of cows. Sheep, pigs too. Not so much chicken, which is good because chickens shit everywhere. The outgoing is freight cars loaded with ice and beeves and mutton. They're shipped to canning or packaging facilities not local to the area or to big meat wholesalers. But you wouldn't believe how much meat goes away. We do run checks on black-market food sales, which is bigger than you might think. But you're talking tons and tons of stuff, while regulated drugs would only be a tiny bit, not even a single car's worth."

"How about rings of thieves? That is, professionals, who steal based on intelligence."

"You're talking a higher class of thief. But we get mostly Fourth District folks, who try to break in and make off with two or three beeves to sell to local butchers. So our boys don't do and aren't trained in Sherlock Holmes types of investigation. Be happy to let you look at the files."

That led, really, to nothing, just mug shots of men, mostly of color or recent immigration, who played a daily game of cops and robbers with the rail dicks. If they won, they got some meat money; if they lost, they got a crack on the head that would raise a goose bump for a month. Sometimes one of them died, but it went unrecorded.

So much for that. He'd wanted a list of usual suspects; he got a peek at dead-eyed zombies.

The next stop—after an hour on the range at police headquarters with incoming agents, again matching guns to hands, and counseling, then supervising—front sight, front sight, front sight—was the Food and

Drug Administration offices, where he ended up chatting with a pleasant geezer named Charlie something. Charlie Olive? Olivo, Olly, oh yeah, Charlie Oliver, once sandy-haired and still a-speckle with freckle, probably as crooked as tracks through mountains, but amiable and willing to cooperate. He was a smiler behind extremely prominent white teeth, which would be of deep pride.

"Yes, sir, Agent Swagger, I do know of and am aware of Dr. Magellan's enterprise. I'm surprised it's still kicking. The man lacks administrative talent. The federal agent in his district has filed several complaints; the doctor has been fined, though I do think the fines are still in adjudication, and he is watched very carefully, again by our Milwaukee Division."

"Does he do much business down here?"

"Not with the bigger companies, who have their own pharmaceutical departments. The low-enders, the boys just hanging on, he'd be on that circuit. The deal is, lower prices but no complaints at mistakes that are frequent and shipping delays, which are common. But there's not a big trade down here, drug-wise. Mostly we inspect, looking for sanitation issues, animal welfare, safety violations. The drugs shipped in would be more or less smallish amounts of anesthesia, which can also be used for animal euthanasia, as you know. Constant, yes, but not necessary in large quantities. It's important for a slaughterhouse to have it around, because even if it's in the business of killing, nobody wants to see the animals suffer any more than necessary."

"That's why Nugent's Best Beef would be a customer?"

"Exactly."

"Did this big order of pentobarbital they received attract attention?"

"It attracted *my* attention. So I went to Thaddeus Nugent and his manager, Oscar Bentley, and we discussed it. He told me he'd found a way to mix a 'cow cocktail,' if you will, that settled the animals on the chute.

That's where so much beef goes bad. Anyhow, when it seemed to work, he told me he wanted to stockpile it while he had a chance and prices were low, the pento being the key ingredient."

"The prices fluctuate?"

"Yes, sir. I could arrange to have you talk to someone who knows much more about it if you want."

"This is just a preliminary check. No need to move to the next step yet."

"I don't know if the deaths were their fault or not. It's possible, I suppose."

"Ah, wait a second. What's that supposed to mean?"

"In a Maine prison where they sold their product, seven men died of some sort of food poisoning. I guessed that was why you're here."

"Don't know a thing about it."

"Thaddeus is very worried."

"He seemed a little flighty when I talked to him. But believe me, I've enough going on. I don't need something else that's not even in my jurisdiction. Besides, I suppose it's meaningless because it was all destroyed in the fire."

"That damned fire sure made a mess of everything," said Oliver.

"Would there be any other possible source of pentobarbital in the Yards?"

"I'd have to check my files. I'd be happy to do that and send you a memo. Is that acceptable?"

"I would appreciate it, yes."

"If you have anything else, I'll be happy to pitch in. Just let me know."

"No, you've been very cooperative. I much appreciate it, Mr. Oliver."

"Now, you could criticize me, I'm sure, for passing on a closer examination of the Nugent situation. I'll provide you with my superior's number and his superior's number in D.C. if you want to follow up in any way or file a complaint, formal or informal. I don't hold grudges and I know you have to do your job. Plus, ha ha, I'll be retiring shortly. Still, I don't want to do a thing to hinder your investigation, and I'll happily give depositions or let you into my files or whatever it is you need."

"Very pleased with your cooperation, sir. Sometimes different government agencies don't see each other as collaborators, but as competitors."

Further note to self: Magellan? Ask Milwaukee field office to run a quick check on him, see if anything pops up.

Next: fire headquarters, Arson Division, Lieutenant Kerley, apparently decent enough and no sense of ownership of fire issues, not a cop-thug like old Muldoon of the yard dicks. Swagger had always liked firemen: they were as tough as cops, but because they confronted the flaming inanimate, they had no need of some kind of bravado that was hard to get through and could be troublesome, and lead them to wrong decisions.

Mild and sunny, portly and earnest, Lieutenant Kerley gave him the basics.

"Unless a fire is started by an idiot using fuel accelerants, arson can be very tough to prove. I look at possible cases every day, but can't press on because there's no meaningful evidence. You can start a fire with a book of matches or a cigarette, and who's to say if it was done deliberately or accidentally."

"In other words, you have no definitive ruling on the big May fire?"

"I can show you where it started, how it leaped animal passageways and jumped from building to building, avenue to avenue, even the big one, Exchange, and how our companies maneuvered to fight it."

"Yes, show me."

"It started here"—he led Swagger to a map of the Yards on the wall, the same one Swagger had seen on every office wall—"in some hay. No traces of turpentine, kerosene, gasoline, or alcohol. Believe me, we went over that area very hard, with specially trained dogs. It was a match, a burning newspaper, a spark, and kaboom, eight million dollars turned to ash on the wind or charred beams and slats and a man killed. You can see this area runs under the Morgan Street frame viaduct, off 43rd Street. The viaduct passes over a warren of wooden cattle pens and pig and cattle runs. It's filled with hay, which is highly flammable, particularly in this hot weather. The best theory is that some motorist tossed a cigarette out his window and it landed in some of that hay. Maybe someone on the ground got careless in his smoking. Then the fire rode the wind, and at a certain point, say here, it became so powerful that it began to leap streets and involve buildings in almost random paths, like an explosion. You just have to meet each attack and put it down."

"Brave men."

"Yes, they are."

"Okay," said Charles, "I'm going to throw a theory at you. Not to convince you but for you to tell me if you think, for some reason I don't know, it's impossible. If you say it is, I'll drop it."

"All right."

"Say you wanted to burn down a building—maybe for insurance, maybe to cover up a crime—and you knew the Yards quite well—"

"What building?"

"Let's just say the Pulverized Manure Company."

"That's everybody's favorite. Always draws a laugh."

"Is under the Morgan Street viaduct a plausible starting point? Let me say up front, this boy was no arson professional and he could have just seen the way the wind would push the fire."

"Let's go back to the map and go back to my files."

Getting the material and sorting it, Kerley pointed exactly to the viaduct on Morgan Street, over-running a spread of wooden cattle structures. Then he consulted a page in his file.

"All right, at 4:15 p.m. the wind was charted at the Chicago Weather Bureau, not two miles away, to be sporadic but blustery at fifteen miles an hour, northeasterly. Now here"—he moved his finger a couple of inches—"is the location of Pulverized, or should I say, the former location of Pulverized. Others on the same block were Zanzinger's Sausage, Nugent's Best Beef, Hartwell's Scientific Slaughterhouse, and Luigi's Italian Pork Sausage Company, all gone, burned flat. The mean distance to Pulverized is less than half a mile, and that street went up very soon, by, say, four-thirty."

"Is it possible he didn't mean to burn down half the Yards but miscalculated?"

"More than possible. Amateurs don't have any idea how fast fire moves. They think you set a fire, it burns for a while, then the fire trucks arrive and put it out, and damage is limited. No, not at all. It's almost a living thing. It's fast as hell, it's completely responsive to wind direction, seems to have a nose for fuel, it can leap surprising distances, and the best firefighters in the world can only advance on a narrow front, limited in their maneuverability by access to water lines. It's commonplace for our units to find themselves cut off, and they have to fight their way out or climb to a rooftop and hope for ladder rescue."

"Could you play my little game and pretend for me that indeed the fire was set to burn down Pulverized Manure?"

"Some days I felt like burning it down. Phew! Can't say I miss it. But yes. Looking at it, I'd say the arsonist was right where he set the fire, knowing the wind would move it fast across the pens and barns to the buildings on the west side of Exchange. But he probably counted on Exchange stopping it. That would have limited the damage considerably. But he had no idea how a fire can leap, and it jumped Exchange like it was a small fence to a big horse. Once on the other side of Exchange, it did its worst damage. The inn, the hotel, the Exchange Building, the amphitheater, a radio station, a newspaper office, whole lot of smaller outfits tucked in there. That's probably six of the eight million right there."

"Given the size of the fire, was it odd that so many folks got out alive? Only one death."

"Only a poor fellow named Isaac Means, a dock supervisor. He saw it early, went off to fight it with buckets of water. We found his body the next day."

"Brave man. But nobody else. Is that remarkable or am I way off base?"

"It is remarkable. But there was another hero. Next to Pulverized is a place called Nugent's Best Beef, and their boss, guy named Thaddeus Nugent, he must have smelled the fire before he could see it. He got his people out in good order, then stayed behind to phone the other places. They evacuated too—nobody in a stockyard messes with fire. I thought Nugent deserved a medal, but he's a modest type, didn't want any publicity."

"Actually, I've met him. Seemed decent. Still, given Means, if it was arson, then it was murder."

"Yes, it was."

"I will take that into advisement. But your bottom-line position would be that while there's no evidence that my theory happened, there's also no evidence it didn't."

"Absolutely."

"You've been very helpful, Lieutenant."

"Please keep me advised. That would be a bastard I'd like to see strung up by the balls."

CHAPTER 21

HE WANTED TO SEE THE BURN. IT WAS LATE, BUT HE HAD TO SEE IT, TO have in his mind an image of how the fire had moved. He just wanted to see the play of the big scorch across the northwest corner of the Yards. His plan was to crank hard to the right just inside the gates and walk one of the smaller, unnamed streets to the starting point at the 45th Street viaduct, then double back on a larger street, to intercept Exchange, following exactly the fire's march, where the ruins of Nugent's Best Beef as well as Pulverized Manure and the other companies lay in ash.

The sun was setting as he parked off Halstead near the castle gate. In the air, cow, lots of cow. In his ears, cow, lots of cow. As he walked through the mud, cow, lots of cow. He didn't call Officer Washington because it was so trivial, more along the lines of scratching an itch than investigating a crime.

He crossed some at-grade tracks, took his right-hand into the devastated zone, and strode along, masking the basic meaninglessness of the task behind a purposeful stride. What he encountered reminded him of nothing, for no visual vocabulary of utter devastation existed. No war had yet educated the world in that kind of destruction. Everywhere, flattened, packed ash. In a few spots charred spars and struts, in a few others fragments of brick walls, attached to nothing, supporting nothing. He'd heard a phrase once, not sure where: *the wasteland*. That was it. Above, as time passed, a waxing crescent moon vectored up from the east and cast a bone-bright pall on everything, giving it a ghastly sheen. That color had no life in it. Bright as it was, it had no warmth. It was the color of ghosts, of maggots, of dead-fish belly, of a corpse before rot sets in. It lit the ash like its counterpart on desert sand.

He found the 45th Street viaduct, still standing and evidently firm enough to bear traffic. Above, cars now and then rumbled down it, advanced by light beams. He saw the site that Lieutenant Kerley had pinpointed as the fire's ignition point. Nothing could be learned from it, just patches of dead black hay where the fire had burned on that hot afternoon and killed Mr. Means. He soon enough encountered a nameless street running back toward Exchange that had to be the way to the Pulverized Manure Company and its next-door neighbor, Nugent's Best Beef, home of the Roasty-Toasty Beef Stew, prison purveyors, and who knew what else.

This is the way the flames had moved. Counting steps, it was about five hundred, and for a raging fire under push of hard wind the obvious route. Wood was nourishment, wood was the meat and potatoes of fire, and, shoved by bursts of the fulfilling oxygen, it would have charged like the doomed boys under Pickett, headlong and careless but willing to risk everything for the sake of a mission accomplished. If you tried, you could imagine the moving wall of heat, remorseless, incandescent, and without pity.

He arrived at Exchange, again took a left, and soon by stink identified what remained of Pulverized Manure, which meant the next ruined lot had to be the Nugent slaughterhouse, of which nothing remained. He surveyed the wastage. Just rolling mounds of ash, the same odd stump of burned spar or rib, a little shaky brick here and there where once had been the wooden complexity of pens and pathways, all leading to the knocker, the man with the sledge. All gone. And then—

There were three of them. They rose like shadows out of the moon-pale ash. All wore long coats and fedoras. He saw pistols in shooting hands and that insouciance the soon-to-kill always show to the soon-to-die.

At least that's how they saw it. What they didn't see was the .45—same one used in Flanders Fields—in his right hand, cocked, and with a snap of his thumb now unlocked.

"You boys must think you're gunfighters," he said.

The moon shone down, hard and bright. Lunar shadows lay across the field of ash, slashing it into random patches of light and dark. It looked like a skewed chessboard. A razor cut of unlit space sprawled in the wake of the odd post, bisecting the fighting field. Defining the arena of the pistol, a feeble stand of brick stood at the left, a charred phone pole to the right, that one dangling wire connected to nothing.

"We been here before," one of them answered.

"Not as many times as me, pegger," said Charles, and then everything went to blur and, sights being too small to see even in the bright moon, instinct shooting, favoring the man with the best wiring for that kind of work.

Charles's speed unleashed the first shot, left-hand guy, and though it may not have been a fatal hit as precision was impossible, the man curled like bacon feeling the pan's heat, and his spin backward told everyone he was out of the fight.

Left to right, Charles pivoted even as the other two shadows bloomed white-hot in muzzle flash and sent whizzes by his ears, though he was dropping to one knee, taking his time fast, not looking for sights but making certain the profile of his automatic was squared up straight, not twisted or canted, and at that point the tip of his finger sent another hard-ball into the ether, and the center fellow sat fast, gripping his midsection as if to plug the hole that had surely been bored there.

A volcano of haze erupted just before Charles as the third man's shot hit and elevated ash. Charles entered vapor. With no target, he went to suppression mode, sending five fast ones into the general area of the shooter, a tight burst that drove the man to ground. Fog was general, and went quickly through nostrils to lungs, and phlegm to throat. Charles fought down the spasm that rose in his gorge and used the used, dense ash to snake backward, backward, backward, even as he smacked a second magazine of .45s into the grip of the .45 and sent the slide smashing home. There was no point in advancing, as number three had also disappeared as the ash cloud thinned and settled. Charles had no need to capture or kill his enemies, only to survive them.

He eased backward even farther, reaching the hard-packed dirt of Exchange Avenue and feeling through his shoes the furrows the big engines had cut in May as they hustled to bring water to the flame. He crossed, then continued, melting further into the fire ruin. He calculated the next move: wait, silent, until dawn. Or hasten to his car, assuming the killers, two hit, weren't in any mood to pursue. The third one? Would he have the balls for pursuit work against a crafty marksman in the dark, through a field of baffling wreckage rendered crazy in the moon's bright show? Doubtful. Charles thus chose to exit, to hawk the ash out of his lungs and wash it off his face, to brush his suit, and to get his shirt into the sink for tomorrow. Besides, he needed a drink.

CHAPTER 22

A WHISKEY MEMORY FLASHED WARMLY THROUGH HIS LIMBS AT 7 A.M. and then was overcome by the percussion of knocking on the door.

"Mr. Swagger, phone for you."

"Got it," said Charles, arising to pull on a bathrobe and slippers, then wobble out the door and to the apparatus on the wall, fighting for clarity the whole way.

"Swagger."

"Agent Swagger, sorry so early, but I just myself got a call. Evidently there was a gunfight in the burned section of the Yards last night. Are you all right? Was it you?"

"It was me, I am fine, except my shirt is a mess. May have to buy a new one."

"Thank God. I will get there fast and see what can be seen."

"Good, Officer Washington. The exchange took place in the ash heap that used to be Nugent's. You might look for tracks, pooled blood, spent casings, footprints, any of the usual shooting scene debris. The ash is fragile to wind pressure, so a lot of it may be gone. Still, it should be checked."

"Any ideas?"

Yes, he had ideas. No, he did not care to share them. Too early, too half-formed. Possibly wrong.

"Men in black. Assassins. Professionals, that's all. Mobbed up? Hmm, my guess is that if it was mob, they would have packed heavier ordnance— Thompson, BAR, Winchester sawed-off. These were pistol boys. Hard shooting a handgun by moonlight, which is why I am here and they are not dead, at least as of last night. Maybe wounded and bled out. Maybe just nicked."

"I'm off."

"Sylvester, wait. Couple of other things. First, at the scene, you'll find my ejected casings. But check to see if the fellows shooting at me left casings. If they did, were they in a little cluster of six, or were they tossed. That'll tell us if they were shooting wheel guns or autos."

"Got it."

"Then check all emergency rooms for late-night bleeders. Hit bad, they might have dumped him there. Also, bodies found abandoned somewhere in Fourth District, dead by bullet hole. Maybe I shot better than I thought. They don't want to drive around with a corpse, so they strip him and drop him in an alley. Maybe an ID is possible from a morgue picture."

"Got it, yes, sir."

He hung up, and the phone rang again.

"Charles?"

It was Mel Purvis.

"Yes, sir."

"Chicago Police say there was shooting last night where you've been seen. Tell me it had to do with Baby Face?"

"I wish I could, but it was this other thing."

"Drugs in Fourth District?"

"Yes, sir."

"Charles, you know how much I respect you, but I can't have you getting winged or killed on some no-count-maybe-could-be drug scandal in the Fourth. Next to Two-Gun Washington."

"He's a great police officer."

"I'm sure he is. It doesn't matter. You're too valuable. Suppose you're laid up and we run into Baby Face, and none of our young people have the sand to face him and finish him."

"I will try and get free of this damned thing as soon as possible, sir."

"You're okay? You could be shot in the guts and not tell us about it so you can keep on going."

"I'm fine, Inspector Purvis."

He managed to get a shave and shower in, but in examining his shirt, he saw it was still a mess, even though he'd washed it and hung it outside to dry. Wrinkly, and the ash was of such fine particulate it hadn't come out in the wringing, so rather than being white it was a kind of mélange of smeared gray. Then another call.

"Swagger."

"Charles, it's Sam. You're okay?"

"Yes, sir. They missed, I may have wounded two of them. Not sure how much blood there'll be. I'll give you details in my next report."

"You're coming in here today, I'm hoping."

"I am. On my way."

"Maybe you could put in more of a presence this week. I am getting vibrations of discord from a variety of sources."

"Yes, sir."

"See you soon."

"I may be a little late. I have to buy a new shirt. Mine got all messy in the ash."

"Charles, do yourself and all of us a favor. Buy two. Maybe three. Get crazy, even, and buy stripes!"

Seven emergency rooms in the 4th District and Washington checked them all. The morgue, of course, and he checked that too. Then street sources, various pimps, gamblers, snitches, reefer boys, what have you just that side of the law, and they, like all the rest, had nothing. No bleeders, no corpses, no floaters, not in the 4th District, at least. He left instructions of the sort that had to be followed: any word on bleeders or bodies, you will notify me soonest.

That done, he stopped for lunch at a diner favored by other black policemen, had the breakfast he'd missed this morning, along with three cups of java to keep from falling asleep on the job, and then went on to the precinct station to check on phone messages or other communications, to hear what the other cops were saying, to take a breather and store up for the hours left on the street. It was a squad room, festooned with mug shots and National Recovery Administration posters and authoritarian mandates such as "Be Snappy, for a Police Officer Must Present Well if He Is to Be Obeyed" and "Your Billy Club Is Your Friend."

A shadow loomed. Washington looked up. It was Lieutenant Marbry, one of the few blacks to make officer rank, though not owing to brilliance or diligence so much as being the cousin of the mayor's chauffeur, and compliant in all the scams and games that were played in the 4th.

"Sylvester," said Marbry, pulling up a chair, "time for a talk."

"I've been waiting for this," said Washington.

"I'm hearing things."

"Can't be a help on that."

"Maybe you can, maybe you can't. This is just a friendly little chat. Everybody knows about you and how you'd not let a thing happen to a brother officer, black or not, clean or not. You are a hero, leading the district in arrests, shooting it out however many times with however many gunmen. Not too many have your reputation."

"I like to do my job," said Washington.

"Yes, well. There's doing your job and doing your job. Do you get my meaning?"

"I suppose I do."

"Let me be clear on my drift here. You can go along to get along, as most do. And make no mistake, such men contribute to the community even if they take a little on the side. You have chosen not to participate, and while everybody respects that, it also means nobody quite trusts you. That is why you do not have a partner or really any friends that I can tell. That and the gunfights that seem to follow you wherever."

"I made my choice. I can live by it."

"Well, this here thing immediately before us is different. First, it's working with a whitey got a lot of folks nervous. They call him 'Sheriff,' his old job. I guess he's a good man, but you don't want to trust him too much. If there's credit, it all goes to him; if there's blame, it all goes to you."

"He sure don't seem interested in credit. And nobody comes to the Fourth District to get credit. It's a one-way to nowhere."

"All the same, this Sheriff might not think as you. He might see things different. He might have a plan he hasn't shared. He might be working a scam that would never occur to you. His interests might not be your interests. In the end, under gunshots, would this fellow risk taking fire to pull your wounded ass to safety? Even if he meant to, he might think, My life ain't worth no colored man's, cop or not. Do you see what I am saying?"

"I do. You want me to pull away on this? It involves serious crimes in the Fourth District, and it appears to be white against black. People are dying, while others, white-people others, are getting rich. Charles Swagger, for what reason I don't know, wants to stop that."

"I'm saying that's a tall order. Mighty tall. No judge or jury's going to hold white for what they do to black. Ours is to abide and infiltrate, and sure enough, our time will come. That is what I am telling you."

"Back off, is that what the word is?"

"It needn't be a hardship." An envelope fell out of his hand and landed on the floor.

"Believe you dropped that. Pick it up. Believe me, this is the best for all, and this Swagger can get back to what he does, which is machine-gun fights with Baby Face Nelson. You can get back to what you do, which is keep the bad boys out of white town, and maybe put a bad man down where he needs to be put down."

Sylvester picked up the envelope, handed it back.

"I don't operate that way. God would not approve, and it's to him I pay my allegiance, not the people who give out money earned from whores, drugs, and gambling."

"All right, then, Sylvester," said the lieutenant. "Go all high Baptist on me. Don't take the money. But take the advice. It won't send your soul to hell."

CHAPTER 23

WAS THERE A MORE BEAUTIFUL SPOT ON GOD'S GREEN EARTH? IT WAS the 16th at Indian Hill Country Club in Winnetka, where the fairway doglegged left around the fulcrum of a pond feathery with reeds and thistles of roses entwined in the rough under the quiet pines. Something about it—the smoothness of the green grass, the trim of the fairway, the greener green of the kidney-shaped 16th not seventy-five yards, a fair 8-iron shot, away—had always calmed him in the deepest part of his soul and enabled him to raise his game toward triumph over the concluding three holes.

Yet this time Thaddeus skulled his stroke, depositing the ball with a tepid sand-splash in the trap that lay hidden just beyond the green. He could still par out, having an excellent short game, but the possibility of a birdie was now formally gone, barring a freak happening.

"Thaddeus, I don't believe I've ever seen you do such a thing," said Tom Ingersoll, CEO of Borg-Warner.

"Doing lots of things I've never done before," said Thaddeus.

It was true. A two-putt from under ten feet on the 4th, a bogie on the three-par 11th, a drive into the rough on the 13th, and now this.

"I wish you'd tell me when you're going south," said Roy Barrett, of

Thinnes, Devonshire & Barrett. "I might just make back some of the damn money you usually take from me."

"I'd have brought a movie camera," said Oliver Heinz, VP and operating officer of Bell & Howell. "Because when I tell folks in the clubhouse, they won't believe it without evidence."

"Any advice, Jimmy?" he asked his seventeen-year-old caddie, a senior at nearby New Trier, where he was captain of the golf team and headed off to Yale quite soon now.

"I just see tightness, Mr. Nugent, that's all. Through the shoulders, somewhat affecting the smoothness in the hip rotation. Only one answer, which you already know: relax."

Yeah, easy for him to say. At seventeen, you have your whole life in front of you, and with Yale on the horizon, chances are swell that it'll be a pretty good life.

"My question," said Tom. "Do you need a massage or a psychiatrist?"

Everybody laughed, including and especially Thaddeus, flattered since the jest was formulated on his skills as a scratch golfer.

"The wedge, Jimmy," he said, handing over the 8 and taking the heavy club with him.

He tried to relax. But it was hard. He looked around. The fairness of the day, unseasonably but delightfully cool for a late Chicago August, the rustle of wind off the lake a few blocks east, which pushed the pines into a swaying rhythm, the soothing buzz of some sort of insect life that had to exist out of God's awareness that wealthy golfers needed such relaxing therapy when the stakes were high.

Could I lose all this? he wondered. He saw a Dickensian future of penury and disgrace, of losing both the big Winnetka house and the smaller, cozier one on Walloon Lake in Michigan, of having to pull his son out of Princeton and maybe college altogether. They'd have to change their names so as not to be tainted by association with the

hated murderer Thaddeus Nugent of Roasty-Toasty Beef Stew infamy.
He'd lose the friendship of other industry titans like this threesome.
God, he'd have to play on public courses! He'd have to play in . . .
Wilmette!

This alarming development had arrived courtesy of a Charlie Oliver
call with info that Detective Whatever-the-name was still poking around.
Worse, he seemed to be on the track of the "Roasty-Toasty Goes to Maine"
scandal. How the hell had he put it together?

He tried to calm down. He knew if he let his mind run away on him,
he was lost, not only here, on the course, but in life in general. Had this
Swagger reached Oscar? Maybe Oscar had betrayed him as a way of
saving himself. Oscar! *Oscar!*

How could Oscar have done such a thing? But who else? No one
else knew. It had to be Oscar and it was so wrong, because Thaddeus
had settled a more-than-tidy sum on Oscar from the insurance payout.
Some loyalty.

He entered the trap gingerly, so as not to muss the sand any more than
necessary. It was like being swallowed by the desert. It seemed everyone
else had vanished and before him loomed only a wall of sand, looking
thirty feet tall, in its configuration almost that of an incoming wave set
to crush him.

He diddled with the club in his hands. In truth, it scared him a
little. It was fairly new to the bag, having of late replaced the niblick.
Invented by Gene Sarazen, the wedge boasted a fifty-eight-degree face,
a forward lower edge sheathed in lead for more weight—it was his
heaviest club—all dedicated to the idea of blasting through the sand
and hoisting the ball high, without spin, and depositing it near the pin.
It took more finesse than strength, more discipline than athleticism,
and more confidence than skill.

Okay, now. He addressed, settled his spikes in the grit for the necessary
anchor, waggled his arms to loosen them, felt his hips load in the back

pivot while his grip remained a crush, as if he were trying to kill a bird. A loose little finger could wreck the shot, the hole, and the day.

At tip-top, he held just a hair of a second, then launched. Being quite coordinated, he loved this part, feeling the glide sliding, the momentum building, the concentration welling, all while his hips led his shoulders which led his arms which led his hands which led the club through the swing, under the direction of eyes riveted not to the ball—this was the secret of the wedge—but to the sand an inch behind.

The extra weight, like the keel of a yacht, carried the club through, building at a speed that has no place in time, a cushion of sand against and thus caparisoned as the fifty-eight-degree blade took and lifted the ball—the contact was solid—high and soft until it ran out of climb, at which point it began its spinless descent. All this occurred in an explosion of sand, for the clubhead must perforce remove that as well as the ball from the earth.

It felt good. It sounded good. But was it good?

He edged out of the trap, handing the club to Jimmy, receiving in return his putter from Jimmy, who would now rake the disturbance his effort had raised, then come up to the green to engineer the flag through the putting process.

"Great shot," said the boy, but that's what the boy always said.

Thaddeus headed to the green, where his three friends awaited his arrival, their putters in hand.

He looked. He saw three balls. He walked to one, then the other, and finally the third.

None was his.

What the—?

"You completely missed the green, Thaddeus," said Tom Ingersoll.

"But—"

"Didn't even touch it," said Roy Barrett.

Goddamn! he thought. His humiliation was complete.

"Yep," said Tom. "Damn you, you hit nothing but hole."

They broke into laughter, having enjoyed their little comedy game almost as much as they'd enjoyed the perfection of Thaddeus's shot, which had landed dead solid perfect in the cup, where it now nested, showing only its white top half to the world.

"Maybe your luck is changing," Barrett called out.

But Thaddeus knew different. God was calling him. It was time to go home.

They sat in the University of Chicago cafeteria, over cold cups of coffee. Charles hadn't said much but nodded when Sylvester Washington reported that while he'd recovered seven .45 casings—Charles's—he'd come up empty on any shells from the three assassins.

"Revolvers, then," said Charles. "Not because they didn't have time to search for the empties an automatic would toss, but because that's what they had."

The blood, contaminated as it was by the ash, told of two men wounded, one worse than the other by the amounts. It was the first guy on the right who'd merely been grazed, as a few spots turning black in the ash indicated. Meanwhile, number two, in the middle, had taken a solid hit, probably in the midriff. He might be dead, he might be pulling through in some Indiana hospital or veterinarian's back room, but he was nowhere in the 4th District.

In summary, the police scan of the shooting site had yielded nothing of value. The tracks were all smeary and too fragile to be captured in a plaster cast, and no other debris was on location—not chewed matchsticks, matchbooks, cigarette butts, tissue papers, Wrigley wrappers, anything usable.

"They knew what they were doing," said Charles.

"Professionals?" asked Washington.

"I would guess, yes. They didn't leave clues, they didn't leave any accidental crap about, they retreated in good order when they saw they'd lost the element of surprise, the wounded didn't cry out, they had a sure exit route signifying they knew the territory."

"How did they get on to you?"

"Had to tail me. Good tail too. I wasn't looking for it, I suppose because I am a dope, but still they never overplayed their hand, and I didn't—this happens to me sometimes—I didn't get any buzz of being looked at. It saved my life several times in the war, let me tell you, but nothing registered yesterday. Maybe I was too dumb to be paying attention—"

"Not never, not nohow."

"Anyway, wherever they are, they're pretty certain they got away clean."

"They may try again."

"Excellent point. Which brings me to what I wanted to discuss with you."

"Go ahead."

"The fact they may circle around for another try and this time get luckier is one strong suggestion it's time for us to move hard against them. But that's not the only one. I am getting hints that have turned into jokes that have turned into orders that I get this thing closed down and go back to work for the Division full-time, what with both Pretty Boy and Baby Face still on the loose. I'm betting you're getting the same pressure."

"I was leaned on hard yesterday. Nobody done leaned on Two-Gun before, and that means everybody is serious. Killing serious, I should say. Certain commands not even Two-Gun can defy."

"So it sounds like we are in a pickle."

"It does."

"Let me get another cup. Sylvester, you want any?"

That was the best thing any white person had ever said to Officer Washington. Fetch coffee? Amazing!

"No, thanks."

Charles left, returned with a cup of steamy joe. He lit a cigarette.

"One of the smartest things I ever heard," he finally said, "was when a salty Chicago police officer offered me two ways out of a shooting I'd just done. He pointed out that the official way of progressing from that spot on would be a nightmare, as politics, prejudice, maybe journalism, certainly office feuds and resentment, all that would play a part. I knew that to be so. He then said, 'Why don't you just walk away, I'll call this a John Doe, and nobody's the wiser.' Do you remember that?"

"I do," said Washington.

"So let me return the favor. I see two ways out of this. The first is the official way. We continue, against the wishes of both our superiors and all of our colleagues, to pursue an investigation. We find what might be called irrefutable proof of who's doing this Night Train thing. We take it to a city prosecutor. Maybe he's reform-minded, maybe not."

"I'd vote not."

"Even if he is, he has to go to his bosses. Assuming we get by all of that, and warrants are issued, we make arrests and the balloon pops. Newspaper boys, lawyers, hard looks at both of us, the novelty of black and white cooperating turning out to be really scary to some. Your people, mine, maybe not ready for it. Then the boys we arrest will put together a legal team, and one of the tricks of that trade is to tear down the accusers, so you've got someone looking through your life for secrets. Don't know about you, but I've got one I can't have out in the open. Maybe all your shootings weren't quite square. Plus, we don't know how high up these boys have ties, and what retribution high office can bring on us. Plus, I can't get back to Arkansas, where I have a frazzled wife and a very ill son, plus another boy off fighting in banana wars for United Fruit, although it was the United States Marine Corps he joined. He could get killed at any moment and his mother would need me home. I'm sure you have stuff like that in your life."

"I do. No wife, but sisters needing my care."

"So, to be dead flat honest with you, Officer Washington, I would have to say none of that is appealing. The only one it benefits is Baby Face Nelson, and if he takes five young agents with him because I'm off chasing folks in the Fourth District instead of on the other side of the front sight from him, that's a weight I don't care to bear."

"I'm guessing where this is going."

"Let me spell it out, clear and simple nevertheless, so you know exactly what you're in for."

"All ears here."

"As I see it, this thing is happening for one reason. That's because someone crooked took possession of four hundred bottles of pentobarbital. Everything suggests it came from the Yards just before the fire. It's probably still here. I believe they set the fire to cover the disappearance, one way or another. With me? Questions?"

"It makes sense."

"So the fastest way to stop the black man from dying by various means because of this stuff is to destroy that supply. A little of it goes a long way, so they're probably not even a quarter through their stash. They could go on for years. If the heat comes on them, they back off for a few months. But it's the stuff that's pushing this campaign."

"Since you raided in the Great War, you thinking about a raid. That also would be the Two-Gun way. That's why I carry two guns."

"We find the place. In the dead of night, we get into it. I know a lot about breaking and entering, as a small-town sheriff sees it four days a week. We find the stuff. Since we don't have access to the Thompsons in our outfit arms rooms, we're carrying cut-down pump or semi-auto 12-gauge shotguns and lots of shells. Number four buckshot ought to be about right. We hammer that stuff hard, blow it to hell and gone. Then we get out as we came in. Anybody tries to stop us, that's their big mistake. Shoot to kill. They are murderers and monsters and they entered this world cold-bloodedly, willing to take life for money, so any chances they took are on them. Maybe some of them get away. That's too bad, but can't be helped. The point is to stop the dying in the Fourth District."

"I like it," said Officer Washington.

"We get out, we shake hands, and it's all over."

"Just one thing."

"Sure."

"We don't know who these people are."

"I do. I've known from the start."

CHAPTER 24

YOU WOULD THINK WITH A NAME LIKE VON LENGERKE & ANTOINE, IT was a law practice, a brokerage, perhaps a florist or an antique store for the refined. But it sold guns.

It was at 33 South Wabash, on the eastern rim of the Loop, shadowed by the elevated tracks. It also sold fishing rods and equipment, outdoor supplies, heavy apparel for hikes or hunts, tents, canteens—all the stuff people, usually men, used to enjoy nature under any circumstances, rain, shine, blizzard, or tornado. But, yes, guns, walls and counters full of them.

"How may I help?"

"Well," he said, "I'd like a pistol. Nothing big or bulky."

"For self-defense, then?"

"Yes, that's it."

"Maybe something a policeman would carry?"

The place had a hushed, sepulchral sensation to it, as if it were a devotional space, hidden under buttresses, sheathed in stained glass and Gothic filigree. A few other customers drifted about, bending to the handguns in the glass counters or playing with a hunting rifle or shotgun from the racks beyond the counter. It was all strange to Thaddeus.

"A policeman, yes."

The salesman, genteel as a parish priest, led him to a particular counter that contained a selection of the weapons. They all looked the same to Thaddeus.

"These are Colt revolvers. One of the oldest names in the business. Colonel Colt started making pistols before the Civil War and—"

"That one," said Thaddeus, his eye caught by one of the smaller issues. He peered harder. It represented some kind of contest in steel between ugly and beautiful. Glossy blue, with a pencil stub for a barrel, it had a kind of streamline to it, starting off straight in barrel and frame, then falling away gracefully into what had to be the grip, wrapped in checkered wood. It gleamed. It wanted to be picked up. It was fascinating in its orchestration of ovals and angles, a weird mingling of both themes, making it harmonic to the hand.

"Excellent choice. That's the Colt Detective Special. It's a smaller version of the Colt Police Positive, which nearly all uniformed officers carry. The Detective is scaled down for undercover men, agents, plainclothes investigators, homeowners. It fits into a pocket, or we can supply any sort of holster, even one that hangs under your shoulder from a harness. Almost every policeman in Chicago owns one, the uniformed officers carrying it hidden for what they call 'backup,' the detectives under suit coat but accessible for fast usage. But you'll also find it in most jewelry stores, bank presidents' desks, anyplace that deals in large sums of cash, as well as on the hips of Secret Service and Justice Department agents."

"Is it powerful?"

"It shoots a .38 special–caliber cartridge, which will kill any man ever born. Yet it's not so powerful that it's unpleasant to fire. It will jump but it won't bite. Here." He bent, opened the cabinet from behind, and removed it.

Thaddeus took the thing, surprised immediately at its density but also how well it fit in his hand. It nestled perfectly in his palm, his finger went right to the trigger, and if he tried, his thumb arrived exactly at the checkered tip of the sharp hammer. It was completely constructed of solid pieces of steel, each machined with great precision to fit together with the others, a three-dimensional jigsaw puzzle far beyond his comprehension. At the salesman's insistence, he pulled the trigger, finding it more difficult than he'd imagined, but fascinating in the rhythm between the trigger and the hammer, which rose and fell with authority. Cocking the hammer to fire "single-action," as the man called it, was much more pleasant. Peeking into the gap revealed when the hammer was locked back was like peeking into the cockpit of American industry, revealing strangely shaped but presumably necessary moving pieces as well as secret, clever pins, pivots, and screws holding all together. Then the salesman demonstrated how to open it, letting its cylinder fall out an inch to the left and hang in space on a kind of yoke. This permitted six cartridges to be inserted in the six circular holes. And the cylinder to then be relocked in the frame with a push of the finger.

"For you," he said, "I'll throw in a box of ammunition. One thing. If you shoot it, especially at an indoors range, be sure to stuff cotton in your ears. It is very loud. That's something the moving pictures never show. Your ears will ring for days without protection. Of course if there's a burglar in your house, you won't worry about the cotton. Saving your life and your family's is worth some ear ringing."

In the end, of course, he bought it. He wrote them a check for $28.70, watched the man find its brown cardboard box, select of box of Remington .38 ammunition, and bag the whole thing.

CHAPTER 25

"**Y**OU WANT TO KNOW WHO, SYLVESTER? YOU ALREADY DO," SAID Charles. "Stop and think of what these fellows had to know to do this thing. It wasn't a common accumulation of knowledge. Only certain people would know the right details to make this happen."

Sylvester nodded.

"They were highly professional," Charles went on. "They didn't make mistakes, panic, overplay their hand. Well disciplined. I'm talking not about the pushers, who were clearly people recruited on a daily basis, from some kind of list I haven't figured out yet. No, I'm talking about the folks who figured it out in the first place, then assembled and administered the distribution of the Night Train. They brought drugs to the pushers. I'm betting they set up surveillance as a means of protection. They collected money at shift's end. They monitored the whole thing and kept it running smoothly. That means they were used to operating in or just outside the law enforcement system. They had to be tough, because they were dealing in a world where thievery, panic, bad decisions, impulsive actions were common. That was their strength, dealing with that. They had to know the street and the type of creatures on it. They were comfortable with criminals and criminal activities. Nothing shocked them, nothing scared them. Do you see what I'm driving at?"

"I do. It seems to lead to—well, you go on, then, Sheriff."

"Obviously, they had a source for the drug. I don't know that yet, either. Maybe Nugent, or his right hand man. Bentley. Maybe Magellan. Maybe somebody we don't know of yet. They also needed a space to set up the jars each day, and a specific destination in the Fourth District. Meaning two things: They knew the Fourth District, knew it well. And there was some sort of signal or code that would tell their customers where they'd be that day. Had to be simple. I do note, it's always just off Halsted."

"I am listening."

"They followed me, skillfully, meaning they'd done that before. They plotted their ambush in a highly effective way. Against most men, they'd have made their kill and vanished. They just didn't know I had done a lot of that kind of thing. They underestimated me, their only mistake. But, at the same time, they knew the stockyards extremely well, even the burnt zones, which would have been newly configured owing to the destruction of the May fire. That's how they got ahead of me to set up, that's how they got out of there so quickly. How'd they learn that so fast?"

"They had to be there."

"Every day," said Charles.

"Everything you've described is straight gangster."

"Think again. The way this is set up, it's meant to outsmart gangsters. It's to come onto gangster territory, supposedly strictly supervised, make a quick cash killing, and disappear before the mob gets there, leaving no tracks, nothing to follow. The way that dentist was used; he sold that one day, made some bucks in an afternoon, then was gone. It would have worked perfectly if Billy the Hat hadn't gone nuthouse and put a bullet across his cheekbone."

"Not gangsters."

"Not cops, either, do you think, Officer Washington?"

"Lord knows, there are plenty of bad ones around. But there'd be talk. I would know. You always know. A police department is no place for secrets. Everybody talks to everybody, all the time. I know, then, that we don't know a thing, only that it's called the Night Train and it's messing up a lot of folks. And that nobody upstairs cares."

"Who, then, Sylvester?"

"Maybe some cowboys that herd the animals in. Maybe—no, they wouldn't have the knowledge of the Fourth District. They wouldn't know how to set up a network of drug dealers in an area like that."

"Excellent. You're almost there. Think of the guns. The guns always tell us something. In this case, revolvers. As I said, the mob seems to have gone to autos. Johnny carried one, so did Homer. Capone had one. When we bring down Pretty Boy and Baby Face, you'll find automatics, I guarantee. The police, as always, are behind. The Army adapted the .45 Colt automatic in 1911 and I'm carrying one now. But the police, they'll be dragging their Police Positives and their Smith M&Ps with them for years to come. So if these three boys had revolvers by tradition, who were they?"

"We just discounted cops. Mr. Charles. I don't—"

He paused. Light came into his eyes.

"*Ex*-cops. They'd have all the cop skills, they'd have the cop guns, they'd have the cop toughness and the hit-first, shoot-first mentality."

"That's right," said Charles.

"I know where there's a lot of ex-cops," he said. "Tough guys, all of them. Know the stockyards. They would have sources of information. They would know things their snitches would tell them. They would know about the drugs at Nugent's, they would know how to break and enter at night. They would know where to set a fire that the wind would take to Nugent's to cover the crime. But they wouldn't know enough about fire to guess how fast it spreads and how big it gets. That would be a surprise to them. But at the same time, they'd know where there was a coop or a warehouse or a shut-down slaughterhouse where they could stash the pento fast without interference. They would know the Fourth District, at least some of them. They walked beats and knocked heads and maybe even shot-to-kill there. They would have seen the way the drug world operates, and they could have modeled their operations on that, knowing up front what the others found out the hard way. They'd know not to set up in a club, a jive joint, some place with mob ownership and lots of mob eyes. They'd know the police beat and patrol routes and how they shifted every day. They'd know to get a new dealer every day, tell him nothing so even if he was caught he'd have no information to give up."

"I think your class just won the Bible."

"It's got to be the Union Stock Yards and Transit Company Police. The yard dicks. Invisible but everywhere. I see it now, Sheriff. Clear as the damn day. But where'd they find these dealers? And where'd they even get the idea in the first place? I mean, as far as I know, imagination isn't big in the yard dicks."

"No, it's not. Yes, there's someone else, someone bigger, smarter, who knew even more and had that imagination. Not sure now, but maybe one of these guys can tell us."

"We're going to visit?"

"Are we ever."

CHAPTER 26

HE LOVED HIS NEW LITTLE GUN. HE CARRIED IT WITH HIM EVERYWHERE, even in the pockets of his golfing plus fours, and in his evening smoking jacket. His fingers grew to know it well, as they always curled about it in the right pocket of his trousers, so as to keep the elastic of his braces from stretching out from the twenty-one ounces of steel he now sported. He loved the friction of the checkered grip, the art deco swoop that went into the hammer, silver on the sides, black on the top. His thumb rested on the latch that locked the cylinder in place, finding it a soothing place. Alone in his home office, he would remove it and just stare at its pleasing lines, its sense of purpose that was nevertheless conveyed in powerfully aesthetic design. He loved the gun sounds too, all the clicks and snaps and pops as it was put through its function tests, each with an accompanying and soon identifiable vibration. It was so beautiful. It was so ugly. It was so charismatic!

For a desperate man, nothing comforts like a gun. It gave him a sense of freedom from his many woes. He did not think explicitly of "suicide," as that idea was too vulgar for him. His preferred term was "escape."

The little gun meant that at any instant he could avoid the train that rushed down the tracks at him, with its freight of failure, of shame, of scandal, of social and financial and familial ruin. A single press on the trigger would send the cocked hammer forward, and literally a tenth of a second later, all the woe would have vanished. There was plenty of money left for Marjory and the boys, and they could remain in Winnetka forever. That was something to be proud of: Winnetka forever! Yes, that was worth dying for, and he took an almost giddy satisfaction that nothing would be wasted on lawyers bent merely on elongating their payday and the godawful journalists who would love to paint him as the capitalist murderer of innocent victims (convicts!) and relish his slow, dramatic destruction. Even Colonel McCormick's *Tribune* would not be able to resist the temptation, and he imagined a front-page cartoon of himself in the dock, sweating bullets in the shadow of the gallows to ride the Roasty-Toasty Express to the death. He would not give that to them.

He pressed the barrel to his head, just above and to the front of his ear. His thumb eased the hammer back against some reluctance from the mainspring, and he felt the subtlest glissando as the hammer's motion rotated the cylinder, to align it with a new chamber. The trigger, drawn backward by the hammer's journey, opened the trigger guard more fully, and it seemed to welcome his finger. When the hammer reached its apex and locked in place, some eccentricity of the mechanism produced not one but two clicks, a shallow click followed by a more serious manifesto of intent. Now volatile, all its springs coiled, the gun had a slightly different feel to it, a kind of rigidity or gravitas. That last big snap reminded him of an ensign's heels smacking together as he popped to, offered salute, and said, "Reporting for duty, sir." The little machine was ready.

With the tip of his finger he pushed gently against the trigger's steel curvature and felt a kind of relaxation, all springs now released, shiver through the pistol in the tenth of a second the hammer fell.

It snapped.

One of these days, he thought, I shall have to load it.

CHAPTER 27

HE FOUND IT EASILY ENOUGH, UNDER THE SHADOW OF THE EAST ELE-
vation of the Loop tracks. The address was 33 South Wabash, and
down the street Charles could see the vertical marquee of the famous
restaurant and big band broadcast spot called the Blackhawk. Prime rib
was said to be pretty good there, and they made your salad from a big
bowl while the musicians of the Coon-Sanders Band played. Nice place
to take his wife, he thought, knowing the prospects of her getting up here
were pretty slim, which of course prompted a stab of guilt, which just as
quickly he buried in stern self-remonstrance and quick reacquaintance
with something called "duty," which he had obeyed his entire life without
ever quite figuring out why, recently suspecting that it was self-deluding
subterfuge for doing what he wanted.

He turned, and a few storefronts down found Von Lengerke & Antoine,
the gun shop and general outdoors store. "For the sport" was the motto.
It seemed posh, more like a jewelry place. Gangsters shopped here? So
the rumors went. Some sport! He entered, finding it the sort of place
where Browning, Colt, and Winchester would always be Mr. Browning,
Colonel Colt, and Mr. Winchester, as required by their peerage. It was
split in two, with all the fishing stuff and checkered shirts and boots on
one side, and the guns, including a still-legal Thompson but also some

quite sleek British game rifles, displayed on the other. He tracked along the long guns on the wall, passing from bolt actions to lever actions to semi-automatics, and finally to shotguns, amid a flourish of wall-mounted game birds, their feathers all spread like a poker hand. It didn't take long before a clerk came rushing over.

"Morning, sir. Can I be of service? Show you something?"

"I'm interested in a semi-auto 12-gauge, and since most of my guns are designed by John Browning, I'd like to stick with that brand. I've heard his Auto-5 is the best."

"Yes, sir," said the clerk, turning, checking, then selecting an Auto-5 from the rack. He snapped the bolt to prove to his customer that it was unloaded.

"Duck hunters swear by it. Those low flocks incoming fast, you can get tangled up or even short-shuck a pump like Winchester's 12. With Mr. Browning's shotgun, it's as fast as you can pull the trigger, five times."

Charles took it, ran his eyes expertly over it, checked for details like the quality of the joinery between wood stock and metal receiver, brought it to shoulder a time or two, rotated as if tracking a low-flying Canada goose in one of Arkansas's many dismal swamps on the way south in the fall, felt the weight, the balance.

"We have the gun in several grades, sir. The higher the grade, the more refined the wood. Polishing is said to be better, Circassian walnut for the furniture; there's gold-infused engraving of a very tasteful manner, and I'm guessing that the people in the factory take more time fitting a Grade 4 than a Grade 1. But whatever, it's a beauty."

It was. It had John M.'s trademark high rear end, an inverted slope rising from stock grip to the top of the action, giving it something of the appearance of Mr. Browning's useful automatic rifle. In fact, it looked like a BAR that had gone to college. Its twenty-eight-inch barrel provided a supreme grace, and, rotating on imaginary birds, Charles felt the elegant barrel leading the gun through its arc. But as much as he loved the gun at once, he understood that so long a barrel was a sharp disadvantage.

"It's barrel length I'm more concerned with. Is this the only choice?"

"In the Browning, yes. However, both Remington and Savage make a variant of the same exact gun owing to some fracas between Mr. Browning and Winchester. Maybe not the cachet but functionally identical, both fine manufacturers. The Savage has a shorter-barrel twenty-inch skeet model, with a Cutts Compensator that can be adjusted to—"

"I'm familiar with the Cutts on a tommy, thanks."

He took his wallet, opened it to show his badge.

"I'm not hunting ducks or geese, but men. I need something to carry in the car that I can get to fast and has a lot of power and speed and can be fired one-handed in an emergency. It should also have a wide shot dispersion, which the Cutts will provide. The Division has heavy guns like your Thompson over there and lots of Winchester 97s, but they have to be signed out, and then signed in. That's hard to do when someone's cutting on you with a drum of .45s."

"I see your point," said the clerk.

And now the bullet. Again, surprisingly dense for its size. Yet there was something equally comforting in that unexpected heaviness. It wasn't nothing, it wasn't anything, it was something. It had purpose in this world, a destiny, perhaps to punch a hole in a piece of paper, perhaps to punch a hole in his own head. Whatever, not to be trifled with. It came from a tray still containing forty-nine others, which looked to his experience somewhat like an egg carton, in the neatness and precision with which it offered its cargo, line by line, five across, ten long, alternating head or tail down, all squished into the tray precisely. The box was sour-apple-green, saying "REMINGTON," and across the rear end, it said ".38 special, 130 grains, lead, round nose."

He examined the killing tip. Yes indeed, proletarian lead but shaped somewhat like a bell, a soft curve to a bluntish tip. That was the piece that killed. As he understood the theory, the powder in the brass case exploded when the hammer struck it, and its force found the way of least resistance, driving the bullet at supersonic speeds down the barrel toward its target. In his intended use, there would be no problem with aim; the muzzle would be against his skull. Yet he wondered about other applications, since his playtime with the gun had acquainted him with the difficulty of marksmanship. It wobbled in his grip, and the tighter he held it, the more it wobbled. Yet if he held it loosely, it would jump from his hand and clatter to the floor. It was a mystery utterly beyond him. The sight was a thin blade that would not keep still when pointed in a selected direction at a selected target. The best thing, he realized, was to shoot it single-action while braced against something. Only then would the damned thing settle down.

Now he did what had been unfathomable a few days earlier when all this was so new and frightening. He plucked that bullet off the table and very delicately, as if it were that egg fresh from the carton, brought it to the open cylinder, aligned it with a hole, and deposited it. The world did not end. Winnetka did not disappear into a rip in the earth. The stock market did not collapse a second time. Nothing happened.

All right, then, he swiftly made five more deposits, then again, with a little girl's delicacy of touch, noting again the theme of circles: the cylinder was circular, as were the holes; the cartridges when inserted and showing only their rear surface were circular, and within them, centered, yet another circle. It was in its infantile way impressive. He gently closed the cylinder into the frame, feeling the tiniest of metallic shudders as the latch locked the cylinder in its place. And behold: a loaded pistol.

He stared at it, feeling both awestruck and awesome. He could this second pick it up and the next second kill somebody—well, himself—with it. So much power. He had no idea that everybody on earth feels that way when he first picks up a loaded gun, but it usually goes away in seven seconds.

In Thaddeus's case, it took nine seconds.

He put it in the pocket of his sport coat and went to dinner.

CHAPTER 28

"**N**OW COMES THE HARD PART," SAID CHARLES. "SOMEWHERE IN THE city of Chicago, they are assembling their goods for distribution. We can't do a thing until we find them. Yet if we put out an alert, surely they'll hear of it, and batten down, and go away. They can wait, we can't."

"And we can't work over a customer. Word gets back to them, they close down. We have nothing."

"The bastard was smart."

"I do have snitches," said Washington. "Remember Old Cracker? He called me the night you shot George Roberts. That's how come I got there so fast."

"Aren't you full of surprises? But I don't think we have the time to run a big snitch network."

"Then maybe—uh, no."

"Officer Washington, go ahead. Any suggestion considered at this point."

"Dogs. The noses on them. Get some hounds, let 'em smell the pento, maybe that—no, everybody sees me with a hound on a leash knows I'm hunting something with an odor. Well, maybe not here in the Yards, but out on the streets. Find us a pusher, then follow him to his handler, then follow his handler to the building."

"That's good, but again, it would take men to run a canvas and these fellows are so slippery. Maybe—"

"Halsted," said Washington.

"I'm not—"

"Lookie here, Sheriff. We know of three distinct places where this thing happened. The first, Roberts in the Yards. The second, the undertaker, Mr. Johnson. The third, Billy the Hat, same dive, off Halsted."

"All off Halsted," said Charles. "Well, that's presuming Roberts wandered in from somewhere looking for prey off Halsted. It was on the Halsted side of the Yards."

"So Halsted," said Washington. "At various crossing streets."

"Really," said Charles, "all's you'd have to know is the crossing street. And it would be two or three numbers, from 1st Steet on out to the end."

"You know, in the Fourth District, numbers on everybody's mind. It's a ticket to wealth. Mr. Eddie Jones, he runs it. It's a lottery. Folks bet three numbers and if their number comes up, they get the payoff."

"Where does the number come from?"

"It's always the total of the betting at Hawthorne Park or whichever track is open. The last three numbers of that total, that is. They call it the 'handle.' And it's everywhere every day, because folks have such hope. In store windows and the newspapers, the lucky number."

Charles nodded. Then he said, "You're the genius, you spell it out for me."

"You bet your number today, say 458. Tomorrow you check, maybe big old 458 come up. Never does, but maybe. But that random three-number group, drop the first one. So instead of 458, it's just 58. That means today the dealer man going to be around 58th and Halstead. What could be easier?"

"We could check the three incidents against—nah, too long. Let's check today's number and see if we can find ourselves a pusher man tomorrow."

They did. But there was no pusher man. Tried again next day. No pusher man.

"So they're getting their numbers someplace else. Where else?"

"Has to be easy and fast to find."

"Temperature? Highest wind speed? Last three numbers of visitors at the World's Fair?"

Who came up with it?

Actually, neither. It was the National League Chicagos who beat the Pittsburghs at Wrigley, 12–3.

Then it was the *Tribune*'s night sports desk editor, who came up with the headline "Easy as 12–3, Cubs Crush Pirates," which stuck in everybody's mind.

Then it was a Mrs. James Pettigrew, of dubious reputation and not unknown to police, who dropped dead in an alley near—

"Halsted and 123rd," said Washington.

"It's the score of the ball game that provides the numbered street off Halsted," completed Swagger. A check verified the correspondence.

They followed him.

They followed his handler.

Not right away, but slowly, they tailed the handler, never pushing it or closing within three hundred feet.

Yes, he returned to the Yards. But then another setback. They had planned to position Old Cracker to intercept the car's arrival and by increments locate its destination. Who would notice Old Cracker?

But the route took them straight through the devastated burn zone— wide-open for blocks.

"Call him off," said Charles. "They'll see him plain as day. Next evening he's the one washes up on the beach. I won't risk that. There's been enough dying. Plus, they go away for a few weeks. We lose a man for nothing."

"How do we follow in wide-open territory, with no cover?"

Airplane surveillance? Long distance from a rooftop telescope? Putting some kind of radio tracking device secretly in the car?

"Hasn't been invented yet."

Ask Yard folk? The dicks would hear and vanish.

Pulling in a dick and sweating him? Against the law and maybe yield no—

"Gold," said Swagger.

Washington looked at him.

"Mr. Charles, I—"

"Chief Mulrooney told me some of his boys were fixed on the rumor that the Jewish owner of a slaughterhouse had buried gold in his place because he didn't trust banks after the crash of '29. That was just cover, in case anybody saw them messing around in the ruins."

"Now that you mention it, them two boys the night of the shooting struck me as filthy."

"Sure, they were on their way back from fixing up that day's dosage. They'd been in a filthy ruin."

"An abandoned kosher warehouse, east of Exchange. How many can there be?"

As it turned out, there was only one.

CHAPTER 29

"YOUR BIDDING WAS AWFUL TONIGHT, THADDEUS," SAID MARJORY.

"I know," he said.

He stood before her in silk pajamas and robe, freshly brushed teeth, ready for fifty pages of *So Red the Rose*, even if he was not in a Civil War mood, just as he had not been in a bridge mood. He was not in a life mood. He was in a suicide mood.

"I hate to lose to Louise. She is such a vixen when she gets even the slightest advantage over me."

"I don't even see why you're friends with her."

"Her daughter is Ted's age, *very* pretty, and goes to Holyoke. Her husband is a partner. You like him."

"Jack's okay."

"It would be an excellent marriage for Ted."

"For God's sake, Marjory, let the kid pick his own wife!"

"Well, aren't you Mr. Grump?"

"I'm fine."

"I know it's not the office. There is no office."

"I'm fine, I tell you."

"Thaddeus, you're not fine. Ever since that detective showed up, you've not been yourself."

"I've never been myself. *Ever!* I was not cut out for meatpacking. I hate cows, manure, beef stew, my father for dumping this thing on me!"

"It served us all."

"Without that damned fire, we'd be in the street! That's how smart I am."

"I think we need a long trip, darling. They say Italy in the fall is magnificent."

He said nothing. Would sleep come tonight? Probably not. Another eight hours of feckless twisting and turning.

AGGGGRRRRHHHH!

CHAPTER 30

"**A**N OLD BUILDING ON DEXTER PARK AVENUE, ACROSS EXCHANGE from Nugent's but out of the burned zone."

"Old building on Dexter Park?"

"Cracker said it was the Goldberg Kosher Corned Beef and Pickle building. Goldberg's closed down in '31, never recovered from the crash. It's just a frame building, ramshackle old place, mostly wood, gone to rot. The company has never found a new tenant."

"Let's look at it on a map."

They did so, the same map that was everywhere. Sylvester's finger found and traced Dexter Park, intersecting Exchange Avenue, where the unfortunate Nugent's and its brethren had been.

"It seems well sited. Close to Nugent's so nobody had to drive around with all that pentobarbital in his back seat. Exit Dexter Park to Exchange, and then, once out, a left or right turn onto Halsted and into the heart of the Fourth District and a meetup with that day's designated pusher man, whosoever he may have been. Again you see someone of intelligence behind it."

"Mulrooney. The chief?" asked Officer Washington.

"Possibly, though he didn't seem to me anybody except a mean, bitter old cop who'd busted too many heads and was just waiting out a retirement."

"Then who, Sheriff? We might destroy the pentobarbital, but it would be so wrong if the fellow that put this whole thing together got away with it and spent the rest of his life chuckling over the Fourth District Negroes."

"I've got two suspects. First, one word: union."

"Amalgamated Meat Cutters No. 173," said Washington. "A tough bunch. Lots of picket-line fights over the years. Kick the hell out of scabs."

"I'm guessing most of them originally worked in the industry. They'd know the Yards extremely well. They'd also be the smarter ones, who figured out after a while that busting cows with a sledgehammer didn't have much future to it. They'd naturally gravitate to the union, and working as organizers, they learn even more about this place. They'd constantly be running into the yard dicks, maybe even drinking in the same bar with them. Imagine a guy there who's lost his idealism about the union movement. He's not a red anymore. So he's looking for an angle himself, because he's not getting any younger. He heard about the big shipment of pentobarbital to Nugent, which would get him thinking. He could see it as easy money, plus it would be a way of expressing his hatred for the meatpacking industry, both the big guys and the little."

"I know some people in 173. If we don't get the connection from the raid, that could take us somewhere. But who's number two?"

"Nugent himself. Had the brains, knew the Yards, wanted out of the business, wanted the insurance money, anything to stay in Winnetka. Men will do a lot to stay in a nice house. He could learn drugs fast, being educated at that fancy college. It's just economics is all."

"Maybe with the help of Oscar Bentley, the man who makes it happen."

"We'll find out tonight. Now let's get back to the map and I'll show you how I see this happening. It's time to have some fun."

CHAPTER 31

A WANING HALF-MOON ATTENDED. IT WAS SMUDGED ORANGE, HANGING in the southwest sky. It didn't cast a bone-white glow as on the night of the gunfight, but more of a sepia tint, like an old photograph, nothing quite clear or clean in it. Its shadows were blurs. No breeze brought mercy. It was killer hot in Chicago, and insect life swept the atmosphere in vast formations.

They crept through it on foot, having parked Charles's car at Halsted and 43rd. Since the big three national meatpackers were located far away, and the two great restaurants, the two hotels, and the amphitheater near the main entrance had all burned, there was little danger of drunken revelers or late-night hard workers wandering in. Thus at 3:44 a.m., 43rd Street had the sense of a ghost town. Here, the smell of the animal and its shit and the smell of the fire and its ruins overwhelmed, combining into nauseous miasma trapped by the jellified atmosphere, almost making Charles wish he had his gas mask from the war. But other than that, this street inside the mile square seemed like any old block of any old city before cement became the rage. The wood was ornate, full of craftsman's pride and filigree. Columns and balustrades seemed to adorn each structure, so in the soft moonlight, shadow was abundant, networks everywhere of light and dark. All the buildings were dark. In the distance the pens seethed with cattle. You could hear them shift and grunt, issue throaty sounds that had no kind of classification, occasionally unleashing bellows or other signals of anger or distress. It could not be pleasant to be locked in a pen with the smell of blood leaking in from nearby.

Charles and Sylvester reached a certain spot. Across the street and down a bit lay the ruin of the Goldberg Kosher Meat and Pickle Company. Its sign, barely visible in the feeble moonlight, had been rotted out in spots so that it read "Goldberg ___ Meat ___ Pickle" and under that a line of Jewish writing. It was dark, its roof looked as if it had lost half its shingles, no window held glass, only shards. It gave no sign of occupation, signifying only the presence of ghosts and memories. Around back would be its pens and chute, where, in its day, the better-grade cattle had been gathered, drawn up the chute, then, as in gentile domains, slaughtered—the knife across the throat was the common method—bled, gutted, hung, halved, and turned into product for the delicatessens of America. The difference was merely that for these folks, blood was taboo, and so not only were the carcasses bled hard and long, the meat was then soaked in water vats to drain whatever few drops remained. Who knew what design changes that would require in the interior architecture of the operation. But it was certain that the cellar or some kind of lower level would be full of tanks of water, to receive such cargo, as well as vats of brine that once received a ton of cucumber a week, to be alchemized into crispy, astringent perfection for the palates of the company's customers. So besides the slaughter mechanics, it was a building of vats, dusty, rusting, maybe empty, maybe not.

"Let's go over it one more time," said Charles.

"I go on across the road and the tracks. And into penland. Four blocks. Then avenue to the right, between pens thirty-nine and forty, there is a cattle trace, which leads to one of the big Armour pens. A thousand head in that one. I head down it—"

"Perfect."

"Take up a position at the gate. Then I wait until your arrival."

"Yes, that's fine. That's good enough."

"Sheriff, you sure you want to do this on your own? What if they come at you in numbers? I am called Two-Gun for a reason."

"I need you where I need you, to do what you have to do when you have to do it. Besides, this evens out the odds considerably."

He clapped the Savage shotgun in his hand, heavy with the weight of five No. 4 buckshot loads in chamber or slung under the barrel in tubular magazine. In each pocket of his jacket he had fifteen more No. 4s. He'd practiced loading the weapon while waiting to move out. It took steady hands, firm fingers, and repetition, but now he could slide four into the opening in the breech under the ejection port in a second or two, the fifth to be inserted into the chamber. It then took but a solid push on the bolt-release button to prime the shotgun, and one had at one's disposal five charges if need be, fast as a prairie fire.

"You take the most dangerous action for yourself."

"This is the sort of thing I do. I ran many raids in the war. I happen to be good at it. I am not even scared, only impatient. So no other option need be considered."

"I still worry about the light."

"I bring a candle and not a flashlight because the flashlight is too bright. It's a giveaway of presence that is immediate. The candle glows, it doesn't beam, and it flickers uncertainly. Men aren't sure if it's there or not. It happens that I have very good eyes and can see more by candlelight than most. I will be fine."

"So be it."

"All right, Officer Washington, if one of us doesn't get out of this alive, no tears are to be shed; that's what we signed on for. Still, whichever way the breaks fall tonight, I have enjoyed working with you to the maximum. Smart, thorough, dutiful, and earnest. The best. The honor has been all mine."

"You are a fine man, sir. To get involved in something like this that is affecting only the black of the Fourth District is beyond admiration, at least to me."

They shook hands, and neither being of ceremony, that was enough. Each scooted off in a different way, for his different mission.

Charles withdrew back down 43rd a bit, then, certain that no observers were lurking, he crossed Dexter Park, split down a gap between two packinghouses, found himself out back. Each was the same, operational or not: a death pen where the selected waited to be driven to a ramp, a chute up into the building itself, and at the far side, a loading dock for the trucks or wagon that would take the final product either to trains or to local wholesale. Moving behind them was mostly about climbing fences. In a few, cattle left over from the last kill stood numbly, uninterested in reality. Now and then one would issue a sound of some meaning in cattle language but none in the human tongue.

Charles reached the last fence, negotiated it to find himself at the back side of the former beef pickle headquarters. As with the others, it featured a pen, a chute, and a dock, though in this case, the curse of decay was evident, even in the dark. Charles tramped through dust—drought had consumed Chicago, which aided in the May fire's violence by a long shot—and scaled the chute. He thought there would be an entrance big enough for steer or heifer, and there was, though locked. He set down the shotgun and took from his pocket a leather packet all breaking-and-entering specialists and most sheriffs carried, selected a tool, leaned close to find a keyhole, and began to diddle. It was not new to him, and through the sensations of the tool, he identified the locking mechanism and its parts. That done, he let the pick return on its ring, selected another, and began to gently poke and prod. The lock was solid but unsophisticated, and it took but a minute or so to find the points of leverage and spring the device. He entered, closing and locking it behind him.

He waited for his eyes to adjust to the slightly reduced light of the interior. No need for candle or match yet as that would ruin his night vision. When he'd seen as much as he could see, he edged forward. The interior seemed to be nothing that he'd expected. At the chute entrance, the death floor was quite small, of grated iron. Peering beneath, he could see the circle of a large vat. It was obviously meant to capture the blood surging from the steer's cut throat. Then, presumably on the muscle and zeal of its operators, the dead or dying thing was shoved a few feet to yet another chute, where it was placed to slide to a lower level. There was no overhead system of roller-mounted line that would be manipulated to pull the carcass to its stations of process. Instead, the carcass slid down the chute to be received by another vat. That one would be half-full of salt water. The carcass would splash in, and sit for a few days to soak out the leftover blood. The vats were all wheeled and could be moved to the mouth of the chute, then replaced as the day progressed. Later, the vats were spilled. Out came the water, out came the beef. Then the animal was processed, and the brisket was sliced thin for aging and spicing and separated for the magic that would turn it into the authentic corned beef.

Charles's eyes swam into adjustment. He figured the boys must have assembled their cotton patches in a solution of glycerol, alcohol, and pentobarbital down here, by flashlight or lantern light, because the lowness of position would have mitigated most of the shine to any would-be late-night onlookers. Thus too the drug would be stored down here. Scanning, his eyes crossed no chest, safe, cabinet, or trunk. He waited a bit, then tried again. In this fashion he moved through the building's length, through a wilderness of vats that filled the central space. But again, no storage unit presented itself, nor were there doors to an anteroom where the work might be performed for that day's delivery.

He realized he had to do what he preferred not to do, light the candle and use its flickering illumination to find his goal. Kneeling, he pulled it out and, closing his eyes to protect his night vision from the spurt, ignited the match. Introducing match to wick, he waited until the steady pulse of heat told him he was okay, then opened his eyes. At this level, the slaughterhouse's lowest, he again waited for his eyes to achieve dilation and then looked to see what he could see. It was just emptiness amid the vats, half a man high. Shadow cascaded this way and that. The place had a stench of death in a wet cave to it, of being subsumed in the queasy damp of the earth itself. Walking as carefully as he could, he patrolled one wall, then another, then back along the third, in no place finding sign of supply storage. Finally, only the back wall remained. That scanned, nothing was revealed.

Damnation! All this work to come up dry. Not a trace of a drug operation. Where would they hide it? He told himself that such a place would have to be accessible, easy to manipulate, meant for a short, concentrated effort, not the slow rhythm of a day's honest—

Had to be in a vat!

The vat had to be easily tipped!

The material was then spread out on the floor and two men did the assembling while two kept watch. Then it was replaced and they headed back upstairs, and two of the men drove away with the stuff, the others disappearing into the complexity of pens and chutes and walkways that occupied the vast center of the mile square.

Charles found it. The shortest of the vats, it was also one of the nearest to the stairway upstairs, which led to the docking area. That made much sense.

He tipped it gently, feeling the material inside shift, sliding upward as the vat was lowered. The contents slid out. Yes, a cardboard packing crate with glass jars wrapped in paper against breakage. Yes, a paper bag, whose interior revealed wads and wads of one-inch-square cotton patches. Yes, a large brown jug of medicinal alcohol, a smaller clear bottle of medicinal glycerol.

And yes, finally, a crate of six levels, each level latticed by cardboard to protect its precious cargo of vials. Lettering on the crate said "The Upjohn

Company, Albany, N.Y." A skull and crossbones proclaimed either pirates or poison. He assumed the latter. And in smaller letters, "pentobarbital, 25 ccs; 400 units." He could tell that so far, only a third of the top level had been used. Much was left, much money yet to be made, many deaths yet to occur.

And he heard, from far above, a door opening and one man saying to another, "Let's get this done. I have stuff to do."

On the cattle trace between Pens 39 and 40 was exactly nowhere. It was just empty fenced lots of mud and earth, some with animals, some without. Other than the knowledge that human labor was needed to build so much fence, no sense of the human race appeared. It was a flat plain, under a vast cathedral of stars, and only at the rims of the visible was there sign that such a thing as civilization existed.

Washington could see, toward what had to be the northwest, the towers of the Loop. Many buildings wore a ceremonial gown of illumination to proclaim their beauty and importance, but from more than a mile, all detail went missing and the brightness was not enough to drown the cascade of stars above and the sinking smear of orange moon. The other quadrants of horizon were darkened, as commerce in even this most commercial of square miles, in this most commercial of cities, had at last shut down for an hour or two before dawn.

The most profound suggestion of life was the sound that leaked somehow from the standing cattle. As before, nothing like a moo occurred, but every other category of animal noise, including grunts, snorts, gulps, belches, farts, low moaning, heavy breathing, the occasional yelp of pain, and whatever else could be construed. At the big gate to the Armour pen, he sensed their packing density. These were much higher-grade animals than the poor rejects of Nugent's low end of the bovine universe. They were hefty, muscular creatures, firm of construction, proud in posture, noble by profile. They stood in majestic torpor and lassitude, as if confident their very presence was warning enough to keep the world at bay. The steers had horns of various lengths and curls, but all had in common the rapier-like tip at the end, which could shred a man's guts in a second. No one wanted to get too close to that possibility, ever. They would feed America, and seemed oddly pleased at the honor, even knowing where it would take them tomorrow. Or maybe not. Who knew? Really, you could gaze for a year into those placid, gigantic brown eyes and learn nothing. Washington certainly had no theories.

He leaned against the fence on high alert. He was flexing both hands to warm the muscles, for the shooting that lay ahead. He had cleaned and lubed each heavy-duty revolver that afternoon, finding them as always almost magical in their complexity and precision, the thickened frame sturdy enough to contain the extra blast of the more powerful .38-44 cartridges, whose speeding bullet would knock a man flat if it hit a bone, shattering that bone in the process. The ivory grips weren't just for show; they provided, being dimensionally larger than Smith & Wesson's standard woods, more gripping space for his large hands. He knew his capabilities—draw from the hip, shoot from the hip and out to twenty-five feet, hit dead solid perfect center.

He checked his watch. It ticked slowly onward, revealing only that it was on to 5 a.m., and if tonight was to produce results, they would be initiated shortly. He breathed, mouth dry, felt the fetid air, looked to the sky to see a far-off airplane, heard a train whistle in the night, tried not to anticipate, and then he heard the fast-as-kettle-drums sound of shotgun shells spewing buckshot into the night.

Now?

Yes, now, before they're down here and set up. Start them off in confusion and they will stay in confusion.

He heard the reverberations of the four heading down the metal stairs at the far end of the room and leaned forward, snicking the safety off the trigger guard of the Savage. He fired five No. 4 charges into the crate of pento. It was like firing a Thompson gun jacked on a saxophone bohemian's noseful of cocaine, and it unleashed discordant percussive notes at burst speed. The flashes, given the shortness of the twenty-inch barrel and the darkness of the room, blossomed incandescent and vast, and the shells rushed through the gun's process as if on an express train, in obedience to a finger that had pulled oh so many triggers. The shells emerged, now empty husks bereft of powder and shot, at blur speed, spinning crazily atop one another as they were flipped out by the ejector. Mr. Cutts's compensator, set to apogee, coaxed each flotilla of twenty-one pieces of lead in the widest possible pattern. The shot tore, shredded, disintegrated, shattered, destroyed. In less than a second, the crate had been pulped beyond recognition, and yielded only remains of tattered cardboard, flecks of which floated heavily in the air, splintered glass vials, and Bakelite caps. The killer fluid itself saturated this mulch of ruin, but Charles flipped the hot gun, slammed four more shells into the magazine (the fifth being too awkward to load), threw the bolt, and hammered all four into the mulch, administering a tide of total pulverization. The folks next to Nugent's would have been proud. This was pulverization of the highest professional grade.

He spun, hearing confusion at the end of the room, as the four dicks were caught by surprise and locked themselves into paralysis as they waited for clarification and decision. While they waited, Charles reloaded yet again, this time taking the extra second for the fifth shell. He spun, braced, and lacking any target except a compass heading, launched all five, the same orchestration of thunder and lightning and buckshot and hot ejected empties. As anticipated, the clouds of shot hit primarily vats and banged off on the ricochet in a pattern of random diagonal trajectories. The men fell back, some stung, all terrified, all lost in near-terminal bewilderment. Plus, their ears hurt and the flashes burned so bright, they saw flashbulbs going off before them in space.

Charles turned, hit the stairway nearest, and clambered up it.

"I see him," somebody said, and fired a pistol bullet.

Revolvers in the dark on a moving target at seventy-five feet: not ideal shooting conditions, and the round hit something metallic with a clang and bounced off. More bullets came his way, all unaimed but for general area, all hitting something metal or wood, all ripping debris into an atmosphere already toxic with chemical death, shreds of cardboard, old paint, rusted metal chips, powder residue, perhaps old blood molecules as stirred by the commotion.

Charles got a final reload in, stood, and issued himself a barrage of covering fire by which he backed out the door onto the loading dock, dropped off it, found a cattle trace running along the holding pen, and headed out as fast as he could. It would be seconds before his antagonists came after him, but he knew absolutely that they would.

Washington was ready now.

He listened harder. More shots, these apparently of pistol, as they had a fragility to them, almost a trifling buttercup of noise against the brute force of the shotgun's blasts. It seemed too much time. Had the unimaginable happened? Charles Swagger's luck had to run out sometime, yet how sad it would be if the killer of Johnny D. had been taken down by a rogue bullet fired in the dark by a no-'count yard bull.

But then Charles asserted his existence and survival with three 12-gauge comets launched into the night. It had developed into a running gunfight in the dark through the endless nothingness of penland, with the shuffle and moan of now clearly agitated cattle rising in turn at the provocation of the gunshots.

Washington held steady, even though he had a tremendous impulse to walk the trace onto 43rd Street and see what approached. Charles, hit, limping, needing help? Charles cornered with the dicks having leveraged the angles on him, able then to throw shots from all sides with no cover in between? Maybe he was even down, and now they stood over him.

But if Officer Washington had any faith in this world, it was invested in Charles Swagger alone. No two-bit Packingtown railroad bull was about to take down Charles Swagger. Washington saw him suddenly whirl about the corner, hoist his shotgun, and in a second he'd sent five flashes flaring into the night, and whatever it would be, the next stage was upon them.

Charles ran through a night of nothingness and flash. It was not in him to run normally, but this action had been choreographed along certain principles, and so he did not stand to fight, but instead swerved this way and that, crossing Exchange and entering the wide expanse of penland. On either side were the blankness of fencing and the somewhat random distribution of cattle, occasionally sheep, occasionally, knowable by their stench, even hogs, who were fouler to the nose than any creature great or small. He was confident he would not be hit, for his pursuers had only their Colt revolvers, a close-range daylight weapon if anything, completely unsuited to shooting down skittering shadows a hundred yards ahead in the dark.

Occasionally he spun, braced against fencing, and cranked off a batch of shells. He didn't aim, he pointed, and he kept his eyes closed during the discharges to preserve his night vision, knowing the short-barreled weapon to launch fireballs against the satiny dark. Not quite an ordeal, the circumstance nevertheless had a dreamlike or memory-retrieved sense to it. Western Front, 1916 and '17, as a sergeant in the Canadian army he'd led raids that more often than not ended with helter-skelter dashes through the endless nothingness of no-man's-land under enemy attack. But this was the comic version, for then the fire had been roaring death beams of 7.92mm centerfire from the German Maxims aimed by experienced gunners, where tonight it was the yard bulls and their popguns.

He reached Pen 39 at last—it seemed a year in coming—and veered to the right, finding next door the pathway between 39 and 40 that led to a back entrance to the large Armour holding yard. He paused, crouching, breathing deeply to reacquire oxygen and also to adjust his fedora. It had tilted a little too far to the right and he did not care for that appearance.

He saw them, spread out across the street, moving remorselessly. They meant to catch and kill him. They understood at a glance that he had destroyed their enterprise and that, worse, he knew who they were and what they'd done, and whatever happened next would not to be in their best interests, so that only killing was left. They clustered, conferred, then began to come toward him.

"Hold off, boys!" he yelled. "Put the guns down and assume the position against the fence. You will at least survive the ni—"

The answer was gunfire, which stated their decision explicitly.

He pointed the Savage upward and fired five, fast as he was able. In the boldness of the flash, he could see them not fifty feet away, just as they could see him. It was an intimate little tableau of the visible after such a long slog through the invisible.

He turned and ran. So intent on him were they that they paid no attention to what else the animal trace contained, and, stopping and calming, they tried to refuel on oxygen. Then they pushed on, seeing how close they'd gotten, feeling they had their man at last.

Officer Washington saw him come.

"Man," he said, "too damn much running for an old man."

Breathing deeply, Swagger took off his fedora and wiped his brow with his sleeve.

"They're here," said Washington.

Swagger turned. The yard bulls stood shoulder to shoulder at the mouth of the trace, pistols in hand, hats tight. They thought they had him trapped, for no man would venture on foot into the packed Armour holding pen. It was sure death by trampling.

"Okay, federal man. Got you now. Time for you to face Irish wrath for stomping out our business."

"You got that right," yelled back Charles. "It's a time for wrath, Paddy. You have fair earned it."

He turned to Washington and said, "You ready for this, son?"

"Been waiting on it my whole life" was the reply.

Shoulder to shoulder, stride for stride, gun for gun, they started the walk down the trace.

"Fuck! He's got that two-gun coon with him."

They could see the gunfighters ahead, walking that steady, serious pace, calm as a breezeless summer day, hats low, mouths flat, eyes hard. In the now grayish light, they looked like cowboy death.

"They set us up for this. I am getting the hell out of here!"

"You stand tight, Jack! Four of us, two of them. Close enough so aiming don't matter. Only guts. Show 'em some mick guts. Close and closer till you can't miss. More guns, more bullets. Then we're clean out of here with a hefty retirement plug. Tomorrow we visit you-know-who and relieve him of what he claimed from us. We also relieve him of ever ratting on us too."

"*Faugh a Ballagh*, me fine boyos!"

Closer and closer.

Forty feet apart.

Enough light to see the others' hard, narrowed eyes.

No speeches now, or imprecations or commentary.

There might have been an instant of calm, and then the doors to hell ripped open as the devil himself dropped in for early breakfast.

Charles saw hands go blurry in a rush, and fired, automatic shucking a shell, muzzle spurting a blot of flash and a chunk of lead and sending a hardball into a man's stout gut. Not being an amateur, he wasted no time on the man's stutter-step toward collapse, but instead cranked to left and fired two so fast it sounded as one, into high chest and low throat of the next paddy, all of this before either could get a shot off.

Simultaneously, all his strength hammered into his strong right hand, Two-Gun double-actioned 158 grains of high-speed lead into the hipbone of an antagonist, shattering it, the next one arriving but a tenth of a second later to pulverize the left ventricle. The last man standing got his only shot off, but it sailed high and the recoil took the muzzle higher, and he was battling in microtime to recover when Washington's fast-mover broke his cheekbone in three and splattered brain tissue into the fetid atmosphere.

Gun smoke, rancid and angry, fought the odor of shit for domination. It curled and drifted and looked for crannies to inhabit. Ears rang. Eyes blinked hard and fast, ruined of night vision by the multiple extravagances of powder burning beyond barrel's end.

"You okay, Two-Gun?"

"Don't think I got no holes in me. You, Sheriff?"

"I'm fine. Need fresh air, bourbon, and a cigarette. That's all."

"Okay, now what?"

"I suppose we call it in."

"Gots a better idea. Sooner to that drink."

"I'm all for it."

Washington led him back down the trace to the gate of Armour's holding pen.

"Now, you stand clear," he said.

Charles mounted the fence.

And with that, Washington unlatched the gate and shoved it wide-open. Even still the bovines didn't notice or seem too clear on what was happening. No one had ever accused them of being smart and no one had ever taught them any tricks. Eventually, if left alone, they might have noticed and begun to trickle out in ones and twos. Thus Officer

Washington drew his second gun, thumbed back the hammer, pointed at the low, orange moon, and fired until empty.

The shots were like a current of electricity zapped through each animal, animating it in a split second to recoil and instinct. They bolted, the ones closest to the now-opened gate the leaders by default, and all drove hard for escape. Chewing up gross tons of dust and shit and straw, their stout legs and sharp hooves in total churn with panic, they bolted toward what to them was survival from the curse of gunshot. How fast an animal goes from stupefied torpor to high-speed action is one of the miracles of animal behavior. Nothing human can match it, as if they become a different species, now one absorbed in the all-consuming drama of escape. Nothing else occupied their minds, to the degree they had minds, only the universal message of instantaneous flight.

The cattle hit the four bodies without much in the way of notice by individual animals. Their brains so narrowly focused, they did not register other markers. The common mechanism of destruction was trauma as applied at full force by the galloping dynamic of the muscular legs moving fourteen hundred pounds on the hoof lost in flight panic. It smashed the four bodies hard, shattering bone in the process. Under the hooves, they were crushed into meal by those driving limbs, slashed by hoof-edge, slicing, ripping, crunching, breaking. Against the energy of stampede, flesh and bone are butter to the hot knife.

Charles and Officer Washington made it back to Charles's car with the dawn. Behind, there was ruckus, as escaped cattle are an emergency. However, once freed, the cattle did not pine to escape. Instead they stood about in ones and twos, gossiping.

The two men rested, breathing hard, each waiting for words to enter his mind. Finally Charles said, "I'll drop you at your car."

"It's over, then, Sheriff?"

"There's a fellow left."

"You'll deal with him."

"I will."

"Will you tell me—"

"No. If you know, Officer Washington, you might sooner or later acknowledge it innocently, but possibly it could reach someone of influence. We don't know to what level this enterprise was sanctioned and who derived profit and what their will toward retaliation would be. So best to leave it alone."

"Sheriff, did you get a look down the street after the cattle were done?"

"I did. Not much to see. Lots of cows standing around. And in the trace, pieces which I take to have once been men."

"Yes," said Officer Washington. "Well, what I saw was justice. Ain't much of it in Chicago, but here tonight, between Pens thirty-nine and forty, was a little."

CHAPTER 32

THE AIR WAS LEADEN. GLOOM OCCLUDED ALL. THE CLOUDS SEEMED TO weep. His skin hurt. Thoughts of golf at Indian Hill and the stately glory of Winnetka were long past.

"Oh, Thaddeus," Marjory had said, "that detective called. He'll be dropping by shortly after noon. He says he has a few more questions."

Thaddeus smiled, thanked her, went upstairs, and took the pistol out of the hiding place in his sock drawer. He rehearsed the steps. Simply cock by thumb on way to head, listening for the last big click, press muzzle against temple, and the slightest touch to the trigger would end all, and forever.

He had been through it many times before. Now once more: it was best. No arrest, no scandal, no shame to family. A one-day story, two at best. So much better than the drawn-out ordeal by pathetic sniveling that a trial would entail, with him in the starring role as the rich murderer who profited off the deaths of convicts. He knew that, in the press, the convicts would be portrayed as angels who'd accidentally misbehaved and were then martyred on the altar of capitalism. The reds would eat it up. His own people would abandon him to obscurity, prison, maybe the gallows. His children would change their name. It would be the end of the Nugent line.

When he saw Swagger's car pull up, he said to Marjory, "Darling, just in case, do know how I love you and the children and I did everything I did for your benefit." Not entirely true, of course, but what else was he supposed to say?

"Thaddeus, my goodness, what on earth are you talking about?"

"Darling, there were some work irregularities. I may have to answer for them. I'm nowhere near as perfect as you think I am." She didn't of course: another myth. "I am, in fact, profoundly flawed." That one was true.

Leaving her befuddled, he went to the door and opened to the knock. The detective was as before: stern, possibly of Baptist denomination, long of leg and trunk and arm, hat low over eyes that saw much and expressed little. Same hot-weather tan suit, much abused since it had hung on the rack at some department store.

"Detective. Come in."

"Thank you, Mr. Nugent."

"Do sit. I am ready for anything."

"Yes, sir. This won't take long."

"Should I have my lawyer present?"

"Ah, no. I don't think that'll be necessary. It's pretty open-and-shut."

"Yes, it is," said Thaddeus.

"I'd like to return to the day of the fire."

"I'm sorry. What?"

"Sir, the fire. May 14, when your building and pens were destroyed."

"Yes, of course. Is there some question of legality here?"

"Not unless you know of one. I looked pretty hard into it, and everything seems to accord."

"Well, then—what can I do for you?"

"Sir, the arson investigator told me that one reason the fire did eight million dollars in damage but only killed one poor soul was that you got your people out fast and in order, and called Pulverized Manure on one side and Western Pork on the other. They got their people out in the same good order. So when the fire devastated Exchange Avenue, all the places were empty."

"We were in fact preparing for inventory. So everybody was on their toes."

Inventory, thought Charles. Interesting.

He went on.

"Officially, the fire is said to have started at 4:15 p.m. Yet you as well as the Pulverized people were out of the building and had moved down Exchange by 4:15, or at least several people have told me."

Were they trying to build some kind of insurance fraud against him? This was suddenly and completely baffling. He had been told time and again that there was no evidence of any kind of ignition signature save accident by discarded cigarette under the 45th Street viaduct.

"I can't say when exactly the fire started. I can tell you when the call came in."

"Call? What call?"

"My secretary got a call, I'd guess around 4:10. She came scrambling in, terribly upset, because she'd been warned of a fire. Get out now, someone had said. We went to the window and saw nothing, except, of course, cattle, but you have to take such things seriously, since the place is a tinderbox, especially in hot, dry, windy weather."

"I see," said the detective.

"I'd happily give you her number and address. She's a rock. Was with me for twenty-five years and never made a mistake. If Virginia Stanton said a fire was coming, a fire was coming, and only a fool would brush it off."

"I may have to talk with her. Did she by chance recognize the voice?"

"No. That was funny, come to think of it. She said he slobbered. His mouth was full of saliva or something. A lisp, I suppose you'd call it, or a stutter, or both. Possibly drunk. Virginia could give you a better description, I'm sure."

"No, actually, that's very helpful. Okay, well, you've been a great help."

The detective rose.

"I thought this was about some other issue," Thaddeus heard himself saying as he rose too. "There were some deaths in a prison that was one of our accounts. I thought there might be questions as to—"

"There might be questions, but I wouldn't be the one to ask 'em. Don't know a thing about it. I did send out a bulletin to our field offices regarding your accounts and any possible irregularities. Sorry, that's my job. Anyhow, here's something that might interest you in that regard that wasn't covered by the Chicago papers."

He took an envelope out of his suit pocket. Thaddeus ripped it open, saw a clipping from the *Bangor Daily Call*, August 19, 1934:

SHAWSHANK DEATHS LAID TO SALMONELLA
IN STEWED TOMATO TINS

BANGOR (UPI)—A three-doctor state panel concluded that seven convict deaths at Shawshank Penitentiary last month were caused by food poisoning traced to a contaminated can of stewed tomatoes inadvertently served to the prison population with a popular beef stew dinner.

The chief medical examiner, William Wright, M.D., said that—

"Sure would like to arrest somebody today," said Swagger, "but it doesn't look like it's going to be you. Have to try something else. Anyway, thanks for your help and good luck on the course this afternoon."

"Yes, sir," said Thaddeus, missing entirely the reality that sometimes even dour cops joke. "Yes, oh, yes, oh, gosh, yes, I don't know what to say. Oh, this is sensational. Look, here, can you take this? Give it to some policeman. I bought it for self-defense, but now it scares me."

He handed over what Swagger saw was a Colt Dick Special. Swagger opened it, saw six brass circles within circles gleaming within the cylinder.

"You're sure on this, sir? I do know where it could be helpful."

"Yes, please, take the damned thing. I don't need a gun. This is Winnetka!"

He bounced to his car, a sprightly old fellow, all dapper and perky. No rain on his parade, no, sir. So much energy. Those white teeth, that straw fedora pushed back on the balding head. Charlie Oliver, Food and Drug Administration senior agent, Union Stock Yard & Transit Co. squad.

Swagger watched, waited till he got in, then moved swiftly to the other side, opened, and slid in.

"Hello, Charlie," he said, smiling. "Remember me?"

After flashing surprise, the old man gathered and said, "Oh, sure, howdy. Named Charles, just like me. With the Division, right? You were investigating some missing drugs, as I recall. Went to Thaddeus Nugent. Pentobarbital."

"Nugent has been cleared of any wrongdoing. The drugs seem to have been in his supply room when the fire struck. They were burned up, like everything else."

"I do wish I'd handled it better, Agent Swagger. And I thank you for not making a fuss with my boss. FDA has a kind of rough reputation these days. And I'm within a few weeks of retirement, after working the Yards for nigh on thirty-five years. Very happy to get out alive. Not all do."

"Damn shame about those company dicks," said Swagger. "Hell of a way to go."

"It's a damn dangerous place, I tell you. Folks don't appreciate that, not even my own wife. Step in shit one second, catch ten inches of horn in the gut the next or, like those boys, get pancaked into the mud."

"O'Malley, Reagan, Dunphy, and Connaghy."

"Sounds like a damn vaudeville act," said Charlie. He clicked his bright white teeth. "Ain't funny, but still . . . the Irish, what can you do? Maybe some whiskey involved, but you didn't hear that from me."

"Don't worry, Charlie. By the way, how's the side? Heal up nicely? Didn't look too serious. I usually shoot better, but it was damned dark that night, and I couldn't see my sights. You were pretty damn lucky, no doubt about it."

"I— I— Sir, what are you talking about? I don't—"

"I figure it was you and two of the Irishers on the ambush. O'Malley, Reagan? The other two were back at Goldberg's Beef Pickle, getting set up for the next day's work."

"Sir, if you—"

"See, it took a man with a wide range of knowledge to put this together. Unique, this fellow would be. He'd know the Yards as only someone who'd worked there for thirty-five years would, every animal trace and pen and shortcut and dead end. He'd know the yard bulls, having worked with them for the same amount of years. They were his enforcement, if he got in a jam, and whenever there was swag, he made sure to give them a taste. But he also had to know drugs and their potential. He had to realize that four hundred ccs of pentobarbital could be turned into a hundred thousand dollars of cash if handled the right way. You have a master's degree in chemistry from downstate; I checked. But he'd also have to have contacts in the Fourth District. That's why it was so helpful that your dentist was Ralph Hughes. Damn fine pair of choppers he made for you, eh, Charlie? You needed upstanding men to act as onetime pushers. Easy work, a chunk of dough, could be trusted selling tickets for a ride on the Night Train. Dr. Hughes's patient list provided the names. Money for everybody."

Charlie said nothing. He clicked his teeth, stared into space.

"Then when you heard Nugent was about to inventory, you knew you had to act. He would have discovered the missing drugs, called the cops, and the whole thing would have been a big deal. Just found out about the inventory yesterday. It was the missing piece. If Nugent brought the cops in, even the Irish would have been smart enough to put missing pento and dying Negroes together. That's when the fire came into it.

"Later, you ratted out Nugent to me on the Shawshank deaths to muddy the waters. You thought maybe the idea of nailing a big rich guy on seven murders might be too much temptation for me to turn down and I'd lose interest in your little enterprise in the Fourth. Too bad I don't think that way."

"You have no evidence."

"The court I'm going to doesn't require evidence. Or confession, or representation. So I'm thinking that when Hughes caught that bullet across the cheekbone, his cover was gone and your whole thing might be over too soon and you had plenty of pento left. So you went to him and you said, 'Ralph, here's the choices. Either the cops or the mob are going to figure you out very soon. Whichever, you're ruined, and if it's the mob, it might not just be you but your wife and daughter too. So if you love them, Ralph, I'm sorry to say tonight is the night you take a swim in the lake. Nobody'll know a thing, all that money you made will stay where you put it, and your wife and daughter will have the life you dreamed of for them.' Am I right, Charlie?"

"He was a decent man. Worst thing I did was bring him in. But the wife and daughter are well off in California, far from all this."

"Here's the final nail, Charlie. When you called Ralph and when you called Nugent's to warn of the fire, you took your false teeth out. That's why you were slobbering and hardly able to say a thing."

Charlie stayed silent.

"I'm going to make you the same offer you made Ralph Hughes," said Swagger. He pulled out the Colt Detective Special and tossed it onto the top of the dashboard.

"Otherwise, I'm going to tell some Italian folks I know. They see that Night Train money as theirs and you as a thief. They won't go easy. Examples have to be made."

Charlie gulped. Then he turned to Swagger.

"Can't you cut me some slack? I kept it in the colored," he said. "Among the dark people. They're animals, let them lose their souls. Nobody cares."

"No slack for you, Charlie," said Swagger. "Too many folks bought that ticket and ended up dead. And guess what? Somebody did care."

He got out of the car and walked off. A hundred yards out he heard the shot. He didn't look back.

JOHNNY TUESDAY

AUTHOR'S NOTE

DO NOT IMAGINE THIS STORY IN TECHNICOLOR. IMAGINE INSTEAD A multi-chromatic palette only the simple would call black-and-white. It is a rhapsody of off-white and near-black, colors without actual names, coal-dust-on-ivory, ebony smeared with Vaseline, dusty obsidian, radiant plum, Wrigley white, all the way to an inky black so black it foretells doom. Such hue and nuance are everywhere: The blinding white-hot muzzle flash of an onyx steel Colt automatic or the satiny luster of the moon glinting off a dead-end puddle in a slum. The soft pale glow of a silk blouse clinging to a woman's alabaster shoulder, or the shoulder itself—gelid, sleek, of weight, of flesh, so smooth and warm to the touch you could suffocate on it, as many have. Or the elegant cumulus gray of cigarette smoke so heavy in the air that it swirls and tumbles. Twisted angles, shadows like blades, crazy jigsaw streets, fog adrift like gun smoke, gun smoke adrift like fog, cops with dead-guy eyes. Such bedazzlement arrives imprisoned in a square cell at 1:37:1 ratio and photographed through the lenses of men named Alton or Metty or Seitz or Musaraca. Enter the noir universe at your own risk. But be aware: once in, never out. That's the house of noir: it's been the ruin of many a poor boy; God, I know, I'm one.

CHAPTER 1

I T WAS FEBRUARY 1945, AND IN THE CITIES OF AMERICA, SMALL OR LARGE, town, burg, village, or hamlet, everybody smoked. Moreover, everybody wheezed, everybody coughed, everybody picked flecks of tobacco off their lips and hawked gobs of incandescent goo from lungs into kerchiefs or the streets, burned holes in suits, sweaters, and pants, set wastebaskets and sometimes houses ablaze. Everybody died early. Nobody noticed, nobody cared.

It was true everywhere, which means it was true without irony of Chesterfield City, Maryland. The town's product, basically, was cancer, as its plantations, fields, farms, sandy loam, ample sunlight, and cheap Negro labor provided the big tobacco companies of Virginia and North Carolina with some of the raw materials to manufacture little sticks of death, to be sold in brightly colored, heavily advertised packages. The more the butts sold, the more prosperous became Chesterfield City.

The war, fought on a high-octane mix of K-rations, cigarettes, and .30-caliber ammunition, was winding down. The weather, middle Atlantic in February, was brisk, but not painful to ears or nose, in the sunny forties. It felt good to breathe, excuse that damned cough. On Chesterfield City's five blocks of downtown, overcoats and scarves shielded citizens from the nip, and the obligatory fedoras turned the street into a river of hats, with brims straight as Hoppy's in the matinees, or pulled down to cover eyes and nape, as if a nor'easter or a film noir were about to blow in.

Out for Saturday-morning errands, the folks stopped for coffee or hardware, bought new sports jackets from Malloy's, obeyed the stop-lights, ducked away from the dark, sleek late-thirties automobiles out for a weekly gas-rationed spin, put a paycheck in the bank, grabbed a plateful of eggs and bacon at Merit's Fine Diner, performed the whatever and whenever of American life in the last year of a global spasm. Many prayed for news from sons in combat; many wished the rationing would finally vanish; a few hoped the war wouldn't be over until they'd killed their own bucketful of Krauts. All smoked.

The city was smallish at thirty thousand, just big enough to be called a city, even if it was stuck on a peculiar peninsula running south from Delaware on down through Maryland to Virginia, cut off from the main-land by a mile of bay on one side and thirty-seven hundred miles of ocean on the other. No bridges linked the Eastern Shore, as it was called, to the Western Shore, that is, America. The only way to get there was the long way; there was no short way.

Some of the Saturday downtowners, but not many, may have noticed the *Chesterfield Courier* truck as it tossed off bundles of newspapers at downtown's four different newsstands and three drugstores, and may have paused at the headline, "MARINES STORM JAP ISLAND," and even read the subhead, "Iwo Jima, 750 miles off homeland, hit by three divisions, casualties said to be light."

But they'd been reading headlines like that for some time, always pivoting on the fulcrum of an exotic foreign place they'd never heard of, and casualties were always said to be light, at least on the first day. Ho-hum, nothing new here. It was the war, that's all, no time to pause for details; you could catch up later on the radio news.

But under the sameness, the niceness, the earnestness, the war fatigue, the cigarettes, and the hats, an anomaly was inventing itself. Something was about to happen.

In the president's office of State Bank and Trust of Chesterfield, two men and a woman were in seated conversation. The office looked like a dream of a don's chambers at Oxford, at least as imagined by seriously moneyed Americans. They'd hung their hats—homburgs, actually, after the fashion of New York financiers—and neither smoked, but the men both wore double-breasted pinstripes in blue, as was expected of the higher gentry; the woman was equally of splendor, in that classy vocabulary of the time that demanded slim legs, platform heels, a neat coif, and eyes that had a sleepy—or was it sultry?—quality to them. Her hair had to be blond, and of course it was, her lips ruby, and of course they were, her lashes full, yep, and her demeanor silky, of class, one might say.

She was Mrs. Raymond Tapscott, her husband was Mr. Raymond Tapscott III, who owned the biggest tobacco plantation in the state, called Bright Leaf. He was an unimpressive man, even if his grandfather, the bank's founder, watched the transaction from the wall, as if to confer blessing. Tapscott III was impressively dressed, with an impressive wife, but he was gravely flawed. Eyes small and watery, chin vague, nose without character. You saw the two of them and you'd think, What explains this mismatch? And then you'd answer it yourself: Money, as in his. Greed, as in hers. And you'd be right.

Raymond was speaking to the bank's president, Neil Oakley, of Massachusetts by birth and thus, both technically and truthfully, an outsider.

"Neil, I needn't explain to you who founded your institution and who owns the majority of the stock as well. The family malarkey aside, my people have been using State Bank and Trust for generations. Please don't disappoint me. This is very upsetting."

"Raymond, I just hate to open the vault before my full security team is here."

A diamond necklace in a velvet case lay on the desk between them.

"John, if anything happened to my necklace, it would break my heart," said Laura Tapscott. "It's an heirloom, representing Tapscott family tradition and history, and it frightens me to have it lying about."

Whatever Laura wanted, it seemed, Laura got. Neil Oakley, like everyone, was in love with Mrs. Raymond Tapscott and could no more deny her than stop dreaming about her shoulders.

"She's your secret weapon, John. All right, Laura, you're very persuasive. I'll take care of it. You come along."

Outside, the street, the river of hats, the rise of vapors, either condensed breath or the issue of cigarettes. Other features immediately recognizable there at State and Main included the vigor of spinsters; the haggard glare of tobacco farmers sure to get fucked again by Big Tobacco come the harvest auctions, but locked into their destiny nevertheless; lots of Saturday errand-goers, these being men in old clothes, as leisure wear had yet to be invented for the taxpaying class. A cab or two, yellow of course, stood out in the torrent of black-and-green thirties Big Detroit aerodynamics oozing along State and Main. An elderly man, his legs wrapped in blankets, propelled himself along in a wheelchair, and families made way, dads pulling their unruly offspring out of his determined path. Nothing was suspicious, except perhaps the old chap in the chair, for why was he in a hurry, and, say, wasn't he a stranger, come to think of it? But for now everything was unchanged, until it wasn't.

A black car pulled up to the bank. Four men, suits and fedoras tilted low, all wearing MacArthur-type aviator sunglasses, got out; two walked awkwardly because they were swaddled awkwardly, lengthy implements under their coats.

They entered the bank. It was a cathedral to capitalism, vaulted, hushed, marbleized, with stately chest-high tables for the acolytes to figure their sums before getting in line, Roycroft wood with that feathery stain everywhere, a frosted glass chandelier atop, like the eye of some munificent god of the American way. Tellers behind ornate cages toiled away earnestly, and behind them various intermediaries calculated or regulated the flow in and out of cash and investments on clickity-clackity adding machines. It sounded like a bowling alley.

The crew didn't notice much. They had been in banks before, lots of them. They saw the president and Laura and her husband, Raymond, standing by the opened vault. Laura was holding a velvet box.

The leader of the crew suddenly pulled an M1 carbine from underneath his coat, waving it around.

"Get 'em up, goddammit, this ain't no picnic," he yelled, the armed authority in his voice quelling all sound.

Clearly it was a well-trained team; each put a zone under gun muzzle, commanding it. A Winchester 97 is not to be argued with, nor is a Government .45 automatic or some kind of large-bore Smith & Wesson hump-backed, blue-steel revolver.

Meanwhile another robber, this one Pete, with the Winchester 97, turned to face the wide-open window, which gave him a vector on both State and Main. Markos, the one with the Government .45, clicked back the hammer, and no sound is louder than the click of a hammer setting into place on a big automatic when it's pointed at you. He looked like he knew what he was doing.

Alarms of confusion arose as robbers shouted and citizens squealed.

"On the floor, on the floor."

"Don't even think about being a hero. This ain't Iwo Jima."

"Faces down, goddammit."

"Please don't hurt me."

"Shut up, lady."

Jack Petrakis—the boss—went to Laura. He was beefy and oily, of olive skin, so you would guess Italian or Greek or something from around the big pond that separates Europe from Africa. Yet he was not unattractive, and he knew it. His strength and lack of conscience gave him a power plant that generated thousand-volt confidence. He thought the world loved him. He smiled, showing unusually white teeth, and one might guess that behind the Ray-Bans, his coal-dark eyes actually twinkled.

"I'll take that, cupcake. Say, ain't you a looker."

He plucked the necklace case from Laura's hands.

"Thanks, doll-baby. Hmm, maybe I'll take a little something extra too." He made as if to plant a smooch on her alabaster cheek, substitute for other things he and all men wished to leave on Laura.

A hero stepped forth. However, it was not Laura's husband, who had turned the color of pewter in the rain.

It was Neil Oakley, preposterously brave, preposterously foolish.

Driven by love in its craziest form, he launched himself forward to place his body between bank robber and classy dame.

"No, no. You don't want—"

Jack let the boy-sized carbine drop to horizontal in his grip and fired four shots. He was so close, marksmanship was hardly a factor. Even with their tiny powder capacity and light bullet weight, the four cartridges did their job, which was to bring death to earth. The carbine had almost no recoil, spent shells popped out of it like brass toast, and Neil Oakley, who had avoided the draft via a variety of subterfuges, connections, and maneuvers, joined the total of world dead by bullets around three-tenths of an inch wide. It would be ironic except that it wasn't. He had his appointment in Samara after all. So what? He hit the floor like a feed bag dropped off a truck and began to bleed through the holes in his pinstripes—aorta severed, spleen splattered, heart pulped, third button left-hand side shattered—like a pig. A few in the audience had been in combat and so were not surprised by the swiftness of the wet, black spew, knowing that bodies are bags of blood and when shot squirt out amazing amounts—but most shrieked, melted back, went even more timorously into submission, thinking *notmepleasenotme*.

Raymond and Laura stepped back, horrified.

"Harry, the vault," spoke Jack, nonplussed by the subtraction to humanity he had just engineered.

Harry went into the vault, and in seconds was out, dragging a canvas postal bag heavy with loot. He dragged it through the blood, which soaked the bag, and as Harry pulled the bag to the entrance it left a smeary track on the tile.

The shotgunner, Pete, had watched and rather enjoyed the exchange. Then he turned back to his job, eyeballing State and Main for the approach of law and order. But law and order was already there: on the other side of the window, evidently attracted by the sounds of what could have been gunfire, stood a patrol officer, in blue, cap squarely upon head, astonishment squarely on face. Behind the curve already, the officer drew a Colt Official Police from a bag-like hip holster and was quite quick on it, firing once, drilling a precision hole in line with Pete's gut. A second later, after a faltering step and a discussion with himself as to responsibilities of lookouts in bank robberies, Pete launched a load of No. 4 buckshot through the pane, blowing a hole the size of a fist in both the window and the policeman, who obligingly went pavement-bound, chest and lungs destroyed. Sirens rose.

"Pete, you okay?" Jack yelled.

"Fucker broke a rib; I can make it, though. Shit, that hurts."

Harry had moved to the front entrance for his own recon on the situation.

"Oh, Christ, must be a million of 'em out here."

A rattle of shots began to bang through the windows of the bank, hitting fixtures, pinging off the floor, puffing clouds of crystal from the overhead chandelier, splintering feathery Roycroft oak. The alabaster walls began to spurt dust from the bullet strikes. People cowered, screamed.

The panes began to web into gossamer filigrees and spidery abstractions as punctured, until one of them surrendered, fell to the marble floor, and fragmentized. The whole world was shooting.

Outside on both State and Main, cops and civilians formed two hasty barricades cutting off the bank in either direction. With a variety of handguns, Winchester lever actions, hunting rifles, and duck and goose shotguns they kept up the fusillade. It was, after all, lots of fun.

Jack crouched behind a Doric column that was part of the bank's temple-like interior.

"Oh, shit," he said.

From the floor, where he crunched the flesh around his wound into a kind of knot, Pete screamed, "I'm bleeding, I'm bleeding bad!"

It looked like they were sunk. But they weren't.

Out on State, the man in the wheelchair furiously propelled himself down the way to get under cover behind the police barricade.

He made it, pivoted to face the spectacle of cruisers arrayed barricade-like, forming a crescent to surround the scene of the crime. Meanwhile, civilians with long guns—10-gauge goose guns, 30-30 lever guns, a few swankier Model 70 Winchesters—ducked between them, eager to shoot something.

He rose from his chair, threw away his blanket to reveal a Thompson 1928 submachine gun with a drum, leaned into the heavy instrument for control, and fired a burst. Clearly, he was an expert. The bullets—tracers and thus almost invisible in the bright morning light—struck the rear fender of a police car and in a second—WHOOSH—the tank went up in a spiral of flame.

He nimbly rotated, lighted up another car. Two columns of roiling incandescence danced in the wreckage.

That's what you call match point. The cops saw they were outflanked and outclassed by the tommy gunner, who had them cold. He gestured with his muzzle, and they threw down their revolvers and raced away.

The gang, one man helping the doubled-up Pete, made it to the car out front. One hat blew off, but all sunglasses remained in place, if a little crooked.

The tail gunner waited calmly as the car U-turned on squealing tires, then rolled up on the sidewalk to avoid the cop cars, and headed to him.

Suave, collected, well-barbered, he looked a cut above the swarthier, rougher bandits. In fact, he was the sort of man who would be called either "Doc" or "Professor." He looked on the devastation he had wrought, all of it bloodless, which made for a good day's work, as he was no psychotic. The abandoned cop cars had been dilapidated by t-gun fire, two of them captured by livid flame, all their windows shattered, all the tires flattened.

He got out a pipe and lit it, enjoying a buzzy blast of oaky vanilla, the car arrived, and he dipped in.

The car sped off.

CHAPTER 2

I T WAS LATE IN THE MORNING WHEN HE DROVE INTO THE CITY. HE CAME
rolling in from the east side slowly, looking all around. He drove a
much-mashed, much-used (one hundred thousand on the odometer,
bought cheap at a South Carolina lot) '38 Chevy coupe. Both man and
car, then, had seen better days. But both had jobs to do.

On the seat next to him lay a newspaper, picked up down the
road at a coffee stop. It was the *Chesterfield Courier,* and the date was
February 18, 1947. Though scrunched in reading, the front page still
revealed its headline news: TRUMAN WARNS RUSS ON GREECE,
and a smaller head, "Two Years After Bloody Robbery, No Clues," and
in a smaller subhead, "Tapscott Necklace Still Missing."

He reached State and Main and obediently went to neutral when the
red turned against him. Glancing around, he just saw America and, not
having been here before, could not note the changes evident. It meant
nothing to him that a few brave souls went sans fedoras, sans ties, sans
oxfords or work boots—but in, God help them, shoes patterned after Nor-
wegian fishing slippers. But he noted that prosperity floated everywhere,
the streets were a-bustle, retail flourished. He didn't know that Malloy's,
the haberdasher, had vanished, replaced by a Buster Brown shoe store
for kids. He noted that State Bank and Trust's vault-like, cathedral-like

building still stood firm and strong, its windows solid, reflecting the sunlight, as behind them the usual run of duties were dispatched, mortgages paid, checks deposited, loans issued. He couldn't know that inside, a plaque marked the tragic death of Neil, uh, what was the name again, oh, yeah, Oakley, or that, above and more meaningfully, all the chandelier bulbs had been replaced and beamed radiance into the hushed, darkened, sacred space below.

It wasn't home to the stranger, but he knew it anyhow, from magazine photos and newsreels seen on smokey islands, shattered atolls, installations splashed on wasteland. It was any small city. This one happened to be on a place called the Eastern Shore of Maryland. The cash crop could be corn or wheat, but here it was tobacco, which the big cigarette companies bought by the ton, mostly from Raymond Tapscott III. He'd noticed the fields of bright leaf sweeping away to the flat horizon as he drove in.

Chesterfield had a movie theater, *The Best Years of Our Lives* plus second feature *Raw Deal* plus Saturday matinee of Buster Crabbe in *Outlaws of the Plains*; a grocery store; a gentry zone where the tobacco money tended to live in quiet splendor behind walls or hedges; a veterans' village of Quonset huts where the boys returning had to live until housing was built; a cheerful, even radiant section for the ever-growing segment of people in the middle; and finally, a Negro section, which was called by all, on both sides of the line, Libertyville.

Libertyville would be either on the other side of the tracks or on the other side of the river. In this case, it was on the other side of a river, across a rickety bridge, and he didn't get there until midafternoon, after a long recon on the city. It was a ramshackle deployment of tar paper shacks, unpaved roads, barefoot kids, decay, and degradation. Even so, it had a certain pulse to it, for all knew the darks to be people of rhythm, music, gossip, laughter, and jive-jumping. They loved to dance and drink and sing, and that's when the devil sometimes took over, so they had to be watched.

The man in the car knew that if he wanted answers, the only place he'd find them was here.

It didn't have a name, but the music pouring out identified it. At the end of the street, nearest to the river, it was where the Negro man went for his weekly injection of whiskey, smoke, and rhythm. Though the place was abundant in all three, plus the odors of sweat and dust—the hard residue of working tobacco for the Man—it did not seem overly packed. The music was hot jive from the year 1937, blasting out of a jukebox that itself had been built in 1937. It belted jazz, honky-tonk, blues, and anything else that was called "race music." Billie was there, as were Louis and Cab, but many just as gifted had but one recorded tune to their credit, and here they were in constant rotation.

A boy in overalls, barefoot, entered, went to one of the drinkers at the scrap-wood bar.

"Nick, man wants to see you outside."

Nick looked at him. Nick was a well-formed man of thirty or so, handsome by anybody's standards, weary by human standards, dressed in overalls over a much-washed denim shirt. His fedora was on the bar, next to his amber shot glass.

"Tell him to come in. I ain't goin' nowhere till this whiskey is gone."

"Nick, it's secret. He gimme a dollar to git you."

"Told you, I ain't goin'—"

"Nick, he's a white man."

Nick was puzzled. White people didn't come to Libertyville. Ever.

"Jesus, can't them people *never* leave me alone?"

He bolted the shot—ah, bliss!—and got his cranky bones up. He went out to something that looked to be a porch in slow collapse. He saw nothing except Libertyville—its crazed streets, its crazy-leaning shacks, its mud puddles and roaming dogs.

"Back here, Mr. Jackson."

Mister! Now, wasn't that a toot!

Nick ID'd the source of the voice as a glade of trees across the muddy road. He crossed the street and saw a figure a little farther back in the trees where the wet slices of the marshes dissolved into river.

Hard to see a face, but damn yes, the man was white, fedora a-tilt, maybe blue shirt, some kind of woolly coat with prickly rows of sergeant's stripes on it, and a fat, short tie with a Hiroshima bomb fireball atop it. He leaned against the fender of an old Chevy.

"Who are you? What you want? I can't see no face. You shouldn't be here. Git me in trouble, git you in trouble, sir."

"You don't have to call me sir. I wasn't an officer."

No white man had ever told him *not* to call him sir.

"Say, how you know my name?"

"I know all about you, Mr. Jackson. A friend in the military told me your story. You were a stretcher-bearer all over Italy and Europe. Nobody over there, not paratroopers, not rangers, not bomber pilots, not tankers, got shot at more than you. But when it was all over, we all went home to parades and thanks. We all got laid that first night back. For you it was Okay, dark boy, you go on back to your crib in Libertyville."

"That's the way it is. I don't like it, but that's the way it is."

"I have a deal for you."

"You pay me more than the forty per I get picking up trash?"

"A lot more."

"Fifty?"

"No money. I'll pay you in something you never had. I'll pay in respect. Shake your hand. Thank you. Call you sir or Mister. Treat you like the man you are, admire you for the hero you are. You never had that, not down here. Joe Louis doesn't even get that."

"Believe it when I see it," said Nick.

"I need to talk to some other dark people. See, here's the play: nobody knows more about this town than the Negroes. They pick up trash, wash cars; they're maids, handymen, butlers, window washers. They go every-where, but they're invisible. I need to hear what they say to each other, not what they say to white people."

"Man, you fixin' to get *killed*. And me along with you."

"You're smart, Nick. You'll figure out a way to keep us alive. Deal?"

"You crazy."

The man came out of the trees. Nick saw a powerful body, though hidden behind a tweed sport coat. Despite the fedora low across eyes, Nick saw a kind of dignity, maybe, a sergeant's dignity to him. He reached out. They shook hands.

"This should be some goddamn hayride," said Nick.

Crime scene photos. Raw, artless, too much flash, but clear enough. He shuffled through them at a rate of about a second each. "CONFIDEN-TIAL," it said, stamped in each corner, "PROPERTY OF CHESTERFIELD POLICE."

The shattered window of the bank.

The street scene outside in the immediate aftermath.

The blood puddle on the sidewalk, underneath the punched-out hole left by the 12-gauge.

The blood on the floor, which bore the smear of the heavy cash bag dragged through it.

The late, though not great, Mr. Oakley, unrequited in death as in life.

"Sir, please hurry," said Willie. "I got to git 'em back before the day shift." They lurked in the men's room of the Chesterfield Police Depart-ment, Willie's professional responsibility as were the other rooms of the station. He was night janitor, charged with getting it sharp for the next day.

"You don't have to call him sir. He don't like it," said Nick.

"Never heard of nothing like that," said Willie.

"Says he's different. We'll see. Won't tell me his name."

"Stretcher-bearer, you're an expert. Tell me what you see." He gave the photos over.

Nick looked. The photo depicted the dead banker, another angle, on the floor in the pool of blood and, above him, smears left by the trail of the loot bag dragged out of the frame.

"A bleeder. High chest, probably arterial. Under pressure the stuff really pours out. The medics told us to leave the guys with the real bad gushers. They couldn't be saved."

"Fool like you probably tried anyway, like to got yourself killed for a corpse," poked the white man.

"Maybe so. A coupla times."

"What do you see?"

"Dead guy. Seen 'em before."

"Anything odd?"

"Plugged four times, when one would have done the trick. Why four, at that range? Was he trying to make sure?"

"Good point. Maybe the shooter was just trigger-happy."

"But everybody say this here a professional crew. They'd done this before, wouldn't do it this way."

"Another good point, Stretcher-bearer. Anything else?"

"That's all I got. You see something?"

"Notice how wide the blood trail is after the guy dragged it through the puddle. Seems wide to me, anyway. Wouldn't that mean the cash had settled and spread and was kind of heavy? Plus, the guy dragged it, he didn't pick it up. So maybe it was. But it was supposedly only five grand. How could it be that heavy?"

"Ain't never had much cash, so I wouldn't know."

"The official story is that this was really a jewel robbery and these boys had been casing Tapscott, looking for a moment of vulnerability to get that necklace. They just robbed the vault because it was open. I don't know what five or six grand weighs, but it sure as hell weighs a lot less than what's in that bag."

"So the necklace *wasn't* what they robbed the place for. You're saying it was what was in that bag."

"That's what I'm saying the photo is saying."

"Please, mister. I got to get this—" Willie said.

"One more," said the stranger. "The cop."

"What for?" said Nick. "Just another dead soldier in a war."

But the white man looked hard at the photo, seeking more than information, seeking meaning.

The officer's face looked to be in repose, at least, eyes and mouth closed as if in sleep. Maybe early forties, one of those Officer Friendly faces. He lay spread-eagled on the pavement in a lake of blood turned black by the harshness of the photography. One black shoe had come off. His khaki shirt was a swamp of solid and liquid in chaotic tumble, neither quite yielding to the other. The squall of buckshot had shredded his tie and twisted his badge.

"It ain't never pretty," said Nick.

She was regal, serene, lit by inner glow. Her home, small, tidy, with unusual grace notes, in the best part of the worst place in town. It was well after dark, and Nick and the white man sat across from her. She had insisted on serving tea, and untouched cups were before each man.

"Thank you so much, Mrs. Fields," said Nick.

"Well, I don't know about this. Mr. Tapscott has always treated me well. Can't say the same for the woman he married. I won't be betraying him."

"Ma'am, no betrayal intended."

"And you, young man. I never. No, I never. Not in my lifetime has a white person visited me or called me 'ma'am.' But that doesn't please me, it bothers me. It suggests you are up to no good, sir, and perhaps our people figure in your scheme. I saw you because I so respect Mr. Jackson. Speak your piece, and I shall decide if I will answer."

"Thank you, ma'am. In that bank robbery, Mrs. Tapscott's diamond necklace was stolen. That is what all the papers said. My question is: *What* diamond necklace? Was it new? Were you familiar with it? Did you see it? Did it make sense to you? Where did it come from?"

Maybe it wasn't the best place to start.

"Mr. Jackson, who did you say this man was? He says he does not require betrayal, yet he immediately requires betrayal. What is your interest in all this, young man? I don't even think I caught your name."

It took him by surprise. He hadn't planned to deceive, but identifying himself might have unplanned repercussions.

"Please call me Johnny. My interest is in repaying certain obligations. Possibly even achieving some little payment of justice. That's all."

"He has no last name, Mr. Jackson?"

"None that I get from him."

"I cannot speak to a person without a last name. Today is Tuesday. He came on Tuesday. His name is Johnny Tuesday, then. And you vouch for Mr. Johnny Tuesday?"

"He ain't like the others. He don't think he's better. It don't show in everything he says or does. It's like he don't notice who's white or black."

"All right, Mr. Johnny Tuesday, the white man who isn't better. The answer is, that old thing had been lying around since before she got here. It was some hand-me-down from his aunt or something, costume jewelry, I believe. She never bothered to lock it in the safe with her fine jewels. More than once, I found it on the floor. So it suddenly becomes 'the Tapscott necklace' in all the papers. That was quite a surprise to me."

Perhaps she would have been more circumspect if she'd known of a fourth visitor to the tea party. He had a last name, which was painted on the door of the large vehicle he had driven to this place on the tip of something strange at Mrs. Fields's house. It said "RENFRO FUNERAL PARLOR FOR THE NEGRO."

CHAPTER 3

I T WAS CALLED THE WIGWAM, AFTER THE INDIANS WHO'D BEEN BOOTED
out of Maryland three hundred years earlier. About eight miles out of
Chesterfield, it lay on as yet unincorporated land, and so no law touched it.
You could get just about anything you wanted at the Wigwam, and since vice
is always a growth product, it was jammed—gambling, drinking, accom-
modating gals, cigarette smoke. Sitting at the bar was a chunky fellow who
beamed with certitude, machismo, and gangster charisma, in a well-fitted
pinstripe suit, his curly dark hair glistening with pomade. He was unusually
handsome. His name was Pete Ontos, of the Baltimore Ontoses, and he
claimed descent from the boys at Thermopylae. He also claimed descent
from Socrates, Plato, Aristotle, and the guy who invented the sandal—maybe
so, maybe not—who would ever question Pete on such a delicate topic?

As Pete surveilled the headquarters of his kingdom, the bartender
approached with a phone.

"Boss, it's that Negro undertaker."

"What the hell does *he* want?"

But as he took the instrument, his tone became more suave. He had
the reputation of a man folks could trust, even love. He could fix anything,
make troubles disappear in a cloud, get a kid into any college. The price:
only your soul and bank account.

He was actually descended from Baltimore Greek crime family aristocracy, several generations of restaurateurs, bankers, lawyers, insurance agency executives, and strip bar owners who, as they prospered, acquired political power and authority, beating the less organized Italians to the controls of the bay city. He was in charge of the Eastern Shore enterprise, and big things were predicted for him if he didn't waste his talent chasing gash.

"Why, Daddy Renfro, nice to hear from you. What can I do for you?"

His face clouded as he listened.

"I hear you. Daddy. White boy agitating, stirring up trouble. Not good you, not good me. But my counsel is for you to handle it. Any way as you see fit. Don't think him being white, your boys being black has any play on this table. You do what you think is right, make it go away quiet, and nothing will be said, I give you my word."

Nick lifted the garbage can and poured tins of beans, beer bottles, Jell-O packages, empty cereal boxes, bloody butcher's paper, chicken carcasses, and the whatever of white civilization into the bin of his truck. What these folks ate! What they threw away! It sickened him because he saw more protein in a garbage can than a dark family got to eat in a week.

He turned to pick up another can and empty it, but suddenly he saw a black Cadillac limo churn down the alley behind the big houses and pull up. Out popped a dapper boy called Jimmy, nephew to Daddy Renfro.

"Daddy wants to see you."

"I'm working, man."

"Best not disappoint Daddy."

The door opened.

Nick climbed in and found himself in conference with Daddy, the undertaker, a gigantic, sagacious man who by his import and reputation was clearly the acknowledged king of Libertyville. He wore the dead-black suit, tie, and shoes of his profession and had dead-black eyes as well, mournful and grief-stricken always.

"And so, war hero Nick. Daddy is hearing things."

"I can't help what Daddy hears."

"I'm hearing Nick has a white visitor. I'm hearing Nick and this white man called Johnny Tuesday are asking questions. People are talking, Nick. The white folks could notice. That is not a good thing."

"What I do is my business. It's a free country. I fought for it."

"That's the problem, ain't it? You went away to war, you thought it would all be different when you got back. And it ain't. On top of that your girl up and left you. Like Bess, she went to the big city, leaving country cripple Porgy far behind. Nick, it ain't hard to see what's under your blanket."

"It ain't being nothing about that."

"Our time will come, Nick. It will, God knows, it will. But not soon. For now, we must keep orderly. In Libertyville we can't let them know how unhappy we is, and how wrong it is. No, sir. If we agitate them, they visit us. I've seen it, Nick. Fine black folks in burning tar, screaming in pain while the white folks dance around them, all corn-liquored up, waiting to get themselves some toasty souvenir fingers. Is that how you see an end to Libertyville, Nick? 'Cause that's where you be heading. And you be taking us along."

"I said, it ain't nothing about that."

"Best not be. 'Cause if you make them white folks angry, before they visit you, Daddy will. You hear me, boy?"

CHAPTER 4

I T WAS QUIET AT NICK'S LITTLE CABIN. FEBRUARY, NO BUGS TO CHITTER, no birds to squawk, no foxes to snarl, no owls to hoot. Silence lay like the dark right there at the edge of the marshes where the land grew toward insubstantiality as it gradually yielded to river.

"ON THE LEFT! GET THAT GUN ON THE LEFT! Nelson, move your squad through that gulch. We'll cover. Get that flamethrower into—"

Shrouded in a hammock on Nick's porch, the man now called Johnny writhed and twisted, then came awake.

Nick rushed to him, the eternal stretcher-bearer.

"Easy man, easy, you okay, war's over."

Johnny blinked, tried to settle.

"What? Huh! What the—! Oh, Christ!"

"You had it bad, man. You's back there."

"I'm okay, I'm okay."

"The screamin'-meemies! Heard 'em in the field hospitals all the damn time."

"I'm fine. I have dreams once in a while, that's all."

"Dreams! Man, you back in hell! Yes, sir. Don't know where you was, but it wasn't no dreamland."

"I scream here, at night. I didn't scream up front. No time for screaming."

"Where were you, man?"

"Makes no difference now."

"ETO? PTO?"

"I'll just say this—they got their money's worth out of me."

He sat in the reading room of the Chesterfield Public Library, with a bound volume of the year 1945 according to the *Chesterfield Courier*, which lay before him. Next to it he'd placed a note tablet, yellow paper, and scrawled some observations: "Bag—how much could it weigh? What's that translate to in $?"

And below that: "Necklace? Insurance settlement? If not, could Tap be HELPING robbers?"

And below that: "Drew Pearson, Washington Merry-Go-Round."

He was done. He got up, checked around to see that nobody paid him any attention, and walked out.

He thought: Okay, now you got some investigating to do.

Next stop: a country store nestled in the flat plains of the Eastern Shore, among acres and acres of tobacco. He parked his old Chevy and walked in.

"Help ya, mister?" asked the storekeep.

"I'll take one of those burlap bags of feed."

"Corn or oats?"

"No matter. Corn, I guess. And . . . you carry magazines? You know, news, sports, gardens, that sort of thing?"

"Behind you. On the shelf."

"Great. Now, syrup. For waffles. I know you got that."

"Yes, sir."

The transaction completed, Johnny headed back to town, lifting a pall of dust in the empty tobacco fields as the leaves themselves, stripped from the stalks, now hung drying in a thousand weathered barns scattered randomly about, built exactly for that purpose. Later they would be cured, then baled into hundred-pound cubes for the cigarette or cigar companies.

A wan February sun turned the fields the color of grits. Lines of leafless trees offered tangled imagery to the picture. Otherwise the only feature was the lack of an only feature.

Suddenly, a truck was behind him, emerging out of the dust, paralleling him, and with a clang of metal bending against metal, it cracked hard against him, pushing him off the road. He skewed to a stop, ripping up more dust and understanding this was no random accident.

Four men, burly heavyweights in overalls, hard-used fedoras, were suddenly on him, eyes the color of pewter, faces tight with the expectation of the thrill of violence. One cracked a baseball bat on his hood.

"You git on out here, bud."

Johnny climbed out, approaching them. Their obvious leader, who was the biggest but had the smallest mustache, which looked as if it had been borrowed from the midway's bearded lady, smirked because he thought he'd be throwing a few punches in the next few seconds. He was wrong.

"Boys, this here's the fella called Johnny Tuesday who done be agitating our damn darks—"

Without a word, a wasted motion, a hesitation, Johnny hit him so hard in the mouth he'd shit teeth for a month. He staggered, nose shattered and producing a sudden torrent of variegated fluids, and went down ass-first into the dust, blood slobbering like drool everywhere.

One man headed back toward the cab, but Johnny Tuesday tracked him. He turned as the baseball bat came on a horizontal sweep for his head. Ducking it, he let it pass by, enjoyed the breeze, then drove a jab into the hitter's left gut, breaking a rib. Which went wider open, the fellow's eyes or mouth? Didn't matter much as Johnny stepped hard into him and pounded that gut to jelly, taking all fight and much hope of a future from him. Down he went, and to add to his woes he began to shit up his pants. The third saw the destruction wrought so far, thought the better of matching blows with such an expert manufacturer of them, and turned to race toward the nothingness at the horizon, lifting dirt with his boots. At that moment the fourth man emerged from behind the truck with a shotgun.

Johnny's hand flashed, again with blurry speed, and out came a .45 auto from a shoulder holster under his sport coat, cocked, unlocked, and leveled.

"You drop that gun, sir, or I will send you on a hayride to hell."

The gun fell; the man shrank.

Johnny strode to the fallen leader, who was nursing a busted head, nearly unrecognizable for the immensity of the blood flow.

"What's your name, you egg-sucking peckerwood?"

"Duane, sir," said the broken man.

"I got you marked, Duane. I see you lurking around me, I will beat you into the box in four seconds flat. You and the other bumpkin shit-kickers, you get so far out of this county you can't find no one ever heard of Eastern Coast, Maryland, or whatever this dusty tobacco country is called."

He turned, picked up the bat of man number two, who was just coming alert again, and contemptuously dropped it on him.

"Here, give this to the girls' softball team, Miss Mary. They sure can hit better than you."

By the illumination of automobile lights, a puddle of syrup oozed across an old wood floor, where it encountered a burlap bag full of old copies of *Time* and *Life* and *Colliers* and soaked it. From the burlap bag's condition, this odd experiment had been run many times before. For guidance, the picture of the bloodstain in the bank lay next to the experimental ersatz maple bloodstain.

The bag was dragged across the floor, where earlier streaks of different density and color testified that someone—the fellow calling himself, what was it again? Oh, yeah, Johnny—wasn't doing this just for the damn fun of dragging a bag through syrup.

"Yeah, that's it. Goddammit!" he whooped on a note of triumph.

Suddenly, Nick's voice came from the dark.

"Thought I'd find you here in this old icehouse. Seen the lights. Jesus Christ what are you—?"

"Trying to figure out how much that bag weighed. If I can get that, then I can work on what was in it and—"

"Man, we got bigger problems. Folks know you're here. Daddy Renfro pulled me out and warned me today 'bout you. This town is full of spies, Mr. Johnny Tuesday."

"Some boys tried to talk me out of hanging around too." He showed bloodied knuckles. "Too bad for them."

"Jesus Christ, you can't go round stirring up the Man out here on the Shore. It's deep Mississippi with a bay."

"Anybody tries to lay a hand on me gets busted up hard, black, white, yellow, brown, green, purple from flying saucers."

"You don't got no idea what you playing with down here. You could get folks killed. These poor dark folks, never been nowhere, never going nowhere, you're gonna get 'em burned out of their homes. What about them?"

Johnny paused. "Well, you know, you are making me see something I didn't—"

Suddenly, a bell started clanging. It wasn't for Christmas.

"Nothing good about a bell in the night," said Johnny.

"Oh, hell. Night Riders. Shit, man, we got to get back into the trees or we get all shot up."

But Johnny had already gone to his trunk and opened it.

"Nobody shoots me up."

He emerged from the trunk with a Thompson M1A1 submachine gun, Marine-style, with a combat sling. He checked the thirty-round magazine before he inserted it, and Nick saw that the cartridges were white-tipped, and he knew what that meant. Johnny cocked the gun.

In a glade of trees outside of Libertyville, Duane, his head and face bandaged, addressed a loose gaggle of country boys with an assortment of rifles and shotguns. Standing next to him in a business suit was Pete Ontos, the Capone of the Eastern Shore, his sleek hair glistening.

"We goin' shoot up the darks," Duane, would-be Frank Nitti, instructed with a saliva-powered yell. "Blast windows, flowerpots, parked cars, anything you see. Dark comes at you with an axe, you blast him too. Self-defense. These people got to be told the way it is. They forget now and then and have to be reminded."

The men muttered in assent, then went to the cars.

"That what you want, Mr. Ontos?"

"That's it, Duane. You do it good, now, you hear?"

"Yes, sir."

The four cars, lights ablaze, moved at a stately, almost ceremonial pace down the dusty approach road to Libertyville, bouncing as they pulled over the tracks. When the convoy was about forty yards from the maze of shanties, a figure rose from a gully before them, heavily armed, heavily hatted.

"This ain't a good idea," said Nick.

"Relax, Stretcher-bearer. I know what I'm doing."

He fired. Flash, a cascade of spent cartridges, a cannonade of smoke—but most remarkably, a line of tracers flew out and hit in front of the lead car, kicking up a spray of dust.

The cars halted. Silence, stillness.

Johnny fired again. This time he stitched up a line parallel to the cars, the tracers filling the darkness with illumination, particularly as they struck stone and bounded away.

Night tracer: like the Fourth of July in hell.

Silence.

"Next burst is low into the cars, leg shots pin you where you are. Then I fire a tracer into each gas tank and you die in fire."

The doors of the four cars exploded as men burst from them, tossing weapons aside, racing crazily away.

"Look at the boys run!" Nick shouted. "Like hogs from the man with the axe!"

Pete, back in the glade of trees, couldn't quite make out what was happening, but suddenly, in raw panic, his Night Riders fled past him on foot, crazy with fear.

Pete grabbed one.

"The niggers got machine guns! The niggers got machine guns!"

Back at Nick's crib, Johnny secured the weapon while Nick watched.

"They'll leave you alone for a while. They'll figure it out soon enough, and it's me they'll want. So I'm gonna get out of town for a while."

"I hope you're right. I don't want 'em coming back with their own burp guns."

"You watch yourself, now. I'll let you know when I'm back, but I won't be hanging out here anymore."

At the Wigwam the next morning Pete, in his suit, his hair pomaded and glinting, sat at the bar, on the phone.

"Baltimore, DA5-2238, thank you."

He waited a second.

"It's Pete. Let me talk to Mr. Dalikos, please."

Another second.

"Gus," he said when Dalikos came on, "we have a situation down here that could mess up all our big score plans."

"Pete, calm down. If it ain't the FBI and it ain't the New York wops, it can be handled."

Pete told his tale.

"I know he's not from New York, but maybe's he's some kind of under-cover man, I don't know, state cop, maybe FBI, IRS, nobody knows. Some-how the name 'Johnny Tuesday' is part of it, sounds like a racket guy, but I never heard of him. He's really good with that gun. I need professionals. You know who I need, Gus."

"I have just the answer, Pete. You worked with them before."

"I'm glad you see it my way, Gus. With them it's four against one and we'll make this go away."

In Libertyville's nicest building, Daddy Renfro sat behind his desk. He was listening earnestly to the sheriff, in khakis, with a Sam Browne belt and a badge.

". . . and you know I believe in white to white and colored to colored. That's why I don't send my boys down here to smack heads, like some do. I like it peaceful, Daddy."

Daddy nodded as if he were listening with deep respect and as if he hadn't heard this three hundred times before.

"Yes, suh. I hears you," said Daddy in his talking-to-the-Man voice.

"We both 'member the bad old days, where something like this happen and a dark man ends up hanging in the trees."

"Yas, suh. Them days was bad, Lord know."

"So you got to take care of this, Daddy. Any agitators down here, you got to run 'em out before no trouble starts. You hear me, Daddy? Nothing but trouble for all of us any other way. You got to get that machine gunner out of here. You hear me, Daddy?"

"Yas, suh. I surely does."

Jimmy stepped in.

"Pete Ontos, line one, Mr. Daddy."

"Daddy, you goin' hear from lots o' folks today."

"That be the truth, Sheriff."

"We understand each other?"

"Yes, suh."

"I leave you be for now, then."

He got up to leave.

As the sheriff turned, Daddy gave him a look signifying contempt. Then he turned to the phone, saying to Jimmy, "Lord, I hate talking to this punk-ass Greek."

Reluctantly, he picked up the phone and went back to his feigned servitude demeanor.

"Mr. Ontos? Yes, sir, I know. I'm very upset myself. Yes, bad business, for white and black alike. I know who it is, I know what has to be done. Yes, sir, that is correct. You handle yours, I'll handle mine. Yes, sir, it will be taken care of," he said, hanging up. He turned.

"Boy, get me Baltimore, the Cat Club."

He waited till a voice answered.

"George, it's Daddy Renfro, I have to talk to your father."

Another second.

"Big George, how are you, brother? Praise the Lord. Yes, you've heard. Bad news travel fast, don't it? Big George, I need a man take care of this business. Yes, that's right, I don't want no guns, I don't want this place turning into no Dodge City. The white po-lice leave us alone long as we ain't shooting nothing up. It's just Willie-cut-Willie to them and they don't give a damn. So I need a fella good with a razor. He don't even have to be named Willie."

CHAPTER 5

THE DOOR SAID, "DREW PEARSON/WASHINGTON MERRY-GO-ROUND."
Johnny entered, took his hat off; a receptionist looked up. He told
her who he was, why he was here. She nodded, then slid through the
door to the next room, exposing the shabby squalor of the newsroom.
At a battered Royal Underwood sat a harried-looking bald man whose
seriousness was expressed not merely in his mopey demeanor but in the
stubble of mustache that pulled his face downward toward hell. In shirtsleeves, tie loosened around his open neck, he sat typing grimly away. The
room seethed with the smoke of the cigarette that hung from his lips and
the pile of them in an ashtray. Johnny caught a whiff of tobacco density
that could flatten a cat.

"Betty," said the writer, the cigarette dancing between his lips but not
shedding itself of a half inch of ash, "you know I'm on deadline."

"Yes, sir. But he said you'd covered him at a White House ceremony
and he wanted to thank you and—"

Drew looked beyond Betty, immediately underwent a demeanor
change, and stood to put out a hand as Johnny came in.

"Mr. Pearson, sir."

"Well, Sergeant. How are you, son? Lord God, what, more than a year.
Come in, sit down, and tell me what I can do for you."

They heard Betty out front answer the phone.

"No, sir, he can't be disturbed. He— Oh, yes, Secretary Acheson, right away."

She came to the door, then entered.

"Betty, no inter—"

"But, sir, it's the secretary of state."

"That old drunk? Not now. I'm busy."

Pearson leaned back in his chair, sucking the life out of his cigarette, looking thoughtful as Johnny unveiled what had brought him here.

"Hmm," he said after a bit, "tell me more. There might be a story in this." When he was done, Pearson said, "Okay, I'll make some calls. Sounds like a good item."

"Mr. Pearson, any idea on where I could get some information on these Baltimore Greek people? That would be damned helpful."

Pearson scrunched up his forehead to suggest concentration, then said, "Can you get up to Baltimore? The *Sun* has a fine library. I'll call Neil Swanson—he's the boss, runs my column—and get you set up. It's at Charles and Saratoga, heart of downtown."

Two sleek black coupes roared down a country road on the Eastern Shore, flanked to forever by flats of off-season tobacco fields. In each pair of front seats sat a man in a fedora and his partner. All four looked smooth and tough—city tough, gangster tough, armed robber tough, Greek tough. Again they wore black aviator glasses, like General MacArthur's, but their demeanor suggested the only liberation they were interested in was their own. Jack, Harry, Markos, and Pete. All were smoking, none were smiling. They never smiled when they worked.

The bus station in downtown Chesterfield still had the glossy art deco lines and tropes of the thirties, when the nation seemed poised on the edge of the magical era of the bus. The magic having never quite arrived, the place looked like a movie set from a musical Busby Berkeley had shot ten years earlier, when Dick Powell still sang and danced, before he turned to gangster movies. A Greyhound pulled in to deposit passengers.

First all the white people got out. Then all the black. Finally, in a flashy double-breasted out-of-season cream suit with a carnation, a straw fedora, and a pencil mustache, a scrawny black man emerged. The sliver of the mustache atop his lip gleamed, and when he smiled, a diamond tooth sparkled. He looked around.

He saw Jimmy and Daddy Renfro's shiny Cadillac limo. With a bebop rhythm slopping musically through his limbs he crossed the street to it, looked at Jimmy like he was a servant, and started to get in the back, in Daddy Renfro's place.

Jimmy grabbed his sorry ass, threw him in the front seat, then went around and got in himself.

At the Wigwam, in the back room, Pete Ontos talked to the four men, who lounged about insouciantly. Duane, with his face still heavily bandaged, sat behind him. He looked like a bitter zombie.

"His name is Johnny Tuesday," said Pete. "It's a racket name, sure, but what town he's from, I don't know. Tough bastard and packing a machino. Means business. We've lost track of him. But I got Daddy Renfro's people looking out for him. When we get a place, Duane will guide you."

"He thinks he's a boxer," said Duane, "but if I get another chance, I'll—"

"Hey, Duane, don't get in the way or you'll need bandages for your bandages."

The boys laughed.

"Duane forgot to duck," said the leader, Jack Petrakis. "Hey, Duane, when we nail Johnny Tuesday, I'm going to let him belt you in the schnoz one last time for old times' sake before I pull down. Professional courtesy."

More laughter. Duane was not happy behind his bandages.

. . .

Outside Daddy's office, the banty, snappy out-of-towner had recovered his dignity and his cool, and was smoothing back his hair with Ol' Colored Joe's Number One Hair Slicker. His name was long forgotten, except by various urban police departments, and he went about under the trade name "Slice." Jimmy watched him apply the smoothing goo, getting it just right, until he was shined up like a dancing shoe, dapper as Fred Astaire, even to the spats.

"Look here, you little alley rat. Daddy Renfro is a great man. You give him any jive, I'll pound you like a tent peg into the ground."

"You be runnin' into this," said Slice, doing a blurry melody with his right hand, to produce a barber's chin-skinner. With a flick, he opened it, and four inches of shiny, shiny blade snapped out.

"So sharp it'll cut through to your neckbone afore you even notices you done been cut and all that red shit on the floor be from you."

Jimmy laughed, then hit him with a dead-ball look that promised mayhem, swift and bloody.

"You ain't so tough, country boy," said Slice.

"You best hope he don't turn me loose on your trash nigger ass, 'cause I like nothing more than busting yo diamond-face, ho-kicking, ain't-fought-no-man, razor-slicing pimp ass."

The office door opened; Daddy leaned out.

"Sir. Please."

Slice smirked, rose, and as he headed in, Jimmy saw that Daddy had a very scared-looking Willie, the police janitor, in there with him.

The town dump was an abscess on the bright pink gums of postwar America. Stench, rot, buzzards, slime, goo, crap, shit, mountains of it, on the theory that it would eventually just disappear, but it never did. The slight chill of a mild mid-Atlantic February seemed to preserve, even amplify, the various categories of disgust, but at least summer's flies and other small monsters were absent, although rats scurried about; it was their downtown.

Nick dumped his last barrel of trash, mostly eggshells, coffee grounds, and used Kleenex and condoms, and watched it tumble into a mess below of similar composition. When the can was empty, he tossed it into the back of the truck without affection, hearing the metal-on-metal boom. He went back to his cab. Now only back to the municipal yards, a quick hose-out, and he was finished with one more day in his glorious postwar life. He got into his cab.

"Oh, hell. I thought it was too quiet round here."

Johnny sat in the off-driver's side seat, smoking.

"Figured I'd find you here. Sooner or later. Man, this place stinks."

"I applied for a job as college president. It was taken, so I had to settle for this. Johnny Goddamn Tuesday, what you want? You sure shook up this town."

"And I didn't even kill anybody."

"You can't stay at my place. Spies everywhere."

"Don't worry about that. I need to get into the bank."

"Say what? You going to get me lynched for sure. You wanna be in the bank, you go in the way them boys did, guns blazing."

"I don't want money. I want information. I have to know what ties that rich tobacco man Tapscott to gangsters. He's the key. It has to be money. I have to see what his financial situation is."

"He's got a Cadillac financial situation. He's rich."

"You might be surprised. Anyhow, you can do it. There's an old colored janitor there. He could get us in late."

Johnny was going through files on the floor with the help of an angle-headed military flashlight. He kneeled amid rows of mute desks, adding machines, typewriters, ashtrays. It was the guts of the bank, where the actual work was done, the percentages figured, the tiny plus-minuses of 1 or so percent figured, always on paper, the sums at the end of each column exactly correct. He was in front of an open file that read "1945." Nick sat next to him, also sifting through files.

"As of February of 1945, there was nine hundred thousand–odd dollars in the Tapscott accounts, and there are references here to other trustee accounts and so forth. So there's a lot of dough."

"What's he doing with gang boys, then?" Nick asked. "Maybe it *was* just coincidence, not some kind of funny business."

"Nick, y'all better hurry," said the janitor. "I's gittin nervous."

"Okay, Mr. Jackson. We're almost finished," said Johnny Tuesday.

"He didn't need dough, that's for sure," said Nick. "Or maybe he couldn't take dough out of his own accounts. So what habits can a man have that he can't control and needs dough for? Black, white, don't make no difference. Only three I know. Liquor, drugs, and a ho."

"Forget hootch and reefer for this nervous Nellie. That leaves whores for Mr. Tapscott. Where's a man go in this town to get laid? I know there's one outside every city in America. It sells the workingman his monthly chunk of sin in rigged gambling, thin booze, and gals you wouldn't take home to Mama."

CHAPTER 6

JOHNNY MINGLED WITH THE WIGWAM CROWD. IT WAS NO SNAZZY PLACE with swells in dinner jackets and broads showing off their frontage—instead, a lot of workingmen, truckers, all drinking cheap booze and throwing their bucks away on roulette and other casino games. Smoke floated in the air, and cheesy jukebox bebop and big band rattled the rafters. Dolls, painted up like the chorines they'd never be, circulated, cadging drinks or other forget-it-alls out of them.

Johnny wandered around the joint, cigarette dangling, hat pushed back, figuring it out. At the craps table he put a few bucks down, lost, and put a few more down. But he was checking out the clientele, and he saw two guys across the table really hard about the bones. They stood out because they were in suits, not overalls, and had that "I, Gangster" look. One leaned forward to toss the dice, a little too intensely.

"Go, Mama, go, Mama, go, Mama, go! Damn, crapped out again!"

As he leaned forward, his jacket fell forward, and Johnny noticed the grip of a .357 in a shoulder rig. Johnny looked to his partner and noted a bulge under his arm too.

He slid up to the bar, where Pete was talking with another mob Greek, maybe a boss, from his deep sense of cool, to use the new word imported from the darks.

He overheard the chatter.

"That boy of yours ain't going flip on us? He shows all the signs."

"Harry's okay. Gets excited when he's loaded and has the dice in his hands. He's a good man on a job, though."

Johnny found an angle to peer inside the man's coat, checked, and saw the grip of a .357. More big artillery, a pro's piece of work.

He sat back, revolving on his stool, and gesturing the barkeep over.

"Say, pal, I'm all gambled out and I've still got money left. Any other action here? What about these dames, are they just decoration or can a fella relax with one of 'em in private?"

"It's a kind of a club, bud. If someone we know don't vouch for you, you don't get in."

Pete, overhearing this, licked his chops at the prospect of a new mark. He leaned in, giving Johnny a once-over.

"He looks okay to me, Chuck. Where you from, pal?

"Down south in Dixie. Been to Biloxi, been to Phenix City, been to N'Awlins. Good places, all. Fella can have some fun."

"What's your business?"

"Ce-ment. I was a Seabee in the war, learned all about it. My firm runs ce-ment trucks to construction sites. Hear the Maryland coast is going to get all developed once they build that bridge."

"You think ahead, chum. I like that. Okay, Chuck, let him go up."

In a room upstairs, Johnny sat with a tired-looking woman in her thirties, going on her sixties.

"Okay, mister, what'll it be. Straight lay is twenty, French is forty, and I'll take you around the world for seventy-five. Well, seventy, because you're cute."

"How much for information?"

"Hey, what is this?"

"I don't expect you to give nothing up because I'm so handsome.

Here's two hundred. Now you lie on the bed and moan like I'm the one giving you that trip around the world."

The gal lay on the bed. Johnny, with his foot, started shaking it, so the mattress springs cranked and clanked.

"AHHHH. OHHHHHH. MMMMMM."

"February, '45. Two years back. What was happening here? I mean with the gals. Anything odd?"

"AHHHHHHHH. Odd, like how? MMMMMMMM. OHHHHHH. The usual crap. Someone gets punched or cut nearly every week. Somebody gets knocked up and goes off to an old lady in Libertyville. AHH-HHHHH. Gals come and go. It's a whorehouse, like any whorehouse."

"Anything about a rich guy and some gal?"

"Hey, who you been talking to?"

"Keep moaning, sugar. You're in heaven. I just figured it out. What's the scoop?"

"I could get killed for this."

Johnny laid another hundred on the bed.

"OHHHHH. MMMMMMM. AHHHHHHH. Her name was Lucille. Colored gal, but real light. MMMMMMMMM. Anyhow, all of a sudden, it was right after that robbery, she's gone. Usually a gal NNNNNNNNNN tells her friends she's moving in with a john or trying a new town. We have a little party. Not this time. Lucille's just gone."

"You say right after the robbery."

"That's right, or right before. I don't remember exactly. No party, nothing. It was like she left town with the robbers. I didn't get no cake."

Johnny walked down the hall, unfucked, sure, $300 lighter, sure, but also $300 smarter. Another door opened and a big man stepped out, suavely buttoning the fly of his blue jeans. It was Duane, his nose still mummified. He and Johnny saw each other simultaneously, but Johnny was pro-boxer fast and nailed him with a power jab in the same nose. Duane took the big fall, all the way down to the floor, spitting blood. Johnny shook his hand, in a little pain.

"You got a hard face, peckerwood. Now you stay down there sucking broken teeth till I clear out or I will come back and mash your nose into grits."

He headed out.

Nick was walking back—a little wobble there—from his drinking in the Libertyville crib, when he heard a whisper coming from the bushes.

"Pssst. Stretcher-bearer. Over here!"

"Oh, shit. You didn't get killed in that place?"

"They tried, but history proves me hard to put down. Listen, you have to find out about some ho named Lucille. She worked at the Wigwam and disappeared about the time of the robbery. Thought is, some big rich white man took a fancy to—"

But Nick's demeanor changed suddenly.

"Say what, Jack? You don't call Lucille no ho, goddammit. White or not, some things a man can't say to me!"

"Easy, there, sir. Didn't mean anything. Don't know who this Lucille could be, except she worked the Wigwam in '44 and '45 while you were off dodging German steel, and she disappeared round about the time of the robbery. Maybe it's tied in, maybe it isn't."

Nick just went blank. He walked off, into the trees, Johnny following.

"She's your girl, I get it. You got a Dear John in a frozen hole in the Ardennes. Man said, Hey, boy, git your ass up, git out there and collect the wounded, and the wounded was you, from the crack in your heart."

"Nobody's damn business. Don't matter a thing. It's all over and done. She go off to whorin', that's what she do, that's what it is."

"Aren't you the tough one, though? But inside, it's still bleeding; I can smell the blood, lots of it. Arterial. Happened to a lot of guys, if it means anything, black, white, hell, it happened to the Japs and the Krauts too."

"No one would tell me. She's gone, that's all. Yeah, I see, she got tired of waiting for her PFC to come home to nothing but the same old shit, and the Wigwam offered something nice, and off she went. Some white man got her pregnant. He probably drowned her in the marsh. Lots of marshes around here."

"What was her last letter?"

"Ain't no last letter. No goodbye, no Dear John. She just up and disappeared."

"What was her last name?"

"Everstill. Lucille Everstill."

"Okay, we got to get back into that bank, see if anyone gave Miss Everstill a chunk of dough by check in February of 1945. If it's so and it's Tapscott, that's all the proof I need."

"Who are you, Johnny Tuesday? Why is this your fight? You going get yourself killed, and me along with you, for what? You after that money or that diamond necklace? Or maybe working for another mob?"

"I got a stake in it, you bet, and it isn't money or diamonds. The day I leave town, unless I'm in a box, I'll tell you, unless you're in a box. The problem now is Tapscott. From him, I find out who planned it, who set it up. That's the man I want."

"Mr. Tapscott ain't goin' tell no white-trash southern fried hick town racket guy called Johnny Tuesday nothing."

"He'll tell me or he'll tell the devil in hell, whichever."

The gal's face, swollen, wet, smeared with mucus, tears, and blood, lay crossways in three beams of light. It was the only thing visible in a room full of men.

A hard slap belted her. She was a tough one, though, and blinked back tears.

"Good punch, Duane. Way to hit a tied-up whore!"

"That Duane. He packs a mean right. Duane, I'll check your knots, make sure she doesn't get up and beat the shit out of you."

Duane, under more bandages, was not happy with his station in life, which was at the end of the shit chute.

"Look, honey, we don't take no joy smacking in dames. Just tell us what happened, what he said, what he looked like, so we can put Duane back in his cage."

"I told you, mister. Straight lay. No French, nothing funny. Didn't talk much. A john, like all johns. He got what he wanted, I—"

Duane hit her again.

"See, it bothers me that a fine judge of men like you don't see the difference between Duane, who's stupid, and me, who's smart. We ain't the same guy. Duane, show her how stupid you are. Count to eight by twos."

"Nine, sixty-four, one hunnerd, 'lebenty-'leven!" some future comedian interjected.

Laughter. Duane was very unhappy.

His fist flew toward the gal, but another, quicker hand intercepted it and pushed him back.

"Easy, Slapsy Maxie."

The smarter fellow leaned in, addressing Zelda from two inches.

"You had three hundred. Nobody pays that for a straight lay. You weren't sweated up, your sheets weren't sweated up. There was no man stink in your room, no sex smell. There wasn't no envelope full of goo in the toilet. Now, I'm about to ask Duane here to check your cookie to see if it's all wetted-up with use. Do you want me to do that, honey?"

"Christ."

"Duane, get ready for the treat of your life."

Laughter.

"Duane's finally going to get some cooch!"

Laughter.

"All right, all right," Zelda said. "He wanted info about a gal who worked here, then didn't, right at the time of that robbery. Lucille, light-skinned dark gal. Someone was saying some rich boy knocked her up, then maybe paid her off or paid someone to take her to the marshes. I don't know. But that's all."

"Thank you, darling. See, that wasn't so bad. Duane, thank the gal for the nice time and set her free."

Duane cut her throat.

CHAPTER 7

IN PETE'S OFFICE, THE TWO EXECUTIVES CHARTED THE SPRING MARKETING campaign.

"The late Zelda gave him Tapscott. If he gets to Tapscott, the whole thing falls apart, the big score is ruined, New York sees weakness and moves in, and this time Uncle Gus can't do a thing about it."

"But we can use Tapscott to set him up. Call that—"

"It's no good."

"Pete," said Jack Petrakis, "make the call and set up a meet with this guy. Only we'll be the ones who meet him."

"I don't want to go that way. The farther I stay from this, the better. How's this? I'll get a dark to go to Johnny Tuesday's dark and say another dark who works for Tapscott has info. He'll have to go for that, and he'll trust the darks; he seems to like darks. We'll get him someplace and that's when you guys gun him."

"That would work. Okay, I'll tell the boys to put on their Texas Ranger hats because we're going to Bonnie-and-Clyde this Mr. Tuesday."

It was a Savage replica of Browning's A5, a humpback five-round semi-automatic shotgun. With a short twenty-inch barrel, it looked like a BAR with a crew cut. Known for ease of manipulation owing to that short barrel, it could launch five 12-gauge charges in less than two seconds. Now its owner carefully began to thread the shells into the tube beneath the barrel.

The owner was Johnny, in shirtsleeves. He carried his .45 auto in an elaborate leather shoulder holster, an S. D. Myres rig that had been well used by his father, as had the pistol, a Great War relic. He was in the ice-house. He set the shotgun down in the back seat, next to his Thompson M1A1, also cocked and locked; a few full magazines were stacked next to it.

Then he heard a sudden noise.

Johnny whirled, drew.

"Whoa, it's only me," said Nick. "Don't shoot. Figured I'd find you here."

"Then that's my stupidity. I shouldn't lay up at the same place twice."

"Jesus Christ, man, you going to war or something?"

"Didn't tell you. There's new guns in town. I made three of them at the Greek's. Big-city boys, fancy suits, packing big bad guns. They're here for me."

"I didn't do much shooting in the war, but I guess I can handle a gun."

"You been shot at enough, Stretcher-bearer. Go home. You're strictly noncombat. This is my kind of play."

"Johnny Tuesday, I can stand and fight."

"You'll just get in the way. Now you're looking for me to tell me something, right? Longer you're here, the more danger you're in, till I handle these tough guys, so give it up straight."

"Fella named Lonnie, who's a nephew of a fellow named Jake, came to me. Jake's a gardener at Tapscott's. Jake heard you were asking about Tapscott. Says he knows something but he's 'fraid to be seen. He wants to set up a meet."

"It's an ambush. I smell ambush all over it. They want it far out of town so they don't attract attention."

"Just telling you what Lonnie told me. There's a truck farm once owned by a family called Nelson, out Jason Road, four miles south of town. Just old rotted farmhouse, outbuildings, and fallow fields. Maybe white teenagers go there to smooch on Saturday night. Lonnie says Jake'll be there at 9 a.m. tomorrow, up at the house, when everybody thinks he's at church. Maybe these boys'll be there instead of Jake?"

"These boys have done this kind of work before. They'll know I'll be fidgety and quick to shoot at the farmhouse. They'll hit me on the road coming up to the farmhouse."

"Johnny Tuesday, you a crazy man. Four on one. Ain't no odds at all. You must think you a goddamned war hero or something!"

"Not at all. It's a joke, Mr. Nick. On them. See, they think they're hunting me. Turns out—I'm hunting them."

CHAPTER 8

I T WAS DAWN. LIGHT FILTERED THROUGH BARE-LIMBED OLD-GROWTH trees. Looked to be a sunny day, if brisk, as late February usually was this close to both sea and beach. A dirt road in flat country; in the distance odd lines of more bare trees cut up otherwise unplanted land. The robbery crew, plus bandaged Duane, stood in the road. Each carried a long weapon, same as two years before, serious professional artillery, mob bank-job style: the leader holding a carbine, a couple with pump shotguns, one with a BAR. Then there was under-gunned amateur Duane with a Winchester lever gun, deer hunter–style. He stood a little apart.

"He'll come that way," Jack said, "turn off the main road, disappear into that little dip for a second, then he'll be here."

"Jack, suppose some other bohunk shows up at nine?"

"That's why Duane's way up front. He makes Johnny, lets the car pass, signals us, and we open up. I ain't taking no chances on this gun boy. When he's up to you, pump him full of everything you got. I want that car looking like Frank Hamer went to war on it, got that?"

"Jack, you know I ain't no good without my morning coffee."

Laughter.

"Duane, you git on down there. Put that rifle away. I don't want you doing no shooting. You're the scout, okay?"

Duane nodded and departed wordlessly. He was done talking, because each time he opened his mouth, one of these city fucks would twist his words in some way and make him the butt of more scorn and chuckles. Being big and fast to fist and boot, he'd never had a taste of such a diet. He didn't care for it, wanted this thing over and everything back as it was, with his bulk making him Mr. Ontos's number one outside guy.

"You trust that hillbilly?" Markos asked Jack after Duane had trotted off.

"Maybe he'll run into a bullet too. Things happen on this kind of job. Let's get under cover, boys."

As he spoke, from the road tree line half a mile out, the quick flash reflection of sun on binocular lenses winked brightly, but the boys were so jived up at the prospect of rat-a-tat-tat they didn't notice.

Johnny lay in the trees in the prone. No tie, no coat. He wore a dark shirt, khaki suspenders, and a pair of lace-up boots blousing his wool pants. He had his fedora on, his .45 in the fancy shoulder rig, and the Thompson before him. He looked like Robert Jordan in Spain. He crouched, watching through the binoculars.

He saw the four boys slide into the bushes, laughingly, as Duane disappeared farther down the road. Each big guy wore tear-shaped dark sunglasses, like the aviators of the war, of whom he'd seen many. Flyers earned their Ray-Bans going against the high sun to hunt and be hunted; when you sported them in civvies you were just a show-off punk.

Looking at the square Bulova watch against his hairy arm, Jack read 9:05 a.m. Someone slapped a bug to oblivion.

"Ow!"

Jack watched down the road, his carbine at the ready.

"Jack, I am getting ate up alive."

"That's 'cuz you eat so much Eye-talian. Bugs love the sugar in the Eye-talian tomato sauce," Markos yelled.

"Shut up, goddammit," yelled Jack, "I see it, boys, git ready."

Clickity-click, clickity-clack, bolts, pumps, slides were thrown, the boys squirmed and settled.

The car, a '38 Chevy coupe, chugged along.

A cloud of birds rose from some trees.

A bunny rabbit looked around, then disappeared.

The bare branches clacked and scraped as the brisk push of breeze rubbed them against each other.

The brownish grass flattened in a little more breeze.

The car disappeared in the dip and a few seconds later came out.

It passed Duane, who leaned forward, eager to see his nemesis.

He saw . . . nothing.

Panic hit him.

The car passed him.

He turned, he ran.

"Goddamn that hillbilly," shouted Jack as the car was upon them without warning. "OPEN UP!"

The men in sunglasses rose and fired.

The car chugged along as slug after slug tore into it. Windows disintegrated into perforations and then cascaded, and the door burst with holes; the sound of the metal tearing and the guns firing was immense.

Each shooter fired as fast as he could, shell casings pouring from the hot breech of each weapon.

The car, its tires flattened, its windows busted out, its body turned into a cheese grater, faltered, lurched spastically to the right, and went into a ditch.

Dust floated about, mixed with gun smoke; the stench of burned powder hung as heavy as stormy weather in the air.

The four men rose.

The engine was still running, and the rear tire, though flattened, continued to rotate in gear as beneath it the other rear tire spun in the dust, kicking up a cloud.

Harry with the BAR ran across road, aligned his weapon, and fired another burst into the cab. But nothing happened.

Jack, Pete, and Markos went to the driver's-side door, popped it open.

They saw a stick jammed into the steering wheel, a brick lashed to the gas pedal. Without thinking, Harry fired another burst into the engine block, the engine finally gave up, the rear tire ceased, the dust was no longer flung in the air.

"What the fuck?"

"Where is he?"

"Cocksucker lit out."

"He must be—"

It dawned on them simultaneously, and they rotated to the right, where the dust and smoke still drifted in the road. Then it cleared, revealing Johnny standing with his Thompson clamped under his right elbow, oriented toward them.

Duane, having come to rest in the bushes with his deer rifle, was one hundred feet from Johnny with a clear shot.

"Oh, shit."

He tossed his rifle away and began to run again.

The four men on the road faced Johnny. A long, still moment passed.

Then they opened up, shooting wildly from the hip.

Mr. Johnny Tuesday brought Thompson to shoulder, aimed, and despite bullet strikes all about him, fired a four-round burst.

Three of the four gangsters ran for the ditch at the side of the road.

Markos seemed frozen, then turned slowly, tumbled to the ground, tried to pick himself up, and saw his chest was smeared with blood. He flattened into the dust.

In the ditch, a jumble of voices arose.

"He got Markos."

"Son of a bitch, kill his ass."

"Come on, goddammit, let's get down there and finish—"

"SHUT UP, GODDAMMIT!"

They quieted down.

"Get the cars," commanded Jack. "We roll down there hunched low in the cars and pull up to where he is. Otherwise, he just guns us in this hole."

Two cars blasted out of the trees, their brakes screeching as they put a stop to the acceleration, then, under control, pivoted to the right.

Two in one car, the third in the other, crunched low to be protected by the heavy steel of the cab, just peering over the lip of the dashboard.

"GO! GO! Let's nail this motherfuck—"

The cars screamed down the dirt road.

Johnny hunched over the lip of the ditch. He had the Savage autoloader against his shoulder. The cars bore down on him; he felt like a hunter facing charging buffalo or a bazooka operator and a German Panzer.

Johnny found his point of aim, fired coolly, the big gun bucking, a spent shell popping from the breech.

The grille of the first car was hit square by the twelve members of the double-aught fleet, and the car shivered, then veered to the left, into a ditch, in a cloud of dust.

The second car bore on.

Johnny fired again, his first shot off, blowing a headlamp away. He fired once more, this time blowing twelve holes in the grille, rupturing the steering, and the vehicle, bereft of control, faltered, then rolled into a ditch in another cloud of dust.

The driver was shaken up, got ahold of himself, and began to slither across the seat to get out the driver's-side door.

By this time Johnny had come around and was directly across from the driver's side.

He fired, punching twelve holes in that door.

Pete took three of the .32-caliber slugs in the low back as he emerged from the car. He went down but was up in a second, drawing a heavy magnum revolver from his shoulder holster and struggling around the car to close with his antagonist.

Shooting from the hip, Johnny put a 12-gauge double-aught into his breastbone, and the charge smacked him so hard he flip-flopped like an acrobat hit by a locomotive.

Jack and Harry watched from nearby trees.

"Jesus Christ, he's got a fucking elephant gun!"

All was quiet.

The road separated the two surviving gunmen from their stalker. Jack still had his carbine, and Harry the BAR.

"Boy, do we need that tail gunner now. Where is the bastard? I can't see him."

"He must be in that ditch across the road."

"Nah, he took off like a rabbit."

"What do you want to do, Jack? This guy is goddamn good."

"Well, all I can think is we got to get him under fire from two angles, cut down his movement. I'll go to the right of Pete's car, you go to the left of our car. He's got to be in that ditch right across the road. If he sticks his head out, we hit him from both directions.

Johnny found a culvert under the road. Tommy gun in hand, he low-crawled through the drainage ditch, coming up on Jack's side.

As he and Harry moved to their positions, Johnny had them flanked.

He fired a long burst, left to right, bringing down Harry in the general distribution of lead. It recalled many such encounters in the Pacific. But his gun ran dry.

Flinching, Jack saw him dump the gun, and before Johnny could get to his .45, Jack leveled the carbine at his guts from a range of fifteen feet.

Another moment of silence, except for the hard breathing of the men.

"Well, the great Johnny Tuesday, out of ammo. Ain't that a shame? Hey, this is for Harry."

He pulled the trigger.

Snap. He was out of ammo too.

Now both men were down to shoulder-holstered handguns.

The leader unbuttoned his double-breasted coat, shucked it to reveal a .357 Smith in a leather shoulder holster, same as Johnny's .45, though, lacking Mr. Myres's tooling, not as pretty.

"You know what, chump. I been here before. I shot over twenty guys in my time. You think you have a chance against me? How many you shot?"

"Somewhere between one and one-fifty, sport. Not counting the ones I got with a bayonet or grenade."

Jack went for the big revolver. He was fast, very fast. But Johnny was just as fast. Both shots sounded simultaneously.

Johnny spun, hit. The leader stood, face numb, but seemingly otherwise safe. However, there was a hole in his left aviator lens. Suddenly blood poured copiously from under the dark glass. He plunged into the grass.

Whatever the war, killing in battle is always exhausting, particularly after the first hundred. Johnny was drained blank.

He sat down on the gully edge heavily, breathing hard, and wiped the sweat off his brow. A brisk breeze played in the bare tree limbs, clacking as before. Nice to be alive to hear it, feel it, breathe it.

He bled: left shoulder.

He pulled his shirt open, saw what would be called a flesh wound. Easy to make fun of if it wasn't your flesh. The wound, a hole in a sea of bruised yellow skin, oozed blood and stung like hornets at a square dance. At least no bones broken, no arteries severed. He'd been wounded before—more than once. Thus the sight of his own blood carried little weight, but it still hurt like shit. Those hornets. He tied a handkerchief around it.

He got up, climbed back to the road. Both gangster cars were inoperable by reason of a forty-five-degree cant into the gully, as was his old Chevy, by reason of holes everywhere.

Gathering his Savage and already wearing his Thompson M1AI on its sling over the shoulder, he realized he had a lot of walking to do.

He took off, cross-country for security. The land was barren, if furrowed by generations under the plow. Though new seedlings wouldn't be laid in until spring, still a few months off, the soil was being prepared by applications of methyl bromide, which sterilized it against bugs, weeds, anything the planters didn't want. It might have killed wounded ex-soldiers too, for the stench of the chemical was like a kind of nerve gas and in time made him a woozy pilgrim staggering awkwardly through the ridged field. At a certain point, he stowed the two long guns in a farmer's shed. Now and then he stopped to rest, re-examined his wound. It was always bloodier; he threw the handkerchief away, ripped off a sleeve, used that as a tourniquet. Then he took off again, through what seemed a doughboy's no-man's-land.

By one, he'd seen the spires—three—of Chesterfield City and, orienting on them, managed to steer around the quality areas to Libertyville.

He watched Nick's place from the trees, seeing finally that it was safe.

He went to it, slid in the door.

Nick was sitting there, in a coat, looking incongruously cold on a mild afternoon.

"Thank God you're here, Stretcher-bearer. I need stitches, fast."

Nick turned, his coat falling open. He was soaked in blood himself from a razor cut that had laid open his shirt and a portion of his arm. His face glistened with sweat.

"Sure. Soon as you stitch *me* up."

CHAPTER 9

"**N**ICK, I COULD GET IN SO MUCH TROUBLE FOR THIS," SAID SOMEONE quite frightened.

"Okay, I'm just about done."

That morning, Johnny Tuesday had been getting set up for his morning trek to the abandoned farmhouse, and he'd told Nick to be far away, not wanting him associated in any way with what might happen. But Nick couldn't be far away in his mind, which was now obsessed with Lucille Everstill—her photo had gotten him through a very tough war—and had to know more. So he'd returned to the bank and the terrified janitor had let him in.

The flashlight quickly scanned the filing cabinets: "Overdrafts (1945)," "Accounts in Arrears (1945)," "Foreclosures (1945)," a whole financial history of the year 1945 at the State Bank and Trust of Chesterfield. He finally came across "Bank Checks (1945)."

He seized it, began to riffle through the canceled checks, realized they were in chronological order, and went straight to February. The dates of the canceled checks approached February 20 and passed it, yielding nothing. He went on to the 21st, noting the gap for Washington's Birthday on the 22nd, and then the 23rd and saw a bank check, not revealing a source, for $5,000 made out to Lucille Everstill.

His Lucille.

He was surprised how hurt he still was. He couldn't blame her, however. Nothing but Libertyville here on the Shore, to be abused by black men, treated like trash by white, fucked hard by both. You deserved so much more, baby. I wanted to give it to you. Was going to, sure enough. That's why I worked so hard to build a good record in the war, so I could come back a somebody, not a nobody, and—

But what was the point?

He put the check back.

Inside an hour later, Nick moved through the shadows, trying to get back to Libertyville unobserved. He ducked when a police car came prowling along the street, knowing they'd shoot first at a Negro on white streets so late at night.

He crossed the bridge to Libertyville, walked its muddy streets, skipped where possible over puddles gleaming with moonglow, and came finally through the cranky shadows to his own rude shed.

Breathing a sigh of relief, he stepped in.

He sat. Too bad the crib wasn't open. Could use a shot of straight brown, and he took a second of pleasure imagining the burn as it—

Suddenly he went to war alert; something wasn't quite right.

He looked out a window, saw nothing.

He turned.

A flash.

A razor whipped through the air.

Blood spattered on the wall.

Blood ran down an arm.

Nick spilled back, jangled, cut bad.

Slice, seemingly from nowhere, had jumped him.

He cackled, fondling the straight razor in his hand, smiling, his diamond tooth showing.

"OOOeee, country boy. My name be Slice, 'cause that what I do.

Goin' slice you bad and deep. Bleed you out like a shoat squirming on a hook."

"Whoa, you ain't cuttin' me none, nigger!"

"Heeheeheee. Just watch, country."

The two stalked each other around Nick's small space in the rising light of dawn. Flash, the arm drove toward Nick, who managed to just barely tumble out of the way.

"You bleedin' dry, country. No blood, no speed. No speed, I's cut you more. More I cuts, more you bleeds, less speed you got. Heeheeheehee, this be yo' last few minutes. Say hello to Mister Saint Peter. Understand he be a Negro, but you gonna know fo' sure."

Swipe. He drew blood from Nick's chest. Nick was breathing heavily, groggy, covered in sweat.

He looked around, desperately, for some weapon, some defense. But every time he moved toward something, Slice cut him off and with a feint drove him back. It took Nick a bit of time to decode this rhythm. Light came into his eyes. It was all about angles.

If he could get a good angle to the weapon, he could possibly stand and fight.

He looked to the right, saw an iron on a shelf, began to ease toward it.

This info registered in Slice's eyes.

"Heeheeheehee."

They both could see the play. Could Nick get to the iron and use it to clonk Slice? Or would Slice cut him deep as he lunged?

Nick looked again at the iron, took a deep breath, and lunged.

Quick as death, Slice cut him off.

But Nick had anticipated this move, and fast as a running back he changed direction, launched himself the other way, toward a cheap bureau, and with a smash, he crushed its top with an elbow and reached between the splintered boards.

Slice corrected his lunge and went hard at Nick just as Nick spun and confronted him with the wicked point of an Army M3 trench knife, just the souvenir a GI would bring back from the war. He flipped off the metal scabbard, revealing the naked blade. It was phosphated black, a piercing streamline of spear point mounted atop a stacked leather grip and an S-shaped hilt, beloved of raiders in every theater.

"Hey, what? You goin' prick me with that pig-sticker, country? Hee-heehee, come ahead, boy, we see if you fast enough—"

He lunged in mid-sentence with a downward slash, but Nick, instead of withdrawing, saw that his survival resided inside the cut, not outside, and instead of backing up, he came off the X, took the cut in the shoulder again, and smashed chest-on-chest with Slice.

Face to face, chest to chest, maybe even nose to nose.

"Oh, my goodness," said Slice.

"You think I ain't used this on Krauts, fool?"

The knife was buried to the hilt in Slice's gut, but by chance Slice had put his hand out to deflect the thrust, and the point had entered mid-palm, penetrated, and under the power of Nick's rage been driven deep through to the body, thus pinning the killer to his own belly. He pulled, under the delusion it mattered, freed the hand at last, yanking the blade free as well, and a great torrent of blood spurted out.

Slice fell, squealed like a gutted hog, and went eternally still, the knife clattering away.

Nick picked up the weapon, looked at the long, dark blade now slathered with fluid.

"Only goddamn thing I got out of the Army."

Johnny stitched the long cuts on Nick's arm and chest.

Blood everywhere. Needlework, thread being drawn tight, slippery little knots.

Johnny had a cigarette in his lips as he worked, and had one eye squinted against the rise of smoke.

Blood on floor, blood on walls, blood on bashed bureau.

"Wouldn't have plasma around this joint, would ya?"

"In the Frigidaire."

Nick screamed.

"Goddamn, man, that hurts."

"Never said I was a surgeon. Ugh, almost, oh, shit—"

The needle had slipped from his slippery fingers, but it didn't fall because of the thread. He gathered it, began stitching again.

Soon Nick was stitching Johnny. Johnny's torso revealed a tapestry of other scars.

"Man, you're a human target."

Through smoke, Johnny said, "I caught some lead, that's all. ACK—"

"Sorry about that, almost done. Say what—?"

He wiped blood off Johnny's bare arm, revealing a tattoo: "USMC Semper Fi."

"Now I get it. A Marine! All them islands. No wonder you so crazy, screamin' in the night. How many islands?"

"I forget. Doesn't matter. You almost done?"

"I think you gonna live, Marine. At least another day. What islands you on?"

"I forget the names."

"Yeah, sure."

"You do the talking: What was worst in ETO? The Bulge?"

"That's what everyone thinks. But no way. You ever hear of the Bullet Garden?"

"Sounds familiar."

"After D-Day, we moved into Normandy. But nobody figured on a landscape more like Guadalcanal. Krauts in near every tree. Snipers. Picking us off like a whale in a barrel. I musta brought a hundred boys with a single bullet in the chest. Most died."

"That bad?"

"It got worse. Those motherfuckers started hitting people at night! How the fuck they done it I do not know. Maybe electric glasses or something. Man, nobody wanted to go nowhere."

"What happened?"

"Some spy people somehow figured it out. Don't got no idea how. But in a single night they killed all them German night shooters. Two days later, old Bradley launched a big attack. We busted through 'em. So much for that shit."

On the floor beneath them, blood pooled and mingled.

The two men were exhausted and depleted, lounging on the porch on a chill night. Under their coats, bandages grew stiff with dried bloodstains. Johnny, of course, smoked.

"We gotta get out of here. That Greek'll send more guys, sure."

"I'll phone the taxi, except, oh yeah, I ain't got no phone and there ain't no taxi."

"Seriously, can you get us a car?"

"Ain't no cars in Libertyville."

"Know any people outside Libertyville with cars?"

"Yeah. All white. They ain't coming to Libertyville."

"Then maybe we can drag our asses somewhere and lay low. Say, out to that icehouse."

"First place the Greek will look. We—"

Car headlights shown in the trees. Both men stared apprehensively. Johnny drew his .45, thumbed off the safety.

A hearse pulled up.

"I guess we died," Johnny said.

"In church, they said it would be a chariot. On fire, all that."

The hearse driver's-side door opened: it was Jimmy Renfro, Daddy Renfro's gofer and nephew.

"Nick, you supposed to be dead."

"Sorry, couldn't oblige Daddy."

"It was a bad idea anyhow. Where's that trash Baltimore nigger?"

"In the trees. He'll begin to stink in a bit."

"I'll haul him into the marshes tomorrow. That white fella, he the one shot up them hoods? The crew from Baltimore? Man, that was some Sergeant York kind of shit."

"That would be me."

"You put a hundred holes in them boys."

"Nothing they wasn't trying to do to me."

"If y'all done bleeding, I'll take you somewhere safe. My sister gots a place down further south, in Virginia, beyond Chincoteague. Nobody look for you there."

"Daddy won't like that."

"Don't matter what Daddy like. Daddy be dead. Either a heart attack or someone sick of waiting smothered him with a pillow while he slept. Guess who own that house now?"

"Congratulations. You the boss now. King of Libertyville."

"Been watching for a time. Seemed right to make a move now. But I'm nervous about Pete Ontos. That's why I need you boys safe and sound. He be thinking of you before he git around to me."

The hearse brought them to a big stone house in the country, with gardens and a circular driveway. Driven by Duane, cleaned up, bandage on his nose still. Pete Ontos got out of the back seat, spiffy in his suit, a fresh layer of pomade in his curly dark hair.

A severe woman opened the door as he approached.

In a voice suggesting she'd rather be talking to vermin, she said, "Around back."

"Thank you, ma'am."

Elaborate gardens and a well-trimmed lawn emphasized the house towering above. A late-middle-aged man in an old tweed sport coat and fedora was cultivating. As he heard Pete approach, he rose, turned, and revealed a face sharply boned, even distinguished, a pair of horn-rims, and a pipe clenched between his teeth. He didn't look like a professional machine gunner, but he was.

"You."

"That's right, Mr. Wentworth. Me."

"I had hoped our association was finished."

"I hoped as much myself, sir. But there's a new gun in town, asking questions about State Bank. I brought Jack Petrakis's crew back to deal with him and he hammered them flat."

"How unfortunate."

"Unfortunate for them, unfortunate for me, maybe unfortunate for you, sir."

"Who is he? What's his affiliation?"

"We don't know. He can't be a New York guy, so maybe he's from some other town, Miami, Chicago, New Orleans. He sure operates like a mob guy, not a cop. Fast to gun, great with a Thompson. Maybe as great as you are."

"Had to happen."

"Somehow he got the name 'Johnny Tuesday.' Sounds mob, but nobody I talked to knows a Johnny Tuesday. Maybe it's fake. Maybe he's some smart freelance crew guy after the dough. Nobody knows."

"I know where this is going. He's got to be killed. I'm the only man capable of killing him. His Thompson versus my Thompson, man on man, my greatness is tested, but in the end I vanquish him. Mr. Ontos, you're quite predictable."

"I'm a gambler. My trade is predictions."

"I don't seem to have a choice here. What's your play?"

"He seems to have vanished. But he'll be back. We think he must have been hit and he's recovering. When he's got his strength back, he'll make himself known. I've come up with a ruse to get him to a certain place at a certain time. You'll be there. He'll be mistrustful, of course, but you can deal with that. You're the best, everybody knows. Look at this place! This is what being the best gets you."

Johnny and Nick were not talking, nor even relating. They were exhausted. One was asleep, the other sat still, staring out at nothing. Beside them a stream picked its crooked way between rocks and vegetation, and behind them a cluster of low trees vibrated in the wind.

No tobacco here. The landscape was marsh, hiding its liquid reality behind waves and waves of man-sized reeds, also obeying the wind's orders, this way, then that. The geese had returned, to fatten on the marsh protein until the fall, when they'd head back south. A salt tang filled the air, and not so far off they heard the surf. It was the Atlantic, pounding its hard, loud rhythm against the white sand.

Absent storm, it was a place where a man could rest up.

Inside the shack, Nick slept, but Johnny was up, talking to a trusted neighbor.

"Anyplace around here to get a car? I want you to buy a car for me."

"Suh, you wouldn't want no car they sell a dark man."

"You bet I would."

"Best thing, take the ferry across to Norfolk. Git a car. Back in a day."

"Can you do that for me, Mr. Cletus?"

"If Nick say you okay, I guess you okay."

Johnny pulled out a roll of bills, peeled off four hundreds for Mr. Cletus.

"Sir, you rich."

"Either that, or I cashed in a life insurance policy. Now, where's the nearest pay phone?"

The phone was at the Accomac general store, hanging on a brick wall of the surprisingly genteel old town. He fed coins, discussed options with an operator, yielded yet more coins, and then waited.

In his office in the National Press Building in Washington, D.C., Drew Pearson, as alerted by his secretary, turned from his Underwood and picked up.

"There you are. I'm hearing rumors from police sources. The papers haven't said a word. Some gangster war down there? Is that you? It sounds like your work."

"If they shoot, I will shoot back, sir. It's how I operate."

"Well, be careful. What a crime to lose a man like you down in hill-billy tobacco country. But I do have some dope for you, Sergeant. Very interesting. When you say so, or if your body washes up in the bay, I'll go into print with it."

"Sounds fair to me."

"The Italian mobs all across America are looking to build themselves a mob city. Gambling, entertainment, whores, hotels, not much law enforcement, friendly state government, easily accessible. They've looked at Hot Springs, Arkansas; Phenix City, Alabama; Las Vegas, Nevada; coupla other towns."

"I may have heard of this," said Johnny.

"You do get around, don't you? But they're very interested in a little seacoast village in Maryland, on the Atlantic, called Ocean City. It's on a barrier island, but in '33 a storm cut it in half. That means you can harbor oceangoing boats on the bay side, go through the inlet, and hit the Atlantic. It's become a big high-rolling marlin spot, and marlin guys want action at night as well as in the day. But right now there's nothing to spend their dough on except ballroom dancing in an old wreck called the Atlantic Hotel."

"So the New York Italians want to sell them action?"

"That's it. A freeway will make the town available from the north, and they're building bridges across the Chesapeake and Hampton Roads to make it available from west and south. The Maryland state legislature is very cooperative: everybody sees money there. The mob has a local guy whose job is to begin buying up land in Ocean City, all legally, before anyone knows and it turns into a boomtown for the uninvited. But how to get this guy money without raising suspicions? So what they did was shipped him a hundred thousand in small, unmarked bills."

"That's why that bag from the bank was so heavy. A hundred grand in small bills must go to thirty-five pounds."

"Yeah. See, they were worried about some crew finding out about it and intercepting it. So they sent it down in a heavily guarded armored truck, but they didn't want to drive at night and it's a two-day trip over bad roads. They made a deal to store it overnight at State Bank and Trust in Chesterfield City. But someone found out anyway and hit it. Perfect timing, real good crew, got away, left two dead. The thought is, it was Baltimore people."

"Baltimore?"

"The Baltimore mob guys have always been outliers because they're Greek. So it's a Greek-versus-Italian thing. The thought is, somehow the Greeks found out about it and hit the place exactly when the money was there. That necklace just happened to be there and that's what the press bit on. It gave them a chance to run pix of Laura Tapscott. She's a dish."

"So I hear."

"It was just a straight cash take. And there's nothing the Italians can do, because they're not sure. They have no idea who ratted them out. They can't go to war because right now their own town is messed up and they won't do a thing till it settles down. Plus they know that the Greeks, unlike the FBI, are stone-cold killers. Spartans, if you will."

Johnny saw it now. Tapscott was the mob land buyer in Ocean City. He got a piece of the action. His reputation and social standing would make all transactions discreet and easy. But he needed money in an Ocean City account to write checks on and didn't want to take it out of his own, which would attract attention, both locally and from the IRS. The untraceable money went to Ocean City. But someone betrayed Tapscott and the Italians to the Greeks.

"Any idea who ratted the Italians out?"

"Good question. I can't answer it. When you figure it out, you let me know, hear?"

"I will, Mr. Pearson. Thanks so much."

Wentworth had always believed that a Thompson submachine gun, Model 1921 with two vertical grips, as manufactured by Colt, was a beautiful thing. Thus he treated his with loving care. He enjoyed maintaining it and had just disassembled it, cleaned and lubricated the pieces—what an amusing jigsaw puzzle!—and reassembled it in a garage, next to a stack of loaded fifty-round drums.

Though of wealthy lineage, he'd been drawn to guns early. He defied parental and familial expectations by going off to the Great War as a private of infantry, became a Lewis machine gunner, and knew immediately that he had found his destiny. After the war, he turned down his father's brokerage business and instead became one of General Thompson's best salesmen, traveling the country in the twenties with a tommy wondergun and five thousand rounds in his trunk, putting on exhibitions for police forces across the country. There was nothing the gun couldn't do when he was on the trigger, including shooting portraits, skeet, and, with tracers, defining a rose against the night sky.

Of course, as his reputation spread, offers began to come his way. He could only turn them down for so long, and the money was good and easy. He lived quietly, married to the woman he'd loved since childhood, unfortunately childless, which was his one disappointment with a life that had otherwise provided him with whatever he wanted. He'd made so much he'd retired three times, but each time ridiculous offers, old loyalties, the sense of being needed, the pleasure of stardom nudged him back into the game.

His wife entered from the other side of the room, across from the beautiful black '38 Dodge glinting in the low garage light.

"I was afraid I'd find you here, doing this."

"Can't be helped. Ancient times beckon."

"The last time you worked for them, you said it would be the last time."

"I spoke too early."

"It's dangerous? More dangerous than last time?"

"Oh, I ought to be all right. Look"—he held up a drum—"I've got more bullets than he does."

Johnny sat on a park bench, in the wide-open, under the noon sun, fedora, sport coat, and tie. He was reading a book.

A shadow fell across the page.

Johnny looked up, saw the sheriff in his khaki uniform.

"I know who you are. You're Johnny Tuesday. Sitting here, you must be announcing you're back in town."

"I am."

"You're the one with the machine gun."

" I don't see any machine gun around."

"Machine guns are illegal."

"Good thing the Marine Corps didn't know that. Those guns came in mighty handy in the Pacific, I'll tell you."

"Someone with a machine gun filled some Baltimore thugs with holes a few miles outside of town. Holes *everywhere*. Know anything about that?"

"Only that nothing ruins a fellow's day like a bunch of holes."

"All them boys was wearing Air Corps–style sunglasses. If I'm not mistaken, they visited our town before, about two years ago. That visit turned out a hell of a lot better for 'em than this one. So I am not all that upset over what happens outside town limits, Johnny Tuesday, to Baltimore Greektown heavies. Suppose I'll get around to investigating it sometime in 1959."

"Nineteen fifty-nine. That soon? Must be pretty important."

"Here's another something I want to ask you about, though it don't seem your style. Found some gals in the marshes, throats cut, probably worked at the Wigwam. One was fresh, named Zelda, the other, a colored gal, she'd been there a long time. Pretty girl from what I could tell. The first girl popped up when the rope tying her to a radiator broke. We looked around, found the other. Know anything about that?"

Johnny looked off; a hard glare came into his eyes and his jaw tightened.

"Poor kids. They got mixed up with bad boys."

"Happens to whores all the time. Still, don't like it. We got a fellow in this town called Duane Duke, works for Pete Ontos at the Wigwam. He likes to hurt gals, I've heard, and whenever you see 'em busted up, you know Duane's the one."

"I know Duane. I have that peckerwood marked good."

"Johnny, long as your business stays out of town, it ain't my business. I'm just telling you how to steer straight so you don't find yourself on the wrong end of a posse, and my posses have machine guns too."

Pages of *Tales of the South Pacific* by James Michener flew by in the sunlight. It was pretty good. You could tell the guy had been out there, wasn't just making stuff up. He was no Marine, but still—

Then another shadow fell across the pages. An old black man in chauffeur's livery stood above him, blocking the sun.

"Sir, the lady wishes to speak with you."

"I don't see a lady."

"The car is parked in the alley."

Johnny followed the old man to a limo—Cadillac, shiny black as the devil's dancing shoes—and climbed in. She was there.

The doll alarm sounded in his head.

You had to be careful with the beautiful ones. They expected, and knew how, to get their way. They made you love them and you didn't focus clearly. He'd seen it close up and knew what black mischief it could release.

Her face was refined, wearing its thirty-five years extremely well, though it had a cold, occluded aspect to it, haughty, unyielding, expecting to be obeyed. Her eyes, when she chose to reveal them behind the sultry weight of her eyelids, were blue and fierce as if all they saw was hers by right of beauty. She had a thick froth of artfully arranged hair, a swirl of blond and brown. Her neck was firm, her chin tight, her nose perfect, her cheekbones high, her makeup understated but exquisite.

"Ma'am."

The limo pulled out, and Chesterfield, then country, rolled by.

"I am Laura Tapscott-Higgins. You are, I assume, the one they call Johnny Tomorrow. Or is it Johnny Midnight?"

"I believe it's Johnny 'Tuesday.' It doesn't make much sense to me either, but people have to call me something."

"I didn't think it was real. It sounds like a hero on the radio."

"It doesn't sound real to me either, ma'am."

"Is there a reason you prefer your real name not to be known?"

"Seems like there's mob business somehow attached to this thing I'm looking into. The less they know about the real me, the safer I feel. Make sense?"

"I suppose. Well, whoever you are, I am here at the desperate entreaties of my husband, who feels he cannot come himself as he could be subject to a murder attempt. If I understand the story, you believe he is involved in unfortunate business connected to that horrible robbery two years ago."

"It starts with the robbery, yes."

"It was so horrible. Neil jumped in front of me and that man shot him—"

"And the police officer. Dave Dunn."

"Yes, Officer Dunn, of course. Insurance?"

"Don't have any."

"No, I mean are you an insurance detective?"

"It's a private issue, ma'am. I'm not an investigator, I represent no agency, I'm sure not mobbed up. I'm just here to settle on certain overdue accounts."

"You're sure you're not from a radio drama? That sounds very melodramatic to me, Mr. Tuesday."

"Can't help how it sounds. I'm only telling you what is."

"For some reason I believe you. I have a keen nose for duplicity, having been brought up in society, which in its way is more violent than the mobs."

"Yes, ma'am."

"My husband will see you, though in privacy. You appreciate the delicacy of his position. You are familiar with the Nelson place, a deserted farm a few miles out of town."

"I had a previous appointment there. I almost made it but was waylaid."

"So rumor has it. You're a capable man."

"I try to stay alive. In Chesterfield, it isn't so easy."

"He will be there sometime in the morning, depending on his schedule. He drives a very fine 1937 Ford convertible. You are to go at dawn, conceal yourself and your car. Hide in the old house. You should have no trouble."

"I'll be there."

"Fine. Ralph, you may take Mr. Tuesday back to the park."

"Yes, ma'am."

They rode in silence and arrived at the town square.

She turned, somewhat disturbed.

"I hope you know what you're doing, Johnny Tuesday. This is far more complicated than you imagine. There are forces at play that don't care if you're a war hero or not. If you get in the way of the Big Score, they will crush you. They've tried, they will try again. You have no idea what people will do for money. It would be so sad to see someone of your courage destroyed over something like this."

"If you know what 'this' is, please tell me. Havana in Maryland, Greeks versus Italians, Vegas versus Ocean City? Maybe a lot of secret money invested by so-called responsible citizens?"

"I see you are nobody's fool, John Tuesday, even if you allow yourself to be called by a silly name. I also see I have no hope of persuading you to leave town now, tonight. I hope your interests don't collide with somebody who's more vicious than you. But I can do nothing more than warn you."

Johnny cleaned his Thompson M1A1, then reassembled it, lovingly fitting it together, bolt into receiver, then that slid into the trigger group with stock attached, springs tested for function, all of it tight and perfect. It had saved his life and the lives of many others all across the wide blue. Next to the gun on a table was a stack of thirty-round magazines, as yet empty, and six boxes of plain cardboard GI-issue .45 ACPs.

Johnny, in shirtsleeves, his pistol in its shoulder holster, his fedora back on his head, smoked cigarette number 432 of the long day.

A heavy car approached.

He set the big gun down, slid the automatic out of his holster, and eased to the door.

The hearse pulled in.

The door opened and Jimmy Renfro got out, went around to the back of the big Cadillac, opened it, and helped the still-shaky Nick to his feet. Absurdly Nick was carrying a German Mauser rifle.

"Say hey, what're you doing here? You're not strong enough—"

"That's what I told him."

They got Nick to his bed, where he lay down, exhausted, sweaty, one of his wounds bleeding slightly under his shirt. Johnny had another thought: Do I tell him about Lucille? It'll come out soon anyway. But now he's too weak. Who knows if he can even handle it? Best to wait a bit.

"I can't move fast," said Nick, "but I can hunker up and offer cover fire."

"I'm a Marine. We don't believe in cover fire. We just like to get in close and blast away. You want to be useful, you load up the mags. Top 'em off at twenty-eight 'cause I don't trust 'em at full spring tension."

"This is going to be one goddamn hell of a hayride."

CHAPTER 10

WENTWORTH WATCHED FROM THE SECOND-FLOOR WINDOW. HE SAW a dark country road, shrouded in trees, and just barely visible a car, lights off. It pulled into the foliage. It was 7:15 a.m., just after wintertime dawn, the world not fully lit.

Nothing happened for a time. Somebody inside was checking things out, though Wentworth knew he was too low in the window to be spotted, even by binoculars.

The door cracked and a man slipped out, hat low, a war-model Thompson in his hands, some kind of bag strapped over his shoulder, heavy from the swing of it. Extra magazines. The fellow, of course, knew. He had to know. It was clear he was no dummy.

This was going to be interesting.

In the trees, Johnny moved slowly until the Nelson house, two stories, wooden but in disrepair and surrounded by uncut grass and an untended garden, became more visible.

Old farm place. Once prosperous, now fallen to ruin for whatever reason—dust bowl, character flaws, scandal, generational disinterest, squeezed out by Big Tobacco for further cultivation? He didn't know; it didn't matter.

. . .

From the upstairs window, Wentworth saw Johnny move slowly out of the trees, again check about, then advance.

Fire now?

Nah. He'd have to rise, mount the gun, find the target before he could open up. A slick operator like this guy, battle-hardened, was used to jump-up targets and wouldn't panic or dive. He'd shoot fast from the hip.

Wentworth waited until Johnny disappeared under the eaves.

Pale sun crept through the trees.

Duane, half a mile from the house, now sporting his smallest nose bandage yet, so small it finally allowed his baby-caterpillar mustache to show in all its splendor, watched through binoculars. His job was to report the outcome to Mr. Ontos ASAP. It pleased him. The nose still felt like somebody had played baseball with it, all nine innings' worth. He lied to himself in thinking it was revenge he was seeking via the upcoming death of this Johnny Tuesday. In truth, it was the relief that Johnny had left the scene, so his nose wouldn't be used for another ball game.

Johnny had slid through the front door, noticed no disturbance in the layer of dust and debris that lay everywhere, and now squatted a few feet back from the front window, peering intently, smoking a cigarette.

Upstairs, Wentworth sat, eyes closed, concentrating entirely on sounds. Smoke from Johnny's cigarette crept through openings in the rotting floor beneath him.

Johnny flicked his butt on the bare wood floor. No sign of habitation. No noise, no disturbance, no floating dust or human smell. Maybe the dame had been on the level, and he would just wait for Tapscott to arrive. But still . . . His finger flew absently to the safety lever on his tommy. He clicked it.

. . .

Wentworth heard the click upstairs. He came out of his sonar mode. He'd been waiting for a metallic sound, sharp and distinct, by which he could get a good location on Johnny a floor below. It was shaping up to be an unprecedented gunfight; the two men would never see each other but would stalk each other firing through the floor, ripping up great shrouds of dust and splinters, and leaving ragged wounds as the bullets pulverized the rotting dwelling. They'd try to outhear and outguess each other.

Wentworth stood, assumed a good firing position, set himself, and aimed at that portion of the floor under which he believed Johnny lurked.

Just as he leaned forward to put his weight on his front foot—proper FBI protocol for the Thompson—the floor creaked. Had to happen sometime. But why now?

Johnny heard it and threw himself sideways fast.

Wentworth fired a ten-round burst, punching in super-time a spew of fractured perforations in the floor, filling the hallway with gun smoke, floating dust, and wood frags.

Johnny came out of his roll, lifted gun to shoulder, made an instant read on the angle of the bullets, and fired an answering five-round burst, chewing a stitch in the ceiling.

The bullets ripped up the floor next to Wentworth, but the angle was a little high, and as he crouched they flew by him and hit the wall, high up, behind him, dust and shattered plaster the only result.

Silence.

Dust.

Shells on the floor.

Heat radiating from the gun barrels, already too hot to touch.

Each man's face taut, aware of the game he was in; each gave himself over to hard listening for a hint of the other. It was like sub-destroyer warfare in the Pacific, with unseen but deadly antagonists improvising for position with only sounds to guide them. Each man tried to control his breathing.

Johnny kneeled, picked up three empty shells. He tossed them to the other side of the room, thinking that their noise would draw fire and give him a read on his assassin's new position.

The shells rattled against the floor; Wentworth brought his subgun up fast, made the calculation, but didn't fire. He realized what had happened. Instead, he guided the gun backward swiftly to the other side of the room and fired a long, shattering burst that bisected the half of the room in which Johnny knelt.

The stitch of .45s, shrapnel, plaster dust, and wood chips exploded from both the ceiling, through which the bullets passed, and the floor, where they hit, just a few feet from Johnny, who again rolled right, just barely escaping, then fired a burst straight up into the ceiling.

The bullets exploded around Wentworth's feet, and it seemed for a second that he was hit, as his head jerked backward. But when he looked, he had a hole in the brim of his fedora, where a bullet had just missed his face as it rose vertically from beneath him.

He hosed another burst into the floor right below.

Johnny had just moved, and bullets hacked into the sector of floor he had seconds ago abandoned.

Silence except for the tick and creak of the old wood settling after sustaining so much damage.

From outside the house, Duane watched with his binoculars. Through their hazy magnification, he could see the house in sunlight, but the broken windows revealed darkness inside. That darkness was illuminated by periodic muzzle flash, first from the second floor, then from the first.

A few seconds passed. In two other windows, flashes ruptured the darkness.

Wentworth was sweating heavily through the wool of his bespoke tweed. He was frozen in place, standing amid a litter of cartridge cases. The floor around him was much shot up, with strings of bullet holes zigging and zagging all over the place.

Very carefully, controlling his movements, he silently removed the drum from his Thompson and replaced it, trying to move the new one into place so gently the locking mechanism didn't snap.

Johnny was similarly maneuvering his new thirty-round clip into place and was similarly rewarded with a snap-free insertion. He reoriented the gun. He too was surrounded by a litter of spent shells and in a miasma heavy on dust; the floor beneath and the ceiling above were much punctured by bullets. From one or two spots water leaked where pipes had been punctured.

Wentworth saw that the shorter floorboards ran horizontally to the center of the hallway, where they reached a central beam or plank that ran the whole length of the house. He reasoned that the short boards were more apt to squeal and give him away and that the wood was thinner, clearly prone to penetration. But if he could get to the central beam, there'd be no creak and the wood might be thick enough to stop a .45.

He took an awkward giant step, carefully and quietly, and got one foot set on the beam, then pulled his other foot over. It was almost too much. Like Harold Lloyd on a ledge, he fought for balance, almost tipping this way, then that, and finally corrected his foot position and got control of his body. The floor hadn't creaked.

Johnny was puzzled at the silence above. He wondered if he could make a sudden dash to the window or the stairway and from that position either escape or get a better firing angle. But every time he'd moved, his antagonist had zeroed him and put a burst ever so close. So, for the first time, he was indecisive, and with indecision comes fear. He tried to shuck it off, but it was there as so many other times, his old fear of fear itself, dread, like a cold toad in his gut, generating clumsiness, inertia, denial, defeat. He looked skyward for some sign of movement. He saw some falling dust, raised to fire, but then noted that actually the dust was falling from all the bullet holes.

Wentworth had changed his position radically, using the solidity of the beam. He had slid his way along the beam to the far end of the house. Johnny couldn't know he was there. Now he took the empty drum in his left hand, brought the Thompson to his shoulder with his right. He'd hurl the drum, it would land and clatter, and Johnny would fire, giving away his position.

He drew back the drum to toss, then flung it. It clattered in the corner.

Johnny, his nerves at razor's edge, heard the disturbance and quickly aligned his gun to fire—but didn't. Too easy. He wouldn't have made a mistake like that.

The two men froze. They were basically one atop the other now.

Duane was so revved he could hardly stand it. Each moment of silence was like the tick-tock on the big clock at Army-Navy, tied 21–21 with but seconds to go, one team on the other's five, no time-outs. He just didn't know who was on offense, who on defense.

Two hands now on his gun, Wentworth saw that his play had failed. He'd pushed forward, again in that FBI-approved shooting position that he had invented, and he recovered to put himself in a more agile situation. As he shifted his foot position, he stepped on a spent shell, throwing him ever so slightly out of balance. His gun wavered and the drum, which extended four inches in each direction beyond the receiver, gently tapped the wall.

Johnny heard the sound straight up. He dived sideways for angle against the center beam, pivoting in midair to land on his back, and simultaneously fired an eight-round burst that blew eight holes in a line in the white ceiling above him, sending dust to cascade and plaster debris to fall like rain.

Silence.

Then a thunk as if something heavy and meaty—a body—had hit the floor.

Silence.

Time passed.

From the farthest hole in the ceiling a torrent of black fluid began to pour.

A second later, from the second farthest hole, a thinner torrent.

From the third hole, a parade, but not a torrent, of drops.

From the fourth hole a single drop; it splashed on the hot receiver of Johnny's Thompson and, with a sizzle, boiled off.

Duane outside, half a mile off, on the binocs, couldn't make out what was happening. The shooting had stopped.

Johnny climbed the stairs slowly, gun at the ready. The stairs creaked, the whole house creaked. It seemed the world was breathing again.

He reached the landing, looking over his gunsight.

The machine gunner was at the far end of the hallway. He was drenched in blood. He lay where he had fallen, half-prone against the wall in a big pool of blood. His body was essentially dead, and Johnny could see from the lame posture of his arms that his spine was broken. His Thompson lay a few feet in front of him.

He was older by far than Johnny had expected, and better dressed. No gun hood from bad streets in the slum or a hardscrabble farm like, say, a Baby Face or a Dillinger. He looked like a banker on a weekend in the country.

Their eyes meet.

Johnny came out of his shooting position and walked to the downed fellow.

He knelt next to him, took out a pack of Camels, lit one up, and transferred it to the lips of the dying man.

"Don't mind if I do," said Wentworth. Enjoying his last pleasure, he inhaled deeply.

Three columns of cigarette smoke rose from three holes in his lungs.

"Nice shooting," he said. "No lateral drift at all."

"Been shooting these things in the Marine Corps for fifteen years now."

"How did you know I'd be here?"

"I knew from the police reports the robbery crew included someone good on a Thompson. Since you weren't with the others, I expected you to be here."

"Find my car in the trees, about a half mile out, the northwest side, can't miss it. I stashed my wallet in the glovebox. There's six grand in there; you keep it. Send my wallet back to the address on that driver's license. That way my wife will know."

"I'm not in this for money. I'll send it back to her too."

"The key is under the left rear. Take it, at least; a '38 Dodge, real good shape."

"I have a car, a jalopy. It's all I need. I'll have yours towed."

"Who are you, Johnny Tuesday?"

"My name isn't even Tuesday."

He leaned forward, whispered into the gunner's ear.

"Never thought a good man would take me. Always thought it would be a bad one. More power to the righteous, Johnny Tuesday."

In his binoculars Duane saw Johnny emerge. His hat was low, his tie tight; a cigarette dangled from his lips and he had a Thompson under each arm. He looked like the Angel of Machine Gun Death come in out of the rain.

Duane pissed up his pants, then ran to his car.

CHAPTER 11

JOHNNY POWERED UP ON THREE MORE CIGARETTES, FOUND WENT-worth's car, and did what was necessary, then headed to his own. It ate up some time, which was okay by him. He knew what he had to do: figure this thing out a little more clearly, which would be easier to do without someone machine-gunning him.

It was, he figured, their move, whoever they were, simply because he didn't have one. That was because none of the pieces quite fit. He had no theory yet of what actually was going on and who Pete was working with or for, or who was against him. Then there were the Tapscotts; obviously in it for themselves, but with or against who? And on top of that he was hungry.

He grabbed a *Courier* in downtown Chesterfield City and headed to the Merit Diner. Nobody paid much attention as the place was jumping and the sounds played off the white tile walls and the formations of mirrors behind the counter. But it wasn't just echo; it seemed the citizens were riled over something and wound up over one another. Everybody had an opinion, everybody was lit up and eager to share. Not his business. He went to the end of the counter, took a stool, and opened the newspaper to see what was happening on February 27,

1947. Not much: "RUSS SCARE TO AIRLIFT PLANES, MAY CLOSE BERLIN AIRPORT."

All right, so what else was new? No ball games, no elections, no wars, no big accidents; he paged along casually, hoping for an eye-catcher to jog his brain. Nothing.

The counter girl arrived. He had the usual, the No. 3. This consisted of eggs wrecked, baccy, bread scorched and greased, hashed spuds, and OJ. And coffee, by the bucketful.

As he waited for the rations to arrive, he considered.

Someone at Tapscott's had set him up. That was the key. You'd first think the woman herself, as she was the one that had arranged the meeting that turned into a Thompson duel. But he couldn't make himself buy into that one. She was too smack-in-the-mouth beautiful. A woman like that had no need for anything because whatever anything was came her way automatically.

Don't get played for a sucker, he told himself. Beauty was no inoculation against the virus of wicked.

But still, maybe someone had overheard—some minion in the household staff, or at Tapscott's tobacco office—and shipped that news off to Pete Ontos for a cash tip or just out of anger at Tapscott for not recognizing his genius. Or maybe Tapscott was the puppeteer himself and had told her to set the meet, then told Pete to get Wentworth the machine gunner. Or maybe Jimmy Renfro had heard from Nick and saw it as a way to ingratiate himself with Pete. It was like pool on an eight-sided table.

Whatever, just getting the shooters of February 20, 1945, wasn't enough. That didn't satisfy the requirements of justice he had set for himself. And he wouldn't be at rest if those requirements weren't satisfied. He wasn't engineered any other way.

The food came, heaps of it. Not as hungry as when he sat down, he picked at it, smoked, returned to the morning paper, and finally got to the comics page and there saw:

WASHINGTON MERRY-GO-ROUND
BY DREW PEARSON

Mob war on Eastern Shore?

The gangster menace spreads everywhere these days. Latest city to find itself in a hoodlum hoedown is bucolic Chesterfield City, on Maryland's Eastern Shore. Long the hub of the Maryland broadleaf tobacco planting empires and a kind of little England or Old South of noble cavaliers and their damsels, the city's peace was shattered a few days ago by "the subgun's rat-a-tat-tat" as that poetess of the wrong side of the law, Miss Bonnie Parker, put it. The rat-a-tat-tat left four Baltimore gangsters in a heap by the roadside.

Word from this column's confidential sources is that the New York faction wants to move in on an area governed by Baltimore Greek gangs and hired an accomplished man-killer from the East Side of New York, a tough Irisher who honed his killing craft on islands in the Pacific. Against such esteemed and proven talent, the Baltimore boys fell like ten pins in a bowling alley.

While the larger issue is who controls the hunk of land below Delaware, soon to be opened up and profitably developed around the burgeoning sport fishing trade and perhaps with gaming and other pleasures, the nominal excuse for the shooting seems to be the unrecovered proceeds from a bank robbery/jewel heist of two years ago, whose authorship—and responsibility for the broad daylight murder of a policeman and a banker on Main Street—has never been established.

If you planned that robbery, Merry-Go-Round hears, you ought to be quaking in your boots because a Marine is definitely going to land.

There went his cover. That jerk Pearson had betrayed him for a cheap headline, even if he'd gotten just about everything else wrong. But Johnny realized one effect of the column would be to put the city in a national spotlight and force the governor to send State Police or even the Maryland National Guard down to quell the violence. The FBI would have to become involved. That would freeze everything in an ice block for who knew how long. Thus it was in nobody's interest to wait. If "they" were going to move, it would be soon, as within hours.

"More coffee, sir?" said the waitress.

"Wish I could, sweetie. But break time is over."

He rushed to his car, trying to think of anything he could have forgotten.

Then, yes, one thing.

He went to the bank, cashed $2 into nickels, then went a block down Main to the Walgreens with an outdoor phone.

He dialed, fed the thing some nickels.

Second ring, "Sunpapers."

"Fred Rasmussen, library."

The clicks and buzzes of vocal transit through a switchboard and finally, "Fred Rasmussen."

"Mr. Rasmussen, it's—"

"Sarge! Boy, am I glad you called!"

"Yes, sir. You said you'd continue to look in the files in case—"

"Well, it wasn't in the files. But we have something called the Society Section, where we run pictures of rich people's daughters when they get engaged or married or go to big parties. See, they own the department stores and buy all the ads. It makes them happy."

"I get it."

"It's not clipped and filed, because nobody cares. But it's run by an old crow named Sally Goodhue who has a memory like a steel trap."

"Old crows generally do," said Johnny, wondering where this was going.

But then Rasmussen explained what Miss Sally Goodhue had remembered from 1932 and he knew where it was going.

• • •

Johnny arrived in minutes to Nick's, to find the man sitting on his front stoop, a German Mauser rifle across his knees, keen on the lookout. A twelve-year-old boy sat behind him.

"Here you be," said Nick, rising, still a bit shaky. "Worried you done been outgunned finally."

"Not yet. Maybe tomorrow. Things are going to happen fast now."

"They already started. J.B., tell him."

The boy stood.

"Sir, Mrs. Fields give me a quarter to come get you. She say, 'Get Nick and that white man Johnny Tuesday fast as you can.'"

"She say about what?" asked Johnny.

"No, sir. Just fast."

"Leave the rifle, Nick. No need to scare folks into thinking a war is coming."

"Maybe a war *is* coming," said Nick, but he put the rifle back in the house, and they drove the three blocks to what would have to have been called the nicer part of Libertyville, knocked, and were greeted with a polite "Do come in, please."

Mrs. Fields, regal as always, sat upon her sofa in her pink living room. She gestured to seats.

"It is a bad situation," she said. "Early this morning, that big corn-cracker Duane Duke arrived at the Tapscotts' with thugs. They forced their way in with guns and locked the help in the kitchen. All except me. They grabbed Mr. and Mrs. Tapscott, treating them rather roughly. They told me, 'You tell Johnny Tuesday and his pet dark, Nick, best get ready to make a deal. Tommy say he can't kill you, so he going to buy you off. You meet him anyplace you say, and he'll be there alone, give Mr. Johnny fifty thousand and Mr. Nick twenty-five, and then you leave town forever and he lets the Tapscotts go. Otherwise he will cut their throats and tell the law the darks did it. There will be hell to pay and a lot of darks and a lot of whites will die.'"

"Crazy bastard," said Nick. "Excuse my language, Mrs. Fields."

"Under current circumstances," she said, "allowances can be made."

"Johnny Tuesday, what you want—"

"Wait, there's more," said Mrs. Fields. "This is for you, Nick, and I hate to be the one to tell you, but I must because in some way I am responsible."

"Ma'am, I—"

"This farmboy Duane tell me with a grin he took care of your Lucille. She was fixing to leave the Wigwam and town and go to Baltimore, where the darks are said to live better. She had five thousand dollars from Mr. Tapscott. He is a good man. He gave her that money because I asked him to. On that recommendation, without hesitation, to a dark gal he'd never seen in his life. He went to the bank and had a check drawn to her. That is the kind of man he is. Somehow Duane found out about it and took care of both Lucille and her money. I am so sorry, Nick. You were away at war. I was only trying to take care of the sweet young thing so evilly used by the worst kind of men."

Nick got a faraway look on his face, swallowed hard. Then, clenching his fist, he said, "I'd like to beat that yellow-livered cracker to wood pulp. I—"

"Nick, calm down," said Johnny. "He told you because he wants you all crazied up. You are probably the designated murderer of the Tapscotts, and he needs you acting like a wild man in front of witnesses. That's why you can't be anywhere near the Wigwam in what happens next. I have another job for you. Justice will come to Pete, and to Duane, and to all the tribe of the Wigwam, I promise you."

"You going to bust in there on your own, Johnny Tuesday, and take 'em all on?"

"Exactly," said Johnny Tuesday.

CHAPTER 12

LIKE A COMMANDER, DUANE WAS RACING ABOUT, SHOOING WHORES out of the way, checking men, particularly their weapons, which mostly consisted of lever-action deer rifles and double-barrel shotguns, examining the vehicles, making sure they were ready to go.

The plan: A call would come, telling Pete where to meet Johnny and Nick for the payoff. Under cover of darkness, Duane would lead the boys out to within a mile, abandon the cars, and set up a half mile out. As the meet time approached, he would begin to silently infiltrate, and when visual contact with Mr. Ontos was made, he'd come to a halt. When Ontos gave over the bucks, he would put hand to fedora, and all hell would break out.

"Tell those bohunks it's an extra five hundred dollars to the one that gets Johnny Tuesday. And it's a trip to the marshes to the one that hits me."

"We are plumb ready, Mr. Ontos. You say when and where and the fellows move out."

"You get 'em, Duane," said Ontos. "We hit this bastard before the FBI or the state troopers move in, and we have won."

Johnny was behind the wheel of his jalopy, fedora tight, smoking of course. No coat: just the dark brown cotton shirt, buttoned to the top, the field pants held up by suspenders and bloused into the hunting boots.

He had tied himself to the seat, essentially securing himself in case of collision. Or rather, in expectation of collision. Next to him were both Thompsons likewise roped tightly to the seat, against the same expectation of collision. Both had thirty-round stick magazines full up, and wedged into his belt along his back were four more sticks. His automatic, cocked, locked, hung in the fancy Myres leather shoulder rig, fast out of the holster, fast to the first shot.

His plan: in one word—now. No sense in waiting, letting it happen where and when they had laid it out. He checked his watch. It was 4:14 p.m. At exactly 4:15 p.m. Mrs. Fields would call the Wigwam and tell Pete Ontos that Johnny would meet him behind the A&P in Easton, twenty-five miles up the road, at midnight.

But Johnny would meet him at 4:16 p.m. at the Wigwam.

Pete Ontos, in his office, waited for the phone to ring. Finally it did. He picked up.

"Sir?"

"What's he say, Mrs. Fields?"

She gave him the instruction.

"I'll be there," Pete said. "Now, you don't say a word about this to nobody."

"I understand. I just want Mr. Tapscott home and safe. He is a good man."

He put the phone down and turned to Duane.

"It's working perfectly," he said.

Eight miles out of town, in a no-man's-land uncontaminated by law and order, he saw the Wigwam. As it was daylight, much of the brightly lit theatricality had deserted the place: the big neon sign on the casino roof, with its blinking arrow to mark the spot, was turned off and could only be seen, by squinting, as a script of dead tubes. All else, shed of light and shadow and therefore allure, was prosaic, a large wooden structure of boxy design housing the main event, the bar and casino, big double doors to admit the suckers by the busload, windows upstairs for Pete's administrative needs, a bunker of attached garages to one side, and another wing, which housed the pleasures of the flesh. It looked less like a capital of immorality and evil than a Baptist church camp. It was surrounded by what seemed acres of parking lot for the pilgrims from all up and down the East Coast who came to sample its pleasures, the lot empty now and merely testimony to the banality of a night building in daytime.

Johnny Tuesday turned into the property. But instead of parking, he accelerated.

They heard the roar of a car as it reached speed and then reached more speed. That brought one of the lounging gunmen to his feet, and he peered out the window.

"Oh, Christ, the bastard is ramming us."

He and a bunch of other boys broke to get out of the way.

The Ford hit the front of the Wigwam, crashed through timber, splintering it. Like a tank, it destroyed all before it, knocking tables this way and that, churning hard against the floor, unleashing a torrent of dust and chaos in the space.

Johnny was jerked by the impact, but the ropes held him secure. His hat flew off; he retrieved it and plucked his .45 from his shoulder holster.

A man came at him blindly and Johnny put him down, flashes showing brightly in the heavy dust. A few shots rang out, one smearing the windshield with a quick fracture, another plunking hard into the auto body. Johnny pulled a knife from the steering wheel, where it had been taped, and cut himself free, then cut both Thompsons free.

He stepped out with a gun under each arm, cocked, safeties off. He looked like the turret on a B-17.

He fired both guns simultaneously and ran a double burst in a crescent across the wall of the barroom, shattering mirrors, bottles, woodwork, a nude painting, energizing yet more dust and fragmentation, pulverizing a wide swath. It was like some ancient Hebrew god of destruction come to earth to wash away sinful Sodom and Gomorrah, free special on fire and brimstone, today only.

"Now, you boys can stand and fight and die in your places or toss your weapons and run like hell. Offer lasts five seconds, then I start killing."

One, then another, then in a scrambling crowd, the townie gunboys abandoned their positions, tossed their weapons, and scrambled out of the shattered barroom. Nobody wanted to face the wrath of General Thompson, doubled.

Johnny stood aside, both guns brought to bear on the scrambling men, but he didn't fire. They were last seen heading in the direction of Spain.

Duane went petrified, as normal, and was too slow out of his mineral state to join the fleeing mob, and so instead pivoted and headed through the nearest door, which happened to open on the stairway that led to the hall that led to Pete Ontos's office. Since it was a path of least resistance, he took it, raced up—but understood too late that he had taken flight into a dead end. He spied a closet, leaped inside, pulled the door shut, went into petrification-as-survival mode again, and hoped Johnny would pass, giving him leeway to flee yet farther—say, to St. Louis or Omaha.

Johnny stopped at the foot of the stairs. He fired two long double bursts up, the smell of flame and sulfur loading the air with bad news, amid yet more weather of end-of-times destruction.

"Last chance, peckerwoods. Come out now and run home to Mama's bosom, or die where you stand."

Two men in abject panic appeared and threw themselves down the stairs, one of them falling but so intent on escape he didn't notice how bad he'd hurt his leg and limped away awkwardly.

Johnny knelt, put a new thirty-round stick mag in each gun, made sure both were cocked and unlocked.

He eased up the stairs, through the smoke and debris.

He came to the top and looked down a long, empty corridor.

Inside the closet, illumination was low, though light streamed in from the crack above and below the door. Duane tensed, waiting. He heard footsteps, one by one, the tread of a careful man.

Johnny eased his way down the hallway.

Duane saw the shadows of Johnny's boots as Johnny passed the doorway.

Duane took a big breath, then burst out of the closet, and Johnny kicked his legs out from under him, and down he went—hard. He rolled over.

Johnny faced him, both guns leveled.

"The idiot always hides in the closet. Didn't you see any movies?"

"Please, sir, I didn't mean no harm."

"You're not worth a single bullet. They cost a penny each. Get your white-trash ass out of here."

Johnny turned, slid down the hall until he confronted the last door, not even bothering to listen as Duane galloped toward escape.

He braced himself against the wall, fired both guns, two parallel bursts that chewed into the wall just below the ceiling line.

He fired again, running the burst two feet below the ceiling line. The bullets ate the wall, ripping dust and fragments, filling the hallway with smoke.

Johnny kicked open the door.

CHAPTER 13

THE AIR IN THE ROOM WAS THICK WITH DUST AND GRIT, AS WAS THE hallway, from the passage of the bullets. But Johnny could see what he could see.

Pete had his arms around the poor, frightened Laura Tapscott, holding her roughly, a Luger against her beautiful head, pulling her tight to him. A terrified man in a double-breasted suit, looking as if he'd gotten off at the wrong stop, was tied into a chair, his mouth gagged hard. He twisted, turned, bucked in powerless frustration and helplessness.

"Drop those guns, Tuesday!" Pete Ontos yelled. "Or I'll blast this dame to hell and still have time to kill you and Tapscott!"

Johnny considered.

"You're not going to shoot her, Greek. She's been your girl since 1932 when you were the stud of the Poly–City College game and she was the queen of the Baltimore Cotillion. You two've been scheming ever since."

Pete twisted the Luger toward Johnny Tuesday, but before he could fire, Johnny hit him three times from each gun, the close-in impact so severe it ripped him from the beautiful woman and sent him backward in a way Poly's line never managed.

His fall revealed a Colt Detective Special in her hand. She leveled it at Johnny.

"Lady, you're not going to fire. You're the type that maneuvers others into doing your killing. The act itself is too vulgar. Besides, you might end up in the papers."

She let the gun drop, stepped over Pete's body, and sat down on a sofa, crossing her legs so that her shiny jodhpur boots glowed.

"I need a cigarette."

"Ma'am," said Johnny, "I have to say, you're a cold slice of tomato."

"It comes from being born into not quite enough money."

Duane went feet-first through a window, hit the ground rolling, but didn't lose a step. He ran, he ran, he ran, until the scrub woods swallowed him and he was safe from the man with two machine guns.

Made it! he thought.

He hit a road that he knew wound this way and that, skirting marsh, but would eventually take him back to civilization. Bus out of town? Nah, too much exposure. He had a sockful of dough and could pick up a car with some of that. Then up the peninsula to Delaware, eventually New Jersey and a fresh start in New York and—

Someone stepped out of the woods ahead of him.

It was Nick, with his M3 trench knife.

He set down the guns, went to her, offered her one from his pack of Camels, lit it with a beat-up USMC Zippo. Then he walked over and untied her husband, who pulled the tape off his mouth.

"Good Christ, Laura, what in God's name is going on? Were you and Ontos—I mean, for God's sake, Laura—"

"Darling, why don't you ask Mr. Tomorrow? He seems to be the only one who's figured it out. God, I could use a martini."

"Sorry, bar's closed. I machine-gunned all the bottles," said Johnny. He sat down too and took a break. He'd earned it. He lit his own soothing Camel and enjoyed the buzz and the unfurling of the smoke before him, turning the room's atmosphere to something familiar and inviting.

"You make a good cigarette, Mr. Tapscott," he said after a bit. Then, still enjoying the butt, he leaned back to relax.

"I just sell them the broadleaf," said Tapscott. "Reynolds does the actual manufacturing. How did you know? How did you know? She was the one giving the orders! It was all her! Oh my god, she was going to kill me! They were going to kill me. Oh, Jesus, my wife, she was going to have me killed."

"Wasn't the first time. They tried to kill you February 20, 1945. Only that idiot Jack Petrakis shot the wrong man. He thought the bank president was you."

It was time for another cigarette. He lit up.

"They say they're going to put a little cork or paper filters on 'em next. But I'll take my tobacco straight, the way God made it. Right, Mr. Tapscott?"

"How did you know? About her, I mean, not the filters, which, yes, could kill our business."

"Baltimore. She was from there, he was from there. She went to a fancy school, but he was a big football hero and played for another fancy school, even though he was only the son of a guy who owned a diner in Greektown. In 1932, there's a picture in the *Baltimore Sun* of them holding hands at something called 'the Cotillion.' Too bad you never saw it. They've been together since then. They saw the robbery as a way to make a fast, easy hundred grand, then saw it could also be a way to knock you off, get your cigarette wealth, get all the land you'd bought for the Italian mob in Ocean City, and move it to the Baltimore Greeks."

"It's all come to nothing. The Italians are moving on Las Vegas in Nevada. I now own a lot of worthless land in Ocean City."

"So I guess there'll never be a mob city in Maryland. I suppose that's something. Let's stand up and cheer."

"But why is all this happening now? I don't—"

"Johnny Tuesday came to town and got the ball rolling by looking into stuff nobody wanted looking into. They had to get rid of him and tried twice. No luck. He was faster, shot better. But they saw in the third time a chance to make it all go away and move on to the happily-ever-after part by getting rid of both Johnny and you at once. They played everybody for the moment when Johnny kicked down the door and was supposed to put his guns down when he saw Pete with a gun against her head. He puts his guns down. Then Pete blasts him, collects the Thompson, and finishes you. So the line is, Johnny went nuts, and Pete saved himself and your wife."

"I told him it wouldn't work," said Laura. "But just like a man, he thought he knew best."

"Laura, how could you?"

"Nothing personal, darling. I do like you. It's just this Shore upper crust. So boring. I couldn't spend the rest of my life here. Mr. Tomorrow, are you sure not a single bottle survived?"

"Not a one, ma'am."

"So unfortunate."

She took a puff of her cigarette, exhaled a flume of smoke.

"One betrayal I must yet present. Try to be manly about this, dear Raymond. I do realize you boys are so looking forward to your witch-burning. But I'm afraid the witch must decline. What would Mother say?"

She revealed yet another pistol, a petite automatic, silver of course, reversed it so her thumb was against the trigger and pressed it hard to her breast. No head shot for a beauty.

She fired.

It was night. Rain hit on the windshield. The bullet hole had been patched by cardboard, the bumper bailing-wired to the frame. Johnny pulled into the yard behind Nick's.

"Okay, Stretcher-bearer, far as you go." He handed over an envelope. "Some dough I picked up in Pete's office. Use it to get out of this shithole."

"Johnny, it's my home. I have to stay. I have to fix it."

"Then you're a bigger hero than I ever was. Shake my hand and get out. I've got a long drive ahead."

"You told me, Johnny. You said if it was over and we weren't in boxes, you'd explain. Who are you, Johnny Tuesday?"

"Did I say that? It was a mistake. You don't need to know a thing."

"You gave me your word."

"So I did. That's always a mistake."

He lit up cigarette number 126, inhaled hard because he wanted the nicotine really deep, way down beneath the cellular level.

"Name's Earl Swagger, former master gunnery sergeant, United States Marine Corps, five islands, five wounds, lots of little wars before the big one. Home, a little town in the South where I have a wife and a son I hope never has to go through the shit I did. Anyway, on February 20, 1945, I took a bunch of boys to an island of black sand, sulfur, and machine guns. Night of that first day, I'm up on the line, checking our positions. I'm in a crater with a gun crew and a Jap grenade hits the ground, smoking away. We were all dead in that moment. In the next, a kid jumps on it. Takes the whole blast. I turn him over. You've seen it, you know what it looks like, Stretcher-bearer. He didn't have but a second left and he said to me, 'Tell my dad I tried real hard.' I said I would. Seems like the kind of promise a man should keep. His name was Tom Dunn. The next day, word came the boy's dad had been killed. He was a cop named Dave Dunn, murdered in some bank robbery, which had not been solved, in Shitapple City, Maryland."

He took another deep puff.

"So I couldn't keep my promise. I didn't like that a bit. I got to thinking and brooding on it, and I decided, you know what, I'm going to set this right. So that's the story and now it's over, and the best thing about it was going into the bullet garden with Nick Jackson."

"A hell of a goddamned hayride, Johnny Tuesday," said Nick.

He got out. The car pulled away and crossed the bridge out of Libertyville and disappeared down the road.

FIVE DOLLS FOR THE GUT HOOK

AUTHOR'S NOTE

GIALLO, THE NOTORIOUS GENRE OF BLOODY ITALIAN MYSTERY-HORROR films of the seventies, is the guiltiest of pleasures. It may be interpreted, cataloged, annotated, analyzed. It may be sorted by components, as in lurid cinematography, frisky camera, spastic editing, childish psychology, the degree of violence and gore (ranging from extreme to blasphemous), even the orange of the blood. One ought to note something that must be called "kill-originality"—decapitation by steam shovel perhaps the highest, arm amputation to yield torrent of arterial spray upon the wall the most highly influential. And who could forget snail attack?

The directors run the spectrum—Argento, Bava, Fulci, Deodato, and Soavi are the geniuses; otherwise it's hit-and-miss. Absurdities deserve their own separate recognition, the silliest being the mystery killer in black gloves. Most titles are dumbfounding: *Don't Torture a Duckling*, *Strip Nude for Your Killer*, and *The Black Belly of the Tarantula* vying for top honors.

There is, however, one thing *giallo* cannot be: It cannot be defended. So I won't bother. Instead, I just wrote one for you.

HOT SPRINGS, ARKANSAS, 1978

CHAPTER 1

I **AM IMPROVING.**

I am learning technique, patience, anatomy (more important than I had anticipated), speed (also more important than I had anticipated), and a certain efficiency after the act.

I saw this one, as before, at the killing chamber. It emerged into the light, unsteady. It was drunk, wobbling back to the hippy enclave where they seemed to come from mostly these days. It thought it was almost home. It had no idea a creature such as me was lurking.

The shadows are all over, the light sources uncertain, a rummage of trash and abandonment everywhere. The walls encircle, the stench is grotesque, the rats scurry and squeak. It is all of a part with the town itself, now shabby, far from the great pump houses that have drawn the people here for centuries and whose bounties seem endless. You could be in a nightmare if you had nightmares, but I never do. I invent them for others.

I lurch from the dark at it. The thing looks on me, and for that split second it considers what it has become: a waif, destitute, end of the road, fallen so far to support a habit it never intended to acquire. If it had parents, a home, brothers and sisters, that's long forgotten. It's mind has no appreciation of the strategic; its span of focus is only the next few hours, in which it must get a hit, some kind of protein, and some rest.

Tomorrow, the same crude application of clownish makeup and off then for another twelve-hour-shift at the suck-and-swallow factory. That is all. Forlorn, forgotten, tenderness eroded, memories destroyed, only a hunger with holes to be filled.

But once loved. Once lovely. Once embraced. Once nourished, once cooed over and cuddled and held close. Where did that one go? How did it become this one? How did it become so disposable?

My hand is a flash, my aim superb. I hook, I yank, I drag to earth. Some fight, some don't. This one doesn't. It gave up the fight long ago, possibly when an uncle or a brother or a father fucked it hard and told it if it told anybody he would kill it.

As usual, the blood is instantaneous and hot. So much of it. It goes everywhere, spurting from the twists of vein and artery that run through the neck. But the same stroke—I told you I was improving—destroyed the larynx, untethering it from the cathedral of the throat, so that there is no noise. Noise can be a problem, even here: you never can tell.

It lies back, and what sounds it produces may not be easily reproduced. Think of gulps too full of liquid to achieve volume, gurgles of extinction if you will, in an echoless overhanging darkness.

Now I hook, drawing the blade hard across, just over the pubis, which doesn't interest me. It is about death, not sex, punishment not recreation. The peritoneum fights me, as it always does, but this is no surprise, so my application is intense. I open a deep cut, and from the multiplicity of blood-bearing entities, now punctured, the gush is flood-like. So much even in such a scrawny creature. The second passage, deeper, pulls the coils free. It takes but a brisk nip at each end to separate them completely from the corpus. Tilting it and giving it a thump, they come out almost of a piece. It's called the gut pile. It leaves a hollow where once the core of the thing was. So violated. So debased. So deflated. Thus was it reduced to offal.

I am tired. Such exertion has a price. I feel wet about hands and wrists, my hands sloppy with gore. I am sweated up hard, short of breath. I do repeat: nothing of orgasm, nothing of satisfaction, nothing of triumph. Only a statement of nature, of who I am, what I do, what pressures formed me, how I became what I became. It was not on me, it was on those who made me. They will know who they are.

CHAPTER 2

WHISKEY DREAMS WERE THE BEST, AND THIS ONE WAS FINE. IN THE words of some song, strawberry fields forever. That is, rolling green serenity against a serene blue sky, with at a far-off edge of the world some rippling purple mountains. Nothing was happening, which was to be appreciated, even savored. Perhaps a breeze, perhaps the fragrance of eternal spring, perhaps children running and playing in the distance. You couldn't ask for more, and at this point in his life, Swagger did not. Some peace, some quiet, some solitude.

But something interrupted.

He groaned, shrugged, perhaps resisted.

The spell was broken, and as if released by a damn breaking, there came a cascade of imagery that always lurked, and was always ready to spill.

Of burning villages.

Of dead men.

Of the stench of shit, human and animal; fuel, either aviation or napalm; blood, coppery metallic, theirs or ours.

Of the empty eyes of the children.

Of a lost woman.

Of a man far-off dropping when nailed dead solid perfect by a 7.62.

Of the reality that at four hundred meters you couldn't be sure if it was a man, a woman, a boy, a girl. You could only be certain that it carried an AK.

Of the pain of a hip blown away.

Of the pain of a friend blown away.

Of the institution to which he and his father had given their lives tarnished and defeated.

Of—

"Bob. Bob, wake up, goddammit. It's nearly four."

He recognized the voice, which belonged to an old family friend, Sam Vincent, the former prosecutor of Polk County.

He blinked, coughed, shuddered, shivered, and fought his way to provisional consciousness, undercut by a desperate hunger for whiskey, tobacco, and obliteration.

Nothing had changed. Same old shabby trailer, deep in the woods of the Ouachitas. Same sounds of forest. Same clammy feel of night-sweat sheets.

Look at him. Thirty-two now, and gone to seed. Wasted, blasted, worthless, no prospects, no place to go, nothing to be. Not the walking wounded, really—the walking dead. He had died in the land of bad things, three tours' worth, except they'd forgotten to tell his body. When would it get the memo?

"Ain't you a sight," said Sam.

"Didn't know I was going on display today," Bob allowed.

"I can't say your father would be proud, boy," said Sam.

"He might know a little of what so rips me up," said Bob. "I think he saw some of it too."

"Earl Swagger never had a day in his life where he didn't put duty first."

"And he got killed for it."

Swagger remembered his father, in a State Police uniform and patrol car, on that last day in 1956 heading down the driveway to join the manhunt for a no-count named Jimmy Pye. That one was never far away either.

"So what's this about?" said Swagger. "Did my alimony check bounce? I thought there was enough in the account to cover it this month."

"No, haven't heard from Mary Louise," said Sam. "She seems satisfied."

The name of his recently divorced wife was like a smack in the face to him. A former Miss Polk County, runner-up to Miss Arkansas, she had expected so much. She married the returning war hero, beloved of time and place, connections to Polk and Arkansas deep and solid, locked into tradition and prosperity. That's what he'd hoped for too, but it was a fifties story and now it had turned into the seventies. Different times, different forces in play. Instead of opportunity and respect, he got indifference if not outright contempt, while the nights hammered nightmares like nails that could only be pried loose by the crowbar of whiskey. It led to one destination. It's not what he'd wanted but it was what happened.

"What, then?"

"Actually," said Sam, "a job offer."

"I could say yes to whatever it is but in a week I'm drunk as a skunk. I need whiskey now and tomorrow and the day after. That's all there is to it."

"Settle for coffee?"

"Black?"

"As the devil's eyes."

Sam handed over a Styro cup, Bob peeled the lid, and the stuff was not only black as hell but hotter than hell. It burned on the way down. Maybe it helped. Maybe it didn't.

"Okay," he said. "I'm as sober as I'll be all day."

"Gonna hand you something. Real ugly. You've seen worse, so have I, but it's still real bad, and nothing a man would want to see before the cobwebs cleared. Strong enough, boy?"

"I doubt it. But let's give it a shot."

Sam reached into his briefcase, handed a photo over.

Bob looked at it. He then looked some more. He looked up and down, sideways and backward. It was what it was.

"Poor thing. Did she fall into a threshing machine?"

It was a photo out of the Garland County—Hot Springs—morgue. Girl, ripped up. Ripped up butcher-style, no mercy, no precision. Just stuff that was supposed to be inside the body now outside. Yes, in the Nam guys got ripped up bad too. But that was war, the whimsy of steel, stupidity, and politics. This was just wanton hurting.

"Human threshing machine," said Sam. "She's number three that they've found. Maybe there's more. Sure enough there will be more if something isn't done. He always does 'em the same way."

"Do they have a name for that kind of thing?"

"Not even if Jack the Ripper did it back in 1888. Only one I've heard is 'repeater.' This guy's a repeater."

"Isn't catching guys like this what the cops are for?"

"Cops are buffaloed. Here, let their head boy tell you." He turned and called, "Chief."

An imposing man in khaki uniform, late fifties, white Stetson, Smith .357 on his belt and star on his chest, ducked as he entered the trailer.

"Sergeant Swagger, I'm Lawrence Bettiger, chief of the Hot Springs City Police in Garland County."

"Sir," said Bob, rising. He knew the name vaguely but had no policy toward it.

"Stay down," said the chief. "I was in the thing in Korea, and it took years to get it out of my head. I've been where you are."

Bob pulled a cigarette out of a pack of Camels on the bedside table, lit it with a USMC lighter much abused over three tours, let the smoke play in his lungs and brain, then said, "So, how's this thing here connect to me? For a repeater, you don't need a sniper, you need a detective."

"We need somebody smart who can look at stuff from different angles and maybe see something our best people have missed."

"Isn't that an FBI specialty?"

Sam and the chief exchanged glances, not a good sign, then the chief took a deep breath and plunged ahead.

"In most towns, yes. But not this one. Hot Springs is special."

Bob actually knew this. But he kept his mouth shut, smoking, gulping the coffee, hoping the headache that pulverized his brain and made his fingers tremble would go away.

"Hot Springs is trying to change. You know it was a gangster town, a whore town, for years. Your own father fought against that."

Bob had heard, although his father had never spoken of it. In fact, his father never spoke of anything.

"It's been decided that the new Hot Springs won't have whorehouses and casinos. That's all moved on to Vegas now. No, Hot Springs will have golf courses, fine restaurants, lakeside cottages, and water-skiing. It's going to aim itself toward families now, particularly with all these new superhighways that can get them here from most of the country fast."

"Makes sense," said Bob, and yes, it did.

"Even certain interests in New York and Detroit and Chicago realize that. So all of the town's owners, no matter which side of which fence they're on, are moving money in that family vacation direction."

"I got that," said Bob.

"Trying hard to get big national outfits interested. Want to get Holiday Inn and Howard Johnson's down here. McDonald's, the burger people. Some pizza places, and even Mr. DiPasquali is behind that one, no matter how much pizza he already sells. Folks have got to eat and sleep if they're going to water-ski and chase a little white ball all day. But the last thing anybody needs or wants is a lot of FBI agents in town, looking into things. A big investigation has a way of turning up a lot more than the thing being investigated. There's some embarrassments need to be ignored, some financial transactions that can't be looked at in sunlight. No matter which way you turn you're going to run into shady information. It don't do nobody good to let it out. So what we're looking for is someone old Arkansas. Your people got here sooner than most."

"Seventeen eighty by family legend," Bob said. "From the war in the east, or so we think. Not sure what brought the man and woman over the mountains, but this is where they stayed and we're still here, even if I'm the last."

"But you would understand things. You would proceed discreetly. You might uncover awkward facts as you look about. You could be trusted to keep them to yourself, track down this monster, and that would be that. A lot of folks would appreciate it, and the identity of some might surprise you."

"And I'm also guessing you don't want to see the town on the cover of *Time* magazine as the murder capital of America. 'Jack the Ripper' comes to hillbilly land, that sort of thing. Not exactly what's going to get Walt Disney to build a Mickey Mouse park here."

"Yep, and that's why there's no press coverage. We've put the lid on it. We don't want panic, attention, a circus of out-of-town press, all that kind of stuff that can happen when you get one of these sick freaks."

"I see how that makes sense," said Bob. "But what don't is me. I'm not a detective, I'm a sniper, and a squad leader, much used hard and put away wet. I got all kinds of shakes. My nightmares nasty as pus. Wouldn't know where to start as a 'detective.' Your own boys would laugh at me."

"Not so fast," said Sam. "You are the progeny of two of the finest detectives this state has ever produced. Everyone thinks of Earl and Charles as gunfighters, which is true enough. But it's only half the story. Besides that gift, they had the gift of seeing things clearly and understanding how they had to happen. They were superb law officers, particularly in the solution department of police work. I know you well enough to know you have not fallen far from that tree, that is when the whiskey hasn't turned your brain into coon shit."

"You see, our boys are hardworking but limited. They don't have no imagination," said the chief. "Including myself, maybe most of all myself. We have come up zero and we are just waiting for this repeater. And if the next one is the minister's daughter on her way to choir practice, we won't keep no lid on that. So we have to find this boy fast and are plumb out of next moves. Bob Lee Swagger is our only next move. He's our last next move."

CHAPTER 3

LATER THAT AFTERNOON, HE THREW SOME FRESH UNDERWEAR AND A
shirt or two, plus the suit he'd been married in, into a bag, then the
bag and himself into his pickup. He managed to say no to one more for
the road. Instead he had a Coke, which was a Dr Pepper, but everyone
he'd ever known had called any soft drink a Coke.

Then: gun.

He knew he had a .45 around somewhere. It was an old one, used by
his grandfather in the Great War, making it by designation a 1911 model,
not the 1923 modification called a 1911A1, which he had carried in Vietnam. The differences were basically meaningless, long as it went bang. He
tried to remember where he'd stowed it—had he sold it? nah—couldn't,
couldn't, couldn't, then did. He found it wrapped in heavy cellophane
under the propane tank out back. He saw the logic in the hiding place.
In case he woke up with suicide on his mind, it wouldn't be easy to find
and it would require a coat to go out and get. Both of those conditions
might keep him alive.

Unwrapping it, he discovered the pistol came in an ornate shoulder
holster. He looked to see the inscription, "S. D. Myres, No. 12, El Paso,
TX, October 12, 1930." He seemed to think Mr. Myres was some kind of
famous, and the piece, though sloppy-flexible from much wear, seemed

still solidly stitched. You wore it like a coat, adjusting the straps around the shoulder for proper width. It fit perfectly. The .45 slid into it smoothly, knowing it well. Maybe modern rigs were now better in design, conceal-ability, comfort, but for now, it seemed fine. It hung under his left arm, butt toward his right turn. It came out fast. He knew he'd have to get some modern ammunition.

He drove the forty-seven miles down U.S. 7 through Polk and halfway across Garland to what was fancifully called the Valley of the Vapors. There, nestled in the flats between two scouts of the Ouachitas, lay the city that claimed to be America's first resort and with its thermal waters had been an attraction to folks, some of them not even crooks, for more than two centuries. He found a room booked in his name at the grand Arlington, the hotel at the northern end of Central Avenue. Like all of Hot Springs, it had seen better times and was about as "grand" as a pud-dle of piss. Peeling paint, the smell of decay and mold, faded carpets and scuffed furniture, a bed dating from the Battle of Pea Ridge, most bulbs out. Most of all, empty. Also: sad, squalid, dusty, staffed by old people who'd lost most reason for living. Once the gathering place of swells and princes, legendary beauties, the place might now be the picture in the dictionary next to the word *shabby*.

The same was true of the town itself. He had a few bright boyhood memories, mostly involving his father, who was a celebrity and treated well wherever he went. In those days, the Medal of Honor was the biggest of deals, and his dad was one of the state's three World War II recipients, plus most knew he'd had a big hand in driving the New York people out of the town. So he had trouble paying for steaks or drinks, and no trou-ble finding tables, where folks came by and shook his hand all through dinner. Those were happy times, maybe the happiest. Lucky is the boy who can look up to his father. Earl was quite a deal, until Jimmy Pye ended it in a cornfield north of Blue Eye in 1956, or so the story went. It was one of Swagger's ideas to look into that thing in the cornfield, but it hadn't happened yet. Hard to investigate your father's death on a pint of sour mash and corn. Hard to find the bathroom on a pint of sour mash and corn.

But he needed to see more. Applying Marine skills, he realized recon was mandatory on a new mission. Driving slowly down Central, he could see the eight stately bathhouses still dominating, reluctant to give up on their glory, even if they had lost much allure with the invention of penicillin, a sure cure for the clap whereas the 101-degree water was more effective in fantasy than fact. The Lamar, the Buckstaff, the Ozark, the Quapaw, the Fordyce, the Maurice, the Hale, the Superior—they looked like castles or forts, their elaborate brickwork and tiles radiating a sure sense of importance in the world. And why not? After all, they had impressed Al Capone and lit up many a postcard.

But two of the houses were shuttered and one had been taken over, informally and illegally, as a kind of three-story teepee for a tribe of anonymous younger folks, who had in common tight jeans, lack of sexual differentiation, desperately bright T-shirts and hair, everywhere, falling toward the earth in torrents and gushes. It was a thing Bob didn't get and never would. It had no part in any America he had left behind three times to almost get killed for. He just shook his head, more in sadness than in anger.

Beyond the bathhouses, he passed through the sordid club district, headquartered on 13th Street, now fallen to a disease called pornography. Where elegant concubines had gotten a thousand a night for their efforts was now mostly a quarter-peepshow slum where that coin bought you a minute's worth of film of some poor woman stripping. The Southern Club was long gone after the disappearance of its owner, Owney Maddox, in 1946 as part of the reform campaign—it was called the Veterans Revolt— whose true violence had never been documented. Swagger suspected it hadn't been as benign as the newspapers made it out to be. That was what his father had been in the middle of.

A few joints remained. The Mardi Gras, the Club New York, the Carousel, and the House of Pleasures were still there, and in them, he knew, forlorn young gals in grown-up makeup tried to push demi-cocktails at $50 a throw, champagne at $200 the bottle. A tip maybe got you a blow job. He'd seen red-light districts the world over, and they always made him sad. The girls got tough fast, learned every angle, it seemed, the first night, and so no matter where, the thing was a big sex casino, where you laid your money down and maybe got what you wanted and maybe got an empty hotel room where you waited for a sweetie who never showed.

Driving on to a more formal "downtown" revealed only that the commercial action had moved out to the edges of the city, and the once-thriving department stores were boarded up. They'd been killed by malls now lurking on the ways out of town, where fast food had also set up, killing the downtown luncheonette scene. Other retail hung on grimly, a shoe store, a few drugstores, a men's clothing store that now catered to the black, here and there a "convenience" store that sold a twentieth of what a grocery sold, but opened earlier and closed later (you paid for that too), a sporting goods store that only pepped up during deer season, still months away. At the far end of Central was a cluster of admin buildings, for even a dying town needed someone to change the lightbulbs and paint the benches, at least occasionally. Here too was the half-and-half public service building, one side given to the firefighters, the other to the cops. He knew he'd spend a lot of time in that one but was not in a rush to come in today. Today would be about Not Drinking Bourbon.

Not easy, but that's why he stayed in his car. If he stopped and got out, all sidewalks would run downhill and end in a dive, bleak and broken, but with a magic cityscape of bottles gleaming behind the bar, a utopia of blur and daze. Didn't matter where you went, there the bottles would be, calling him with their mute beauty, their amusing shapes, their sharp-colored labels that all read one thing: "Drink Me!"

I want to, he thought.

It built, it rolled uphill, it crushed all before it, the beast called The Thirst was pure mercy for the woeful, the terminally depressed, the abandoned warrior. It made the voices go away, the pictures stop, the throbbing in his steel hip quiet down. Death—but, before that, disgrace—was also on the road, and he knew it. And he knew it didn't matter. Death sometime, even soon and in shame, weighed little against the mercy of the now. Most days he wasn't strong enough to fight it off, and today hadn't been decided yet.

To fight it, he let his eyes roam. He turned arbitrarily down a street that in a few blocks turned residential, lined with neat but small houses, most well-kept but the occasional abandoned one looking like a black tooth in a mouth of white Chiclets. A few people were out and about, here and there kids in games, yielding the street as he came by. All seemed healthy, happy, of good feature and well loved now. He thought of a man with a knife closing on them to issue wounds of the sort he'd seen in the picture, and the rage perhaps drove some of The Thirst from him. Tomorrow, when everything was official, he'd have to confront forensic reports, morgue pictures, crime scene charts, all of it, and begin to try to make some sense of it.

But he allowed himself a little reward for making it this far without a drink: a fantasy of drawing down on the guy with the knife in his hand. He had his granddad's .45, now tucked into the ornate old shoulder holster from Mr. S. D. Myres of El Paso. Drawing from it and putting seven hardballs into the boy with the knife would be so rewarding. It would be worth staying sober for.

CHAPTER 4

A MEETING. OF COURSE A MEETING. BUT ONE LOOK AT THE HOT SPRINGS
Homicide Squad told him exactly why they'd been so bested by this
killer. It would be the squad where they sent the guys who were too old
for the street and its head-busting duties, yet too young, by a few years,
for retirement. It's where unsuccessful careers went to die, exemplified
by men not quite good enough to move up to Little Rock's more professional, more highly paid entity, but who would not be defeated by the
town's generally self-explanatory homicides. You didn't need deduction,
interpretation, advanced forensics, or anything of the sort to solve the
one where the husband had a frying pan stuck in his skull and the wife
was crying. The gang days long over, there were likewise no tommy-gun
rubouts or raid gunfights that needed the highest of detective tactical
skills. But Swagger was not inclined to be judgmental; not being reformist
or ambitious by nature, he had no need to fix the situation. He just hoped
it wouldn't get in his way. That would be enough.

He faced them, they faced him, in the dowdy squad room, decorated
with wanted posters of those whom these guys would never catch. They
were equally dowdy, equally downcast, late forties, early fifties, lumpy
suits—well, the one piece of news was the youngest, a black man, whom
Swagger appointed his assistant because he seemed to have some energy

and he had connections into the prominent Rollins clan, the family that ran the town's small black population.

"First off," he said, "I'm not pretending to know it all. In fact, I know nothing. But that's why I'm here. The chief wants somebody who can come up with new approaches, as it seems the old approaches haven't really panned out. Moreover, because of the delicate situation in the city's financial development, we know we have to go after this real low-key. We all know it's a special kind of a case, to be solved in unconventional ways, so I will be the right man for that because I don't know what the conventions are. If I do something really stupid or overlook something really obvious, I can be corrected. I ain't pulling no rank or doing no yelling or firing, and I do not want to mess up anybody's career. I thank you ahead of time for your patience and forbearance."

This elicited no comment.

"So, can someone bring me up to date so I don't repeat work?"

It was Bill Canton, nominal head of the squad, who spoke next. He was a tall, reedy man, with wire-frame glasses and a soft voice. He did have big hands, helpful for smacking folks around. But he seemed tired; none of the pep and gung ho of a leader. He wanted retirement, not far away, more than he wanted this killer.

"Sergeant, I've gathered up all the files and the forensics, the photos, the coroner's report, all the paperwork, such as it is, for you to familiarize yourself with."

"Good work, Lieutenant Canton. That'll be real helpful."

Canton then said, "Let me sum up, if I may. Get things off to a fast start."

"Go ahead."

Canton pointed out that the usual steps had been taken, as one would expect. Even Bob could have figured them out, off no experience. First all those in the city's records for crimes of a sexual nature were visited, braced, put through ringers of varying sorts depending on how they struck whichever detective was visiting. There were twenty-seven such miscreants, some self-exposers, a few rapists, a Peeping Tom or two. None of them had a past of violence, and none of them impressed his inquisitor as being the sort capable of this kind of thing—even the rapists, who weren't head-bangers but oily persuaders who wouldn't take a no. The same was repeated on a larger scale for wife beaters or abusers, though this was even further off the profile of the murderer. All local institutions for the mentally ill were quietly visited and canvassed for reports of escapees or runaways or recent releases. Nothing there of note. Informally, Canton had also canvassed the state, looking for similar crimes in other venues. He found nothing. Here is exactly where the FBI's national reach was called for, and its absence was clearly felt. Then a detective had spent a day in the archives of the *Arkansas Democrat-Gazette*, looking for anything similar in the thirties, forties, or fifties. Nothing.

"May I ask," said Swagger, "have you made any contact with the psychiatric folks? Maybe a head-doctor could help us develop a profile and we could go at it that way."

The silence answered the question. He realized that these guys probably didn't have the knowledge to ask the questions, much less understand the answers.

"We have increased patrol activities in the 13th Street area. Had to pull 'em in from the edges, but there haven't been any killings since. Maybe he's noticed and called a halt."

"And I'm getting that you've found no physical evidence off the bodies themselves. No footprints, cigarette butts, nothing dropped?"

"That's the number one problem," said Canton. "There ain't no evidence. All three grave sites have been slick as a whistle."

Silence and then Canton said, "This cocksucker knows what he's doing. And my bet is he wants to keep doing it."

Yes, he'd seen it before. What angry steel can do, whether traveling at two thousand feet per second or arriving at the end of a muscle-driven power stroke. Your first reaction is disbelief, always, because bodies are not supposed to be rearranged like that. It takes a second to get it organized and relate what is there to where it should be. You need orientation spots for that, having to find the chin, the chest, the pelvis, sometimes buried in slop, sometimes simply askew. A few were of the body coming out of the ground, a few more, including the one he had seen, from the slab. More detail from the slab, as the lighting was better.

"He takes time to bury them?" he asked.

"Not only bury them," said Detective Eddie Rollins, "but bury them well. We wouldn't have found the first if a hard rain hadn't fallen, and enough dirt washed away for an old lady's dog to kick up a fuss. A patrolman scuffed at the spot with his foot and uncovered an elbow."

Rollins, a youngish guy in horn-rimmed glasses, seemed eager and peppy enough, and Swagger thought his racial identity would give him the outsider's perspective that might be helpful. He might not be locked into the old ways like the others.

"So that would tell us that he doesn't want to get caught. He doesn't want to be famous and enter the headlines and then textbooks."

"Except for the body, neatness counts for this guy. You can see that, with the girl, he was having too much fun to keep it tidy. It doesn't make much sense to us. He cuts the shit out of them and then he turns into Betty Homemaker. That's where we're stuck."

Swagger nodded.

He'd been through the files now, three times. He'd learned that this poor girl was the original find, but it was so out of line for a Hot Springs homicide, the chief had made the decision to send out dog teams in wooded areas abutting but not within the national park that occupied the hills. If the mutts went all barky, the team called in a forensics guy with a methane probe. They'd found two more in the same rough woodsy area. None had been identified, as no clues remained on the desecrated body. They were so decomposed that they were difficult to read for time of death, though all had been cut hard in more or less the same ways. The assumption was that they were gals from the few remaining clubs, but it was hard to track, since the club business was strictly cash-only; nobody took names, nobody kept records, and the girls came and went somewhat haphazardly, most being addicts in need of dough for a fix. And the sheriff had decided not to send a detective to the clubs with questions or a morgue photo of a dead face, for that would stir alarm and turn the town into a circus.

Bob wasn't sure he agreed with that decision. It put the town before the girls, in that the ruckus might save a life or two but would, as all feared, break the story out and God knew how that would play. But it was his first day. He said nothing.

"So these aren't the crime scenes actually speaking," said Bob. "These are the burial sites. He's moved them. Ballsy guy, clearly has a car stashed in the area; after he kills her he moves her. Maybe the hole is pre-selected, pre-dug, to minimalize his time on the last part of the operation."

Rollins nodded. Then he said, "Not bad."

"Rollins," said Bob, "I know you're probably pissed at my arrival. *I'm* pissed at my arrival. I'd rather be pouring down my fifth JB about now. But here we are and maybe I can make a contribution. I appreciate you and the boys not rolling your eyes when I say something, until I leave the room."

They sat in a little office off the squad bay of Hot Springs' little Homicide Division.

"Sergeant," replied Rollins, "we're your biggest fans. We know we need help and we know it isn't coming from the FBI because, well, because. We know about your grandfather and your father, and we know about your three tours, your bad wound. But we also figure a sniper has probably got moves we ain't seen, and so you'll find us very cooperative."

"Good to hear. So here's my first order. I want the boys to conduct a discreet foot search for holes along the woods line. Or recently disturbed earth. I want this real low-key, say 6 a.m. to 8 a.m., before the town comes awake. If they find anything, quietly mark it, and we'll check it out that night. Maybe we'll get lucky. Since we don't have any idea when he's killing them, we don't know when he'll probably go next. Sound okay?"

"Sounds good," said Rollins.

"Then I want dogs to be run along the streets leading away from the clubs. My idea here is that he's cutting them in alleys or even, that time of night, on the street. He cleans up the blood, but he can't clean up the scent. Maybe if we find heavy scent that's the killing spot, maybe there's some clues—forensics, I guess you call them—there. Make sense?"

"Yes, sir."

"Please don't call me sir. I wasn't an officer in the Marines and I'm not one here. Call me Sergeant and I'll call you Detective and we'll get along great. Now I guess I'm going to the morgue."

"You want me along?"

"Yeah, if only to keep me outta the bar afterwards."

There she lay. The cabinet opened, the shelf rolled out, the body transferred to a slab and moved to the center of the room, then bag unzipped and peeled, Mary Jane Doe, all that remained of her, exhibited much of her private world—her interior—to the clinical fluorescent light that beamed down from above and the audience of three men in masks. She had been adroitly peeled open so that every last privacy was exposed.

"I've read the description," said Swagger to the coroner, Dr. Ebbet Conklin, "so I don't need to hear it again."

"I don't want to repeat it again," said the doctor. "Compiling it was enough."

"Maybe some highlights. No, not the right word at all. Some eccentricities, something unusual? Unique to this guy?"

"He likes knives."

"He sure does."

"I'm really an anesthesiologist," said the doctor. "This is part-time, because normally there's not enough business to keep a full-time guy going. Not like the old days. I only took a course. I'm not board-certified."

"Yes, sir," said Swagger.

"I say that in case you think I missed something. I probably did. But it's been explained to me that at this point we don't want to bring in any heavy hitters from Little Rock. Or Washington, D.C."

"We're all operating under that reality," said Swagger. "Me especially. So go ahead, do the best you can."

"First thing I see is a lot of ripping. Yanking. Pure strength against the tissue. It starts at the throat. Larynx all but pulled out. Not chopped, not penetrated, actually whole, but just sort of, er, removed."

"Strength?" said Swagger.

"Not sure how much it would take. Would it take a strong guy? Or could a normal or even scrawny guy do it on anger, or hopped up on drugs? Again, nothing definitive."

"Well," said Swagger, "it's a start. Rollins, you got anything?"

"I've seen a few knife deaths in our black town. It's not a white thing. Whites tend to shoot, not go to knife. But—"

He paused.

"Go on."

"When one black kills another, it's usually by stabbing, not slicing or cutting. It's an extension of fist-fighting, which most of us are good at. But they throw the point at you just like it's their fist, they duck and weave, they throw jabs and uppercuts and flurries, they block with the nondominant arm, they go for boxing targets, like the solar plexus, and quite a bit to the head. A strong man can drive a strong blade clean through a face. I've seen it. I don't see that here. I don't see anything but throat slit and gut ripped."

"Is the anatomy sound, Dr. Conklin? Did this guy know what he was doing?"

"Well, assuming the throat is first, it cuts out the noise. It also opens the aorta and the jugular, which go to and from the brain, draining it fast so you get a collapse in seven seconds. I'd guess the gut activity is postmortem."

"Do you see any signs of knife talent? Could he have been a surgeon, or even a butcher, somebody who's cut before? A chef? That's a Jack the Ripper angle."

"Nothing here says that. I just see rage. And then he dumps her guts."

"So he doesn't just want to kill 'em. He wants to empty 'em?"

"Yes, but oddly, he stays away from the vaginal areas. It's all lower entrails. He doesn't remove anything reproductive or sexual."

"So you wouldn't call him a sex maniac."

"Well, I can't go that far. Man kills young women brutally, has to be sex in it somehow. But in this case, not directly. It's odd, it's like he treasures the cooch, like it's holy or something. I don't get it. That's screwy."

"Maybe it can't make sense," said Rollins. "He's just a crazy sick fuck, that's all."

"There's got to be some sort of principle here, we're just not smart enough to see it," said Bob. "Something here that might lead us in a certain direction. Either of you guys get a read, say, on the knife from what you see here?"

"Plenty sharp, I'll tell you," said the doctor.

"Somehow I don't think 'real crazy sick fuck with plenty sharp knife' is going to get us very far. Is there any way you can measure the punctures to the damage on the inside of the gut and get us a length?"

"I tried," said the doctor. "It's too hacked up, and you can't be sure which entry wound leads to which internal wound. It could be a butcher knife, a hunting knife, a pocketknife, a letter opener, even a sword or bayonet. Not an axe. He's not an axe guy because the blows push the bones aside, they don't shatter them as I'm guessing a solidly applied axe head would do with all that weight behind the blow."

"He's a real ripper, then. Not a chopper, not a hacker, a ripper, but he steers clear of the lady parts. Rollins, you went to college, tell me what that means."

"No idea, Sergeant. Can't get any further than crazy sick fuck."

"Just because there's a saying 'There's a method in his madness' doesn't mean there's always a method in his madness," said the doctor.

"Good point. Maybe I'm trying to make too much of this. Okay, I guess we can—"

He paused.

"Well," he finally said, "because I don't want to come back here again, Doc, can you sort of poke through, top to bottom, and I'll bend over and look real hard."

"Sure. Detective, can you secure the body at the shoulders so we don't get any roll or twist?"

Swagger did what he felt he must do. Face just inches from the gore, he tried to read it like a landscape in which the sniper was to operate, looking for valleys, defilades, plains, any geographical feature that would suggest the way the enemy would come. He learned nothing except to confirm what he already knew about the plasticity of flesh, the autumnal turn of old blood into something like dead brown leaves, the presence, everywhere, of moisture and sloppage, all amplified by the smell of formaldehyde and the discoloration of the blue-pink overhead fluorescents. Finally, there was nothing left to see.

Still, he had a buzz.

"I'm seeing something I've seen before," he said. "Not sure what it is, can't get a fix. But I'm feeling a ringing in my memory."

"Do it again?" asked the doctor. "I have an operation at four, so I've got plenty of time."

"No, maybe just the top. Up there where he snipped whatever that is—"

"Esophageal pipe into the stomach?"

"Yeah, he started there, right? It's like the slide stop on a .45 automatic, a pin that holds everything in?"

"Well, I've never heard it so called, but yes, in principle."

The doctor probed and found the cut and, with a set of fine pliers, pulled it out for closer inspection.

Bob looked, observed, tried to read it.

"The cut seems, um, I don't know, flatter, straighter somehow. No twist, no sliding, really a very trim cut. Different blade?"

"Maybe."

"I know that cut," Swagger said. "Dammit, I've seen it before."

But he didn't know where.

CHAPTER 5

YOU COULDN'T CALL THEM CITY FATHERS, FOR THEY HELD NO PUBLIC jobs, they had never been elected, they rarely gave interviews or let themselves be photographed. Call them city owners, perhaps.

There were four of them, men in dark suits, white shirts, ties tight. All were bankerly, in fact, and exquisitely manicured and shaved. The suits didn't come from Hot Springs, maybe not even Little Rock, New Orleans, or St. Louis. Neither did anything else they wore.

"We're going to be straightforward with you, Sergeant Swagger. Not friendly, not flattering, not charming. We wish we didn't have to meet you. But in order to get it all clear, we believe this meeting is necessary."

"Yes, sir."

They were in one of the underused banquet rooms at the Arlington Hotel. His attendance had been required by Chief Bettiger. "Part of the game," the chief had said. "You know how it works in Arkansas?"

Bob did. "I do," he said.

Now one of the four explained things to him. "All of us have considerable money invested in this city, as it is now, and in hopes of how it will be. Do you understand?"

"I do," said Swagger, nodding. Faces were hard to read. Most looked more prosperous than ethnic; most looked calm, deliberate, far from emotion. Nothing would move them except results.

"It's been explained to you that the city is trying to transition to a family-oriented resort, with big play on Lake Hamilton for boating, the mountains for walking, restaurants for dining, and golf courses for the game. It's difficult, because the words *Hot Springs* conjure gangsters, whores, and gambling. Your father would know about that."

"I'm sure he did."

"He was before our time but not our fathers'. But we know him to have been a talented man of the gun, which is why he prevailed. But needless to say, we cannot have gunfights here."

"I don't like gunfights any more than you do, sir. The last gunfight I was in blew out my right hip and got a wonderful kid killed."

"We do worry, however. You know the line: if your only tool is a hammer, all problems are nails. Would that not be so if your only tool was a pistol?"

"For some, yes. Not for me. I've seen too much of it and I don't need any more. I only carry now because as a police officer, even a special sort like me, you can sometimes attract violence. Only then would I resort to violence. I don't care to die in Hot Springs. I speak as the son of two officers killed in the line of duty, each not twenty-five miles from this spot."

"Fair enough," said the one who did all the talking. "We would have no problem in that case.

"The rest has been explained? No interviews, no photographs, no press releases. Low profile. It's hard to operate that way, but it has to be that way. Especially now, as we are at a delicate part of our negotiations. Much property is still owned by out-of-state concerns. We're trying to nurse their way out of our town for good. But they will not at all be happy if lots of attention still comes the town's way, especially if it brings with it outside investigators."

"I do get it. My people have never been reformers. We want things to run smooth, we want what's best for all. I take on principle that the ultimate goal here is prosperity in the form of new jobs and a bustling economy for everybody. The American way, you might say. Worth fighting for. That's in store, right?"

"Far more under us than under previous administrations," someone said.

But then the seeming leader had another point. "There is another issue here I should explain."

"Okay. I'm all ears."

"You may think we're a little paranoid in our cares and misgivings. But there is an actual threat. The current state's attorney, said to be sure to run for governor in the fall, is a young man of great talent and ambition. If he catches wind of our little problem, it's almost certain that he'll see it as a way to put himself in the statehouse, maybe on the national stage. That would be in his best interests, as the national stage is where he hopes to go. It would not be in ours. We'd lose potential investors, gain the worst kind of notoriety. So your real job isn't to catch this killer, but to keep Bill Clinton out of Hot Springs. Remember that name. You'll hear it again."

"Clinton," said Bob, as if committing the name to memory.

Swagger left, went to his truck, and headed back to his office. He checked, making sure he was not followed—who knew these days in this place?—then turned and headed out of town, went to the new McDonald's, and got dinner. When he got back to his car, Detective Rollins was there.

"You get 'em?" he asked.

"Yep. I recognized two. Judge Thornhill, Fifth Circuit, old, old Hot Springs. Then Art DiPasquali, the Pizza King. Said to be the richest man in town. My uncle will know the other two; I should have that for you when the pictures are developed tomorrow."

"Nobody saw you?"

"No. Took off my tie, rolled up my sleeves, and I was just another invisible black man in this town."

"Good work. It's always important to know who's actually pulling strings and making decisions. So tell me about this DiPasquali."

"Got here early sixties, out of New York. Invested money in a chain of pizza parlors, moved on to strip malls, gas stations, restaurants. Owns a lot of stuff now."

"Any Mafia ties?"

"Only rumors. Italian, money, there'd always be rumors. I'm sure he knows some New Orleans made guys, but he doesn't hang out with them. Big golf nut, three handicap. Gives a lot to charity. Probably involved in some of the shadier 13th Street activities, but they all are. Married to a beautiful woman, used to be a dancer, Maria, used to always be in the society pages, was great for charity balls and the like, even some Negro organizations benefited from her activity. Very handsome couple. Not a blemish on the record. Big donor to the Democrats. Adapted real easily to what you might call the Arkansas way. Made it work for him."

"So he's a prime mover in this retooling of the town?"

"He's the one who sees what it can be, and he wants to be there, raking in the dough, when that happens. If others get rich too, that's fine with him."

"Maybe we ought to look into him?"

"Sergeant, it's all right to say that to me, but my advice is, don't say it to anybody else. If you end up moving in that direction, play it very cool. DiPasquali has big heat in this town, and he could bring it against you fast."

"Good advice, Detective. I will take it. Now, on to hippie land. See what happens there. Then tonight, going to try the 13th Street scene, before I get known and talked about and folks clam up when they see me. Tomorrow I'm going to the university to talk to a professor about psycho types, so I know the territory."

"Do you ever rest?"

"I'll rest the day after I put a batch of hardballs into this sick fuck."

CHAPTER 6

NAME OF TAD WILLIS, THIRTY-FOUR, OUT OF SEATTLE BY WAY OF PORT-
land and L.A. Two warrants out on him for possession in dealer
quantities. Otherwise, clean, meek, seemingly mild. Red-haired, that
thick gush of solid fiber from some secret source in the Scots gene pool,
snarling over pale skin and a froth of freckle. He wore a faded T-shirt,
once red, blue jeans that looked like they'd been dragged by a truck on
the drive out from Seattle, scuffed army boots he'd never gotten from the
Army, and a Tonto headband. Said to be bright by Narco, and not on their
bring-down-hard list. Bob assumed, therefore, that he knew the game,
had connex up high enough, and just wanted to go on as is because as
is was pretty good.

They sat out back of the old one called Buckstaff, and invasion by
hippie hadn't destroyed or degraded it. Whoever these kids were, they
kept the joint neat and did the lawn work, weeded the flower beds, cultivated the earth around the bushes. Maybe it was far from its snazziest
during the three decades where Capone may have been the patron for
the magic waters that bubbled up into it from the fires below and brought
their mercy and purity to the surface, so that after a day on the links, a
couple of hours of thermal ablution, Alphonse was ready for a night of
whores and blackjack.

Nothing of that attended to Tad. He was as un-gangster as a man could be. Flower child? Peacenik? The new male? Whatever, he was open enough with Swagger.

"Here for a nice hot bath, Detective?"

"Not exactly," Swagger said.

"Then what?"

Swagger had the natural charisma of a leader. It was just the sense of him knowing who he was, particularly useful in his previous profession as a sergeant, where his professional obligation was to get young men to do what they didn't want to do. He thought he'd lost it to the whiskey, but it suddenly reasserted itself as he put four-bore macho charm on even the wan Tad, and even the wan Tad responded.

"You know, Tad. I did three tours in the Nam. One thing I learned fast was the smell of marijuana. It was everywhere. I would say 95 percent of the enlisted and 40 percent of the junior officers were midnight tokers. Never went that way myself as I'm from whiskey people, and if I want to get knocked out, it's gotta be something from a brown bottle. So when the door opened just now, I smelled what seemed like twenty kilos of Mexican ditch weed. Hit me bang solid. Made me want to move to San Francisco and put some flowers in my hair."

"Well, maybe there is some illicit weed on the property. I do have the impression that owing to certain arrangements I have with certain people we weren't going to be bothered as long as we behaved. That kind of accommodation was why we—can't tell you who 'we' are—relocated to Hot Springs."

"Don't surprise me a bit. I'm old Arkansas and know how the town operates. And I don't really have the power to violate your arrangement. It would stir up a lot of dust, which nobody wants. But I ain't stupid. I know that Buckstaff is the center of marijuana trade in Hot Springs and that the shit comes up out of Mexico via Texas. I know that it's lucrative and that certain folks get a cut in exchange for their protection and that nearly everybody benefits. I ain't here to tear up the arrangement, run a raid, and put marijuana kingpin Tad Willis on a plane back to Seattle for five dank, cold, wet years in a Washington state pen."

"But you want a cut, is that what this is about? You want a taste too. Why not? It's Hot Springs. Everybody gets a cut. I just thought I had protection from freebooters cutting in. I might have to make some phone calls and we'll see what the big guys make of your idea."

"I'm going to surprise you here, Tad. Don't want a dime. Not here for dough. Not a money grabber. Never meant much to me. Only whiskey. Hah, hah, joke's on you."

It was baffling to Tad, whose youthful face knit in bewilderment.

"See," said Bob, "I'm a special kind of detective. I am legal, you betcha, but I didn't come up through the police way and I was never at no police school. They brought me in because of two reasons: first, I'm old Arkansas, as I said, and know the game. But more important, they got a kind of a special problem and the old ways of doing things don't seem to be working. So I'm here as an outsider to find new ways. So for a little while, as long as they think I'm special, I do have some power and I could make a case for shutting this place down. I'm thinking you probably wouldn't want that."

"Nobody would want that. What's the special problem?"

"Well, one of the special things about it is that it has to remain secret. News gets out, you get bad dust and attention, and that's where nobody wants to go. Just take it from me: it's special."

"Okay, so—"

"So here's one of my ideas. I believe this thing I'm working on to be outside the normal underworld, so that all the in-town snitches and spies, they're of no use. No bail bondsman is going to hear anything on this baby."

"I know where this is going."

"Smart boy. Bet you do. I want you to listen to your kids. They go everywhere, they linger and loaf and smoke, all hours of the day or night. They might see something. They're not of the sort who goes to the police with such things. But they talk among themselves and probably know as much about this town as any street cop. So your new job is to monitor that chatter and if you hear of anything weird, strange, out of sorts, I want to know about it fast."

"What sort of things?"

"If I give you categories, you concentrate on those categories. It locks your mind up. You miss everything outside of those categories. That's no good. So it's wide-open. If it's enough for Billy-from-Houston to tell Suzie-from-Denver, then Tad-from-Seattle has got to tell Bob-Lee-from-Blue-Eye. I'm going to give you a phone number, you call it. Don't think something is unimportant. In this deal, there is no unimportant. You do that and you'll never see the inside of a Washington State cell. Got it?"

"Yep."

"Another thing. I'm sure you got kids coming and going all the time, hard to keep track of them. You don't keep records, right?"

"It's not a motel. They don't sign a register. They hear about stuff on the road and come and crash for a few weeks or months, then hit the road again."

"Well, I'd guess if Susie wanted to try Phoenix, say, she'd tell her friends, her boyfriend, everybody would say goodbye, it'd be formal. You'd play her favorite Dylan on the tape deck as a goodbye tune. But what about this: she just disappears. Her stuff is still here. Nobody knows what happened. The presumption, Hot Springs being a gentle-on-my-mind kind of place, is she met a fella and took off. Or her folks tracked her down. Maybe she called them all of a sudden because she was sick of the tramp life, whatever. Sudden, unexplained disappearances or—"

He stopped.

Something was at play on Tad's face. His eyes went up to the corners of his sockets as he closed this world out and tried to make some other connections, recall some fresh data.

"Three weeks ago. We had one of those. Very sweet girl. Pook, I think. I told her not to go to work in that place. But she did and one day she just vanished."

CHAPTER 7

FROM HER LEFT-BEHIND BELONGINGS, A NAME. JEN MACY, TWENTY-ONE, of Raleigh, North Carolina, called "Pook" by friends, pretty but quiet, dropout from UNC, recently into cocaine, which destroyed her life. She needed it in a bad way, lots of it, now. So she got a job—so sad—hustling drinks at the Mardi Gras club to pay for all the white girl she just couldn't say no to.

From the Raleigh police, a recent photograph, pre-hippie. It was from her sorority at school, where she'd been something called a Kappa. Regular features, frost of blond hair, wearing a sweater and a little circle pin and a string of pearls. Hard to reconcile this image with the gaunt, haunted face, still distended by bruising, Bob had seen in the morgue but after a bit of study he and Eddie Rollins agreed it was the same young woman.

This was treated as a sort of major breakthrough, and Chief Bettiger was extravagant in his praise, which Bob discounted because the chief was over-relying on his supposed detective talents inherited from the two previous Hot Springs Swaggers.

Later, alone with Rollins, looking at Pook in the Kappa house—she reminded him of his wife, Mary Louise—he couldn't help blurting angrily, "What a waste."

"That's not a cop thing," said Rollins. "Cops don't make emotional contact with a homicide victim. They're just pieces of furniture. It muddies things if everyone gets weepy because each one is weepy. Just telling you."

"Same way in the infantry, where kids die all the time. I saw a lot of it—too much, in fact. Sorry, all the booze must have rotted my brain more than I thought."

"So what now?"

"Going to the Mardi Gras."

"You sure? Start asking questions about a missing gal and it might get around, exactly what we don't want."

"I won't go as a cop. If this is illegal, keep it to yourself. I'll go in as a private investigator here from Raleigh to search for this girl. Ask questions that way, nobody connects it with anything going on in this town."

"That works, only the Mardi Gras folks then got no obligation to cooperate. If you're a cop, they know you can bring trouble, but a dick from out of state? They're going to have to be convinced to get on board, and the kinds of folks that work in that place are going to take a lot of convincing."

"Good to know. Maybe I can come up with something."

"Then there's the booze. Everyone knows you had a bad problem. You go into that place, all the bottles, everyone else belting it down and laughing it up, full of smoke from cigarettes and maybe joints, everything loosey-goosey, maybe the temptation yanks you off that wagon."

"That's why you're going in first. You see me sip a drink, you dig out your patrolman's billy club and give me a hard smack on the head."

Eddie laughed, thinking it was a joke. But it wasn't.

Bob sat at the bar, nursing a scotch and soda, chosen because he was a bourbon drinker, and hoped that scotch held no allure. So far so good. Four chairs down, Eddie nursed a beer. Was he known as a cop? Hard to tell, but nobody had paid him much attention except for a black bar girl who thought she'd hustled him for an expensive piña colada and now sat next to him, whispering untrue secrets into his ear. That at least told the room he was occupied.

On looking around, Swagger saw a few desultory patrons sitting with the girls who were equally desultory in sequins and faded silk and torn stockings and several Broadway shows' worth of makeup on their faces. In fact, they looked like cast members of *Cats* if that show had been called *Whores*. A couple girls had already floozied up to him, and he'd waved them away with a smile and the utterance "Maybe later."

Everybody smoked. Some kind of cheesy lantern threw beams of colored light randomly around the room, which was itself aswarm with paper streamers and other crude crepe-paper constructions. It looked like New Year's Eve in hell. A set of smallish tits with a girl attached stood at the other end of the bar waltzing with a pole. It was indifferent to her, she was indifferent to it.

He'd worked it out that the bartender was also the manager, as the little shadow people who administered the place seemed to bring him a flurry of messages, which he'd adjudicate, and they'd head back to whatever part of the empire they commanded, to put his policy to work. "Don't care how sick she feels, tell her to git her ass on the pole"—that sort of thing.

Bob gestured the good old boy over for a closer look. Yep, exactly what you'd figure on: big in body, thick in neck, tattooed on his bulked-up forearms with all sorts of tough guy bullshit, a spew of dark hair tied in a pony tail, a hefty Jesus necklace in gold hanging around that endless neck.

"Another round, bud?"

"Still working on this one, brother."

"The way it works, you rent that stool by buying the drinks. House rule."

"Oh, I see," said Bob. "Don't want to be no trouble. Yeah, another, only do me a favor, this time put some scotch in it."

The big bruiser shot him a snake-eyed look, suggesting he didn't appreciate the jibe. You got complaints? Tough shit.

But soon enough he returned with another pale imitation of a scotch and soda, put it down next to the untouched first one, and said, "That'll be twenty dollars, bub."

"Whoa," said Bob. "Thought there might be a discount on the second one."

"You got complaints, go to the manager. Guess who the manager is?"

"Big guy, stupid look on his pig face because he's stupid. Got arms all turned to purple haze, a mule ponytail, some kind of fairy strap around his head. That the guy?"

"Pal, you are looking to get busted hard. Guys like you end up in a drainage ditch, facedown."

"Okay, bub, I hear you. No offense meant. Me and my big mouth. I was trying to be funny is all."

The guy continued to lay hurt by eye on him.

"Let me show you something," Bob said. He opened his wallet to his car insurance card, flashed it, then said, "That identifies me as a private detective out of Raleigh, North Carolina. I am in search of a young woman whom we have identified as an employee of yours until she disappeared two or three weeks ago." Swagger pushed over the Kappa picture. "Take a look at this, will you, and see if you remember. Of course, she looked a lot different when she was here."

The bartender pushed it back.

"What you think this is, bud? Directory information? The missing persons bureau? Finish your drink and get the fuck out of—"

Bob hit him so hard in the snout, he broke the nose and knocked out two upper fronts. The big man stepped back, amazed at the pain and the dizziness that descended fast upon him like a shroud from heaven, and was only a little into recovery when Bob drove the broken nose upward with the thrust of his palm, and the fellow twisted, teetered, and went down hard. The first was the snake-head punch, with two knuckles extended like a reptile's prow, maximizing energy in a small area; the second was called the palm-rocket strike, meant to drive nasal bone up and in, occasionally for fatal consequences. Both had been popular in SOG circles, '68, near the Cambodian border. They were not unfamiliar to Bob.

He looked around. He had the room's attention.

"Y'all go about your business," he said. "This ain't none of yours and I know you ain't even going to remember it tomorrow." He winked at the astounded Rollins.

Then he walked around the bar, climbed on fat boy's fat belly, and smashed him three more times in the face. More palm-rocket. The nose was a dumped cup of pudding, and few other details were available under the copious amounts of blood and flaps of torn skin now blown outward over big-time trauma inflation. Fatness wouldn't stop bleeding and swelling for another half hour or so.

Bob leaned over to his ear.

"See, I don't take no smart from trash. Got that? If I ask a question, you answer. Fast, clean, honest. Or more pain ensues. I do enjoy pounding the shit out of goobers like you who think they're tough."

"She had a bad coke habit. But she was a good one. She did the job, she never gave no blow jobs in the back, she moved a lot of booze."

"Did she have a special customer?"

"No, sir. We don't encourage that. It leads to complications."

"Did she give notice? Did she tell anyone she was leaving?"

"No."

"What about friends? Anybody here close to her?"

"No, she kept to herself."

"Where'd she get the blow?"

"Not here. We don't mind grass, but blow fucks everything up. We keep the dealers out. We run a tight ship, no crap, we protect the girls. Nobody messes with them."

"How do they come and go?"

"Some walk, some drive, some are driven. They come in, they go home, they just look like shop gals. They put on the whore stuff here and wipe it off when the shift is over."

Bob thought: so she didn't look like a whore on the street. The guy wasn't going for a whore he'd gone to hard-on over in a club. He was just looking for a young woman to kill. Again, the killing, not the sex.

"Okay, put some ice on that face. You'll look human again next fall. If I come back, I'll expect you to answer without me having to fuck you over. Get it, bumpkin?"

"I am not nobody. I am Badger Grumley. You have put yourself on the Grumley revenge list," said the man. "We will catch you sooner or later. We always do."

"Well, Badger, my father used Grumley for kindling. I'll do the same if any Grumley dogs me. And I will always see Grumley before Grumley sees me."

CHAPTER 8

THE DOCTOR WAS PERTURBED ABOUT THE HAND.

"Has anyone seen that, Detective? It looks bad."

"Sometimes the job involves roughhouse," said Bob. "Last night, for example. Anyway, soaked it in disinfectant before I taped on wrap. Aspirin works on the pain, more or less. I can move my fingers, so I don't think anything is broken. I just don't have time for the emergency room."

"I'd hate to see the other guy," said the doctor.

"So would he," said Bob. "I think he'll be staying away from mirrors for a little while."

They were in the doctor's office at Texas Christian University Medical School, a four-hour drive from Hot Springs in Dallas. The room, artfully disguised as a standard office, was a standard office—books, degrees, files. By trade the doctor was a psychiatrist, and an advisor to the Texas Parole Board on issues of convict mental health, which was how Bob had found him. He'd had the Hot Springs police MD liaison make the call and set up the late-afternoon appointment.

Walking from the parking lot to the building in warm midafternoon Dallas sun, Bob had seen more than a few young women, supple, lively, full of life and hope. It broke his heart. They seemed so far from the forlorn creatures on which his quarry preyed, but maybe not. The Hot

Springs killer was a testament to the fragility of it all. You learned that fast in a war but forgot it just as fast when you got back. The killer, however, reminded everybody. Stuff can just whip in on the wind and waste you totally, and there's nothing that can be done about it. The Ripper man is everyfuckingwhere, all the fucking time. He came when he wanted and did what he wanted. He was random death, only in human form. Best hope was that someone untarnished and unafraid would follow on and deliver justice, however late, and thereby stop any further such horrors. Without that, the world would be too tragic to endure. Bob hoped to be the someone.

"So maybe tell me explicitly your needs," said the doctor. "Once I start yapping, there's no telling where I might go."

"Three killings in Garland County, Arkansas," said Bob. "I won't show you the pictures because they'd ruin your sleep for months. That's what they've done to mine, and I did three tours with the Marine Corps in Vietnam, so I've seen some things."

"Okay," said the doctor, bracing. "I only did one, but it was with FirstAirCav at an advanced field hospital in the A Shau. So I've seen some things too. But do go ahead."

Bob liked that immediately. Whatever, it meant the guy had seen some shit. He went on, trying to stay dispassionate as he took the doctor through the three bodies uncovered, with emphasis on poor Pook, the last. He set forth his conclusions, patchy as they were, then felt a need to explain.

"I've inherited this thing under special conditions owing to things I can't control. I'm not even a trained detective. On top of that, I can't bring in the FBI, don't have access to first-class forensics, can't put out bulletins to other outfits for similar patterns."

"That's why you've come from out of state?"

"Yes, sir. It's all political bullshit, but there you are. So I'm just groping. I've told you my findings and they're not much, even if I ID'd the last victim. But I'm still buffaloed by one thing: the guy is crazy. What he's doing makes no sense. He's not a part of any underworld, there's no escapees from asylums in the region, nothing in our files or the Little Rock files connects or infers. I was hoping you would see some things I wouldn't and could come up with some principles I could use to produce some results."

"First off," said the doctor, "I'm going to suggest you stop using the dichotomy 'crazy-sane.' It's not helpful at all. The lines between conditions will vary deeply between suspects, may even vary day by day. If you convince yourself you're looking for one kind of guy, the part of him that's the other kind of guy will get away. For example, maybe his proposition—what he thinks the killings will say or accomplish—would strike us as crazier than hell. But inside that, everything is rational, logical, carefully thought out by high intellectual application. So which is he, crazy or sane? Conversely, maybe his proposition is quite sane: he wants to save the wetlands, say. But his solution is violent anarchism. Again, which is he? Even I'd have a hard time figuring which side of the crazy-sane line this guy is on. It's all blurry, and in the blur it's hard to find a sensible way to investigate."

Bob nodded.

"Here's the dichotomy I would advise and that I think is most useful. I would make a distinction between organized killer and disorganized killer. That can be known from the forensics, whereas the crazy-sane can only be diagnosed after apprehension, observation, and extensive interview."

Again Bob nodded. It made sense.

"The out-of-control killer is probably driven by rage. Something has happened to him of a deeply traumatic nature. Both consciously and unconsciously he wants revenge, or maybe redemption, or to erase a stain on his identity. That's when he goes into the cutting frenzy. But even still, you see a pattern. No sexual organs. Nothing to the face, no decapitation, nothing to the limbs. The throat, to shut her up and to give access to her body, and then the midsection for—well, for what? Emptying, I'm thinking. Somehow the ceremony being carried out isn't random, but under the gore is quite precise. What does emptiness mean to this guy? He wants them empty. I have no idea, but it does seem to me that that's a theme you might find in other aspects of his life. He's been emptied, he wishes he had been emptied, he saw something or someone get emptied. Any idea what tool he's using? Is it designed for emptying? What would such a tool be, where would he be exposed to it, why would it be so meaningful to him? There's a pattern there that means something to him, although supposedly sane folks like you and me could look at it forever and make no sense of it."

"That give me some ideas," said Bob.

"But then there's this other aspect of his personality, the organized part. No rage there. Rather a need to control. Everything in its place, or else. He wants tidiness. He wants alphabetical, he wants discrimination by size, by shape, by color. I'd bet he rehearses very carefully. He goes to the murder site several times and under differing circumstances so he knows how it'll look, day or night, rain or shine. He watches the police patrol patterns. He has several escape routes. If he drives to it, he knows where to park, he'll always have gas and never get a parking ticket. He probably has a timetable, knowing when he's vulnerable, when he's not. He does not want to improvise. He's probably familiar with others who've played this game, from Jack in 1888 all the way to Leopold and Loeb in 1927. He knows what they did wrong, what they did right. He won't make the same mistakes. You'll have to bluff him into making a new mistake. Anything I'm saying making an impression?"

"Empty. Yeah, that's it. She's already dead, so it's not the killing. Why does he waste the time and the energy? Pulling all that stuff out isn't easy, as any deer hunter can tell you. But it's important to him. It's the act of emptying."

He got a buzz off that statement. What? It was like the cut he'd seen before. Something there, behind the screen. What. *What?*

"So you have to reconcile these two parts. Can he be both enraged and precise? I believe it would be a first. But somehow they fit together, they enable. Without them both, he couldn't function. With them both, he's become the whirlwind."

"Maybe I'm overmatched."

"Sergeant Swagger, I was over there when you were. You never heard of me, but I sure heard of you. Bob the Nailer overmatched? Not a chance."

Driving back in the twilight. Trying not to think of whiskey. Dead girls ripped open will do that to you.

Whiskey.

Whiskey.

Whiskey.

Bam, it hits you with a mallet. When you come back, everything has softened, gotten funny, is happening slowly. Voices are quiet, memory gone to sleep, aches and throbbing vaporized. That thing under the shoulder in the old piece of leather isn't a pistol, it's a kind of nostalgic antique, maybe recalling other Swaggers, other issues. The images of the dead reduced to primal gore—here, there, everywhere—are gone.

He thought he ought to get something to eat, as he hadn't had a bite yet today and it was near on six. He looked to the roadside, saw fast food, but he'd had so much of it lately, and he wanted to avoid places with the temptation of the hooch. On the other hand, some nice family place would still offer beer or wine most probably, and maybe he'd treat himself to a sip and wake up in the middle of next month married to a Filipino lady with seven kids. Mindanao was said to be nice this time of year.

In the end, he pulled into a 7-Eleven—for the ambience, of course— and got a tuna salad sandwich, a pack of chips, and a Coke, i.e., an Orange Crush, and consumed it lounging on the fender of the truck. He'd been offered a squad car, but somehow that didn't feel right. The bad thing about the truck was no radio, so if he was out, he had no contact with Eddie or the department. Thus, when he finished, he thought he ought to check in and went to a pay phone next to the store. He had an 800 number, to save him the hassle of a pocketful of coins. He dialed it, got the switchboard, and the op recognized his voice and put him straight through to Rollins, but no answer. He then tried Canton.

"Homicide, Canton."

"Detective, it's Swagger. Just—"

"Sergeant Swagger, you best get in here fast."

"On my way. What's up?"

He read the edge in the old cop's voice. Maybe it was fear.

"We found another one."

CHAPTER 9

SOMETIMES IT FIGHTS, SOMETIMES IT DOESN'T. WHICH SUGGESTS—DOES it not?—how unevenly is distributed the will to survive in our sad little species?

The last one simply yielded and waited for the inevitable. It was the perfect victim. This one, however, was a damned wildcat. Perhaps I didn't get the blade in deep enough on the first stroke, and the blood flow wasn't copious enough to quickly enervate. Perhaps it came from rough circumstances and was used to assault—hence no shock, no stunned surprise, no panic. Instead, the fight reflex, no thought wasted on the instantaneous change of circumstances or the unfairness of it all, no *Why me?* occluding its movements.

It twisted away, stumbled, went down, and tried to squirm to safety as if safety were an option. I sprang then onto its back, pinned it with both knees, tried to press a shoulder against the ground for the upper-body stillness I required, and made ready for a better stroke to the neck. But it wouldn't stop squirming. It was like riding a rabid pony.

It bucked and fought, and its surprising strength rode through the thighs and buttocks and nearly tossed me off, bronc style, this in spite of the wound in its throat. I fought against that, could hear its scraped breathing, its cursing.

"Fuck you, fuck you, fuck you," it kept saying, and inadvertently drove an elbow into my thigh, which gave me a bolt of pain—first, aside from minor abrasions, in my campaign. I knew I'd bruise up like a rotted piece of fruit tomorrow, and that would involve difficulties to be dealt with then. But it was no time to relent.

I planted my left elbow into its back, just below the neck, and gave max pressure, stilling it for a second and that gave me enough time to get a fully expressed launch into the neck. This time the blade worked brilliantly, and I could feel the frisson as it slid through the flesh; I pivoted for the hooking action, caught what I needed to catch, eased off on the full-body pressure, and this time gave it a full-strength outward yank. Things cut, things were torn, things fought but then gave with a sense of popping.

I rolled it over, not wanting to see face but to get at the throat more fully. I did more work, rather messy but urgent even as I could hear its breath spluttering, as if contaminated with excess fluid. It gurgled, it bubbled. I thought of drowning, but full exsanguination took place before the lungs could fill to dysfunction by ingestion.

Now, dead, it lay slightly curved. It was time for the next. I gathered. I rearranged clothes, pushing up blouse, pushing down panties. There it was, all of it. I took a deep breath, set the blade properly, and did what I had so desperately to do.

I emptied.

CHAPTER 10

THE EARTH YIELDED HER RELUCTANTLY, AS IF OUT OF REGRET. TWO masked patrol officers with trowels scraped away dirt, trying not to disturb what it was the dirt concealed.

It was the same thing, only more private. This time, the killer had hidden her a short way out of town, in some bushes behind a strip mall. But the same mechanism applied: somehow some rain had washed away some dirt, enough to expose part of a foot. This time it wasn't a dog who made the discovery, but a fourteen-year-old boy who was looking for a baseball that had entered the vegetation from the other direction, from a playing field behind a housing development.

Swagger stood aside, watching as the men continued in the headlamps of three cruisers arranged to bring illumination. It was a ceremony of sadness, as no one there had done, even conceived of, such a thing. It was ripping their guts out too.

The coroner supervised, though softly.

"Be careful, now. Don't pull or yank. Before she's anything else and after she's anything else, she's evidence. You don't want to be the one who screws up the investigation."

"No, but I'd like to be the one who pulls the switch on this guy at the Varner Unit," said one of the patrol officers. "I'd fry him up real slow."

"All right, Tommy," said the chief. "We all feel that way, but let's stay professional."

In time it began to drizzle. Cop jackets came out; one was handed to Swagger, and he pulled it warm against the wet and the chill. It seemed to take hours. It did take hours. But the deployment of a photographer to capture images of the exposed body in the ground intimated the conclusion of that phase.

"Okay," said the coroner. "Now let's get her onto the gurney."

Gently yet numbed, the two officers did their duty, including the disconnected gut pile, which might have been the hardest, then faded off to smoke and dream of the switch on the chair at the Varner Unit.

"So let's see if she has anything to tell us," he said. "Now before we move her any more and the temperature changes. This rain won't hurt her."

The little clump of men surrounded the girl's blasphemed body.

"Christ," said the chief, "I ain't ready for this. I'll see the report tomorrow." He bolted for his car.

That left Bob; Rollins; the older guy, Bill Canton; and the doctor, however reluctant they may have been.

"Sergeant Swagger, you mind if I stay? Seen a lot of murders, maybe I can pick something up," said Bill Canton.

"Please," said Swagger. "Much appreciated."

The coroner ran the beam of his flashlight up, down, and around his target. After a while, the circle of illumination seemed to reveal something gone toward abstraction. Nothing made sense, nothing was real, it was just a swirl of red with some kind of solid waste looping through it.

He lifted one arm. Abrasions ran down its inside, from wrist almost to armpit. The elbow was bruised, clearly dislocated.

"This one fought," he said. "The others were so overwhelmed they just yielded and went quietly. But not this one. She was a tiger."

"God bless her," said Canton. Then he said, "Doctor, maybe check under her fingernails. She may have ripped him. If you can get some of his blood, we can at least get a type. That'll help sort out suspects later on."

"Very good," said the doctor.

They examined a few more minutes in the flashlight.

"Seems to me he wasn't as neat up there by the throat as the last one," said Bob.

"Maybe the struggle threw him off," said Eddie. "Poor fuck was all tired out."

"He will be dissatisfied with this one," Swagger said. "It didn't go as planned. That means he'll try again soon. He'll want to correct for his mistakes this time." All that, of course, was based on his conversation with the Dallas shrink: if their boy was a control freak as part of his killing need, he'd require perfection and regard anything else as failure. "Could he have been rushed? Maybe surprised?" Bob wondered.

"Maybe check patrol patterns, talk to the officers. They might have almost stumbled across him, just missed, but scared him into sloppy work," Canton said. "That way we find the murder site. Maybe more forensics. Something to take us the next step. Doc, am I right, you conclude this had to be the same boy?"

"I believe so," said the doctor. "Throat, abdomen, removal of lower colon coils, no damage to sexual organs. He's not interested in the vagina. She's not to be raped, she's to be torn."

"Emptied, would you say?" asked Swagger.

"Yes. For some reason I can't fathom. But that's common to all four cases."

"Could you come in close on the cut at the top and the bottom?"

The doctor brought the light close to each zone, let it linger. Bob bent and almost got his nose in it, focused hard. He felt a buzz. Somewhere, somehow, not so far off, but from a far different world.

"That cut again," he said. "I noticed it the last time. It's more like a snip. It's a clean pull through. No sawing, no slipping, somehow it's different than the other cuts, which are more punctures or rips and twists. Or am I seeing things?"

"No," said the doctor. "Our boy again. Could he have two weapons, one for stabbing and slicing, and another for cutting through thickness?"

"Maybe a pincer for snipping," said Eddie.

"Good, Eddie. Electrician?"

"More a gardener."

"Yeah, vines and stuff."

"Unfortunately it's in every gardener's basket. Must be ten thousand of them in this town. Lots of flowers."

"Okay," said Bob, "but if this guy is a planning freak, he'd have the best tool for the job. No Chinese Walmart crap for him. So maybe go to high-end garden shops and see if someone has ordered special pruning clippers from someplace like Europe or Japan."

"I'll put people on that first thing tomorrow," said Canton.

"It's not much, but it's something," said Swagger.

If ever there was a night for whiskey, this was it. He'd tried, he'd failed. Another young woman horribly murdered while he drove around in circles, coming up with trifles of nothing. So stupid. "Emptying." "Snipping." "Dogs sniffing out murder sites." "Checking for pre-dug holes." "Organized versus disorganized." "A buzz on a particular cut."

None of this shit advanced the investigation, no matter what anybody said. ID'ing the body of the poor girl from North Carolina had just been a freak and, since it appeared her death had nothing to do with anything in Raleigh, was irrelevant.

Lord God, he wanted some hooch. Lying alone on the bed in his room in the Arlington, staring at a ceiling untouched since it was built in 1904, feeling the swish of the slow-moving rotary fan on the ceiling in a web of shadows from the lights outside on Central, he knew this would be a bad night, even if it was already half-gone. Sleep was still a long goodbye away.

And even in sleep, there was no mercy. It was the jungle dream again. He had killed men in so many landscapes it was hard to keep them straight, but at least a little part of the time he operated in triple-canopy jungle, a wet mesh of tangles and vines and huge, clawing elastic leaves, only glimmers of sun getting through the three layers of leaf, the ground beneath a kind of soup. But it was the vines that were the worst.

They snapped and whipped and tugged. No ordinary machete would work, because they were so elastic that when its blade struck them, no matter how hard, they didn't sunder, they retreated, bunching together, growing thicker, more impenetrable. He remembered then thinking of his father on Guadalcanal and realized anew what he had always known, how tough a campaign that had been, how brave his father had been to get through it. Nothing in Nam, he believed, was as tough as Guadalcanal or Tarawa.

He seemed to remember something else. Not sure if it was real or imagined, as the two frequently intermingled in his brain. As he either remembered or invented it, he had dropped a main force sergeant on a crooked trail through the heaviest stuff but was surprised when a squad came out of the walls of jungle just off the path through it. They were not guerillas, they were trained soldiers, first he'd seen in this part of III Corps. They laid down a blanket of suppressive fire, and the brush around him lit up with AK strikes, the dust rising, bits of wood and leafage going supersonic, pelting him with beestings and blood-yielding punctures.

Time to get the fuck outta Dodge, buster.

He back-crawled, pivoted, and headed out. He'd opened a pathway coming through in the first place, but if it speeded him it would speed them. He could not get into a firefight because besides his Remington .308 he had only a .45 auto. He hadn't brought his grease gun because he knew the jungle would be so dense the subgun would catch and twist on the vines. He'd left his spotter behind for the same reason. He had but one chance, and that was to flee. And the only way to flee was to chop.

He hit the vines over and over. They snarled, they lashed, they wrapped, they shackled, trying to pull him down as if he were caught in barbed wire. They wanted him dead. They were as much the enemy as— And yet suddenly they yielded. They melted. They went away and he didn't know why. It was as if there was a blur at that part of his dream or memory, some secret that was not ready to reveal itself.

Real or not? What did it matter? It was real in his dream, which was all the reality he had at the moment.

He could hear men behind him, he could hear chopping, he could hear heavy breathing as the effort wore on his pursuers as well. It had devolved into the most primitive of athletic contests, the death race. Could he outrace them, or tire them so much they gave up? Nothing elegant about it, and he thought they enjoyed an advantage, as the jungle was their natural habitat, where he himself had grown up in hardscrabble Arkansas hill-brush, which might cling but generally gave way to a thrust from a knee or a yank from a hand.

Oxygen? What's that? You take it for granted until you can't get enough of it. Then your lungs scream for it, the pain scalds your brain and death seems preferable. But somehow he kept going, now and then cutting hard against a tangle of tendrils that worked for the other side. It became incoherent. It was an ordeal without end, without even a clear direction, a clear vision, a conceptual end in sight. The rifle kept banging against him, as did the canteen. Dump them for speed? But both might be necessary soon enough.

A river.

Had he crossed it?

Was this the right way?

Was there safety on the other side?

Where the fuck was he? His map might hold the answer, but there was no time to unsnap the pouch, unfold the map, and orient. Instead he blundered, sloshing into the water, feeling the coolness up to his thighs.

Then: idea?

From where?

Who knew?

From somewhere, and that of course was good enough.

He splashed in loudly, stomped ahead, but then instead of crossing, he moved upstream perhaps fifty meters. He was afraid they would come upon him halfway across, and then enjoy the turkey shoot.

At a certain point, he veered, returned to the bank he had left, and found a solid prone position in some thorny stickers whose pain he did not feel. He waited. He waited.

There were five of them, the khaki of the Army of the Republic of North Vietnam, complete with pith helmets. Each carried an AK with a curving magazine; it looked like a scythe, not a gun. They were otherwise costumed for the festival called war, with bayonets and grenades and even—this would be the guy in charge, probably—a Tokarev pistol in a black leather holster. They took up positions on the bank, and the man in charge considered. Follow the American across the river? Catch him, kill him, escape? Give up the chase? It never occurred to him to send men up and down his bank, in case the American had doubled back and was settled in for his own ambush. Too stupid? Too untrained? Too greedy for American blood or a medal or revenge for the sergeant Swagger had already killed?

Whatever, in time they headed across, holding rifles above head, treading carefully as the water rose until it was halfway up the chest. The current seemed not to be so bad, but the sucking mud under the surface pulled hard on their boots, slowing them with suction and weight.

He waited until they were more than halfway across, then shot the first one in the head, threw the Remington bolt, watched as the scope came out of recoil into recovery, and settled on another, stopped still in shock and confusion. This one too took the shot to the brain and launched back in a froth.

The surface of the water was calm after those two, as the remaining three men had wisely taken themselves below the surface. He scanned through the scope, looking for bubbles signifying escaping air, or turmoil, thrashing, anything indicating oxygen debt and the panic of being underwater with oxygen running out. One suddenly exploded midstream firing upward, sucking desperately at oxygen, getting it, and then a bullet through the lungs. In that turmoil, the smartest of them, having ditched rifle, helmet, belt, bayonet, grenades, and canteen, came blasting from underneath in a spray and clambered ashore. Bob tracked, but the shot never became clear, and so that was one point for the enemy team. There went the shutout. He pivoted to his side, realizing that the last one must have gone the other way, across the river, and he found him just as he squirmed into cover, and the shot may not have been fatal but it was certainly damaging, tearing through what appeared to be buttock as the man disappeared.

He waited. Gun smoke, not a lot but enough, the smell of burned powder, drifted in the humid air and on the surface of the water, ripples still radiating outward from the sites of men splashing hard under the imprint of death. One of them floated by, facedown, clouds of floating blood furling and unfurling in the green water. He waited again. He waited.

Finally, an hour later, it was still quiet. Dark was still half a day away, too long to wait. More bad guys might show up at any time, so he felt he was stretching it. He felt the cleansing wash of the water, coolish, against his clammy skin. With as little of him showing as possible, he made it across, slid into the brush, and waited again for signs of ruckus. None coming, he blinked awake, covered in night sweat and the twist of sheet—soaked—around his legs. It was like the water pulling him down, but in a second he realized where he was. In his room at the Arlington. Dawn just behind the low mountains through the windows. A cool breeze over the living. It was 0530. Oh, how he wanted a whiskey.

And then he had it. From nowhere—or an unknown somewhere. A memory. A mercy. A break. It was like a pal reaching in to pull him out of somewhere unpleasant, a burning vehicle or a collapsed hole or under a fallen wall. Yep, there it was, saving his life: if not an answer, a beginning to an answer.

LC-14-B.

CHAPTER 11

NOBODY SPOKE. THAT WAS THE GRAVITY OF THE MOMENT. UNCLE LESTER rarely issued summonses these days, preferring to remain mysterious in his Ouachita lair, but now and then, stirred by outrage, he gave evidence of his existence and his power.

Daddy's F-150 ate up the miles between Hot Springs and Batesville, a hundred odd of them north. Next to Daddy sat Daddy's brother, Emerson. Uncle Em didn't speak either. Both looked ahead, and, for large men, they looked rather uncomfortable. Each smoked heavily. Each had pushed his hair back under the greasy discipline of Murray's Superior Hair Dressing Pomade. Each man wore a fresh white rayon cowboy shirt, pressed jeans, and pointed reptile-skinned Lucchese boots, shined. Daddy had a bolo tie in the shape of a steer's head, while Em's collar was open, showing a thatch of bristle.

Badger Grumley sat in the back. As junior to both as well as the object of this ceremony, he knew better than to talk. He breathed through his mouth as the chunk of bandage and plaster reshaping his ruined nose had no openings for nostrils. That itself was torment, and many a time in the night, Badger would awaken, choking for oxygen. Additionally, although the swelling had receded, the vision in his left eye was still blurry and watery. The doc had told him it might clear up or it might not. New dental plates shone where the old ones had been broken by a fist and fallen to earth. That was the only improvement among Badger's litany of grievances, for the new ones were whiter and actually seemed to fit better.

At Batesville they jiggered west, toward Mountain View. It was somewhere up here, nearing Missouri, while being swallowed by the Ouachita, that Badger lost track and sense of direction as the truck rose ever higher, passing through small towns, thickening forest, catching the occasional quickly glimpsed vistas of the flatlands left far behind. Somewhere, not here, not there but only somewhere, Daddy turned on a little road, tracked several miles still on the upward incline, came to gates, pulled through, and the land flattened into plateau, revealing a large brick house, all gables and picture windows, surrounded by lush gardening and, visible on the approach, a large swimming pool out back, amid the several barns and out stations, pens and corrals and whatever else it took to raise things that went moo in the night.

They pulled in.

"Now, you don't give Uncle Lester no lip," his father said fiercely. "Remember, you exist at his pleasure. In olden days, a boy who done what you done would pay with more than a stern talking to. You might find yourself serving as a water-ski boat anchor in Lake Hamilton."

"Yes, sir," said Badger glumly.

They parked, entered. Admitted by a stone-faced cowboy who might have been a bodyguard, though no weapons were visible, they walked through a heavily air-conditioned room decorated in high-end bunkhouse style and were finally admitted to an office where Uncle Lester sat behind a desk, reading a report. He didn't look up, letting them stand twitching. Then he did.

Moses? Some Egyptian god? One of them Greek fellows on a high throne? Badger was not only impressed by what he had seen getting there, but by the majesty of the man himself. He wore a wide white cowboy hat, Stetson custom if you knew your hats, and had a mouth surrounded by frosty hair, both of the mustache and goatee variety. He looked like Buffalo Bill, except that if your name happened to be Badger, you probably didn't know what Buffalo Bill looked like.

Finally, he lifted his eyes, then said, "Tillman, Emerson, you run off now. Rex'll take you to the kitchen, have some nice lemonade or a Lone Star. Mamie will fix you a sandwich."

Daddy and Uncle Em left.

Uncle Lester's eyes turned toward, then leaned hard upon his miscreant second nephew or whatever he was, Grumley family lines being somewhat complex, then gestured the fat boy with the nose hiding in a mummy's wrap to sit down in a leather chair built of cattle bones.

"What am I going to do with you, Marvin?" he finally said, using Badger's proper name, for the first time anyone had done so in several decades.

"Sir, I am sorry," said Badger. "It's just he hit me from nothing, and I'd never have guessed such a scrawny fellow could lay one on me so damned hard."

"You were given that job to keep you out of the trouble you otherwise seemed to always be in, boy." He looked through some papers a law firm had collated for him. "Let's see here, breaking and entering, assault three times—good heavens, all that fighting and he still licked the bejabbers out of you?—burglary, six separate drunk and disorderlies . . . Why, boy, you are a one-man crime wave."

"I just get angry is all, Uncle Lester."

"This sort of thing does the Grumley no good."

"Yes, sir."

"When we break the law, it is for something. There is a goal to it, and a reward. If we fail and do time, that is how it goes with a Grumley. In prison, other Grumley will stand by you as you will stand by them. All of this care and observation is premised on the notion of family, not the sugarcoated style the flatland people believe in, but family as we mountain folk know it, as tradition, as organization, as team, as reliant outside of and beyond what is commonly called society. Am I going too fast here, Marvin?"

"No, sir."

"A true Grumley would have known who that fellow was who nearly castrated you. He'd have been set and ready, with other Grumley nearby, knowing the history, and when the first strike came, he'd have slipped it, and with the other Grumley hell would have been paid out, not received."

"Yes, sir."

"Do you yet know who that fellow was?"

"No, sir. Said he was a private detective from North Carolina."

"Yet I'm guessing he possessed no North Carolina accent, but one of pure Arkansawyer, as he and his people have been here quite a spell, and morever, I'd bet even Badger, hiding from his Grumley heritage in the Mardi Gras, has heard of the name and the reputation."

Badger felt his face go all confused-like in ways he could not control.

"A proper Grumley would know when a new face dropped into town, and what dangers that fellow represented."

"Yes, sir."

It went silent. Uncle Lester opened a leather-bound case on his desk, removed a long, sweet tube of Cuban-rolled tobacco, snipped off the tip, and lit it off a gold-plated lighter. He puffed, exhaled, blew smoke in rolling, tumbling waves into the room.

"May I smoke, sir?" asked Badger.

"No," said Uncle Lester, truly enjoying the pleasures of the transaction between burning fiber and brain.

"His name," he finally said, "is Swagger. Ring a bell?"

It did, sort of.

"I think—um, it seems, uh—"

"He is the progeny of near two hundred years of his people living here. He is, moreover, son and grandson of Polk County lawmen known not merely for their skills with a pistol but as well their acuity. That is, their brains."

"Yes, sir."

"I'd say you were overmatched. As I understand it, he has been a United States Marine, fought in Vietnam over three tours, came back decorated but severely wounded. Bob Lee Swagger. Remember the name."

"Yes, sir."

"He is here, I am informed, because there is a killer about. A monster bringing savagery to our young women. Even Grumley see such evil must be stopped."

"Yes, sir. Is that what happened to—"

"Alas, yes. Kept secret because Hot Springs is attempting to redefine itself as family-oriented. Grumley are interested in that transformation as well. Obviously we cannot become the charnel house of the virgins by national reputation."

"Yes, sir."

"However, long term, Bob Lee Swagger could turn out to be a thorn in our sides. He has that kind of temperament. And a natural aversion to our sorts. As did his father and grandfather."

"Yes, sir."

"Thus, Marvin, you have a new mission in life. You must accomplish it if you wish to return to favor among Grumley. You might say your future depends on it. If exiled, do you think you'd fare well in a new town?"

Both knew the answer, not worth giving.

"Observe Bob Lee Swagger comfortably. Learn his ways, his habits, his nuances, his wants and how he feeds them. Once he has done what he must do for us, then you must do what you must do, also for us. That is wipe out the shame by wiping out the man."

"It's going to be a pleasure."

"I doubt that. He's sadly better than you, 'Badger,' if that is truly the name you go by. Faster, smarter, braver, cleaner, thinner, and he dresses better."

"Yes, sir."

"As I see it, 'Badger,' you have but one choice in the upcoming confrontation. You must play very dirty. Now, boy, go away. The next time I see you, it had better be in celebration of your success or a funeral mourning your death."

CHAPTER 12

UNCHARACTERISTICALLY, SWAGGER WAS LATE. HE DIDN'T ARRIVE AT the station until ten thirty, but he seemed more energized than normal.

"Eddie," he said, "can you find the chief? And I guess Canton has horned in on this enough to be included. I may have something." He carried some object wrapped in old newspapers.

"Absolutely, Sergeant," said Eddie, rising and rushing into action.

Three minutes later all three had gathered in the chief's office, found seating, lit up, and turned to Bob.

"Okay," he said. "Had a bad dream last night. No sense telling about it, but it put something that had been hidden in my mind up front again. So I left at dawn this morning, drove back to my trailer in Polk County, and after some effort found what I was looking for. Maybe this'll give us a direction rather than just a hope."

He picked the package up, unwrapped the papers and revealed a bladed tool zipped into a triangular olive-drab canvas sheath. He unzipped the sheath and deftly removed by its wooden handle the strangest damn thing any of them had ever seen.

"LC-14-B," he said. "By 1940 Marine Corps designation, 'multipurpose tool.' Manufactured and sold to civilians after the war as the Woodman's Pal."

It looked like the progeny of a love affair between a sickle and a machete. Whichever way you turned it determined its role. Held one way by its wooden grip, it was a straight-edge chopper, a whacker, a hacker, suitable for small branches and trunks or Japanese necks. It required only strength, energy, maybe anger. Turn it, however, and it became a more precise device: one deployed its sicklelike hook, edge sharpened to murderous spinosity, to cut sharply selected vines or branches it had trapped in its curve.

"I carried this one in Vietnam for jungle clearance. You see, in the jungle the toughest barrier isn't the limbs or the leaves but the vines. They're everywhere like a spider's web. When you whack them with a conventional machete, you just push them back. The blade doesn't cut because the vines have so much play in them. You have to cut them individually or pull them up. In other words, you're not going anywhere fast.

"With your Woodman's Pal, you swing vertically down and the hook gathers them up in a bunch. At the end of the stroke, you've got them locked on the ground, neatly collected. Then you put a boot on them, clamp them tight, and give a hard upward yank, and you cut through them all, and you keep going. Saved a lot of lives from Guadalcanal all the way to III Corps."

If it was hard to imagine, he gave a quick demonstration, pantomiming the downward sweep, the crush of the boot, and the firm upward pull as the sickle blade cut through the captured twine of weeds. Then he handed it around, and each man gripped it, swung it, mimicking the downward stroke, more or less acclimated himself to it.

"Heavy enough to do some serious hurting," said Rollins. "You put a blade this thick and this sharp at the end of a good, strong swing, the momentum and the energy it delivers on contact is going to be powerful enough to split just about anything living."

"You think that's the weapon he's using," said Canton, with a hint of disbelief still lurking in his tone.

"I do," said Bob. "The cut we've found on the two girls, the upward one that releases the esophageal tube from the stomach and the lower one that releases the anal tube from the lower colon, that's the sickle cut I saw in Vietnam on the jungle vines. Smooth, no sawing, nothing ragged. Just the pure power of the edge defeating the secured vine. First he hits 'em in the throat, severs their jugular and carotid, then he rips sideways after hooking their speaking apparatus for removal. Then he opens her up across the middle with a slash of the straight blade on the other side, which gives him a long, deep rip, then he flips the tool back to the sickle edge"—he demonstrated—"hooks the coils, and pulls hard across the body. In that way he captures what he's freed up and pulls it out in one swoop. It's how he 'empties' them, which is what I believe he's doing as the point of his exercise."

There was silence.

"So," said Bob, "that narrows the pool from anybody everybody everywhere to Vietnam returnees, especially out of the southern parts, where the jungle was thick. Think also of hunters, trappers, outdoor folks who would be familiar with this instrument. So I'm thinking we visit veterans groups and outdoor or surplus stores, we find out if anyone has purchased one, we get names, which we cross-index with the list of sexual deviants and other violent offenders. We also check any sanatoriums for patients who might have had some kind of blade fetish and might have known about this thing, or tendencies for violence against women and some contact with the two groups I already mentioned. I'd say we do this, and we do it fast."

"It's real good, Sarge," said Eddie.

"It seems that cross-racial crime is quite rare," said Swagger, "but it can't be discounted, Detective Rollins. Maybe you could look into the black areas and talk to some people and see if you could come up with folks that were in the jungle or had a brother or a cousin who served. Maybe like I did, he brought his LC-14-B home."

"I will get right on it."

"Detective Canton, I see doubt on your face." Would he ever please or impress this old galoot?

"Well, first off," said the older man, "I do believe that's a fine piece of investigative work. You're right, we've now got leads and it's up to us to apply the shoe leather and turn the right lead into an arrest."

"But?" Swagger put out.

"Two things, then a third. The two things relate to size. That is a big old tool. To operate it you need full leverage. A big swing, in other words. The bigger the swing, the faster the blade; the faster the blade, the deeper it cuts. To open somebody up with it, you need to deliver it to the flesh at the end of a roundhouse wallop. Now, you say this boy is a planner. Then it would seem he has some way to lure them into an area large enough to do his work. Probably the same place. We have to find it. That's one thing."

Swagger nodded evenly. Yes, that was something he hadn't seen or thought of.

"The second thing is also a size issue. Hiding it would be tough. Not impossible, but tough. Whatever solution he came up with would be awkward, slow, involve unwrapping, or pulling a long way out of his pants or from a coat, and in this hot weather, who's wearing a coat? So, again, don't you think he has to have a butcher site where he does his work with room to manipulate and no need to hide the weapon?"

"Good point," said Swagger. Another one he hadn't thought of. The old bird knew a thing or two.

"But, and here's the real but, it did put me in mind of another thing, and I wouldn't have gotten there without it."

"Go ahead, Bill," said the chief.

"Sergeant Swagger, you deer hunt?"

"My father was said to be the best deer hunter in Polk County. I was lucky enough to go to two deer camps with him before he got killed, and I took my first buck under his guidance. After that, I went with Sam

Vincent, the Polk County prosecutor, and his boys. They made me family and I took more than a few over the years. I'd hoped someday to get back to it, maybe introduce my own son to it."

"Good for you. I hunt the critters hard myself, have every fall for forty years. In deer camp, I have seen—not every time, but occasionally—a special kind of knife. It follows the principle of the Woodman's Pal exactly, except on knife scale. It has the two sides for two tasks, the blade for cutting, the sickle hook for gathering and yanking. Maybe eight inches long. You'd carry it in a sheath, just like any knife, wear it on your belt, no one would suspect it was any different. Being smallish, it's maneuverable in tight spaces, and it's powered by direct application of strength. No need to swing and build momentum and speed. You just put your biceps and pectorals into it. In concept it's probably as old as the Stone Age. Bet the Choctaw had them chipped out of flint. You cut the animal's belly from chest on down through the gut deep and hard, open it up, then flip the knife, and with the hook get good leverage on the large colon up top and the small colon down low and, with a yank, get through them. Then you hook into the intestines and pull them out and dump them on the ground. There's your gut pile. There's your emptying."

"I've seen it a hundred times," said Swagger, remembering. Gut pile. Yes, exactly.

"This knife," Bill said, "would mostly be used by professional guides, because they're the ones who clean all the game their clients shoot. A local hunter wouldn't need it, because he's only going to get his one buck and clean it once. He can do one fine with his hunting knife and his hands. But if you're looking at cleaning more than a dozen, more than two dozen a year, this tool is necessary to your livelihood."

"So we—"

"We check all the guides against the list. If they're clean, we go to all the guides and see if they had clients or heard of clients who used this thing. We go to all the sporting goods stores that might carry or could order such a thing and see if they've sold one recently, and, if so, to whom."

"I have to say," said Bob, "Detective Canton, you are a sly old dog."

"Maybe so," he said, "but I sure wish I'd thought of it earlier."

"Might check to see if it's been used in other crimes, not here in Arkansas, but nationally. Maybe this guy moves around."

"That's good, Detective Rollins," said the chief.

"By the way," asked Bob, "does this thing have a name? Like 'Woodman's Pal'?"

"Yes, sir," said Canton. "It's called a gut hook."

CHAPTER 13

IT WAS HIS FOURTEENTH STORE, HIS FOURTEENTH FAILURE. MICKEY'S DRY Goods, Fishing Equipment, and Beverages, a hole-in-the-wall in Mount Ida, nearing the end of the list. No, said Mickey, he hadn't sold a gut hook in ten years. He sold mostly to local boys anyhow, and he'd vouch for them 100 percent. He showed Bob the one he had in stock, even volunteered to give it to him as his contribution to law and order, but Bob had no need. He thanked Mickey and stepped out to his truck.

She was lounging on the fender.

About twenty, give or take a year, crowned in red curls so blinding you couldn't miss them or forget them. What you'd call cute in spades. Jeans, a polo shirt, sneakers. She looked like Little Orphan Annie all grown up and a Kappa at Duke—his wife had been a Kappa at Duke.

"Hi there," he said. "Hoping you let me use my truck. I'll bring it back when I'm done."

She smiled. Killer. Too bad he'd given up on love and all that messy stuff that seriously interfered with his quest to sample each bourbon in the world—twice.

She said, "Hi, yourself. Last time I saw you, you were rearranging Badger Grumley's face. It's got to look better now, though I haven't seen it yet. Badger's in shameful hiding."

"He'll be around, I have no doubt. He's the sort of man you either leave alone or kill. So doing neither was my mistake, and yes, I will no doubt encounter Badger again, at his convenience. But that would mean you work at the Mardi Gras. You don't seem the type."

"It turns out there is no type. Unless you consider forlorn, bruised, beaten, abused, and a serious drug habit a 'type.' Most are dumb but not all. They don't process, for some reason or other. They are from everywhere. Some used to be princesses, some have always been whores. This is where the road dumps them. It's part of underground America. They can make enough most weeks to keep the monkey off their backs and they've fallen so far, that's all they care about."

"Sure doesn't seem like you."

"No monkey on my back, except for the nicotine in Winstons. No blow jobs in the little booths upstairs. No touching. But I sure can hustle the rubes into fifty-dollar ginger ales with some bar wash for flavoring. Amazing what cheap makeup, bad clothes, and a blonde Marilyn Monroe wig can do for you."

"You don't mince words," he said, "I like that. My name—"

"Swagger. You're a detective, but somehow different from the normal lunks in this town. I know. I found out. I find things out. Here's one, for example. The last girl he killed, the one who fought? Her name was Laura Kazynski, from Denver, Colorado. Seventeen. She didn't hang out at Tad's but at the Razorback Pagans Motorcycle Club, off U.S. 7. Cycle gal, all the way. Her boyfriend showed up last night looking for her. If she wasn't there and she wasn't at the Mardi Gras, there's only one place I'm sorry to say she could be."

"That's very helpful. We'll drop by the clubhouse and check her out, notify her local police, see if she had any entanglements that got her killed in Hot Springs. But aren't we missing something here? Namely you?"

"My name's Franny Wincombe. I used to go to Vanderbilt. I want to be Joan Didion."

"Who's Joan Didion?"

"A writer. In L.A."

"What's so special about L.A.?"

"Nothing. Her point exactly. She makes it very well. I want to be her, despite the fact that she's already her. But to be her you have to have talent and guts, and you don't learn if you've got either at Vanderbilt, in the Theta house. So I decided to dedicate a summer to adventuring, hitching across America. This is as far as I got."

"Miss Wincombe, I have to tell you that's not a good idea. Very dangerous. You don't know what kind of scum is out there. Vanderbilt may be tame, but nobody's going to rip you up for crazy psycho reasons. Have you eaten a good meal in a while?"

"I get by."

"Let me buy you a nice dinner. Not a date or a pickup, a recruitment. You've been places I can't get. You see things straight on. You see patterns. All that's helpful. You know a lot about this thing. If we're out here in Mount Ida, we're close enough to Blue Eye, and I know some good, clean places."

"Good, clean sounds good. We can discuss how we're going to catch this guy."

"Are you a celebrity?" she asked.

"Old Arkansas, old Polk County. My father and grandfather were legendary peace officers in this county. Each died in the line of duty. I'm basically a drunk. I've spent the last three years in a trailer in the woods, trying to empty the world dry of bourbon. These folks are coming by to shake my hand by way of checking that I'm sober."

"Are you?"

"Seventeen days running now. Maybe I'll stay on the wagon, but I want to at least remain aboard until I put this guy away."

"Because your dad and pop-pop were so good, they think you're good?"

"That's the idea. I haven't proved it out yet, however. Okay, enough about me. Let's get to the Mardi Gras before the meat loaf arrives."

A joke. She'd ordered fresh trout with baked potato, he'd gone for the strip steak. The place was called Wilhelmina's, after a Dutch queen but also a play on the origin of the name Mena. Said to be Blue Eye's nicest, it had a good fifties feel to it, meaning the gravy was thick as sin in New Orleans, the atmosphere was full of butter and salt—it was almost an entrée—and the salad dressing didn't come out of a bottle.

"I'll tell you what I've learned."

"First, do you think anyone at the Mardi Gras is doing this?"

"No. They're having too much fun abusing the girls or trying to peek into the dressing room. So, yes, creepy voyeurs, but basically harmless droolers. Whoever's doing these things, I bet you agree with me, has to be at least strong, lithe, maybe athletic."

"I'm not sure where you're getting your details. You're right, by the way."

"I won't tell you his name, but one of the patrol guys is sweet on me. He has no idea I'm Joan Didion, he just thinks I'm a down-on-her-lucker. He's going to save me. I'd tell you his name if it was important, but it's not. "

"Fair enough. Are the girls scared? Do they know? Do they talk about it?"

"No and no. Girls come and go in that business. If one goes, it's no big deal. She's gone off with a boyfriend, she caught a ride headed where she needs to go, that boyfriend is getting violent and it's time to disappear, she's pregnant and can't afford an abortion, that sort of thing. So when the first one disappeared, then three weeks later the second, then four weeks ago Jennifer vanished, they never saw a pattern. They never heard about any of them. They're totally in the dark. That was just before I got here. I happened to get her makeup table. There was some Pook stuff there. Nothing much. But I asked and it seemed suspicious. Then Billy the cop started hanging around. I leaned on him, he talked. He made me not tell anybody because it was a secret blah blah blah. Then he told me they were bringing in some Marine war hero said to be smart. They thought maybe he'd be smart enough to figure it out. When you built Badger his new face, I knew that you were that guy. So I sat on a bench outside the station and started following you in my '64 Volkswagen bus. Living at the Arlington. Eating at joints, mainly no-hooch joints. Twelve-hour days. Sometimes you stay up all night, or at least someone does in the Arlington, sixth floor, corner suite."

"So far I haven't come up with much," said Swagger. "I have some ideas where this is going—"

"Tell me."

"Not hardly."

"Bully."

"Go on."

"No, it's you. What you learned."

"Well, so far we believe we know what kind of weapon he's using, and it's rare enough to go after hard. That's what I was doing in Mount Ida. And I've got a theory about what's going on in this sick boy's mind."

He told her about "emptying," as discreetly as he could. She wasn't, however, repulsed, as he'd expected, but fascinated.

"You don't think he's cleaning out the gut pile like a hunter? Say, to preserve the kill's freshness, which is why a hunter does it?" she asked.

"But then he buries them. Gut, then bury. The two don't go together. That's why I discount some kind of psycho hunter."

"Okay," she said.

"My main problem is the Mardi Gras. I can't raid, bring 'em all in, sweat 'em all. That would alert the whole town something's up, especially the killer, who'd fade like smoke in a wind.

"I'll be your spy," she said. "But, see, I'm floundering too. I'm not sure what to look for. I'd hate to get nabbed just for randomly searching. Tell me what you don't know."

"Listen to me, Miss Wincombe. You *will* be careful. You push *nothing*. You have a fake story already made up so you don't babble if caught. You call me *every* night. I will watch you go to the place every afternoon. You take *no* chances, is all that clear? I think this is a very bad idea, but it's unfortunately the *only* idea. And when it's done, I'm going to give you a chunk of dough, and far, far away you go. L.A., maybe, to hang out with this Joan Diddly."

"Didion. Are you rich?"

"I have a nice piece of inherited property that I'm renting out to a very good farmer. Then there's disability from Uncle Sam. So there's some dough, yeah."

"So what am I looking for, then?"

"First, where is he getting his intelligence? He must have ears into the club. He knows when a girl is leaving and how she'll go, so he can be there. That suggests somebody in the club."

"But they're all morons."

"Maybe they're telling somebody."

"I don't see how it could happen so fast. Say it's the janitor, he goes home, tells his brother the killer. How does the brother have time to get out there?"

"That's as far as I got on that one, too. I believe there's more to this than it seems. That's why I warn you to be careful."

"Got it."

"Second, we have no idea where he's killing them. We've had tracking dogs looking for blood scent, come up with nothing. There would be a lot of blood; he couldn't wipe it all away."

She nodded. Then she said, "Here's one thing I know that you don't. Usually, the girls just leave and walk down to Central. It's risky with all the drunken, horny idiots around. But as far as I know, nobody's had any trouble."

"Makes sense."

"Some drive, some take cabs, some live so nearby it's not a problem. But here's some other way that once in a while a girl will use."

She said nothing for a time.

"I haven't found it yet, but I think there's a tunnel."

CHAPTER 14

NOTHING.

Then again, nothing.

And finally, nothing.

The great gut hook search failed, despite the whole department rallying behind it. Swagger could fault none of the officers, only his own misguided thinking.

"That's how it always is," said the chief. "You just throw stuff at the wall and see if anything sticks."

"Nothing stuck this time, that's for sure."

He sat with the chief, Rollins, and Canton in his little windowless room, tabulating the results. Even off-duty officers had pitched in, and in all, in the greater Hot Springs/Little Rock region over forty sporting goods and gun stores, twenty-two surplus retailers, twenty-two professional deer hunting guides, and ten National Park Service rangers had been consulted on the topic of either the gut hook or the Woodman's Pal. Nobody had anything to say about it.

What was the next step?

"Nothing has come in on similar 'gut hook' murders?"

"Yes," said Rollins. "But all the killings are domestic, mostly poker fights in hunting camps during hunting season. Nothing suggesting a repeater on a campaign."

"Nothing from big cities?"

"Not a thing. Well, something goofy out of New Jersey. Atlantic City, there was a mob guy called the Fish Hook Killer, back in '56. I guess they saw 'hook' and decided to send it along. Five snitches were killed in a span of a few weeks. The New Jersey State Police believe the weapon was a big fish hook, you know, used for shark, marlin, that sort of thing. Big game fish, lots of it out of Atlantic City. Easy to find a hook big enough to snag an elephant. It was said to be a warning to other guys not to open their yaps, nothing to do with our thing. Never caught the guy. There's a State Police detective named Lou Pistolli who seems big on it."

"I'll look at that, if I may."

"Then Chicago, a Polish guy used an actual gut hook, cut up his wife, but didn't kill her."

"Hmm," said Swagger.

"Unfortunately it was in 1931."

And that was it for news. The dog hadn't found any blood scent, according to Tad none of his girls had anything to say, nobody in the black part of town knew a thing.

Suddenly, three weeks in, there was no next step.

"Anybody else got anything?" he asked.

Silence.

"This is small," said Canton. "Almost not worth bringing up. But it goes to the organized/unorganized thing we keep butting our heads against."

"Let's hear it."

"Looking again at location. Three of the four bodies—not the last one—were found very near the National Forest. Not in, but almost in."

"Okay," said Bob, "so, uh, so what? Is there—"

"Yes, there is. If it's found on federal land, it goes to the National

Park Service and then it goes, fast, to the FBI. I suppose it could just be chance, but maybe not. Maybe he knew that. Not a lot of people would."

"That's another one for organized," Bob said. "He didn't want Big Fed with all their gear, manpower, forensic sophistication, on his tail. Us, he can outfox. The feds, probably not."

"It could also be one for the Chamber of Commerce," said Canton. "It could be argued this guy knew the big Hot Springs retool was going on and was somehow behind it. And—"

"All right," said the chief. "Bill, let's not go there. Your implication, then, would have to be that this killer isn't some 'sick fuck,' as you say, but someone in the business community, rather high in fact, and is playing his impulses off in tune with our hopes for the future."

"Well," said Canton, "I actually hadn't worked it out that far, but maybe—"

"Unless you have serious reservations, Sergeant Swagger, I'd suggest we steer away from the business folks. Get them upset, they could turn on us; who knows, our whole investigation could get shut down."

"Yes, sir. I told you I'd play by the rules. No complaints here."

"If you should happen to come across some really *hard* info, bring it to me and we'll figure something out. Make sure it's solid. I don't want Art DiPasquali on my ass. No more free pizza for anyone. Plus, we'll all end up on patrol beats."

"Not me," said Swagger. "I'd just go back to the bourbon-and-trailer lifestyle."

That got a laugh out of the spiritless men.

"By the way," said Swagger, then paused.

"Yes, Sergeant?"

"Just a thought, nothing—"

"Sergeant, you've done more than anyone in this room to advance this investigation," said Bill Canton, "so if you've got something, even small, we ought to hear it."

Swagger paused.

"This just popped into my head when Detective Canton pointed out we've mainly been concentrating on the last two bodies, not the two found first."

"Correct."

"It was the third, butchered identically to the first two, that convinced you that you had a repeater here. Doing the same thing, time after time. True?"

"Absolutely."

"So let's think for a moment about the first one. Where? How?"

"That was the FedEx guy, right?" asked Canton.

"Yes, sir," said Rollins.

"FedEx on delivery found a bloody smear in the street. Quite a bit of blood, too much for a blister or a cut. He was puzzling over it when a cop drove by. He signaled the officer down, showed it to him. The officer said he'd take a look around, headed up a slope to the tree line—just off Central, the slope goes up to West Mountain, which overlooks the city—and he saw a bit of hand washed out of the mud. That's what got the bus rolling. Isn't that right, Rollins?"

"That's what I recall. I think it was Officer Miller. We could get him in and—"

"No, that's not where I'm going," said Bob. "It's not the discovery I'm interested in, it's the response. At that point you had no idea this was a repeater. You thought it was isolated, and you thought that, despite the brutality, it would easily be cracked. It would be some Donna Jean or Mary Louise done in by a drunken angry husband, boyfriend, pimp, something domestic, not random. Someone would report her missing, or there'd be a clue on the body and you'd have it wrapped up and in the books by 5 p.m."

"Correct," said Canton.

"What that means is that maybe you didn't apply the full effort to that crime scene you applied to numbers three and four."

"Possible. In fact, almost certain."

"This was, when, February? March?"

"No, actually April. The 19th if I recall."

"Yes, sir," said Rollins. "The 19th."

"It's real simple, then. Maybe you missed something. Not meaning to blame anybody here, but at that point everybody assumed it was routine. Who could know otherwise? Then also, remember, this could have been his first job too, so maybe he wasn't yet as slick as he was to become. He was nervous, jangled, excited. And they do drop stuff. It's not unknown."

"As I recall, the Leopold kid dropped his glasses at the site of the Bobby Franks body, it was a rare prescription, and the next day they rounded him and his buddy up," said Canton.

"Good, good," said the chief. "I like that one. So let's go back. That is, you three, now. Again, I don't want to get a big sweep going, with a dozen men on hands and knees picking through the grass and mud, but the three of you, go now, before dark, and give it a thorough once-over."

Grass, a slope, three hundred feet up to the beginning of serious pine vegetation and another three hundred to one of the walking trails that snaked through the federal park. On the other side of Fountain Street, which branched off of Central, forming the wedge of private land on which the Arlington was located. Bob could even see the window of his room from here. Looking back, he could see down the broad Central Avenue—"America's Broadway," it had been christened—to the looming, now abandoned Army-Navy Hospital, and a little that way the Majestic and the DeSoto Hotels. Smack in the middle, like a front sight in the wings of the back sight, was the art deco masterpiece called the Medical Arts Building.

Orienting on the site in the bushes where the body had been found, Swagger divided the sloped lawn into three zones. Each fellow took one, and up and down they went, an hour's worth of careful trudging. The effort yielded about 75 cents in change, several candy wrappers and Pop-sicle sticks, but zero on the prescription glasses front or anything else that could be construed as evidence, much less a break in the case.

Good light remained, however, so next came careful probing of the brush and dirt where the forest began and where the body had been found. The site itself, located from Rollins's memory, was without feature, and in the surrounding brushes, nothing had nested. Again, it seemed quite—

"Hey, hey!" shouted Rollins.

He'd moseyed afar and was a good ninety feet north from the site of the body. Clearly, no one, including himself, who had been part of the original investigation, had ventured that far from the body. But on the theory that the repeater might have exited the area via the brush line, rather than plunging down the meadow, in plain sight of anybody who might have passed by or been gazing his way from one of the hotels, he'd given it a try. It was his idea, so all praise and credit went to him.

"A footprint," said Bob.

And there it was, quite clear indeed, the familiar elongated oval of a man's shoe sole, complete to the complexities recorded of the texture, pattern, and minor damage. This one had a nick halfway in, halfway down, where its owner had stepped on something sharp enough to cut either rubber or leather.

"We're lucky," said Canton. "And maybe he's unlucky. It's shielded by that tree from the same downpour that washed the dirt from the hand. It's melted a little, but I think we can still get a good cast of it. Gives us a pair of shoes, a shoe size, maybe from the depression some genius can calculate a weight."

"Sarge, you want me to call it in? Get our forensics team, all one of them, out here."

"Do that, Eddie."

Off he ran.

Bob got on his knees and eyeballed the print carefully. Guessed it was about a ten and a half, the ripples running perpendicular across the sole, perhaps something unique.

"Look familiar to you, Bill?"

"I'd say," said the old detective. "Look at this, Sergeant."

Canton twisted, lifted one foot, and showed his own sole.

They were identical.

"It's a Bates Police Oxford," he said. "I've been wearing them for thirty-five years. I expect to be buried in them."

Swagger looked back at the print. Momentary confusion here, an inability to add two plus two, but then he got his four.

"Jesus Christ," he said. "It's a cop."

CHAPTER 15

SHE TRIED SO HARD TO BE ONE OF THEM. SHE WROTE LETTERS TO DAR-la's lawyer about the divorce, because Darla hardly knew her ABCs. She drove Mary Claire to the county health facility when one of the tests came back positive, and then found her a doctor and made sure she kept the appointments because Mary Claire's no-account boyfriend was probably drunk. She applied makeup to Marty's eye, after the ice had driven the swelling down, because if she had a black eye she couldn't work, and if she didn't work she didn't get any money, and if she didn't get any money, she couldn't feed her two-year-old.

On and on it went, harder and harder, it seemed. The endless expression of male rage as played out on the female body, and the sad thing was, for these girls it was normal. It was just the way the world was. They had to get nude for a few bucks, they had to throw in a blow job for the occasional big spender at the Mardi Gras ($350! And she only got to keep $100!), they had to make nice to Skip, who so far hadn't beaten or raped anyone like Badger, but at the same time, as one could tell, he wasn't hardly the type you'd go to for a shoulder to cry on.

"Why don't the girls trust me?" she finally asked, straight out, to Lily Jean, whom she was driving in her rattling '64 Volks bus to the pharmacy to get Kotex to deal with an unexpected issue.

"Because you're smart," said Lily Jean, bespeaking a fundamental truth. "You know so much. We all can't hardly keep up with you, way you talk, stuff you know."

"It's just the way I am," said Franny.

"But, see, you don't have to do this. You could work in a store, a library, teach at a school, anything. But no, Franny down at the Mardi Gras, shaking her ass for the truck drivers and the out-of-town salesmen and the low-rent bondsmen for the same tip money as us. You got no scars, you got all your teeth and they're shiny to boot, you watch things and record things, you don't take no drugs—"

"I smoke too much."

"Everybody here smokes too much. You make jokes that you laugh at but nobody else even understands."

"The curse of irony," said Franny, making a joke that nobody would understand.

"You don't do no blow jobs, even if they say you been offered as much as five hundred dollars. They say you don't like dick."

"I just don't like to be touched by a stranger. If a guy gets thirty seconds of tit in exchange for fifty dollars, I suppose I can get used to that, even though it sickens me. But I'm not going to do any sex stuff for anybody, not for all the money on earth."

"See, you are way different. To us, sex is just what we do. It can be good, I suppose, though I never had me none of that kind, but it's part of being a woman on the dirt side of the poor-folks line in the South. Then there was that time you were with a bunch of us and we noticed the Medical Arts Building. And you said, 'I love deco.' And everyone just looked at each other. Girl, what were you talking about?"

"Okay, I get it," she said, pulling into the parking lot of a strip mall with a Rexall between a DiPasquali's Pizza and an Ace Hardware. "Do you have enough money?"

"For the stuff, yes. Not for no cigarettes."

"Okay, here," said Franny, handing over a five. "For the cigarettes. I want change, Lily Jean. If you kept it, you'd only give it to Ralph and he'd spend it on whiskey."

"He is my man. He says all this will change. He's working on a big deal."

"Of course," said Franny, sarcasm being another feature that marked her as different from the other girls.

Off Lily Jean went, for Kotex and menthols. Poor, wan creature, little wren of slight bones and a mere spray-paint of flesh. She'd get her stuff and get back to the Mardi Gras by four, spend an hour painting herself up in lavender eye shadow, pushing Ping-Pong balls and wadded Kleenex into her otherwise barely occupied bra in order to simulate cleavage, applying several coats of hot orange lipstick, and greasepaint to eyebrows, squeezing herself into some fool's idea of a sexy costume—heavy on sequins, pretend satin, tightly cut to curves, etc., etc.—and if she was lucky, she'd come out the other side with $75, on a real good night $175, if there was a blow-job extra payment. All she could look forward to, maybe, was a promotion to bar dancer. They usually got a good $300 a night.

Franny sighed at the wickedness of the world, knowing there was little she could do about it, but willing nevertheless to give it her best. She lit up a Winston, which no longer tasted good, like it should, and waited for Lily Jean to come back.

And then she waited some more.

And then a pickup truck squealed as its brakes halted it just to the right, and Lily Jean was dumped from it. It sped away so quickly that Franny didn't think quickly enough to get a look into it, but as it roared away she saw its back license plate: "BDGR-1."

She opened the door, went to the fallen Lily Jean, and saw that the girl had taken a hard punch to the left eye, which was swollen closed and looked like a grapefruit, yellow and blue, Krazy Glued to her head.

"Oh, baby," she said.

"He come up on me and pulled me into his truck. Then I started to scream and he hit me hard upside the head. 'You shush, you little bitch,' he screamed. Then he leaned over and whispered, 'You tell that little'—and I don't want to use that word he used for you—anyway 'that little you-know-what that I seen her hanging around Swagger, and when the time comes and she's there, she's gonna end up going down hard as he will.' Then he drove me here and dumped me."

"He is a greasy fried piece of shit," Franny said. "He wants to beat Swagger, but he doesn't have the guts, so he beats on a girl who's, what, ninety pounds, dripping wet?"

"Ninety-two. My head hurts."

"Gotta get you to the emergency room. And call a cop."

"No, no," said Lily Jean. "Please, Franny, no. There's paper on me from Yell County, they might take me away. Who'd feed my boys? I need that money real bad. I have to work tonight."

There you had it in a nutshell. Beaten but couldn't go to the cops because there was some charge against her. What, stealing chickens? Maybe a tube of perm? So she had but one choice, which was to shut up and take it and hope that convenience store ice could lower the swelling enough and Piggly Wiggly makeup could cover what was left, so that Skip would let her hustle tonight, so she could feed Baby Jim and Baby Carl. Maybe she'd get real lucky and a blow job would be on the menu.

They stopped at a Walgreens, and then a gas station for ice, and in a parking lot, Franny did what she could for Lily Jean. The ice, held hard against the puffed cheek, did some good. When the swelling had gone down as far as it could go, the makeup came out, and Franny tried to be an artist, and again, somehow, the illusion was established. The puffiness seemed to diminish under the magic of the cheesy drugstore pancake, layer after layer, applied as gently as possible. Fortunately, the skin hadn't split, so no blood seeped across the cheek to give Lily Jean's wound away.

"Okay," Franny said. "I think that does it. I can't get you better looking."

Lily Jean popped up toward the mirror, gave herself a once-over, and saw that in the dim light of the Mardi Gras she'd pass. That meant her seventy-five bucks was secure, and only a shift of tit-rubbing away.

"You have saved my life, Franny, no matter who you are. You're good people, not stuck-up like some say."

"It's nothing. Glad to help."

"You can count on me to pay you back."

"Then you do one thing."

"What's that?"

"Tell me about the tunnel."

CHAPTER 16

THE LOCAL ISSUE HAD TO BE DEALT WITH, QUIETLY, FIRST. OF HOT Springs' fifty-six policemen, twenty-two wore ripple-soled Bates Police Oxfords. Within twenty-four hours and without a lot of fuss those twenty-two volunteered their right foot for quick comparisons to the print found at the first body site. No matches. Four even volunteered to bring in their old Bates shoes, but the chief didn't think that was necessary.

After all, the process had already delivered good news, he joked. Out of roughly 4 billion people on earth, twenty-two could definitely be discounted. More important, it meant the possibility that it had been a cop investigating the first killing had wandered that far off the site.

"We're gonna have to go to the State Police," said Bob. "They'd have the resources to do it, and maybe quietly. Little Rock, the rest of Garland, Polk, Hot Springs, and other adjoining counties. Take two or three days. Do it of a sudden, so nobody has time to switch. Is it worth it?"

"They still remember your father Earl," said the chief. "Maybe if you came with me to Little Rock and explained our situation to—"

"But, Chief," said Bill Canton, "they'd want in. And once they're in, it'll get out and go big. They'll nickname him 'the Hot Springs Slasher,' to build him up so there's more glory to be had when they bring him down with all their resources. And this poor town gets nothing for its trouble and loss except the fun of seeing the Disney people tripping all over themselves running away."

"Bill," said Bob, "that's true, but it's been a while and he's getting itchy. We can't let him kill another girl, stripper or not."

"I agree," the chief said. "But Bill's point is well-taken, even if political. So let's say another forty-eight hours to work this angle, and then if we don't—well, then we go to state. Just to be sure, I'll check city hall. See if they'd be okay with it."

"They won't be," said Bob. "It's money they're thinking of, not justice. What's the big deal over one poor white trash kid getting whacked versus Hot Springs staying in the dump forever? Think of the DiPasquali Pizza that would go unsold."

Sarcasm. Actually these guys didn't get it either.

Afterward, Bill pulled Bob over for a hallway chat.

"I didn't want to say this in front of the others because I don't want to be thought of as the bad guy."

Bob sensed more criticism coming. Fine, Bill was smart, and entitled.

"Go ahead," he said.

"One thing."

"Only one?"

More unrecognized sarcasm.

"It's just that this is an extremely odd crime for a cop to commit. I know there are crooked cops, more than a few in our own department even. But when a cop commits a crime, it's almost always about money. You can see why. He works his ass off for ten years, gets all banged up, sees all the sights of the world's asshole, and he realizes sooner or later that it really doesn't matter. The bad boys go on being bad or new bad boys come on the scene worse than the old bad boys. The stupid keep making stupid decisions. He knows there are fellows in his own squad room on the take and nobody is saying a thing. He knows that without political pull it's highly unlikely he'll end up chief, or even an inspector.

The whole thing is pointless, rigged, and also dangerous. So he thinks, Why shouldn't I take care of number one? Then he sees how easy it is, how nobody really cares. And that's when it picks up. And in time, nothing matters."

"But this is way different?" Bob said.

"Yes. No money I can see in it at all. What would the money angle be? It just don't make no sense."

"If you throw in crazy, it doesn't have to make sense."

"Could be, sure enough," said Bill. "But again, that's not the kind of crazy a cop goes. The ones drawn to violence from the start for whatever reason, and I know they're there, guys like that usually sell their experience to the mob. If they're tough, they become enforcers. They collect debts. They deal with squealers. Anytime blood needs to be shed, they're the ones to shed it, because violence doesn't scare them. Or maybe they become burglars, having learned the breaking-and-entering trade. But it's always for a payday."

"Maybe a guy who wanted to be a cop but either failed or got booted early. The resentment builds and builds. It finally cracks him and . . ."

He stopped. Even he saw through that one. The failed cop was, what, killing girls—not even just killing but gutting them—to show up his bosses and get revenge for his own unfair treatment? Not impossible, but so improbable, it didn't pass the laugh test, except maybe in grade B Hollywood. It was thinner than the paper on the wall.

"Okay," he said. "Good stuff. As usual. Let me think on it and try and figure some way it might make some sense. And you do that too."

"I sure will," said Bill.

Whiskey.

He dreamed of it.

No, wait, he wasn't asleep so it couldn't be a dream. Then it was a fantasy. As in the Land of Bad Things, when home and safety seemed a universe away, and tomorrow was just another bad day in the bush—that is, if you didn't get killed tonight. That's when the fantasy of home came to you.

Now a fantasy of whiskey, in its own way a fantasy of home. You take the pint of Jim Beam out of the paper bag. You feel it slosh as you set it down on the table. It is brown. Its cap is yellow and will take but a crank to unsnare. You feel it crack and yield as you twist. You pour a couple of fingers into a hotel bathroom glass, where it splashes and ripples, then quickly calms. Limpid pool. Without quaver, without disturbance. It's just whiskey sitting in the bottom of the glass.

You raise it to your lips, maybe giving it a little slosh to hear evidence of its liquidity. You sip it. It tastes, uh, somehow not like it looks. It looks like butterscotch, it tastes like flame. Gargling it numbs your mouth, then down it goes, and wham-bam-thank-you-Jim, in a split second the world is fuzzier and friendlier, the edges not so sharp, the furniture not so shabby, the tomorrow not so bleak.

There was no whiskey. There was nothing except this little room in a half-empty hotel in a dying city where someone hunted not to kill but to desecrate. The emptier? What immortal hand or eye could frame its fearful symmetry? Line of poetry from somewhere, maybe some kid in a platoon had read it aloud one evening before they got hit. That's what made it memorable. It had stuck because it questioned the existence of God, as did all combat soldiers who had administered death, and all homicide cops with a knowledge of what a man could do to another. It was the ultimate degradation. We kill. Some of us like it. Some of us—

He sat alone under one light in his room. A ceiling fan beat its way in circles from above, humming softly. Outside, the night passed. Maybe a whisper of dawn could be seen across Fountain Street and beyond West Mountain across the way. The city was dead. It was the darkest moment of the night.

Get back to it. Think, you worthless son of a bitch. There is a certain way all this random stuff can be arranged so that it makes a crazy kind of sense.

An unorganized killer.

An organized cleaner.

A cop.

A knife for gutting deer.

Everything was from some other place, and none of it fit together. It was incoherent. Maybe there was no pattern, it was all random. Those who look for pattern go mad. No other place to go but mad. I'll end up as mad as he—!

—!

—!

—!

The world ceased moving. The atoms stopped vibrating. The air no longer circulated.

I got it, he thought. And in the second before he started writing it down, he had one more clear thought: I got you, you motherfucker. Your ass is mine. Bob the Nailer time.

CHAPTER 17

I MUST BE STRONGER. HOW CLOSE I CAME TO DISASTER. THE LAST ONE was a tough little piece of gristle and bone. It fought and clawed and almost kicked free, even if losing blood from the rip in its throat.

But who knew how much blood it could lose and still live? I expect it depends. Suppose it had kicked me in the face. I am unconscious. I drop the knife. It manages to get up and stagger away. It screams. Someone is nearby. By the time they get there, it may be dead, but the police have been alerted. They arrive quickly, dragnet, and there are limited hiding places.

It is true that to some degree I want to get caught. There is much work left to do and I can only do that from a certain place. But I want that to happen on my terms, exactly as I planned. I do not want to get there until it is time, I am fully prepared, I have learned my lines, I know my role in the theater of infamy that will ensue. Then I will have done my duty, achieved my revenge, brought justice to the world. Then I become legend. That is worth my life, easily enough, and I can die satisfied.

Thus, I exercise for strength. I have no need of heavy weights in a gym, or a trainer or anything radical and pattern-breaking like that, and besides, people would notice.

Why are you doing that?

So when I jump a victim, it has no chance of getting away.

Oh, okay. Just wondering.

That simply would not do, especially not so close to the end.

Thus, in the privacy of my bathroom, I perform a morning series of calisthenics meant to strengthen my arms and chest. The push-up, for example. Three sets of fifteen. Not pleasant, especially the last few, but necessary. Hardens the biceps, hardens the pectorals. Then sit-ups. Hardens the stomach, makes certain kinds of lifting or dragging easier. Then stretching my hamstrings. They were the strongest to begin with, but they can be improved. I stretch them to get them warm, then I hook my ankles under my bed and try to lift both legs. I can feel the burn.

In the end I am sweaty, out of breath, but oddly satisfied. I never knew such exertion was a kind of drug itself, and the harder you worked it, the more you wanted it. And the better you felt.

It seemed to clarify a lot of issues. In the beginning, the goal was a hazy possibility, and only the electricity of the act itself carried me through it. But with each successful effort, it came into deeper focus and seemed more morally necessary. It is of a higher morality than that implied in church or in the lawbooks. There are certain laws that cannot be violated, and when they are, punishment must be inflicted. Unfortunately, some who die will be innocent, as in war. Bomber pilots, cannoneers, machine gunners know what I mean. This cannot be avoided, on the old ends-means argument. I will willingly pay for those sins, as I should. But I will have my justice, no matter the cost.

Now it's just a matter of waiting for another phone call.

CHAPTER 18

H E WAS LIKE A REDNECK MORON IN A CANDY STORE. OH, WAIT, HE *WAS* a redneck moron in a candy store, which was actually the Grumley-owned Hunter's Supply of Texarkana.

"I like that one," he said, pointing.

"No, no, no," said a Grumley relative of kinship far too complex to be explicated, name only of Ben.

Badger had pointed to a hand-engraved Peacemaker, with ivory grips boasting a bas-relief stallion with a ruby eye.

"That's a used custom gun, cost over fifteen hundred dollars, and easily traced to its original owner, who would give me up in a split second. Are you dumb, boy, or are you just dumb?"

"It's the prettiest."

"It is, but pretty don't count for this job, as I understand it."

It was well after closing time. Before him on the wall hung perhaps fifty handguns, not big items for Hunter's Supply, but in small volume they were steady sellers. The place also served as arms supplier and repair installation for any Grumley enterprises involving lethal force as delivered by smokeless powder. Being the somnolent seventies, demand had not been terribly high in the past few years.

"Look at new revolvers," said Ben, thinking Badger might by confused by the mechanics of an automatic. "New, because the serial number isn't known yet to the state. No chain of ownership can trace it here, if you should get nabbed, killed, or caught, and the pistol recovered. They have to go to the manufacturer to trace it, and maybe the manufacturer is feeling cooperative and maybe not. Also, a new gun will always work, whereas with used, you never can tell what secret abuse it has been put through. It could blow up in your face. Finally, it don't pitch empty shells that can link it to a certain gun. Are you listening, boy?"

"I am, Mr. Ben." He was also breathing. The steel shank that had been taped hard to his nose was now off. He almost looked human. Stupid, but human.

"Best bet, I'd say, is that one. It's a standard Smith and Wesson Highway Patrolman, in .357 magnum. N-frame, biggest they got. Our troopers use them, that's how reliable and powerful it is. However, you don't need power, as I understand it, because you won't be shooting through car doors. You'll be loaded up with .38 Special. A fine man-killing round. If you're close enough, you won't even have to shoot twice. Once in the heart. Don't try for the head, as it's quick to move, and since this fellow is known to have his business down pat, he could evade and draw and shoot, and that would be it for Badger. The world would go into deep mourning for at least seventeen seconds."

"It's ugly," said Badger. It was, sort of. The defining quality was its thickness. The barrel was extra thick to contain the magnum blast, and under it was the ejection-rod housing, which looked like another barrel, and contributed immensely to the "thick" accusation. Some found that look damned interesting, but Badger was not one of them.

"That one," he finally said.

"I should have known," said the mystery Ben. "The most expensive. Boy, you better not lose it, because I will tan your hide for sure."

He reached out, took the revolver off its hooks, gently opened the cylinder, and handed it to Badger.

"Colt's best. Called a Python. Highest grade of royal blue finish. Highest-grade walnut stocks. Best adjustable sights. Softest, sweetest trigger pull. So accurate you could—well, *you* couldn't but some could—shoot the eyes out of a gnat at fifty feet. Yes, and pretty as pretty can be."

Even Badger got that. The revolver gleamed, highlighting its extra touches, such as a ventilated rib that ran along the four-inch barrel, and the figure eight of the cylinder release. But it was more than those details. The goddamned thing was just a masterpiece of harmonies and balances, slopes, planes, and flats, and when he put it in his hand, it seemed to live of its own volition and point ahead.

"Try the hammer," said Ben. "Gently, now."

Badger put his thumb on it and drew it back, finding smoothness, ease, but also sound effects.

Click-click-click-click.

"It's said old Sam Colt designed it so when you cocked it, those four clicks spelled C-O-L-T. Not only this gun, but all Colt wheel guns going on back to 1836 have that characteristic. Like a theme song, you might say. He was a genius, which you surely ain't, boy."

Badger loved it. The feel, the look, the way it fit his big hand, the checkering on the grip locking it tight into the flesh, the way it pointed, the way it *wanted* to shoot.

"Now, don't let this go to your head, boy. You ain't no Clyde Barrow. Don't do nothing stupid and get yourself killed or the object of a three-state manhunt."

"Yes, sir," said Badger.

"When time comes, you just walk close up behind him, point it, and pull that soft trigger six times fast. Then you turn and run like hell. No teasing, no boasting, no playing around. It don't matter to nobody if he knows it's you. Killing is serious business, and it can go wrong a hundred different ways. Got it?"

"Yes, sir."

"Do not think you can fight this polecat. He knows more tricks than a magician. He is slick as they come. He's done a whole lot of this kind of work."

"Yes, sir."

Ben went behind the counter, reached under it, and came out with a green box of Remington .38 Specials, the 158-grain police load.

"Go far out into the country. Make sure it's plenty private. Load up, and fire six. That's so you know what it'll feel like and it won't be no surprise. But don't spend the afternoon working on your marksmanship. You don't need marksmanship. You need guts. Got that?"

"I do, sir."

"And bring it back. It goes back on the wall after I clean it. If you want it, you'll have to buy it at a hundred fifteen dollars. Do you understand?"

"Yes, I do, sir."

"Now get your sorry butt out of here. Go show us you're a man!"

CHAPTER 19

MEETINGS, OF COURSE.

First with Eddie and Bill. He told them what they had to know, not quite all he knew, of course, because it always helped to hold certain things back. It went exactly as he hadn't expected. The cynical and wise homicide cop Bill, who'd poked holes deftly in every single thing he'd offered, was immediately positive in his response.

"That's damned good, Sergeant. You found the meaning in it. I see it all fit together, I see exactly what you need, and I will get on it right away to make this happen and we can nail this sick fuck but good."

Eddie, on the other hand, was shy.

"Seems like a lot of supposin'."

"I guess," said Bob. "But you have to suppose at a certain point. You can't just wait around for somebody to call in a tip."

"Most that are solved are solved by tip," said Eddie.

"Yes, but they are crimes of the community. Someone who knows a lot of people is feuding with and kills someone else who knows a lot of people. All those people talk. They understand the feud. It's part of their everyday life. One of our guys drops a dime, calls the right person, and a name is mentioned. We round up that fellow, sweat him, he cracks. This isn't like that. It's someone's deep down secret, hidden and protected so far, the deepest of deep, ugly secrets. Nobody literally knows a thing except a very few who are so involved they cannot speak."

"But you say it has to be a rich fellow. That's going to upset a lot of people. Maybe best to let the rich alone as they provide for all, in one way or another."

Swagger saw that Eddie, though black, was in many ways more wired into Old Hot Springs than was Bill. He had his job via connection with the black power structure, which in its way depended upon, and served and was in turn supported by, the white power structure. Hence, Swagger's proposition threatened all that. It was like a puff of breath against a house of cards, and once things started happening and cards began falling against other cards, nobody knew what could happen. It could take everybody down.

"I get that," Swagger said. "That is why I am proceeding very carefully. I will not go ahead without the chief, and he will not go ahead without the approval of certain people. That's why we have to get going now. It's going to take a few days."

"Well," said Eddie, "I don't know nobody could bring this off but old Arkansas—what year again?"

"Seventeen eighty. The Swaggers, from over the mountains. From the war, we presume. They never said. All the Swaggers since been here and each served something, either town or county or state or country. I am hoping to do the same."

"Sergeant, you know I will always be with you, no matter what."

"I knew that the second I saw you, Detective. You were a man I could trust."

Then on to the chief, who, no dummy, grasped not only the reality, the possibility, even the probability of the Swagger theory, but also the same danger that Eddie saw. It could upset a lot of people and bring lots of people down. This was unsaid, but it lay beneath them as they sparred in the chief's office.

"And you've tested and eliminated all other possibilities?"

"All Bill could come up with by usual police means, and all the crazy ones I came up with, with no preset attitudes at all. And the longer we wait the more likely it is he strikes again."

"Maybe get a wiretap. Listen in, pick up intentions that way."

"Yes, sir. But in the meantime girls are dying. And when you go to your city attorney to get the wiretap, you knock up against the system. No matter how you think it works for you, it does have leaks. People talk to people and suddenly we're on the front page of all the Little Rock papers. The next day, all the New York papers. You know as well as I do these folks love 'rippers.'"

"A tradition since 1888," the chief said. "I know the history."

"I do have a suggestion."

"More than welcome, Sergeant."

"We go to Mr. DiPasquali, the pizza millionaire. He seemed sensible when he and I had our little sit-down a month ago. He was the one who informed me of the Bill Clinton problem, which if anything is worse now that it's clear Mr. Clinton is gearing up to run for governor in the fall."

"That is certainly true."

"My thought is that if we can bring the town's most powerful figure in, get him briefed and believing, get him behind us, get him ready to go into support when we make the arrest, it makes this move feasible, no matter who it turns out to be. And all the rich folk are less inclined to go tribal and see this as an assault on them as a class, but just as the necessary housecleaning as the city pivots toward tourism and family fun."

"You think ahead, don't you, Sergeant?" the chief said.

"It's a sniper thing. You've always got to have an escape route," said Bob.

Bob knew Arthur DiPasquali had come to Hot Springs eighteen years ago with nothing but a pizza recipe, a beautiful wife, and a few thousand bucks. Now he practically owned the place, with interests in hotels, real estate, restaurants, a lot of retail, many of the new strip malls booming out near the interstates. He was generous to the Democratic Party, he was generous to the educational establishments, he was generous to the school system, the hospitals, the factories, even the old-Arkansas farmers still making a living in the hinterlands, if barely. He gave loans through his banks and never called them in. If your family had been there over a hundred years, your credit was good forever. Meanwhile, his wife represented the cultural half of the noblesse oblige of the millionaire class, active in grants to ballet and museums and local drama. She also was on the board of the hospital and responsible for its new wing, named after her: the Maria DiPasquali Pediatric Wing. If they were Mafia, as some said, they sure didn't look it, smell it, or taste it.

It figured, then, that he would occupy a modern building, sleek but not showy, respectful in the way it did not compete with Hot Springs' ornate historical structures, but modest and purposefully unimpressive. The chief's driver let him and Bob off for the 7 p.m. appointment, and a doorman took them through the lobby to the elevator, and punched the button for 5.

"Wish I'd bought a new suit," said Bob. "Been wearing this one for four weeks."

"You look fine. Mr. DiPasquali doesn't care about snobberies like that."

Office hours were over, and another assistant escorted them through the emptiness of DiPasquali Enterprises, again low-key and without formal adoration of the man who invented it all. They waited in an anteroom, and Bob saw the pictures of the man's ascent and, particularly, the evolution of his style, from curly-haired Italian pizza guy to corporate swank in pinstripes, under a smooth back-sweep of luminous black-gray hair, horn-rimmed glasses, and a sense of majesty.

"Come in, come in," the man himself said, bringing them into his office, which afforded a panorama of all downtown Hot Springs, looking like a Camelot as it rose above the contrasting greenery of the forested Ouachita foothills. You could see it all from here: the lights of Central, the precision and elegance of the bathhouses, the art deco splendor of the Medical Arts Building, the bulk of both the Army-Navy Hospital and, far away, the Arlington Hotel.

"Do sit," he encouraged. "Nice to see you again, Sergeant Swagger. I hear you've made some interesting progress."

"We think so, sir," said Bob. "I wanted to share it with you. Your support would be important and I don't want to drop any surprises on you."

"It is appreciated, believe me. So, proceed. Let's hear it."

"It's somewhat strange, I'm told. Usually you have suspects, which you narrow down until you've only got one left. I have no suspects. I don't know who it is. I have no idea why he is doing this. I don't even know where he is doing this, much less how. I have no snitches. On top of all that, I have no theories as to why he would choose to butcher four young women working in our 13th Street district. I'll leave that to the psychiatrists."

"They'll have a field day," said DiPasquali. "Do smoke, by the way. I'm about to light a cigar. Care to join?"

"No, thanks," said Bob, popping a Camel from the pack.

All three tended smoking issues for a quiet minute, then filled the air with torrents of twisting, curling smoke.

"So what do you have, Sergeant?"

"I know how we're going to catch him. And I know when. Tomorrow night."

C-O-L-T.

The four clicks told Badger he now held a Python revolver, fully cocked in his right hand. He felt like one of the ten kings of hell. The revolver was everything he wasn't: classy, brilliant, powerful, impressive, and the well-chosen implement of a serious man. You didn't need it to beat the shit or fuck the brains out of B-girls, or smack a bad-acting customer in the head prior to power-walking him to the street and dumping him, hard, on its cement. It was no pimp's gun, flashed to quell rebellion among the girls or sudden recalcitrance among their customers. Any old Saturday night special from the last century in .32-caliber, suitable otherwise only for dogs and hos, could handle that job.

This was a gun for bank robberies, the king crime among armed raiders, and one he had long yearned to commit, but he'd been forever limited to running a third-rate cooch bar in a dying slum of a dying city, where everything smelled of the green Odor-Rite cakes in the urinals, as bathed and brought to full bouquet by piss. Had he lived, a Dillinger would have surely been of the Python cult, as would Baby Face. Other criminal trades beckoned under the spell of the revolver's charisma: an assassin, closest ally of Uncle Lester, who would sweep into the appropriate venue and dispense order in the form of murder on competitors, snitches, police detectives, even politicians.

In accordance, then, with the majesty of the gun, Badger had already broken his pledge to Cousin Ben. He had stopped at another sporting goods shop and bought a small box of .357 Magnums, designated +P, 158-grain semi-wadcutters. The plus designation meant these were true high-power man-killers, meant to splatter into lead frags as they plowed through flesh. Each was a tiny grenade in a bullet. He had to give the gun the dignity, the respect, the adoration, of letting it loose at pedal-to-metal speed, and these 158s filled the prescription. He imagined that, attendant upon the flash and the roar, he would shatter rocks or dismember trees. It was so cool.

He looked about in the twilight. He was in the Ouachita National Forest, up a trail and down another trail, far from civilization. The lights of Hot Springs blinked in a valley below. Otherwise, no human existence revealed itself and no cars sounded on the nearby roadway. It was the zone of gray, twilight not yet devolved into night, the orange smear of the sun still warm at the western horizon. The forest rangers were probably in for the night, since the place closed at six and was locked up, though, as a Grumley, Badger knew secret entrances.

Now came the time of thunder and lightning.

He braced himself solid, assumed a gunfighter's pose, locked in his elbow, and gazed at the front sight through the wings of the back sight—mandated protocol of the handgun, he knew—and gently touched—

When he woke up, he could feel the blood running down his face. He stirred, tried to remember what and how, and only the image of a world-ending atomic flash and in the next instant the whack of a punch harder even than the ones thrown his way by the devil-dog Swagger reminded him of what energy he had just released. The smell of burned powder hung in the atmosphere.

Jesus Christ! he thought.

Bob quickly took Mr. DiPasquali to the discovery and identification of the ripple-soled Bates Police Oxford with the cut in one of the ripples.

"A police officer!" said Mr. DiPasquali.

"Well, it didn't make no sense to us either. As Bill Canton says, when cops go bad, it's usually money involved. They want theirs. But there seems to be no money angle in this thing. So it left us with an order of high implausibility: a psycho repeater maniac cop."

DiPasquali nodded.

"Then it struck me hard. Only way to organize this thing so it made sense."

"Go on," said DiPasquali.

"There's two of them."

That took the air out of the room. Nobody said a thing. A clock ticked, a far-off train whistle blew, a car horn honked.

"Maybe it's units, not men. See, this has baffled everybody from the start. How could this guy go so butcher-crazy in the killing, and then turn into a different type of man altogether, and scrape the crime scene dry of forensics? Among other things, to do that scraping you'd have to *know* forensics, as would a cop, particularly a homicide detective."

"This is very interesting," said DiPasquali.

"And if that is the case, as I believe it is, it opens a series of other doors which I believe will lead us to him."

"Go on, go on."

"The cop—or cops—are getting paid. Only big dollars would get them on such a gig. I mean, *big* dollars, bank-job numbers, white-collar numbers. It would be a nauseating thing, not only the physical reality of doing such work itself, but the psychological work of suppressing every instinct for justice following an atrocity, no matter how money-crooked they'd become. A cop of this kind knows these attacks put him in league with the most hell-bound of criminals, the lowest of all the dogs in the pound. Not even the cons will hang with the girl repeaters, I'm told. You want a man to do that, you have to pay up."

"Logical," said DiPasquali, who had leaned forward over his desk, listening intently.

"So the next question is, where would you find a cop for such a job. Maybe import him? Fly him in from some big city? Then he's a stranger to the area. He doesn't know the streets, the patrol patterns, the competence level, the context of any of it. That means mistakes. There can't be no mistakes. Mistakes are heavily lethal in this game."

DiPasquali nodded.

"Then locals? Where to find them? Bill Canton, as usual, had the answer. In Hot Springs Village, that development on the lakes, there's a neighborhood where a lot of retired cops have gone, called Elk Cove. They fish, they smoke, they play golf, they play poker, they drink, they joke about the old days. They are most comfortable, as are Marines and millionaires, among their own kind. They would need money, more than the hardscrabble pensions their thirty years had earned them. They would also know the stuff necessary for this job. They might figure, I done enough for the community, whatever that is. What the fuck? What's in it for me? And the cost is a few gals on the very far edges of society. Once every month or so.

"Who would hire them?" asked DiPasquali. "I assume you're about to tell me one of my friends. A person of high economic means. A Hot Springs mover and shaker."

"It has to be. Either he is, or he is the steward of, a killer personality, a maniac. I'm guessing a son. For many reasons, including both scandal and love and all stops in between, he cannot send this boy to prison, to an asylum, or to Sparky at the Varner Unit. A son at least. Maybe a brother. Certainly not a wife or a daughter, for there's an issue here of strength, and I don't believe a woman could manage the violence so efficiently."

"Our Mr. Big—I've probably had dinner with him and cigars—sets up this monster thing. He lets the boy kill, but he employs the ex-cops to hide the bodies and erase the forensics. All this, of course, premised on the worthlessness of the victims. They won't be missed. Nobody cares. Better for all that the family, the father and the son, maybe the mother, and the business of the town, especially at this pivotal moment of the town's evolution, go unaffected."

"That's it, sir," said Swagger.

"You were right, Chief Bettiger. This fellow *is* a great detective like his father and grandfather. What's your plan now, Sergeant?"

"Bill's already been to Elk Cove. He knows more than a few out there. He's looking for someone that's suddenly come way up in the world."

"Any luck?"

"Yes. The retired vice commander of Little Rock Homicide, named

Phil Green, has just moved from Elk Cove to Mountain View, a much more exclusive area. Big house, now drives a Cadillac convertible."

"Every cop dreams of a Cadillac convertible," said the chief.

"Has a pool, six bedrooms, a lake view, a boat. Joined a better golf club. Come way, way up in the world in the last few months. So we track him. We show up discreetly every night at two. One of these nights he'll get the call, he'll assemble the team. We'll follow from behind, and I believe Detective Rollins is known to be a good car man."

"He's had a lot of narcotics experience," said the chief. "That's a game where you're always following suspects to a dealer in the dark."

"In all likelihood they go to a preselected spot. They have made preparations. Maybe they've already dug the grave, just filled it with loose dirt. They empty it. Then they go pick up the body. They want to be on-site with the body for the least possible time. Into the hole she goes, the dirt is quickly shoveled back in, the area cleared, and they get out of there."

"Except—"

"Except we take them. We follow, we raid out of the night. They will understand quickly that if they don't want to ride the needle at Varner, they better cooperate. They give us the boy and the kill site. Maybe we can get there before another doll goes to the gut hook, maybe not. Sure try hard, but losing a fifth might be the price we have to pay. I'd hate that, but it is what it is."

"And you want my support?"

"I do. The final arrest could make a splash, unsettle folks, divide the town, bring in this Bill Clinton. We'll try and underplay it, but there are things that can't be controlled. Much better for everybody if the town's leading citizen is telling folks to calm down, these things happen, let the police do their job."

"I only say, it's so much better if there's no violence," said DiPasquali. "When you jump them, we can't have gun battles in the woods."

"I understand. That's why, instead of assembling a squad of heavily armed combat vets, it'll be just Bill, Eddie, and me, no special weapons, no night-vision. Not even shotguns. Just my grandfather's World War I .45 and whatever it is the other two carry—.38s, I assume."

"Do it, then, Sergeant. Put these beasts down."

CHAPTER 20

S CUNGE.

Scum.

Toilet bacteria.

Stain on underpants.

The worst?

There was no worst anymore. They were all the worst.

How much longer could she take it?

The dialogue that ensued between the three of them—him, the person he thought she was, and the person she actually was—followed a well-worn track.

"Ain't you pretty, though?"

Ain't you a pig in shit?

"Why, thank you, sir."

"You mind if I set with you a spell?"

Why not set your socks afire and dance yourself to death?

"Why, I'd be pleased."

"I do so like a blonde."

If you can't see this is a cheap wig, you are dumber than a fence pole.

"Why, thank you, again. Come from a long line of blondes."

"You seem of higher breeding than some that are here."

Compared to you, the lowest girl here is the Queen of Sheba.

"My mother would be so proud to hear you say so. You'd be buying me a drink? That's the rule here."

"I'd be pleased to do so, pretty gal. You pick it!"

She gestured to Skip behind the bar. She held up two fingers, meaning "Polynesian Hurricane No. 2," $50, which was ginger ale and rum-soaked lemon with Reddi-wip atop, as opposed to "Polynesian Hurricane No. 1," also $50, also ginger ale and rum-soaked lemon, but with—big change ahead!—a lump of vanilla up top.

"I sell threshing machinery for Farmfriend Inc. The Japs own it, but it's still American-run."

Who gives a fuck and a half?

"Fascinating. Tell me more."

And he did.

On and on it went, the history, mechanics, derivations, culture, and higher sociological meaning of the Farmfriend Inc. Threshing Machine, with a new $50 Polynesian Hurricane No. 1 at each change of subject. Even this clown here got a bit buzzy on the traces of rum he was consuming. That's when the hands thing started, petting her hand with his fingers, running his hand down her arm. Why, he thought he was doing pretty good and in a few minutes would be in a pink bedroom with the blond gal of his *Playboy*-inspired dreams.

"Pat," his name, "Pat, I have to run to the potty. I'll be right back. You don't let any of these others gals steal you from me. I have seen them eyeballing you hard."

"Susie, I am yours forever."

"Forever" was the thirty-nine seconds it took her to detox in the showers. Her friend Pat would now be hit with a $600 tab, no "Susie," and Skip's billy club to kick him the hell out after the credit card ritual.

• • •

She lay in the darkness in the back of the dressing room, on a cot behind a curtain. It was late. No diminution in the smoke, the smell of the Odor-Rite, the bad disco piping in, the hustle and jingle of the girls moving fellows in and out. But tonight was not her night. The drift of human carnage was too oppressive; it enervated her. She felt jellified, slugged out, without hope or future. It truly sucked.

They were locking down.

Skip rolled in.

"This weren't a good one for you. After that thresher man, you hid in here. Could have run two or three more tricks through the machine. We need the dough, you need the dough." He was a tall stretch of human foulness, a tattooed stringbean with the usual shabby-hippy hair that hung down over his ears like straw on which a goat had pissed. His eyes looked like the trout's on the mantel. Compassion? Maybe when he took a crap, but only then. The one impressive thing about him was that there was nothing impressive about him.

"I have a headache," she said. "Namely, you. Leave me alone. I produce more than any girl here. I can take a slow night once in a while."

"You smart ones. You is always trouble. Badger warned me on you. Just remember, I am watching you hard."

He vanished.

Time passed.

Another form drifted in close. It was Lily Jean.

"Hi, baby. What you doin' back here?"

"Brooding. It got to me tonight, for some reason."

"I hate to see you sad, baby. You the nicest anyone ever been to me."

"Just trying to be a human being, is all. Not much of that in this bad old town."

"I always want to see you happy."

"Some nights it isn't in me. How's the eye?"

"It went down. It's okay. I got my kids fed."

"That's great."

"Been thinkin'. You wanted to know about the tunnel?"

Franny took a deep breath. Don't blow this, she told herself.

"I did. Just in case, you know."

"You almost had need of it tonight. That fellow Pat, he made a skunk. Skip had to conk him hard, twice. Hope he don't die."

"Busters like that don't hardly never die," she said, remembering to fracture her English into hill patois.

"So here it is. It don't never hardly happen to you because you're too smart. But most of us being dumb, we don't lay our cards right. Sometimes a guy thinks he been promised more and he gets stubborn as hell. Dangerous. Killing dangerous. The girl worries he may be outside. He may feel it's right to rape her, as he was promised. And them things often go wrong, she ends up dead or broken for life. Well, there's a tunnel here. You go in Skip's office, it's right there, in the closet. But it's locked. Skip got to go with you, Badger before him. He unlocks. Then you feel your way through about a hundred yards. Be careful. Then it comes into a big Hot Springs tunnel—lots of 'em from the old days—that runs on down to the old Hot Springs–New Orleans train station in that depression in the middle of town. There's more light there. You go about a half mile, you come out the other side of Central, where nobody ever goes. You think you be on the moon. You cut left, you go up the slope, and you're on Central. Flag a cab, or walk, any way you do it, you're out of the 13th Street zone and on the way home, safe. See?"

"So a trick's got to freak on you? That's the issue? That gets you into the tunnel?" Franny asked.

"Yes, baby. Then you home free."

CHAPTER 21

SWAGGER ROSE EARLY, HAD A NICE ARLINGTON BREAKFAST, AND THEN went to his truck. It was an hour and a half back to his part of Polk County, off Route 7. His trailer seemed fine, and nobody had tried to break in or spray-paint "Baby Killer" on it. He opened up and began his search. You would think years of Marine Corps discipline would have kept him organized, but instead his mental disorder and all that Jack D. had chosen the trailer by which to express itself.

Not good. Started over, looking in some of the same places he'd already looked, realized he was competing against his own drunken self to solve this mystery. On the way, he found a hidden bottle of hooch, a half pint's worth. That'd be enough to get him going. But he was now thirty-two days without a taste and he didn't want to give that up. No strength of will, no higher moral purpose, no lecture from God or the temperance gals, just the meaningless streak of thirty-two, which he didn't want to break.

He poured it down the drain, then remembered he had a canvas sack or something atop the kitchen cabinet, reached up, pulled it down, and by its weight knew he had found what he came for.

Another hour and a half had him back in Hot Springs, and from a pay phone he called both Eddie and Bill, who were off today in anticipation of the night's business. He told them to meet him not at the station but at a coffee place halfway out of town.

They showed, they ordered coffee and, Bill being old-school, a nice old doughnut. Then it was time to scrape down to the brass.

"Why here?" asked Bill.

"Because who knows who's telling folks what in the station and what gets out. We keep this to ourselves, okay?"

"Sure."

"Bill, I know you hunt. So you must have deer rifles."

"I'm not a big gun guy. Been using a Winchester 70 since I got back from Korea. Never had need to change. Thirty-aught-six. In twenty years, I've gotten twenty bucks without a second shot needed."

"How about you, Eddie?"

"Nothing. But I know a fellow with an M1 carbine. Could get that, ammo, some spare magazines."

"Load the magazines. Bill, bring two or three extra boxes of ammo."

"What's going on?"

"We will be ambushed tonight. The plan is for all of us to be killed. They know we're coming. Right now they're loading up."

That was greeted with deep breaths, looks of disturbance and foreboding, some doubt, then, Eddie speaking for both, "Are you sure?"

"Dead sure. He has to end this right here because he knows how close we are. I told him where we'd be so as to invite this attempt, which'll clinch it, give us prisoners to turn on him and make the arrest. That's also why it'll be tonight. It's nerve-wracking to him; he's got to kill it now."

"Who?"

"DiPasquali. He's the gut hook killer."

Both sucked air hard, swallowed. Again, "How do you know?"

"Here's his life story. I've been working this a couple of weeks, off that letter from the New Jersey State Police detective Lou Pistolli. DiPasquali was the Atlantic City Fish Hook Killer of 1958. He ripped the guts out of five mob snitches. He didn't use a fish hook, though, he used a gut hook. How do I know this? I called that detective, who was still all lit up over the fish hook case. Wanted bad to solve it. We shared some stuff. I told them we had info on DiPasquali which could lead to the fish hook killings. For their part, I wanted an agent to visit all the sporting goods shops around AC. They did. On the third shop, the owner found an invoice dated March '58, for an Antonio Spellini, for one hunting/specialty knife, $3.95. See, it was cataloged under hunting, not fishing, so nobody found it in the first investigation. Jersey records show Spellini as a minor hood, a felony assault, two weapons charges, known as a knife guy. This Spellini went to town with his new toy. He cut the five spies to pieces real fast. That made him a mob star. He was called up to Manhattan, where he worked for the Galante outfit. They were trying to knock out the Gambinos and he fit right in. He did well. He changed his name. How do I know? It's all because of this State Police detective. He already had it half put together. He figured it out to check death certificates, and started with DiPasquali. He came up with an Arthur DiPasquali, born 1937, died 1940, of 2230 13th Street, Atlantic City. He checked that against duplicate birth certificate requests, found one for Arthur DiPasquali, November 1961. That's when Tony Spellini became Arthur DiPasquali, taking over long-dead Arthur's birth info."

"The state cop is a champ."

"He did the work, on the promise that we'd send the gut hook to them when we recovered it. Maybe there's some kind of evidence. He mentioned they now use silver nitrate to bring out old fingerprints and that he could build a case on DiPasquali off that sort of approach."

"What happened to 'empty'?" asked Bill.

"Maybe it was nothing. A shrink I talked to came up with it and maybe I ran too hard with it. Maybe it cost us time and effort. My apologies."

"None called for. Nobody's right on everything."

"Speaking of right, Sergeant, you were onto DiPasqauli from the start," said Eddie. "What tipped you off?"

"In my first chat with him he had to tell me that the real enemy was the ambitious attorney general of Arkansas, guy named Bill Clinton, who would use a big case like this to take him to the governor's office. What he didn't know was that I knew Bill Clinton. Back before he was the attorney general, just a law professor, he used to give speeches everywhere, just to get his name and face out there. He came to a vets group I was part of in an attempt to quit drinking. He heard I was a big hero and all that shit, and related to Earl and Charles, and we met. Decent young man, I thought, will go far. We smoked a cigar on the porch. He told me what DiPasquali didn't—that he was *from* Hot Springs. He was *of* Hot Springs. He was created *by* Hot Springs. No way, then, was he going to go *after* Hot Springs. His job would be to *protect* Hot Springs, because too many folks here know too much about him."

"So why did DiPasquali lie to you in the first place?" Bill asked. "What did he gain? Guy like him always is on the gain."

"My theory," Bob said, "is that he wanted to make sure I understood the rules about not upsetting the Hot Springs applecart. That was piling on, I suppose. But he wanted to steer me away from digging into Hot Springs itself, and the connections of various folks to various folks. I might see how much he was behind, and that might make me curious enough to find out about Anthony Spellini and his proximity to the fish hook killings. He couldn't afford that."

Both other officers nodded.

"Young man, you are much slyer than you seem to be," said Bill.

"Nobody pulls the wool over Gunnery Sergeant Swagger, USMC," said Eddie. "But the big question isn't who—"

"It's why, for sure. My guess is he's always been psycho. He likes the knife. He likes to cut. There are crazy folks like that. He invented himself twenty years ago in that murder spree. Not only did it make him famous, make him a mob star, get him the boss's wife—her name was Maria Angelo, daughter of an Angie Angelo, killed in New York February 3,

1954, in an unsolved mob hit—but it got him sent to Hot Springs in an executive position in 1961, with the responsibility of modernizing and transforming. So that's his best time. Now he's made it, he's in the clear, he's a heroic success in both his lives, public and mob, and he's been keeping this inner psycho part of him bottled up. It's finally busted out. So he sets out to indulge, but safely. He's got the money to set this up. He's got the guile, the cunning, and the organizational ability. He knows ex-cops. It's so much fun for him. It's more fun than he's had since '58. He thinks he's earned it."

CHAPTER 22

TAD GOT IT. THE IDEA OF A NEW LOOK, A NEW PERSONALITY, A NEW stage on which to perform, appeared to enchant him. He wouldn't stop burbling about the details of his performance—the haircut, the beard trim, the fake tattoos, the boots and jeans, the bandanna.

They sat out back of Buckstaff, on the lawn furniture, in the sun, hidden from reality by a screen of bushes. Franny was earnest, Tad was buoyant.

"You don't want to go too far into this," she said. "This guy is a creep through and through. He likes to use that billy club and he's damned good with it. He'll tap you so fast you don't see it coming, and it puts you in exactly the right state of consciousness. You're not out cold, quite, but you're so groggy you have no resistance. Then he leads you to the door and gives you a boot in the ass and you wake up at seven in the morning with a headache and no memory. You do not want that."

"I'll take care, you'll see. You'll be surprised at how adept I am at something like this. It's you that I worry about. Why is this trip necessary?"

"I have to get into that tunnel. I think it's the butcher shop for the sick fuck killing girls. I think it's a festival of forensic evidence and if we find that, we find him."

"But now that you've buddied up with this detective, why don't you just get a warrant, burst in there, and examine the tunnel with a squad of armed men in backup? Seems safer all around."

"If we get the warrant, how fast does that word get around? We know someone involved in this does not want it to be discovered. If they know in advance, they might themselves clean up the forensics or, worse, poke the tunnel until it collapses. We'd have nothing, I'd look like a fool and I'd never be trusted by Swagger again. I have to be sure."

"Trying to talk Franny out of something she's decided on is like arguing with a tornado. You are something else, girl."

"I suppose so."

"I don't even know who you are. I know you're not some wild gal of the road, a hippie chick with a coke monkey on her back, wandering the country for chills and thrills and powder. You're too smart, too organized, too settled on where you're going. You'd never let yourself go the way of the powder. That's for victims, and whatever you really are, you are not a victim. That's why you're not like anybody who's been through here in the last three years."

"Everybody's got their secrets, Tad. Someday, when this is over, we'll laugh about it over a beer."

"That's a deal!"

Franny checked her watch. Close to five. She was due at Mardi Gras at six for the late shift.

"Franny," came a call from the house, "someone on the phone for you."

"See you tonight, Tad."

"I'm off to get my props."

She went in, to the community pay phone.

"Swagger," the voice said.

"I was just about to call you. I think—"

"Never mind that, for now. I believe we've broken it, and we're taking aggressive action tonight. I don't know how it'll play out. But in the meantime, I want you a long way from the Mardi Gras tonight. No way of predicting anything, and violence is not out of the picture."

"Everybody is worried I'm going to get killed. Believe me, I'm *not*."

"You don't know how many kids your age I've heard say just that. They went home, God rest and bless their souls, in a box the next day."

"Bob, listen to me. I believe I have found the tunnel. It will hold the answers to all our questions. It will give us our guy. Tonight, I—"

"No. No, again, no! Not tonight. Tomorrow night, we'll go check it out. As a present for you, I'll break Skip's face into seven pieces. You'll enjoy that, and so will I. All right? Not tonight!"

"I feel like I'm arguing with my father about the prom."

"This ain't no prom, believe me."

"All right, all right. Good luck tonight. I'll go to the mall and see *Saturday Night Fever* again. Maybe this time I'll even like it."

Of course she had no intention of going to the mall—or seeing *Saturday Night Fever* again.

She had to see that tunnel.

CHAPTER 23

SINCE SWAGGER HAD THE BEST NIGHT VISION, HE SAT UP FRONT WITH Eddie, who in fact did drive well, even with the lights off and from two hundred yards behind. Bill sat in back with his deer rifle.

Ahead, far ahead, somebody's Ford station wagon buzzed along. It moved steadily and without hesitation, as if on a shopping trip.

"They *want* us on them," said Bob. "That's the point. They're taking us somewhere they've already seen and are familiar with. They want the landscape working for them, not us. Our advantage is that they don't know we know they know. They think we're dopes walking into a setup. Our job is to ambush the ambushers."

"How—"

Bob pulled something long and tubular out of his canvas bag.

"This is what's called a starlight scope," he said. "All the snipers in Vietnam toward the end were issued them. It was in my stuff, and when I was hit, it was just scooped up and sent back with everything else. The truth is, it's basically no good. Short range, won't stay in zero, hard to get hits with. Most guys just dumped theirs. But it's not for shooting tonight. I'll use it for spotting. I'll try and see how they've set up so we'll be able to approach from a blind angle, designate their positioning, and jump them hard. I'll do that part. If it comes to shooting, I can handle quick shooting in low light. I just need them thinking we've got a whole platoon coming their way."

Silence then, except for the radio unit Bill had installed in the car. Crackly, almost indecipherable stuff, only a cop could understand it. Mostly squad cars reporting in via terse, epigrammatic declaration, occasional requests to attend scenes at addresses, but nothing that wasn't normal. The three men breathed hard, not listening. They were men about to go into battle. Each had an interior drama going on; none chose to share it. Bill and Swagger smoked, Eddie just concentrated on keeping the right distance from the vehicle he was following. He could see just well enough, though there was a bad minute where it appeared he'd lost them, but a quick calculation down another block brought them into contact again.

They took Malvern southeast, out of town, a long, straight shot, then turned down Carpenter Dam Road, which ultimately led to the construction that had created Lake Hamilton. Not much out here, so Eddie let the distance widen to three hundred yards while Bob used his gift to keep them in view.

"Can't see a thing," said Eddie.

"You're fine," said Bob. "He's slowed way down; Eddie you slow down too."

Eddie eased off.

Swagger glanced at his watch: 3:30 a.m., in the middle of nowhere, the only sounds issued by night birds and predators moving about on business.

"Okay, pull off," Bob said. "He's found his spot."

To the right, the land had started to rise, forming a ridge of wild grass and scrub brush, a few low pines. They waited. The big car, Bill's Chrysler Brougham, ticked as it cooled. The wind came and went, the grass waved this way, then that.

"Okay," Bob said. "Here's the play. We go up to the crest, move along it Indian file, bent low. When we see their car in the road below, I'll try and find them in the scope. Assuming I can, we'll split up. Give me a few minutes to get around to the other side, while you work your way down. Maybe when you see me in the scope, I'll give you a signal. You announce police, demand hands up. They will open fire. I move in. You cover. Eddie, when you fire that carbine, do it in bursts of five or ten. Fire high, so you don't hit me on the other side. The noise and flash will scare them. They're cops, not soldiers."

Both were quiet.

Bob reached into his bag and removed its last treasure. It was a Savage 720 shotgun, off the original Browning semi-auto design, with a twenty-inch barrel and a Cutts compensator. It had been around forever during his youth, even if it seemed unfired, and no one had ever told him anything about it, such as why it was necessary. But it had been necessary then and it was necessary now. He slipped four double-aught bucks down the magazine tube under the barrel, then flipped it and added another one to the chamber. He touched a button and Mr. Browning's obedient design snapped the bolt closed. It was serious man-killing machinery. Hardly anybody could stand against it if, double aught, it came in bursts; the game was over. He added a few more shells to his pocket, where he also had five magazines full of .45 hardballs for his granddad's Colt, hanging as it had for a month in the ornate holster under his left shoulder.

"Let's do this thing," he said.

Same as it always was, a Swagger led men with guns across a dark landscape for an appointment with a gunfight. They climbed through the knee-high wild grass, finding the going easy and the slope forgiving. Up top they paused. Above them, the dome of stars, far-off, ageless, patient, pinwheels of incandescence uninterested in what passed below. A little sliver of moon, low to the southwest. In the distance to the northwest, the hot glow of the city of sin despoiling the satin-black sky.

Bob rose and signaled them on. Bent double, long arms in hand, holstered pistols unstrapped, loaded, heavy, rocking back and forth in holsters, they advanced maybe two hundred yards. Bob raised a hand. They dropped to their knees.

He had wedged the starlight scope in his waist, held secure by his belt. He pulled it out—a tube about sixteen inches long with various boxy square control panels and battery cases arranged chaotically along the thing. Who had ever thought this contraption was suitable for anything? He shook his head. It weighed about six pounds and was difficult to manipulate and, lacking a rifle on which to lock it, hold steady. He flicked it on, improvised a position by clamping it between his knees, and aimed it at a glade of low trees halfway between the road and the crest of the slope, as designated by the station wagon parked on the side of the road.

At first, nothing. Just gray fuzz. It was like looking in pea soup for the monocle that fell off your eye. But then, as he at last found a position of relative steadiness, the device caught and amplified enough ambient light to cook up an image, which was the group of trees, and four blurts of light in a semicircle facing the road. In time they came to resemble men prone behind rifles.

"Four, not three," said Swagger. "They're oriented toward the road. They expect us to pull up and cross open ground, right at them. All have long guns. They're set to mow us down."

He passed the scope around, and both men had a chance to look through it.

"Okay," he said. "You guys hold here for about five minutes. I'm going another fifty yards along the crest, then belly-crawl down until I've reached their little woods. You'll see me signal. You sneak down halfway and that's when you yell. They'll panic because they're outflanked, and they'll try to set up on the new perimeter. You lay down cover, then squirm out of position because they'll zero on your muzzle flash. Bill, revolver first, six fast, then move and set up on your rifle and cover. If it's moving fast it's probably me, so don't shoot. Otherwise, anyone behind cover, you drop him. Eddie, after the initial fusillade, you go to the west and try to come in by the rear. If you see someone standing, don't shoot him, because that's also probably me. Stay low. Keep your eyes open. I'll get in among them and try to end the party one way or the other. Got it?"

"Bob, you don't have to be the hero," said Bill.

"Yes, I do," said Bob.

CHAPTER 24

TAD DESERVED AN OSCAR. HIS RED LOCKS GONE—TALK ABOUT METHOD acting!—his head cue-ball bald, he had reduced his beard to an evil red goatee that made him look like Satan's firstborn. Amazing how sharp his features were without the softening effect of the hair. He had cheekbones like warheads, wore a Confederate headband, a Schott leather biker's jacket crisscrossed with zippers and pockets, over a sweatshirt that said, "KILL 'EM ALL, LET GOD SORT 'EM OUT," tight, beaten-to-a-whiter-shade-of-pale jeans, black engineer's boots. It was the look that said, Psycho Viking from hell, Harley-powered, drug-fueled, switchblade armed. To see him was to wish to be in another universe.

He stormed into the Mardi Gras as if he owned it, looked immediately to the gals cruising, saw Franny, and went and grabbed her.

"You be with me tonight, Blondie," he said loudly.

He dumped her at a table, gave her a wink, and turned to the bar. "Hey, barman, some of your best for your best," and lay back with the satisfaction of an NKVD officer after a nice kulak massacre.

"So, bitch," he asked loudly, "what's it going to be and where's it going to be?"

"Easy, easy, sir," she said. "Let's not get way ahead of ourselves here. Let's talk a bit. Don't even know if I like you."

"Don't matter if you like me," he said. "Most don't. But what matters is how much green I've got, and for someone cute as a pony dancing in daisies, I got plenty."

Cute as a pony dancing in daisies? Who wrote this stuff?

She tried not to laugh, though it was hard. Skip brought two pink barely fortified ginger ales, and Tad gobbled his down, ordered another. Meanwhile smoke rotated in the blue air, on the bar a girl in a sequined bikini clung to her pole while she imitated an orangutan, disco thundered so loud it squashed both humanity and the civilization it had created, and, ho-hum, it was another night at the Mardi Gras.

Good thing the ginger ale was so un-ginned, because Tad had five of them at $50 a crack and feigned drunken belligerence on an increasing scale as the night proceeded. He was like Al Pacino on amphetamines. Finally it was time for the grand finale.

He stood, grabbed her, and pushed her hand into his crotch.

"No way," she screamed, yanking away.

"What you mean, whore? I paid. It belongs to me."

"Nothing belongs to you but what you drank," she said.

"Honey, your ass belongs to Rocky. I am Rocky and I means to have what's mine by cash payment."

He grabbed her and tried to pull her toward the stairway that led to the private rooms upstairs.

Skip, however, closed the gap quickly. The prospect of thudding someone into a coma had him all het up.

He grabbed "Rocky" under his left arm and gave him a rattling good shake. Then he said, "Bud, now, you calm down, don't want to get rough with you," meaning, of course, Bud, now, don't you calm down, I really want to get rough with you.

"Rocky" made a spastic lunge at Franny, and as his arm shot out, Skip whacked it with his billy club. It retracted in pain and then curled up as if set aflame.

"Ow, shit," "Rocky" yelled, "that *hurt!*"

"Supposed to hurt, you moron. Now, you come on with me or you'll get a lot more. No grabbing the gals here, got it?"

"Rocky" squirmed to yell at her, "You bitch, I will get you, goddammit, I bought you fair and square!"

That earned him a poke in the guts from Skip, and he crumpled. Then Skip pulled him to the doorway, threw it open and him out. He landed with a crunch.

Skip came back to her.

"You okay?"

"Fine. What a creep."

"Closing, you come see me. These guys sometimes hang around. I'll get you out of here a secret way, no trouble, no matter what this clown does."

She nodded, watched as he headed off to the bar, where his first move was to make a phone call.

Hours passed, Mardi Gras time being inferior to real time, as it went three for every one second on the clock. Franny used one of her breaks to leave Swagger a message with the police operator detailing what she had learned about the tunnel and her intention to explore it tonight. She told him what she knew, not what she suspected, but at least that Skip controlled access. Then she returned to her duties.

Finally the last losers staggered out and Skip blinked the lights, signifying to the girls it was time to close up shop. No more beating down paws of drunks or accepting wet, boozy kisses smearing their makeup. Franny watched the end-of-night ritual as each girl got in line to pass by Skip at the register, and for each $50 Polynesian Hurricane No. 1, she got $20, for each Polynesian Hurricane No. 2 at $35, she got $10. Blow jobs? None tonight, but $100 of the $350 on the rare occurrence that it happened.

Meanwhile Franny went to the dressing room, wiped the childish makeup off, peeled off the cheap satin dress, removed the tennis balls from her bra, tossed the blond wig, unpinned her red curls to hang free. Then she pulled on jeans, a T-shirt, and her Nikes. And last, she picked up her heavy purse.

She went back to the big room and waited till the last of the girls were done. Then she went to get her money.

"Good night for you," he said. "I have you down for eight big ones and three small ones. That's $190." He counted the bills out. "You know you could make a lot more money if—"

"No way," she said. "Now get me out of this place. I have to walk tonight, the bus is in the shop."

She was left alone with him. That itself was a little unnerving, because if he decided he wanted a frolic, he'd just take it and no power on earth could stop it or cared. But evidently he'd gotten himself well satisfied by the clubbing he'd laid on poor Tad.

"Okay," he said, "you come with me."

He led her back to his office, such as it was, and opened the closet door. She could see a door in the closet wall, padlocked. He took his ring of keys, selected one, and unhitched the lock. He pulled the door open to reveal nothing but black.

"You have a flashlight?"

"No," she said, "I didn't plan on this tonight."

"Okay," he said, going to his desk and returning with a light. He tested it and it proved steady if wan.

"Here's how it works. It's real easy, you won't have no trouble. You use the flashlight to get down the stairs and you use it to get along our tunnel. It's low and be careful because about fifty yards or so there's a bunch of pipes. You'll see them if you're alert, and you'll have to duck under to get by."

"Got it," she said.

"A few more yards and you'll come into the big tunnel. It runs under

Hot Springs. You turn left. Probably won't need the flashlight anymore because the tunnel exits a half mile down and a little light leaks in. But if you feel safer, go ahead and use the light. Your choice."

"Okay," she said.

"Nobody alive hardly knows this is here. Won't be nobody down there. You just take your time, though, no rush, because you don't want to fall. If you hurt yourself, I don't know who'd know for a couple of days."

She nodded.

"Then that's it. See you tomorrow, usual time."

"Fine."

"Oh, and remember, we don't talk about this way out. Not even among the girls. It's your safety that's compromised if it becomes widely known."

"I understand," she said. And with that, she turned on the flashlight, found the stairway down, and set off into the enveloping darkness.

CHAPTER 25

THE LOW-CRAWL DOWN THE SLOPE TOOK LONGER THAN HE'D ANTICI-pated, because low-crawls always do. His least favorite mode of transportation, it seemed mostly for movies and drill sergeants, as in three tours he couldn't recall doing it once. But now he did, swimming through the high grass, building up an oxygen debt and a thirst—that's what canteens are for—but eventually reaching his goal, which was the edge of the low pine colony that had randomly spouted up here in this remote part of Arkansas.

He stood behind a tree. Peeping around, he could see occasional movement in the dark, hear the low rustle of men shifting position to keep the blood from collecting in their lower extremities. He marked them: two to the left, crouched low in underbrush; two farther away, on the right. Or was that fourth one just a log? Hard to tell. No way to know until the lead started flying and the muzzles spurted flame.

He stood apart from the tree, hoping he was in range of the starlight scope, and raised both hands. I am here. Start the show. I am ready. Let's do this thing.

He went back, waited, couldn't remember if Bill and Eddie'd already moved down the hill or that was the next move.

"Where the fuck are they?" a voice came out of the darkness.

"I bet he missed the turn. He's farther down Malvern. He'll figure it out and return; it's just another—"

"POLICE!" came Bill's cry. "You are under arrest. Stand up, freeze, show hands, and you won't be hurt."

Coming as it did from a completely unexpected direction, the announcement sent a bolt of panic through the gunmen, unleashed a torrent of cursing, and the two on the right pulled out of their prones and raced to take up positions facing the new threat.

"We are police too," came a response. "You stand up and show your hands."

"Vince Lincoln, I know your voice. You are on the wrong side, goddammit, and I do not want to shoot you. We have a lot of guns all around you."

"Bill, you'd have said yes to this deal too."

Vince fired.

Bill fired.

The three other gunmen fired.

Eddie fired.

Bob moved.

He low-sprinted to the end of the line, came across a man leaning into a lever-action after having let a shot go and was now looking for a new target. The idea was to get up close, smash him in the head, and move along the line, but he must have made a noise, for the man rolled toward him, and the rifle muzzle came at him.

Bob sent a double-aught charge into him, feeling the recoil hard and hurtful, but seeing the buckshot kick up a squall of disintegration that absorbed the man, at the same time somehow rearranging him in micro time. Bob turned, another one came for him, fired a hip shot that missed and that Bob answered with another charge of big buck, and this one, unmoored to earth, went all floppy-doll airborne. Bob assumed the other two would follow and squeezed off his own artillery support, three more fast shotgun blasts at his estimation of their positions.

Eddie let his carbine go through fifteen, and the bullets whipped through the trees, shredding leaves and branches, adding their own riff to the crazy. Bill had gotten another reload into his Colt and fired a six-round spray of .38s, also high. Gunfire cut and destroyed the silence, the loudness of the things always shocking, driving nails deep into ears. The smell of burned powder rose and drove out the oxygen. Frags of bullet smacks against wood or dirt rocketed high, turning the site hellishly bedazzled, its dusty magic destroying visibility, clarity, distance, possibility. It was the maddest dance of all, men in battle.

Swagger dropped the shotgun as reloading was now problematic, rolled to the right while he drew the .45 from the S. D. Myres No. 12, and dashed ahead, looking for targets, hoping not to be one. A man rose before him and Bob fired twice from the hip, his honed instincts putting the man down.

Suddenly he was crushed. He went to the ground, tried to rise, but realized he'd been head-bashed hard. He rolled over and saw a figure above him, rifle up, about to smash his head again, but at that second the guy folded and toppled backward as Bill's .30-06, from fifty yards out off a sitting position, put him down for keeps.

God, Swagger's head hurt. Oh, fuck, he had taken one full in the head. Dizziness swooped in and took over and time ceased altogether as he tried to squeeze some sense or at least some clarity back into his brain. Then he realized: it was over.

"You hit?" Bill asked.

"The guy skulled me before you dropped him. That's all. The buzz will stop in a year or so."

Bill offered him a recovery cigarette, which he accepted eagerly; the smoke in his lungs perhaps would outbuzz the pain in his head. It brought him back to a semi-reality.

"Guy over there is Vince Lincoln. In Homicide fourteen years. Good man."

"Dead?"

"Let's see."

They ambled over while Eddie checked the others. Vince was still alive. He breathed hard, occasionally spit some blood. He lay broken in the brush, two of Bob's .45 hardballs distributed throughout. Live or die? In God's hands, and the skill of the as-yet-summoned ambulance driver.

"Bill, don't you lecture me none," Vince said.

"Do you know what you did?" said Bill. "Do you know what these people you helped were doing?"

"I had a sick kid. I did the calculus and decided I'd go to hell for my son. Them other guys bought houses on lakes with pools. The money was immense."

"You'll spend the rest of your life at the Varner Unit unless you come clean."

"I'll tell you anything," he said, "as my loyalty is now released since Audie Murphy there blew away—"

That was when Eddie arrived.

"I don't know if this is good or bad," he said, "but that guy over there? Shotgunned as he rose? That was Mr. DiPasquali."

CHAPTER 26

AT LAST THE CALL CAME. THREE RINGS, THEN A HANG-UP. THE SIGNAL. At last the hour of the knife.

I changed, got the thing, and went out. Everything was as it should be. The house was silent. I drove through the deserted town, parking as usual in the alley behind a closed DiPasquali's Pizza. Getting down the slope and into the tunnel unseen was no problem this late. Only the club area still had a little life left in it, and that was blocks away.

I entered the tunnel. When would it arrive? Hard to know, as there are so many variables. Sometimes soon, sometimes not until nearly dawn. It didn't matter. I enjoyed the waiting. I was alone in the subterranean damp, and in a moment of fantasy, it seemed to me as if being palpably present in my own subconscious, where all my demons resided.

But it was only an abandoned tunnel. No demons. Not even rats, not that I had ever seen. Now and then you'd hear some animal noise—what, I don't know, cat, raccoon, insects, whatever they have in dark, wet tunnels in Arkansas.

Yes, it was him. DiPasquali had taken the blast full in the chest, and the impact of nine .32 slugs—the double-aught load—had bowled him back, twisted into loose-limbed stillness. He worked his whole life to get out of the gutter, and here he was, in the gutter, chest shredded, eyes glazed open, smeared in blood and dirt.

"I thought he paid for this kind of work," said Bill.

"Not this time. Too much at stake. He had to be in on it, do it, see it, know it. It's what made him such a good executive. And such a good killer."

"How the fuck is this going to play?" asked Eddie.

"Hey, it's Arkansas," said Bill. "They'll figure out a way. It'll be downplayed, somehow. Hunting accident, heart attack. The whole thing will go away. And by tomorrow at five, someone'll be in from New York to take over DiPasquali Pizza."

"At least the gut hook killings will be stopped. Arkansas will be Arkansas, but no more girls getting cut to pieces."

"Hey," came the cry from Vince Lincoln.

They walked back to him.

"I heard what you said. You mark this down. DiPasquali never killed anybody. I don't know who chopped up those poor girls, but it wasn't him."

"Then who?" asked Bob.

"If you hurry, you can find out yourself. There's a girl in the tunnel tonight. And someone waiting in the shadows with a knife."

I took out the knife. It's not that I particularly have a fetish for blades, or even cutting. It's just that whatever use it is to the hunter, its intended end-user, it is at the same time perfect for my purpose. It's heavy enough to cut deep at full swing, like a machete. Its point is sharp enough to penetrate the layers of subcutaneous fat that surround the lower thoracic cavity. Its hook is barbed enough to sweep up miscellaneous coils of the lower intestine, ripping them from their fragile moorings. The edge inside the barb is more than enough to snip the esophageal tube itself, and as well to snip again its emergence from the complexities at the anus. The whole piece is well balanced and fits to the hand well enough to yank out in one pull all that roiled mass of inner plumbing. That done, emptiness is again achieved, and sooner or later, someone will read the message in the absence of entrails, and the end game, with its delicious ironies, surprises, and critiques, will begin to emerge.

It's a brilliant plan. Yes, I am mad. I could not do this otherwise. Yet it is the madness of purpose, not the madness of random frenzy as driven by hate. Give me that, even as you execute me. My hatred is as intense but much more focused. Its meaning will shortly become apparent and—

I hear it. Still several hundred yards out, but persistent in its traipse through the drain water. Then a cough, a sniffle. It is getting closer. This one will be so much better than the last. No more sloppiness like the last one. This one will be perfect.

CHAPTER 27

SWAGGER SAID, "I'VE GOT TO GET IN, FAST. I'LL TAKE THE CAR. I'LL CALL it in, and other units will be here in no time."

Eddie handed him the keys. Bill said, "There's a dashboard flasher unit in the trunk. Just plug it into the cigarette lighter. Don't worry about the car. Now go, go."

Swagger spun and began his mad race to the vehicle. His strength amplified by anxiety, he ran through the high grass, zeroed on the thing by the side of the road a few hundred yards out. He ordered his steel hip not to betray him, and for once, it obeyed. He felt the .45 banging against his side as he went, and the weight of spare magazines in his suit coat pocket. He took comfort in the gun, but at the same time his fear for Franny was piercing, agonizing, and deep. He tried to drive it out. He could not.

What if he was too late?

What if it was done and the killer was gone?

The pain of such a world was incomprehensible. He'd already lost someone he loved to an enemy, his spotter in Vietnam, Donnie Fenn. It had almost killed him. He couldn't go through that again. That's when the .45 would really come in handy.

He reached the car, got the flasher out of the trunk, and set it up. He turned on the engine and the radio came alive. He picked up the micro-phone and pressed the send button.

"All units, all units, officers need assistance, officers need assistance. A mile down Carpenter Dam Road off Malvern Avenue, need ambulances, crime scene teams. This is Swagger."

"Swagger?" It was the chief. "What's the situation? Did you make arrests?"

"Gunfight. Lots of shooting. No officers down, but the suspects are shot up bad. Need medical."

"All right, good, it's on its way. All units, including State Police and suburban, please respond to this call."

"Sir, can you patch me to the telephone operator?"

"Sure."

It took a second, but she came on.

"Sergeant Swagger?"

"Was there a phone message for me?"

"Yes, shall I read it?"

"Yes, yes."

" 'Entry to tunnel Skip's office. He has keys. I have figured a way in. Talk tomorrow.' It's not signed."

"I know who it is. Thanks and out."

He threw the big Chrysler into gear, took a U-turn that tore up a tornado of dust, then hit the pedal hard. The Brougham was Chrysler's fastest and biggest model in 1977. That meant a V8, 440 hp, a large piece of Detroit iron. He floored it, the dashboard flasher strobing red and blue, angled around Carpenter Dam and onto Malvern. It was a straight shot into the city. He hit 115 miles an hour, the darkness a blur, passing incoming police vehicles and ambulances under light and siren, headed to the shooting scene. The car was a beast, floating on heavy shocks, not lithe enough to be an oval racer but without turns to ease it into drift, a straightaway machine to reach warp drive. In no time, it seemed, he was in city streets, intersecting Central just a few blocks south of the club district beginning on 13th. He slowed, though not much, and took the turn off Central onto 13th hard, this time the big body of the vehicle swaying as it rode its springs, the tires screeching Irish banshee–like against the night. He glanced at his watch—3:50 a.m.

He saw the club up ahead, sealed up tight, even though its sign still blazed, throwing orange-and-blue light on everything. Inside, lights burned, suggesting habitation. He decided to knock on the door with 4,700 pounds of automobile.

The car hit the doors at a seventy-degree angle, blasting them wide-open, and was stopped from further penetration only by the brick walls, the left fender crumpling into a broken accordion, the light going out, the axle shearing, a rubble of bricks instantly spewing clouds of dust. He was out, not letting the shock of the impact throw him, leaping over the ruined fender and toward the office.

That door now opened and out stepped Skip, baffled but armed, a shotgun in his hands.

Swagger drew on him, flicking off the safety of the .45. The pistol was pointed at Skip's forehead.

"Drop the shotgun, Chickenface."

The shotgun fell to the floor.

Bob put the muzzle of the pistol one inch from Skip's nose.

"Get your keys and open up that tunnel, Chickenface, or I will paint this room with your brains."

"Don't want no trouble, sir." For once his eyes betrayed compassion—for himself.

"You'd best open fast."

Skip backed up and on palsied legs led Swagger back into the office. He went to the closet and opened the door to reveal the second doorway, padlocked.

"You better have the key."

"Y-yes, sir," said Skip. He took out his key ring and bent to find the lock. Swagger could see the key shaking in his fingers as it ticked against the lock. Finally, he got it inserted, pulled the lock open, and ripped it off. He yanked the door, revealing darkness.

Trying to buy mercy, he said, "I have a flashlight over here."

Swagger let him pass, get the light from his desk, and hand it over. It worked, though weakly, casting a light like the moon through smoke, a blood-orange.

"If anything has happened to that girl," he said, leaning close, speaking from his deepest reptile brain and meaning every word, "I'll gut hook you to the ceiling and watch you bleed out for a week."

"Sir, please, I ain't done nothing. I just done what they told me."

Swagger took the light and advanced to the stairs. Then, light in one hand, .45 in the other, he began his journey.

CHAPTER 28

I T WAS SLOW GOING. SHE EDGED THROUGH THE COLD WATER, FEELING the claustrophobia of the tunnel enclosing her. She'd gotten under the pipes, turned the corner into the larger tunnel, and now picked her way along. No sign of human habitation yet, but now and then the sound of something animal moving through the darkness. The weak circle of her flashlight had revealed a raccoon, its eyes bloodred in the reflection. It froze, considered, and dashed away. The light also revealed strange underground vegetation, maybe from outer space.

Far away there seemed to be a light source. That had to be starlight and streetlamp, and enough glow got in to illuminate a blur of gray. Yet it seemed to get no closer, and she couldn't rush, fearing a fall or a clunk on the head from something overhanging the passage. The air was moist, the stench not of the toilet but still unpleasant, perhaps of death, perhaps of blood, perhaps of rot or decay. It reminded her of—nothing. There was no preparation for a dark night's trek through an unknown tunnel. She tried to keep it together.

Not much farther. No problems yet. I am fine. I will find what I need to find, I will do what I need to do. I will destroy the beast, one way or another. You will not escape justice, you will pay in pain for the pain you have caused.

In a bit of time, the wetness of the tunnel seemed to vanish, and she was on dry ground. She breathed hard, feeling it marked progress. The gray light seemed closer, maybe brighter, and perhaps that was a whisper of fresh air.

This is where it was done, she thought. Right in here, close to the end. Then the boys who cleaned up came, dragged what was left to somewhere, and buried it. Experts, they scrubbed the burial sites of forensics. Who knew how long this had been going on? Who knew how many girls had simply vanished, without anyone anywhere knowing or caring, or looking? The lives meant nothing human to anybody.

She wanted to cry. The monstrosity was of itself such an affront it weighted her down with grief. So sad, so—

It had to be here. The opening was now only twenty yards away; there was plenty of room to swing the gut hook, and plenty of privacy. She focused the cone of light here and there, bringing illumination to the shadowed corners, the unseen walls, the floor of earth. She knew: she was in the butcher's church, at the altar. She saw brownish flakes of blood showing in the wan orange of her light. Splatter and spray, dribble and pool, the blood had gone everywhere. They'd had no need to clean this area. Who would ever in a million years stumble across it? She was at the dark center of the blasphemy. She hugged her purse closer to her. She felt the vibrations of murder.

A figure rose before her. Ninja? Witch? Banshee? Night hag? Djinn? All in black, face half-swaddled, eyes unseeable. A figure out of the darkest of all girl dreams, the early medieval nightmares of killers in the dark that turned the brothers so Grimm, here to prey on weakness, panic, fear so strong it was an animal, all in a studied choreography of cruelty to flesh and soul.

Against the circle of gray light, the killer raised an arm, and Franny saw the knife, with its barbed hook designed for guts.

"I'm sorry," came the voice. "You are the sacrifice."

The knife flashed toward her throat.

Skip could not stop shaking. He knew others would be here soon, that it would soon be over for him and that what followed would be an eternity in the penitentiary. So many sins now to be revealed. "I only did what they told me" would get him nothing, because he had taken money for it.

The police would be here soon. He went to the bar, reached under it, and took out the one unopened bottle of genuine J&B scotch he had. His poison. His release. His pleasure. He cracked the seal, unscrewed the lid, and poured himself six fingers in the nearest hurricane number one glass he could find.

He drank two fingers' worth.

It hit him like a flaming punch to the head. It knocked the world blurry. It numbed brain, it enfeebled fingers, it weakened knees, it amplified dizziness. He sat on a stool, thinking he needed more of this artificial mercy. He did two more fingers, feeling each molecule trailing napalm as it rushed to his gullet.

Outside, he heard a car pull up, then another. Strobing blue and red filled the room from the bashed door and the car wedged into it. He heard doors opening, shouts.

Then an idea, rare for him, but not entirely without precedent.

He reached over and back under the bar and removed the telephone. Placing the receiver to ear, he managed to get a finger into the dial. He hoped he remembered. His mind was blank. But then he had it. He dialed the number.

It seemed to ring and ring, but only because the hooch turned time elastic, dragging each second out several lifetimes.

"Who the fuck is this?" came the bellow, its maker torn from sleep and pissed as hell.

"B-B-Badger, it's Skip. At the club."

"What the fuck you want this time of night, goddammit?"

"You still hunting Swagger?"

"I am."

"He's here. He's down in the tunnel finding God knows what."

Badger said nothing.

"I think it's falling apart," said Skip. "I think they know."

"Fuck," said Badger.

"Cops outside now."

"Fuck," said Badger again.

"Swagger be coming out down by the station pretty soon. No one around. The cops don't know about the tunnel yet. Swagger coming out, you could get him easy from behind, then get away clean. Maybe with him gone, the heat is off us."

"How long ago did he—"

"About five minutes."

"Good man," said Badger, hanging up.

Two cops flanked Skip. They grabbed his arms and without love cranked them behind him for the cuffs. They shoved his face to the bar, breaking his nose.

CHAPTER 29

SWAGGER PROCEEDED. HE WAS INTO THE BIG TUNNEL, HEADING toward what appeared to be a smudge of gray light. He didn't want to yell because he had no idea what a yell would produce. He didn't want to race, for it would rile the water into heavy froth. He didn't want to turn on his flashlight, for that too would have unknowable repercussions. He just forged ahead, fast yet in careful control of his body, trying not to make any disturbance, smelling the rot, the moisture, sensing the enclosure of the tunnel, cringing at the thought of Franny alone down here, being hunted by the man with the gut hook. That produced a near aneurysm of anxiety and almost knocked him to his knees, and he tried to close it out and concentrate on movement and action.

Beyond, the light grew larger, brighter. He could take it no more and broke into a run, closing the distance in seconds. Against the light he sensed disturbance and waited for focus and clarification, but then he could wait no more and flicked on the light, locking his knees, locking his wrists, locking his elbows, locking his hands, drawing his pistol up into a strong supported position to make a long shot if necessary. He clicked off the safety, felt the trigger against his finger.

Clarity.

What he beheld astonished him.

• • •

The knife flashed toward her throat.

It didn't make it.

It was interrupted mid-slash by the LC-14-B, swung with full practiced force, the edge slicing through the joint at the elbow.

The arm fell into darkness.

The killer rotated in agony to the right, the scream barely human as it expressed both pure pain and the awareness of obliteration. The heart pumped a mighty spasm as he turned and from his new stump spewed a crescent of blood against the orange wall, and the smear disorganized itself into dripping spatter instantly.

Franny twisted the implement in her hands, came around again with all her strength, and planted the hook deep between the hip bone and the lowest rib, that soft area of vulnerability common to the mammal of all species. The hook pierced and caught on coils of tubing, and Franny herself rotated for leverage, pulling it across and through, feeling it rip, gather, advance, and repeat. This message in the entrails was clear and without irony: I am killed. The repeater fell, facedown, oozing a life supply of blood into the raw dust.

Then Swagger was next to her.

"Jesus Christ, are you all right?"

She started to cry. She buried her head in his shoulder. He squeezed her hard, hoping to fill her body with a surge of life. He could feel her heart beating.

"It's okay. It's okay," he kept repeating. "Go on, sweetie, cry. You earned it. I never saw a Marine with guts like yours. Cry, cry, you so earned it."

A few minutes passed. She seemed to settle down.

He said, "Let me check this guy."

"He isn't a guy," said Franny. "It's Maria Angelo DiPasquali."

• • •

Almost dawn.

They sat on two rocks just outside the tunnel entrance in the empty basin, in gray light and low mist. There seemed to be no other life on earth. The air was fresh and good.

"You picked up the Woodman's Pal from my truck, I guess, when we went to dinner."

"I thought I might need it more than you."

He held it in his left hand. He'd already washed the prints off it. Now he applied his own, everywhere.

"I'm going to drive you back to your place now. Get some sleep. I don't want you involved in this next bit of crap. I don't want your name even mentioned. Tomorrow I'll drive you to the airport. You go back to wherever you came from. North Carolina, you said, but I don't believe that any more than I believe your name is Franny Wincombe. I don't even want to know your name. I don't want this thing following you around your whole life."

"Can I have a cigarette?" she said. "I dropped mine."

He got out his Camels, flicked one out for her, and took one for himself. He inhaled deeply, as did she.

"When did you know?" he finally asked.

"Remember 'emptying'? That was so right. Any woman would know it. It means abortion."

He nodded. "Never thought of it," he said.

"If abortion is at the heart of it, you say 'Who's?' DiPasquali's wife was childless, not by chance either. I asked around. An old gal who worked in the original DiPasquali's Pizza told me that when she got here with him twenty years ago, rumor was she was pregnant. But it was a terrible time for him so he must have bullied her into the procedure. Procedure? Well, it was hardly that. It was 1960. She went to some back street butcher, who cut her badly. Pain and blood, I'm sure, but worst of all, she couldn't have any more children. For the butcher it was all in a day's work, for her it was the end of the world."

"So this thing, it was—I'm still not sure."

"It grew and grew. It tipped her into craziness over the years. So she came up with this plot. It was aimed at her husband. She knew he was the Atlantic City killer. She found the knife. Her way of punishing him for murdering her children was to commit these crimes and eventually be caught. Her story would come out and the scandal would destroy him here. Then the knife would be related to Atlantic City, and he'd go to prison for the rest of his life. In her mind, for murdering her children. What happened to her didn't matter. Overwrought? Remember, these people are Italian. They invented opera."

"That hangs together," said Bob.

"You see the rest?"

"Yeah. He knew when she got caught, everything would fall apart."

"That's it. Hence, he had three choices: He could have her committed. He could have her arrested. However, both those involved massive scandal at the peak of the city's delicate pivot toward wholesomeness. Moreover, she would give him up for his crimes in Atlantic City.

"Number three—he could cover them up," said Bob. "Yeah, he is the one who hires ex-cops for their homicide scene expertise, and for the price of one poor working-class girl every four to eight weeks, he keeps the lid on, at least through the pivot, satisfying both city elders and Mafia overlords. The whole thing was predicated on Hot Springs Homicide's unprofessionalism. He knew that if the FBI or state cops came in, they'd pick it apart."

"It's straight *Godfather*. Remember Barzini on drugs at the meeting? Switch one word. 'The *murders* will be allowed, but controlled.'"

"It makes the most sense."

"What'll happen to him?"

"He'll be buried. I put a blast of double-aught into him an hour or so ago. I'll send the knife back to Jersey and maybe they can close that case off it."

They tossed their cigarettes.

"Okay, let's split."

They rose, they turned, they started to move out.

They heard some scuffling in the brush behind them. And then: C-O-L-T.

Skip was scum, no doubt. He was a rapist, an abuser (of wives and children, namely his own), an armed robber, a thief, a felon, a misdemeanor champion, a murderer (nobody knew), a bad-check artist, a scammer. There was paper on him from four states going back thirty years. When he was in the sixth grade, he hit another kid in the face with a tire iron. He had prison tattoos on about 40 percent of his body. He used marijuana, cocaine, heroin, amphetamines, to say nothing of J&B scotch and unfiltered cigarettes. He had seven teeth. He was stupid but cunning. To him, a life spent busting shit up was a life spent well.

While not a Grumley, he was a Grumley vassal. He had served the clan his entire Arkansas life, as it had served him. He had a Harley Shovelhead, a Camaro four-speed painted primer black, and two pairs of Jet Skis.

He knew the ropes, and because he'd been in trouble his whole life, nothing in the justice system particularly scared him. He could do time, brutal prison guards, public shame, exile, and the occasional rape by a larger man that were part of the dirty white boy prison lifestyle. It was okay. It went with the territory.

"Mr. Johnson, you could be charged with accessory before the fact to murder in the first. Given your previous record, that could play out to the rest of your life in prison. You'd best cooperate and maybe slice a few years off."

The interlocutor was Bill Canton, who'd done this a few times himself.

"You don't got nothing on me. I'm sitting there doing my bookkeeping and some crazy cop crashes through my front door in a fucking Chrysler

Brougham and points a gun at my nose. He demands to know some business secrets. He ain't got no warrant, he's abusing the badge, he's known as a violent man. I'm just going to sit here till a public defender gets me sprung, then go on vacation. If you try me, you will come up—"

"Did you knowingly arrange for girls to be killed by an unknown but powerfully connected sociopath? Did you accept money for such work? We have all day, and you're not going anywhere until you open up."

"Where's the public defender?"

"He's not here yet. When he gets here, I expect he'll be tied up in paperwork for hours and hours. He's not going to save you."

"Do you know who owns the Mardi Gras? You're the one who should be scared. When Mr. DiPasquali finds out, he's going to bring fire and brimstone on your little hick department. You're all going to be looking for new jobs while I Jet Ski my way around Lake Hamilton every day. I might even take up golf."

"I'm sure you'd be welcomed at some of the city's better golf clubs. By the way, DiPasquali is dead. He won't be of much help to you. Currently State Police detectives are at his headquarters going through his books and records under instructions from Attorney General Clinton, whom I have called. Another team is going through his house. Think they'll find anything incriminating?"

"I got nothing to say."

"Where is Swagger?"

"He got bored, I guess. He went home."

"Anything happens to him goes against you. The same with that girl. You might end up with consecutive life sentences. That's a long time to wait for a trip to hell at the other end."

"What time is it?"

They told him.

Okay, an hour had passed.

Badger had done his deed. More importantly, Skip had done his job.

He'd alerted Badger, then protected Badger. By the criminal etiquette that dominated his life, he'd performed to the highest standards. He thought he was a hero. He had betrayed no one. Badger would take care of him.

"Okay," he said, and started spilling beans but good.

He had them dead cold, the Python cocked. He stood three feet behind them. The world was empty of everything but gray light and killing fury.

"Get them hands up where I can see them."

Both Swagger and Franny raised their hands.

"Okay, Swagger, who's holding the cards now?"

"I believe you are, Badger. Let this girl go. She hasn't done a thing."

"Dumbass. She's witness number two; she never liked me. She thought she was better than me."

"Dumbass. She *is* better than you. In fact, she's better than me."

"You've sent a lot of folks across. How's it feel to be there now?"

"Didn't they tell you not to waste time bullshitting?"

"Yeah, but I am so beyond that. I can make this last as long as—"

At a speed that had no place in time, Swagger's right hand flashed to the .45 in the old S. D. Myres holster hanging under his left shoulder. He didn't bother to draw it. He had no spin move; he didn't duck or evade against a cocked Python with a hair trigger and a psycho-moron's finger on it. He knew that from his position he couldn't clear leather, get around, and fire, even if he ducked or dived or did similar movie nonsense. This was not a movie.

The holster was so old and flexible it yielded to the power of his hand. He slid it in, flicked off the safety, twisted the buttery leather up, and fired. The bullet destroyed the holster, it destroyed his suit coat. One thousandth of a second later, it destroyed Badger's aortic valve.

They both turned. Badger wasn't down but he was about to be. From center chest poured quite a bit of his blood, gurgling messily toward the planet Earth. Splatter, bubble, pool, and puddle. Then he sat in the red mud he had just created. Then he lay down. The Python remained in his right hand, still in condition C.O.L.T. He had lost interest in shooting it. He had, in fact, lost interest in everything.

"Boy, you are good with that thing," said Franny. "By the way, you're on fire."

So he was.

The muzzle flash had ignited whatever cotton-rayon-polyester blend of petrochemicals had made up the suit coat. It smoldered, issuing a ripe stench of blue smoke, a flare of ember, and injecting a lot of pain into his flesh. Second-degree burn.

He jumped, doing a little idiot dance, ripping the thing off, flinging it away.

"Are you all right?"

She looked, saw that his shirt was torn apart by the bullet and scorched black. The holster's muzzle had been blown open, blossoming into four or five petals, all its beautiful hand-tooling equally defiled by burned powder. Underneath the wreckage she could see blisters forming on his raw skin.

"I'm fine," he said. "Aspirin and Vaseline will fix everything. It always has. Now come on. Very shortly the whole Hot Springs Police Department is going to come crashing out of that tunnel. Let's get you out of here."

CHAPTER 30

I T TOOK THE BEST MINDS IN HOT SPRINGS TO INVENT A COVER-UP. THEY almost invited Charles Portis in, as he was known as the state's best novelist. They needed his narrative talent, as displayed in *True Grit*.

Still, they did all right. Mr. Portis would have been pleased. Arthur DiPasquali had been kidnapped by a cabal of embittered ex-cops living in Elk Cove, Hot Springs Village. Hot Springs police officers had intercepted them on Carpenter Dam Road. In the ensuing gunfight, Mr. DiPasquali was tragically shot and died on the scene. Of the ex-cops, two died and one survived. In the meantime, in learning of her husband's death, his wife, Maria Angelo DiPasquali, committed suicide. No service was planned and both bodies were cremated. Everybody would accept it; it was the Arkansas way.

End of story, except the part where Bill Canton retired with a medal and full honors and Eddie Rollins was promoted to sergeant and got a medal too. No formal acknowledgment was made of outside help.

Swagger picked Franny up at Buckstaff at eleven and drove her in his truck to Adams Field, in Little Rock. They didn't have much to say, as emotionally both were wrung out.

He pulled into the drop-off zone.

"They gave me some money," he said. "Here. You take it. I don't need it."

"I've got money," she said.

"Then take it anyway. Just to make me happy. So something good came out of this. You can use it when you're out visiting Joan Didion."

"I'm not going to visit Joan Didion. I'm going home."

"Don't tell me where. The less I know the better. Nothing that happened here should ever be a part of your life again."

"I wish it were that simple. For a smart man, Sergeant, you missed the most obvious thing."

"Maybe I didn't miss it. Maybe I didn't want to think about it."

"You knew?"

"Only thing that could explain you. Pook—Jennifer Macy—was your sister."

"She was. Best big sister anybody ever had. When I was a freshman in high school, I was chubby and had bright red Little Orphan Annie ringlets. I was bullied hard by certain people. 'Chubette,' 'Miss Piggie,' 'The Blob.' Pook found me crying in my room. Next day she went to those people and she put the fear of God into them. They never said a word to me again. It was like that all the time. She watched over me."

Swagger pretended he had nothing to say. But then he said it anyway.

"What happened to her?"

"Taylor Stanton starts dating her. She was a virgin. He was cool. His deal was cocaine. He used it to get sex off girls and then dump them, and laugh about it to the boys of Phi Delt. She was his big challenge. He did that to her. She'd never done drugs, she had no experience. It just took her over. She was ashamed and destroyed and hopelessly addicted. She left town with some hippies on the way to get more powder. The road is cruel. She ended up in Hot Springs. I think the late Badger Grumley was her supplier. I got a postcard from her a week before she died. I had to find out what happened. So here I am. Now it's done."

"You have a job left. Your job is now to live a life she would be proud of. Make a contribution. Do good. Make the world better. Consecrate her memory."

"I'll try."

"You'll succeed. Now go, go, go."

She gave him a hug, being careful not to squeeze his blisters. Then she left the car with her little bag. He watched her disappear into the terminal.

EPILOGUE

THE CAR WASN'T HARD TO FIND. IT WAS MEANT TO BE NOTICED. IT WAS a bright red '77 Pontiac Firebird convertible, top down, license plate "QtrBk-11."

It was a soft, sultry night in Chapel Hill. A wind whispered over the parking lot behind Sorority Row, pushing the dogwood and the elm, and above, stars seemed to drift and blink, under no particular mandate to do anything except drift and blink. Music—the Pretenders, the Eurythmics, Stones, some BeeGees, "Louie, Louie"—pulsated from behind the trees that shielded what appeared to be an English manor house, as at the same time social hubbub in the form of giggles and jokes and riffs provided the dominant soundtrack.

The Delta Gammas were having a mixer, strictly no booze allowed (no checking in blazer pockets, however), and it seemed everyone was having a good time. It was a fabled era to be an American undergrad at a big state school like UNC; no ten-ton issues, like a war or a political scandal, crushed the life out of the campus, especially here in the mild mid-South. Par-tay, par-tay!

Bob lounged against the fender of the Firebird. It sure was a beauty. He enjoyed the night, he enjoyed the breeze, he enjoyed the music and the sound of social interaction. No disco. It reminded him of a path he didn't take, and if he didn't have regrets, that didn't stop him from the sort of fleeting if fraudulent nostalgia people feel for places and times they never experienced. It just fired off a lot of what-ifs in his mind, not that there was, or could be, any going back.

He was on his third cigarette when he saw them on the approach. Evidently it was a sort of get-acquainted party by which stud upperclassmen were introduced to DG's latest pledges for reasons both good and bad. Good: again DG attracted the most beautiful girls. Bad: sometimes the upperclassmen had more on their minds than friendship. But it was an ancient tribal ritual, unlikely to be eliminated under any circumstances.

There were three of them—all blond, all in gray football T-shirts and shrieking madras shorts, sockless in blinding white athletic shoes, all more or less handsome, square-headed like comic book supermen. They had battleship jaws and hands big as basketballs. They had a swagger, of course, plenty of artfully arranged hair down across ears, and muscles everywhere, carefully cultivated in hours under heavy iron. They all looked like they should be named Chad.

"Say, bud," said the central figure in the jock triptych, "that's no park bench, that's my car."

Bob smiled.

"Sure is pretty. Damn fine car."

"Yeah, okay, but it's not here for the amusement of drifters. You just go on, now. We've got places to get to."

"You know," Bob said, "I think I know you. You'd be the football hero, Taylor Stanton, right? What a privilege to run into Taylor Stanton."

"Yeah, yeah," said Taylor. "You want an autograph, pal? No problem. I'll sign something and you mosey along. Everybody's happy."

"Actually, no, that's not what I want," said Swagger.

"Ty, let's shitcan this loser," said one of Taylor's friends, looming in on the exchange.

"He'd be your right tackle, right?" asked Bob.

"Left. Now, let's go. Tommy here doesn't like—"

Well, it didn't really matter what Tommy liked. Tommy, a second later, was on his ass. Tommy's nose had been turned into the Bridge on the River Kwai after the explosion. It wasn't Tommy's damage or pain, or his groveling, however, that now flavored the transaction. It was the sure knowledge, based on the velocity of the punch and the precision with which it had been delivered and the confidence and experience that drove it, that they were suddenly in a different part of the universe.

"You know," said Bob, "I do so like hitting big guys. Always have. They go down hard every time and getting bad hurt takes the starch out of them."

"Do I know you?" said Taylor, through a dry throat across a dry tongue and out dry lips.

His right tackle began to edge back, out of the confrontation. It was one thing to face ACC linebackers for Taylor, but not tough-as-shit Green Berets, as this guy could only be.

"We have a mutual acquaintance," said Bob. "Her name was Jennifer Macy. Everybody called her Pook. I think you were her boyfriend for a while."

"Look," Ty said, "I am *so* sorry for what happened to Pook. She was a great girl. I had no idea she'd take it so hard. It was the last thing I wanted. Are you here to serve me papers or something? I'll give you my dad's lawyer's address, and if you want to sue or bring charges, we can work something out."

"See, I don't work that way. Takes too long, and for someone like you, being rich, being a star, being a hero, there's nothing the law can do that does you any hurt. Lawsuit? Your daddy writes a check. Charges? You'd get the best lawyers in the state, plus the governor. And you just go on your way. So what would be the point of that?"

"Look, I don't want any trouble."

"Son, too bad for you. I *am* trouble."

He smiled. He hit Ty in the mouth. Teeth, expensively straightened, flew far into that good night. Then he hit Ty under the left eye. Snake-fist, mostly knuckle, as before big in SOG in '68. In three minutes the impact zone would turn a sort of purple-yellow and bloat to pumpkin size. All-American? He'd look All-Monster for another three months. Swagger hit him once more, fist snap, flat of the hand below the knuckles, lots of flex in the wrist, more a street thing than martial arts. The nose. Now a cow pie. It too would become gigantic.

Ty lay on the ground, blood, snot, phlegm, and drool all over his stud T-shirt and his madras shorts. His offensive line had backed way off, in silence, the one punched trying to stanch the blood.

Swagger bent close to Ty.

"I could bang on you all night, Ty. I could kill you, I suppose. Bare-handed, maybe in one minute. But let's just leave it this way. I know you. You don't know me. I'm going to pay attention to you. If I hear you're up to your gal tricks, I'll have to hurt you some more. Next time it'll really be bad too, not letting you off easy like this time. So you learn from this. That's more of a chance than you ever gave Pook. You deserve far worse, but in her gentle memory I'll let you off the hook. That's the only bit of mercy I got in me for you."

He rose, and nobody made any effort to interfere.

He turned and disappeared into the night.

ACKNOWLEDGMENTS

FOR *CITY OF MEAT*, THANKS TO MY WIFE'S BROTHER-IN-LAW, GLENN Kerley, who drove us down to the Stock Yards site on a wet Saturday, Chicago in December. Not much is left except that ludicrous gate, more Disney than Chicago. Also, hey, Chicago, get a plaque up for Isaac Means, the yard watchman who died in 1934 trying to put out the fire with his hands. He deserves it.

For *Johnny Tuesday*, which began twenty years ago as a screenplay meant to be the perfect film noir, thanks to all who read it then—wish I could remember their names. I know the late Jay Carr was one of them—a great guy, miss him badly. Thanks as well to Fred Rasmussen, the *Sun's* great obit writer, for help with *Sun* history from 1947.

For *Five Dolls for the Gut Hook*, thanks to Dave Dunn, who came up with the Woodman's Pal idea and pretty much saved the story from wandering off into the mists. Thanks to Bava, Argento, Fulio, and Martino for the guilty pleasures that took over my imagination for the last four months. And by the way, the "13th Street District" I describe in the story is basically Baltimore's Block, which remains a tawdry wonder years after Blaze Starr has moved on. I have no idea if Hot Springs had such a zone. That's the point of being a novelist: you get to make stuff up.

For all three stories, thanks to friends, beginning with the great

Gary Goldberg and moving on to Mike Hill, Dave of course, brother Andy Hunter, Lenne Miller, Jeff Webber, and Barrett Tillman, who pitched in with advice and spirit-reviving good cheer. And as usual, thanks to my wife, Jean, who made the coffee, which basically lubricated every story.